Empire and Ashes

Jeryn's Dagger

D. L. YOUNG

aethonbooks.com

JERYN'S DAGGER
©2025 D.L. YOUNG

This book is protected under the copyright laws of the United States of America. No part of this publication may be reproduced, stored in a retrieval system, or transmitted, in any form or by any means, without the prior permission in writing of the publisher, nor be otherwise circulated in any form of binding or cover other than that in which it is published and without a similar condition including this condition being imposed on the subsequent purchaser. Any reproduction or unauthorized use of the material or artwork contained herein is prohibited without the express written permission of the authors.

Aethon Books supports the right to free expression and the value of copyright. The purpose of copyright is to encourage writers and artists to produce the creative works that enrich our culture.

The scanning, uploading, and distribution of this book without permission is a theft of the author's intellectual property. If you would like to use material from the book (other than for review purposes), please contact editor@aethonbooks.com. Thank you for your support of the author's rights.

Aethon Books
www.aethonbooks.com

Print and eBook layout, formatting, and design by Kevin G. Summers.

Published by Aethon Books LLC.

Aethon Books is not responsible for websites (or their content) that are not owned by the publisher.

This book is a work of fiction. Names, characters, places, and incidents are the product of the author's imagination or are used fictitiously. Any resemblance to actual events, locales, or persons, living or dead is coincidental.

All rights reserved.

ALSO IN SERIES

EMPIRE AND ASHES:

Jeryn's Dagger

Xamorian Path

Unending Stars

Calling all SciFi fans: be the first to discover groundbreaking new releases, access incredible deals, and participate in thrilling giveaways by subscribing to our exclusive SciFi Newsletter.

https://aethonbooks.com/scifi-newsletter/

Want to discuss our books with other readers and even the authors?

JOIN THE AETHON DISCORD!

PROLOGUE

"WHERE DID YOU GET THIS?" THE ARRESTING OFFICER DEMANDED, tossing a cloth bag onto the table in front of Jeryn Lorsi. The heavy thud and elongated shape left no doubt as to what was inside: Jeryn's kukri blade.

Leaning forward in his seat and furrowing his brow, Jeryn studied the object for a moment, then said, "I've never seen that bag before."

The officer didn't appreciate the humor. "I'm not talking about the *bag*, citizen," he sneered. The pale-skinned man struck Jeryn as the prim sort. He had a thin, neatly trimmed mustache and a perfectly pressed uniform with shiny brass buttons. "And I wouldn't recommend making things worse by trying to be clever," he continued, standing and glaring down his long, slightly bent nose. "You're in a lot of trouble."

Jeryn didn't disagree. He was definitely in trouble. Of the very deep variety. Hours earlier he'd been arrested—along with a dozen others—and charged with trafficking illegal goods. The police had raided a local smuggling operation, and they'd done so right when Jeryn had been unloading his illicit cargo of Tehodian whiskey from a neighboring system. He'd been in the wrong place at the wrong time. It happens.

The arresting officer had confiscated Jeryn's blade and locked him inside the small, windowless interrogation room, leaving him alone and then returning after what Jeryn guessed had been about an hour.

Now the officer gingerly opened the bag and poured the blade onto the table with a clank. Jeryn tried not to stare at it, tried not to let anything in his expression betray the weapon was his most prized possession.

"It's an antique," the officer said. "A fairly valuable one, according to our scans."

"You're kidding," Jeryn said, trying his best to feign surprise. "I had no idea."

The officer rolled his eyes. "Sure you didn't. Now tell me, who did you steal this from? A governor? Some wealthy merchant?"

"I didn't steal it," Jeryn said, which was the truth. "I bought it at a junk bazaar somewhere," he added, which was a lie. "On Galaway Prime, maybe."

"A junk bazaar," the officer snorted. "I don't think so."

Jeryn stared at the weapon. It was within easy reach, and the temptation to grab it was strong. But the officer had a holstered plasma blaster on his hip. The man could easily draw the firearm, discharge it, and burn a hole through Jeryn's chest (and the wall behind him, if the setting was strong enough) in far less time than a blade-wielding detainee could attack. They both knew this, which was why Jeryn made no move for the kukri, and why the officer didn't look the least bit worried.

"Did you know," the officer said, "that someone matching your description is wanted in connection with that slave revolt a few years back in the Mutara system?"

Uh-oh, Jeryn thought. He shook his head. "No, I didn't know that."

Nodding at the blade, the officer said, "Someone who used a weapon very similar to this one." The man folded his arms. "This far out in the Realm, we don't get a lot of blademasters. Hence my curiosity."

"I'm no blademaster," Jeryn said with a shrug. "I just bought the thing at a bazaar, like I said." Until now, he'd hoped to be able to talk his way out of his predicament. Or at least (and more likely) grease his way out, as he'd done so many times in the past. Local police in remote systems like this one were notoriously underpaid and usually quite easy to bribe. But now something told him that with this particular officer on this particular planet, things might not be so easily resolved. The man looked at Jeryn with an eager, knowing stare. Like he was on to something. Like this arrest might turn out to be a lot more than a workaday smuggler's bust.

Jeryn began to worry, really worry, about what might happen next. If the man brought in a lie-detecting wrist band to compel the truth from Jeryn, or if he managed to figure out his detainee was using a false identity, things would go from bad to disastrous pretty quickly. Jeryn had to do something, and he had to do it now.

"It doesn't look it," the officer said, gesturing to the blade, "but it's so old our scanners can't even identify the tech it's using."

Jeryn swallowed, thought for a moment, then said, "It doesn't have any tech. Your scanner was wrong. It's just a regular blade." He reached for the handle, then stopped halfway. "May I?"

The officer moved his hand to his blaster's grip, then gave his detainee a single nod. "Watch yourself."

Jeryn wrapped his fingers around the handle and lifted the

blade, feeling its familiar weight and balance. He gripped it, turned it over a couple times, and said, "See, no tech. It's just an old knife." He set it down again. "I don't know, maybe it is worth something. Maybe that dealer on Galaway Prime didn't know what he had. Sometimes valuable stuff falls through the cracks and ends up in a junk bazaar. It happens." He pushed the blade toward the officer. "If this is my ticket out of here, that's fine by me."

The man smiled, shook his head. "It's funny you think you have some leverage here, citizen." He glanced down at the blade. "But I think I'll wait for those reports to come in from Mutara 3 before I cut a deal with you."

"Reports?"

"My cousin's a fellow officer in the Mutara system," the man said. "I just got off a hypercast with him. According to him, they have a few geneprints from that slave revolt that have never been identified. Sourced from a few drops of blood left on the scene, apparently. He's having the reports sent to me, and they'll be here any minute now. And if your geneprint turns out to match one on the report...." He shook his head ruefully. "You're going to have a lot of explaining to do."

Jeryn tried to slow his thrumming heartbeat. "I don't know anything about a slave revolt," he lied, then dropped his gaze to the blade. "And I've only had that knife a few months. I don't even know how to use it. I just saw it at a bazaar and liked the way it looked."

The officer pondered the blade. "It is a beautiful weapon, I'll give you that."

Come on, pick it up already, Jeryn pleaded silently. He imagined police reports from the Mutaran authorities traveling through subspace, traversing light-years almost instantaneously and arriving at the precinct where he sat now, all but helpless.

Then the officer reached for the kukri's handle. Jeryn held his breath in anticipation.

"An exquisite piece of weaponry. I've never seen—"

Every muscle in the officer's body stiffened. His face froze, features contorted into a mask of agonizing pain. Immobilized except for a jerking twitch jolting his entire body, the man looked as if a reactor's worth of energy were passing through him. The pain had to be excruciating.

The officer's geneprint didn't match the blade's owner, and his bare-skinned grasp on the weapon's handle had triggered the kukri's nerve-induction countermeasure. Jeryn had seen the defensive capability activated only a few times over the years. It was an easy one to avoid since just about any glove could thwart it. The officer, seeing Jeryn handle the weapon, had assumed it was safe for him to do the same. A tremendous blunder.

Jeryn reached for the blade. The kukri's countermeasure instantly deactivated to his touch, and to his great relief he felt no trace of the defensive tech. He snatched the blade from the officer's grip, and the man collapsed limply to the floor. The countermeasure didn't kill, it only incapacitated. The officer's lights would be out for several minutes, and afterward he'd have one heck of a headache. Jeryn tucked the weapon into an oversized pocket in his jacket's lining.

He took a moment to gather himself. *All right, now how do I get out of here?*

Leaving the room, he closed the door behind him and found the corridor empty. He turned right and walked, expecting an alarm to blare at any second or a stampede of officers to round the corner with their blasters drawn. If the room he'd just exited had been monitored, one or both of those things would happen in pretty short order.

Thankfully, neither did. The officer must have switched off

whatever monitoring tech the room had in place. A pretty common practice, in Jeryn's experience. For a variety of reasons (none of them good ones), backwater police often ensured their dealings with detainees weren't recorded for posterity.

Jeryn spotted the restroom he'd noticed earlier at the end of the corridor. He entered, finding it empty. And better still, on the far wall there was a pane of frosted glass at head height. An outer window just large enough for him to crawl through. As he approached, he realized the glass wasn't a proper window you could open and close. There were no latches or opening mechanisms.

He'd have to cut his way out.

Removing the kukri from his jacket, he pressed a sequence into the finger grooves. A familiar vibration briefly tickled his palm as the blade took on a glowing red sheen. He approached the window, running his eyes over the outer casing where the glass and wall came together.

His kukri made short work of the casing, cutting it neatly along all four sides. He then carefully pried out the glass and placed it on the floor. Deactivating the blade, he sheathed the weapon and shimmied up and out of the building's newest exit, dropping down into an alleyway. Still no alarms, no sign he'd been noticed. He headed toward the open-air bazaar at the end of the alley. He could lose himself in the crowded marketplace, but he wouldn't breathe any easier until he was out of the city and off the planet.

"Stop right there! Don't take another step!"

He didn't turn to look at whoever was shouting from inside the building. He sprinted madly for the bazaar, arms pumping, head down. A brilliant flash of yellow lit up the darkened alley and the crack-sizzle discharge of a plasma blaster filled his ears. The shot missed, but not by much. Stonework exploded near

Jeryn's head, showering him with pebble-sized debris and dust. He was out of the alley before a second shot could be fired.

The large plaza was packed and bustling with late-afternoon shoppers. A knot of locals, hearing the blaster fire, surged instinctively away from the alley's entrance. Fear and confusion filled human and nonhuman faces, stares shifting between Jeryn and the settling debris cloud a few meters behind him.

Covering his head with his jacket hood, he quickly strode away from the onlookers. He had to disappear in the crowd. Taking a quick backward glance, he saw no one following him. Maybe whoever had shot at him hadn't been able to climb up and out the window.

A commotion over at the police precinct's entryway caught his attention. Officers brandishing weapons poured from the building and fanned out into the busy, teeming square. Wonderful, Jeryn thought. Word had gotten out. They were after him. Suddenly, losing himself in the crowd no longer seemed like the best plan.

He made a beeline for the plaza's nearest exit, a towering redstone archway. The crowd, already reacting to the police presence, began to evacuate the plaza in a rushed frenzy. A sense of confusion growing into panic filled the air.

"What's happening?" someone shouted. "Is it Teg terrorists?"

"Is there a bomb?" another person cried. "Did anyone see a bomb?"

The fearful clamor of human and nonhuman languages grew louder as Jeryn found himself carried along by a current of moving bodies. A Xamorian clutching her offspring to her chest stumbled into him, nearly knocking over Jeryn and a few others.

"Watch where you're going, you stinking geck!" someone barked.

A pair of arms shoved the Xamorian from behind, sending the sentient reptile sprawling to the ground. The Xamorian lost her grip on her three younglings and the creatures tumbled away, their tiny, long-tailed bodies vulnerable beneath a blur of scrambling legs and stomping feet. The parent shrieked in panic, then nimbly dashed through the crowd on all fours and recovered two of the three. Swinging her gaze all around, the parent shrieked again, frantic to find the third youngling.

Sickened by the thought of an infant trampled in front of its parent, Jeryn searched the ground around him. He spotted what looked like a small ball, then realized it was the third baby Xamorian, curled up in a defensive posture. Pressing his way through the swarm of bodies, he scooped up the tiny thing, who'd somehow managed to avoid being stepped on. A stinging bite to his finger was the only thanks he got as he returned the child to its parent, who clutched the youngling tightly and then disappeared in the throng.

Regaining his bearings, Jeryn realized he'd been pushed back toward the center of the plaza, the opposite direction he needed to go. A few meters away, a pair of uniformed police, their weapons raised, moved in his direction. He put his head down and strode straight for the archway exit, knifing through the sea of bodies and hoping the officers hadn't spotted him.

Seconds later, he passed under the archway. Beyond it the crowd dispersed among three broad avenues stretching away from the plaza in different directions. He risked a backward glance, relieved to find no one pursuing him. The panic from moments before began to dissipate into something less fearful as the crowd seemed to sense the danger in the plaza was now safely behind them. For his part, Jeryn felt far from safe. He needed to put more distance between himself and the authorities scouring the area. Scanning up and down the street, he grunted in frustration. There was never a taxi around when you needed one. Maybe he could catch a ride the next block over.

He cut through a side street, his head still covered, eyes still down, trying to recall any surveillance tech he'd noticed since arriving on the planet hours earlier. Some places had every square inch of the city under constant watch. The older, core worlds usually. Other worlds monitored public places very little or not at all, depending on how robust local privacy laws were. He couldn't remember where this world fit on the high-privacy, high-security spectrum, so he judiciously kept his head hooded and his gaze to the ground.

Reaching the next block, he gasped as a ground car abruptly stopped in front of him, nearly clipping his legs. Long and black with darkened, opaque windows, the vehicle blocked his path as it floated on its repulsor field, gently bobbing up and down. The back door slid open.

"Get in," an artificial voice behind Jeryn said.

He turned to find two Thracites towering over him. The two-meter-tall insectoid bipeds stared at him through luminescent honeycombed eyes. Each sported a universal translator on their left shoulder, or what a human would call a left shoulder. Jeryn wasn't sure what it was called on a Thracite.

The nearest one uttered a series of clicks, and a moment later the tinny voice from the translator said, "Please enter the vehicle and make no attempt to flee."

Jeryn's instinct was to make a run for it, but he realized any such effort would be pointless. Thracites were far faster than humans. The pair would be on top of him before he could take three steps.

He turned again to the ground car, a sudden curiosity striking him. The long, sleek machine looked more like a private vehicle than something you'd see in a police fleet. And then there were the Thracites. They surely weren't police. Every world Jeryn had been to didn't allow Thracites to be employed by law enforcement. Their hive-oriented minds didn't adapt very well to police work, he'd heard somewhere.

But if not the police, then who exactly had caught him?

He felt a sharp nudge in his back. "Get in," the translator's voice repeated, this time more insistent.

"All right, all right," he said, climbing into the car and sinking into a cushioned seat that wrapped around the spacious passenger area. Whether the vehicle was automated or operated by a driver, he didn't know. A solid divider separated the back from the front cabin.

The only other occupant sat across from him, an ebony-skinned human with short-cropped, dark hair and a neatly trimmed beard, both gone partly gray. The man appeared to be in his late sixties, if Jeryn had to guess. You could never be too sure about a person's age, especially someone older. Gene-based rejuvenation therapies were banned, but if you had enough money there were plenty of underground rejoo clinics around, even on a backwater world like this one.

The man wore elegant clothes, a smart business suit with a matching cloak folded neatly and lying on the seat beside him. The garb wasn't local, Jeryn noted. The man was from a core world, based on the cut and style of his suit. What could a stranger from the core possibly want with him?

"I'm not with the local authorities, as you've no doubt surmised by now," the man said, his voice as relaxed as his posture. "And you're not under arrest."

Jeryn didn't know what to think. "I'm not?"

"I must say I'm impressed," the man said with an approving nod. "I'd very much like to learn how you managed to escape. I was only moments away from having you released."

"Released?"

"Yes, in the event you didn't manage to free yourself. I thought it might be interesting to wait a while, see if you could find your own way out. And here you are. Well done."

Jeryn couldn't remember the last time he'd been this thoroughly confused. What exactly was happening here?

"Sorry, you were *waiting* for me to escape?"

"Of course," the man said. "You've absconded from custody seven times in the last five years, and from much more seasoned police forces than this lot. It was reasonable to assume they wouldn't be able to detain you for long."

This strange man, whoever he was, struck Jeryn as someone born to wealth and privilege. His manner had the relaxed confidence Jeryn associated with the rich and powerful. Upper crust poise, he'd once heard someone say, was as solid and unbreakable as the hardest stone.

"So what is this?" Jeryn asked.

"This," the man said, "is… an interview of sorts, I suppose."

"Interview? What kind of interview?"

The man leaned forward a bit. "Tell me, Jeryn, are you enjoying your chosen profession?"

Jeryn wasn't sure which surprised him more: the odd question or the fact that this stranger knew his real name. Who in the bloody stars *was* this man?

Before he could answer, the man continued. "It can't be a very rewarding existence, living hand to mouth, always on the move, trying to stay one step ahead of the authorities. Correct me if I'm wrong."

Jeryn shook his head, his confusion mounting with each word the man spoke. "Let's back up for a minute. First of all, who are you? And what exactly do you want with me?"

The man smiled patiently. "You like to get right to the point, don't you? I envy that. If only I could be so blunt in my profession. It would save so much time and effort. But I'm afraid in my world, tact and discretion are the necessary forms of engagement."

"And what exactly is your world?" Jeryn asked.

"If things proceed as I hope them to, you'll find out soon enough." The man smiled again and nodded. "I'm being vague, forgive me. It's no easy thing to speak candidly when you're so accustomed to the opposite. Let me try to be more clear."

The man fixed Jeryn with a steady, unblinking gaze. "My name is Whitmere Everfeld. I manage the largest intelligence operation in the Realm, and I'd like you to come work for me."

PART 1

1

SMUGGLING DEFFLIN

"*Inspection team en route,* Starhopper. *ETA five minutes.*"

"Copy that, customs house," Jeryn Lorsi replied over the comms. "Standing by." He muted the connection, sighed, and turned to Defflin. "Not the best turn of events, I know. We'll just have to deal with it. When they get here, stay calm and let me do all the talking. Got it?"

Defflin swallowed, then nodded. "I understand."

Jeryn did his best not to convey his worry. Defflin, his bald, pale-skinned passenger, looked nervous enough for the both of them, and the customs inspectors hadn't even arrived yet. This was not good, Jeryn thought. Not good at all.

They sat in the cramped cockpit of the *Starhopper*, a cargo vessel Jeryn had chartered under a false identity. The ship carried foodstuffs and mechanical parts acquired on Primus 7 over the last couple of weeks. His cover identity was a workaday inter-system merchant, so he'd stuffed the hold full of wholesale goods commonly traded in these parts. The *Starhopper*'s only passengers were him and his human contraband, Bourke Defflin, a military officer who'd had enough of the local authoritarian regime. Defflin had cut a deal with Jeryn's boss, trading dirty little state secrets for a free ticket out of his home system and a new life on a distant and hopefully less repressive world.

Smuggling a defector out of their home system was supposed to be an easy job. A low risk, high success rate kind of gig. And this one had been going perfectly to plan until a few moments ago. Now there was an inspection crew on the way that'd board his vessel and, if he was lucky, they'd only audit his cargo to make sure it matched the manifest. If he wasn't lucky, if somehow their cover had been blown, the inspectors would storm aboard with blasters in hand and an arrest warrant for one Bourke Defflin. There was no way of knowing which scenario might play out. And in a well-used fifty-year-old cargo ship with outdated everything, making a run for it wasn't an option. All Jeryn could do was wait for things to unfold and try to keep his jittery passenger from losing it in the meantime.

Jeryn gestured to the enormous structure floating in space beyond the cockpit's viewport. "Have you ever seen a gate up close?"

The man shook his head. "I've never been this far out before." He moved his eyes across the interstellar gate, which at this proximity took up most of their visual field. Marker buoys floated in the void, blinking green and tracing the gate's perimeter at hundred-meter intervals. The translucent surface of the gate shimmered, glowing with a soft purple hue some called lavender and others referred to as amethyst. Beyond it, no ships or stars or planets could be seen, only what appeared to be an empty void.

"You've seen others?" Defflin asked.

Jeryn nodded. "I have."

"Is this a big one?" Defflin asked.

"Actually, it's fairly small, as gates go," Jeryn replied. The Primus system gate measured two thousand kilometers across at its widest point. Most gates were at least twice that size.

"A small one," Defflin murmured, awestruck as he stared out

at the gate. The distraction seemed to have worked for the moment. "And why do they vary in size?"

"No one knows, really." For a moment, Jeryn found himself sharing the man's sense of wonder as he gazed out at the colossal mystery.

The gates had been in use for thousands of years. And how they did what they did—impossibly connecting star systems light-years apart like a doorway connecting adjacent rooms—was still an unsolved riddle of science. Cosmologists couldn't even agree whether the gates were a natural phenomenon or constructed by some alien intelligence who'd long since abandoned them. But no one disagreed that without them the Realm couldn't exist. With light speed's unyielding limitation, far-flung stars and civilizations—without interstellar gates—would be inconceivably distant, requiring years or decades of travel time, even between the closest neighboring systems. But the gates had changed that, cutting a ten-light-year journey to a week-long burn between habitable zones, enabling an interstellar empire to develop and flourish until eventually the Realm's banner flew over cities on thousands of worlds.

Every time he approached a gate zone, Jeryn reflected on how strange it was that such a vital component of an empire's existence was an unresolved enigma. A paradox of everything known about the nature of space and time.

Or maybe it wasn't so strange. Primitive cultures expertly navigated oceans while being utterly ignorant of the science behind shifting currents. Birds glided on air thermals without the faintest notion of how atmospheric temperature worked. Were the gates any different? Did civilization really need to know *how* they worked, as long as they invariably worked as expected?

A proximity alert beeped, rousing Jeryn from his thoughts. He brought up an external view on a holo display. The customs house shuttle was three hundred meters to port, feathering its braking thrusters as it approached the *Starhopper*'s docking bay.

Defflin cast a worried glance at the display. "How often do cargo ships get boarded for inspection?"

Two percent was the answer. That was the prevailing inspection rate for this gate's customs house. Jeryn had learned the statistic during his prep work. He considered lying, telling his nervous passenger this sort of thing was quite common in hopes it might ease the man's nerves. But then if Defflin looked it up on his terminal (the data was publicly available) and discovered the truth, the man's nervousness might spill over into panic. And the last thing you should do while emigrating illegally was panic.

"It doesn't happen often," Jeryn answered, settling for a vague reply. "But it happens. Look, we're fine. Our IDs are solid, our ship manifest is in order. You've got nothing to worry about."

"*Starhopper, this is Primus Gate Shuttle A6. Docking in sixty seconds,*" a voice over the comms said.

Before Jeryn could reply, Defflin asked him, "Have you ever been boarded?"

This time a lie was definitely in order. "Sure I have," Jeryn said, projecting a confidence he didn't feel. "Plenty of times. Never once had a problem." In truth, he'd been stopped by Customs and Borders only twice since coming to work for the Agency, and on each occasion he'd only narrowly avoided arrest. He tapped the comms. "Understood, A6. We'll meet you in the docking bay."

Starhopper's crew of two stood before the docking bay's airlock doors, waiting for the pressurization cycle to finish. Jeryn had silently debated the wisdom of bringing Defflin along, finally deciding the man's absence might make the inspection team suspicious. He glanced at the military officer. The man's forehead was beaded with sweat, his features knotted with worry. Maybe he should have left him behind after all. Would Defflin remember his cover name under stress? Would he hesitate to answer questions, or worse, would he stammer and avoid eye contact like some amateur thief caught red-handed? The stars only knew. Jeryn readied himself to catch any balls the man might drop in the next few moments.

"The inspector's a Rauk," Jeryn said.

"How do you know?" Defflin asked.

"I recognized the accent on the comms."

"They let mutts serve in C&B?"

Jeryn shot the man a stern look. "Rauk," he corrected. "The agent's a *Rauk*. Get the word 'mutt' out of your head or you might use it by accident. You don't want a customs agent angry at you, believe me."

Defflin nodded vigorously. "Right, yes, right. Sorry." The man took a series of long inhalations and exhalations.

Mutt, Jeryn thought angrily. Humankind had belittling slurs for every nonhuman species in the Realm. You heard them more in some places than in others, but no world inhabited by humans seemed to be free of them. And it went both ways too. Humans were on the receiving end of their own harsh epithets, uttered in every nonhuman language throughout the Realm. Jeryn had little patience for any of it. Unlike most citizens, he'd traveled extensively, and he'd long since come to the conclusion that people were people, no matter where they lived or how many legs they walked on or if they were warm-blooded or not. A decent person was a decent person, human or otherwise. Sadly, he'd also found the opposite to be just as true. Every species, without exception, had its fair share of fools and deplorables. Ignorance and depravity, it seemed, were universal.

But now wasn't the time to chastise the man. Anything that gave Defflin *more* anxiety would only make things more difficult.

Above the airlock doors, an indicator panel blinked PRESSURIZATION COMPLETE in green letters. With a soft hiss, the doors slid open.

The Rauk stood in front, towering head and shoulders above the two human assistants behind him. The mottled gray fur of his hands and head was neatly brushed and trimmed in a fashion much shorter than the dozen-centimeter length preferred by most of his kind. His tail hung to the backs of his knees, plaited in the tight braid Rauks typically wore in the workplace. The large upward-pointing ears pivoted toward Jeryn and Defflin, and the inspector's black canine-like nose flared in a quick succession of sniffs.

All three agents wore the blue-with-yellow-trim uniform of the Customs and Borders service. Only the Rauk, however, sported the C&B's stars and planets insignia embroidered onto the shoulders of his jacket. A marker of his seniority.

Jeryn also noted the plasma blasters all three wore at their sides. They were hard to miss.

"Permission to board," the Rauk said, but he didn't wait for a reply, striding forward into the corridor.

2

STARHOPPER INSPECTION

MINUTES LATER, JERYN, DEFFLIN, AND THE LEAD C&B inspector sat in the ship's only meeting room. The small space could accommodate up to four humans, or as it did at the moment, two humans and a Rauk. The junior officers waited in the corridor beyond the closed door.

Wuden was the inspector's name, and his eyes shifted between the *Starhopper*'s two crew. While he gave off a distinct air of stern authority, the Rauk seemed less than interested in the contents of the ship's manifest, which Jeryn had pulled up on the holo display. Granted, Rauk facial expressions were difficult for humans to read. Jeryn couldn't say for certain what he saw in the inspector's gaze. Boredom, condescension, suspicion? It could have been any of those. Could have been something else. Inspector Wuden also hadn't stopped sniffing since he'd stepped on board, his nose twitching constantly in a way that you *never* openly compared to a dog's behavior if you valued your life.

Before Jeryn had scrolled through half of the manifest's contents, the Rauk waved him silent. "Yes, yes, that's fine." He removed a hand terminal from his jacket and extended it. The red, white, and black banner of the Realm glowed on the device's face. "Please transfer the contents so my team can begin the physical audit."

"Of course," Jeryn said, gesturing a copy of the manifest over to the inspector's device.

"If everything's in order, we'll send you on your way without further delay."

"Thank you, Inspector," Jeryn said. Beside him, Defflin sat quietly. Thankfully, the man seemed to have calmed down a bit. He no longer had a nervous sheen of perspiration on his forehead, and while he still looked uncomfortable, it was nothing compared to the conspicuous anxiety from earlier. Uncomfortable was fine with Jeryn, because uncomfortable was plausible. C&B inspectors always made merchants uneasy.

"You may begin the audit," Inspector Wuden said into his terminal. Outside, the junior officers' footsteps could be heard, heading in the direction of the cargo bay.

The way an inspection was *supposed* to work and how it actually went, as Jeryn well knew from his smuggling days, were often two very different things. Standard operating procedure entailed a simple audit, inspectors matching up a physical count of goods in the cargo bay with the ship's official manifest. Any variation between the two meant fines, duty penalties, and in extreme cases, arrest and prosecution. In reality, though, fines and penalties were almost never paid, and arrests were a rarity. Payoffs were the most common way interstellar traders resolved audit infractions with local officials. Here in the Primus system, no different than anywhere else in the Realm, bribes were the grease that turned the wheels of commerce.

"Are you both from Primus originally?" the inspector asked, his stern tone softening into something more conversational.

"I grew up in Vanommia," Defflin said. Jeryn gave a silent thanks the man remembered the right system from his false identity.

Inspector Wuden lifted his chin. "Vanommian? Your accent sounds local to my ears."

"Oh, well," Defflin stammered, "we, ah, emigrated when I was very young."

"And you?" the Rauk asked, shifting his gaze to Jeryn.

"Zankara," Jeryn said. "Born and raised."

"Lovely planet, Zankara Prime," Inspector Wuden said, nodding. "I know it. Twin moons, green sunsets. I had the good fortune to be stationed there years ago."

As they waited for the audit results, the inspector made small talk, mostly around local inter-system commerce. There was a pending merger between a pair of (former) rival trade syndicates, and the Rauk ardently believed the proposed consolidation violated the Realm's monopoly laws. If the Assembly of Regents approved the union, he insisted, it would be disastrous for Primus and its neighboring systems. Prices would go through the roof on the raw materials used in shipbuilding, a vital local industry employing hundreds of thousands.

"An economic disaster in the making," Wuden said, shaking his head.

As the C&B inspector spoke, his obsessive sniffing went on unabated. Jeryn had been around Rauks enough to know incessant sniffing signaled nervousness or anxiety, but in this case that interpretation hardly made sense. The inspector was in charge of the situation, his authority empowered by interstellar law. He had absolutely nothing to worry about. Maybe it was an unconscious tic? Jeryn tried not to stare at the Rauk's shiny, quivering nose.

Defflin seemed to relax, engaging in more banter than Jeryn would have liked. Idle chitchat could be dangerous if you weren't careful. Jeryn had seen covers blown with nothing more than a carelessly uttered word or two. But Defflin talked on, and the more he conversed with the Rauk, the less anxious he appeared.

Which was... odd. If anything, Jeryn reflected, it should have been the other way around. Defflin had been a jittery ball of nerves *before* the ship had been boarded by the authorities, and now, sitting here face to face with someone who could send him to prison forever, the man seemed utterly relaxed. Inexplicably relaxed.

Something wasn't right. The Rauk's constant sniffing. Defflin's sudden and improbable composure. Both behaviors felt out of place, unnatural.

Then it struck him, a feeling in his gut that explained everything. *These two know one another.*

Jeryn stood and said, "Will you excuse me for a moment?"

"Wait, where are you—" The door slid shut behind Jeryn, cutting off the inspector's words. He sprinted down the curved corridor for the escape pods, hoping he could get there faster than the junior officers, who'd no doubt already been summoned to arrest him. Or shoot him.

He scrambled to a stop as he reached the row of pods. His pulse racing, he slapped his left hand against the bioscanner. With his free hand, he reached under his jacket, instinctively releasing the snap on his power blade's sheath. Not that it would do much good against plasma guns, but the weapon had saved him on so many occasions—both in his former life as a smuggler and his current one as an Agency operative—his hand automatically reached for the kukri blade in moments of danger.

"Come on, come on," he whispered desperately, waiting for the pod's hatch to open. From beyond the passageway's bend, rapid footfalls clapped against the floor and grew louder. He turned to see both junior officers appear with their weapons drawn just as the hatch hissed open. He dove into the cramped pod, feeling as much as hearing the pulse of the blaster fire that struck the bulkhead where he'd been standing a moment before. The hatch sealed shut behind him.

"Emergency jettison!" he panted.

Before he could strap himself in, the pod launched, pressing him awkwardly against the seat. He gritted his teeth against the sudden weight of thrust gravity. Pods were too small for artigrav generators, so you either floated weightlessly or got pinned down by acceleration. A few stomach-turning moments later, the thrusters cut out and the elephant sitting on his chest was gone. His lungs no longer compressed, he gulped down a couple deep breaths and buckled himself in.

The comms indicator was already blinking an angry red. "Starhopper *pod, you are in violation of Primus Gate Zone navigational procedures. Stop your vessel immediately or we will open fire. Repeat, stop your vessel or we will open fire.*"

He gestured up the navigation display, checking his position in space. A green triangle icon represented his pod. Two blue dots were the *Starhopper* and the C&B frigate whose shuttle had ferried over Inspector Wuden's team. The frigate's transponder broadcast its name as the *Resolute*. A grid of twelve red dots floated between the pod and the gate. Automated sentry guns.

The voice from the *Resolute* barked at Jeryn again. "Starhopper *escape pod, this is your last warning. Stop your vessel immediately or you will be destroyed.*"

Scanning the display, Jeryn quickly worked the math on an escape route. He was a one-minute burn from the gate, and by law the local jurisdiction wasn't allowed to chase him through into the next system.

"Maximum burn for the gate," he told the pod's nav system, "on this course." With his index finger, he quickly traced a path through the sentry gun field. "Engage thrust now."

The explosive burst from the pod's engines roared in his ears as an enormous invisible hand shoved him hard against the seat, pressing down on his chest so hard he could barely breathe. His eyeballs felt like they would burst under the pressure as the pod rocketed for the gate. He told himself all he had to do was hang on for one minute and it would be over. Then again, it might be over in less than a minute, a morbid voice inside him added.

A bright point of white appeared on the display, emerging from the *Resolute*'s blue icon. The display chirped a loud warning and flashed MISSILE LOCK.

"Come on, *move*," he grunted, watching the display.

Most escape pods, like the one he was in at the moment, were little more than airtight lifeboats. They had no combat capabilities or defense systems whatsoever. The pod could track an incoming missile, but it couldn't do much to evade one.

The little vessel rocketed toward the gate, the missile in pursuit and the sentry guns ahead. Jeryn pictured the railguns floating in the void, their enormous cannons tracking his thin-hulled pod.

This wasn't exactly how he'd expected the mission to end up, he thought bitterly. Unbidden, an image of Everfeld's disappointed face appeared in his thoughts. He forced it out of his head; he had to focus on survival. Shame and professional embarrassment could wait.

"How long until we're in sentry gun range?" he asked the system.

"Twenty-three seconds," the system replied.

"External view, aft," he said. At the bottom of the display, the pod's rear-facing visual feed appeared, showing a wide view of space behind him. For the moment there was only blackness and a field of stars, but he knew that would change soon enough.

Straining against the thrust, Jeryn glanced at the tactical portion of the display. The white dot was closing in fast on the pod, a wild dog on a rabbit. A painfully slow rabbit. It was going to be close.

"Put a countdown to sentry range on the display," he said. The number seventeen appeared above the red field of sentry guns. Sixteen... fifteen...

Each second seemed to take an eternity as thrust gravity compressed every muscle and bone in his body. The blood in his veins surrendered to the heavy pressure, retreating from his extremities. Suddenly, he was lightheaded, and his hands and toes began to go numb. He knew he had only seconds before he blacked out. Gritting his teeth and grunting, he bore down to force blood back into his head as he watched the countdown reach nine, then eight. He had to wait until the last possible moment to utter the command. If he did it too soon, the crew of the *Resolute* might be able to counter his move somehow. The edges of his vision went black. He couldn't wait any longer.

"Security override three five seven," he groaned into the comms, "countersign *Fond Farewell*."

On the rear-facing visual feed, he spotted the incoming missile coming on fast. The projectile itself was still too small to be visible, but its long exhaust plume glowed bright against the black void. He watched the missile's tail grow larger and brighter. His vision blurred and began to narrow into a shrinking tunnel.

Then the feed lit up with what looked like fiery whips slashing through space. All twelve railguns had opened fire on the missile, each gun discharging hundreds of incandescent rounds per second. The deadly projectile erupted into a bright, brief explosion the vacuum of space quickly snuffed out.

The emergency override, the last resort he never imagined he'd have to use, had worked. Everything around him became hazy and unfocused, and he was vaguely aware of the voice from the *Resolute* cursing him over the comms.

Smiling weakly, he lost consciousness moments before his pod passed safely through the gate.

When Jeryn came to, the first thing he was aware of was a throbbing headache. The second thing was a change in the view through the pod's small porthole. Where there had been the massive swirling surface of the interstellar gate before, now there was the interior of a docking bay.

A familiar docking bay, thankfully. He'd made it through. Blowing out a long, relieved breath, he sat up, his body feeling light now that the hammer fist of thrust gravity was gone. The pod's hatch slid open with a hiss, and a large head of messy gray-and-black fur poked inside.

"You've looked better," Bhokken the Rauk said.

"I've felt better," Jeryn replied, rubbing his temples. "My head's killing me."

The Rauk smiled. "So, how'd the mission go?"

"That's not funny."

Bhokken reached inside and grasped Jeryn by the upper arm. "Let me give you a hand. There you go. Easy now."

Steadied by the Rauk engineer's strong grip, Jeryn stepped out of the pod on wobbly legs. "Thanks. Are we in the clear?"

Bhokken nodded. "We are. Everything's fine. As soon as you came through, we snatched you up and burned out of there. Next stop is Corren 5. We'll be there in five days." He scratched behind his ear, then added, "Want to tell me what happened?"

"Not really. Maybe later."

"Well," the Rauk sighed, "at least you made it through with your hide intact." Bhokken ran a clawed digit over the pendant hanging from his neck. "Fifteen be praised," he muttered.

Jeryn frowned. "I didn't think you were religious."

"I'm not," Bhokken said. "I'm superstitious."

"What's the difference?"

The Rauk shrugged. "I'm not really sure, to be honest."

Bhokken threw an arm around Jeryn's shoulder. "Come on, kiddo, let's go find something for that headache in the med bay."

3

DIRTY BUSINESS

Whitmere Everfeld hurried down the corridor, his cloak fluttering behind him. His mind raced, trying to come up with a reason behind the emergency meeting with the CM. He failed to imagine any good ones.

Normally, an audience with the consul minister, the Realm's highest-ranking state executive, was planned well in advance. Weeks, even months ahead of time. An urgent, unscheduled summons like this one was almost unheard of. Even for Everfeld, who'd served as the Agency's director for nearly thirty years, impromptu meetings with the CM were a rarity.

A young officer in military uniform greeted Everfeld as he arrived at the executive conference suite.

"Director Everfeld," the officer said, motioning to an open doorway, "we have a secure connection ready for you. This way, please."

"Thank you."

Inside the suite with the door closed behind him, Everfeld waited for the CM's office to initiate the hypercast. Slightly out of breath from the rushed, five-minute hike through the complex's underground tunnels, he was grateful for a quiet moment to collect himself. He stood with his hands clasped behind his back, a holo display a few meters ahead of him. The standby icon, a tabletop-sized Rockets and Stars banner, waved in a nonexistent breeze.

Try as he might, he still failed to come up with an explanation for the hastily scheduled meeting. Something urgent, clearly, but what? He'd find out soon enough, he supposed. A small part of him worried that perhaps one of his covert operations—the ones he hadn't sought approval for and only he knew about—had somehow been discovered.

A minute later, the icon dissolved into an image of three people gazing at him from the CM's communications office. Familiar faces all. Consul Minister Pettine Amarania, the longest-serving CM in the Realm's long history, stood in the center of the trio. Now in her middle seventies, she still wore her hair in the intricate braids associated with her homeworld of Gannebron 5. Everfeld had first met Amarania over thirty years ago, when those same white braids had been a fiery red. On Minister Amarania's left stood Subminister Clevon Jakaan, a longtime friend and colleague of Everfeld's who'd served as the CM's chief of staff for the last decade. Bronze-skinned with a shaved head, Jakaan wore a business cloak over his suit and stood with hands clasped in front of him. Opposite him, to the CM's right, was Pallat Menic, Jakaan's deputy chief of staff. A short man with a round face and salt-and-pepper hair, he'd held the position of Jakaan's most senior and trusted advisor for as long as Jakaan had served the CM in the same capacity.

"Minister Amarania, good afternoon," Everfeld said, nodding in deference. He then shifted his gaze briefly to Jakaan and Menic. "Gentlemen, good to see you. I hope you're all doing well."

"I'm not, to be quite honest with you," the CM said with characteristic bluntness. "I'm tired, Whitmere. I can't ever remember being this tired, frankly."

She looked it, Everfeld agreed inwardly. And though it was the first time he could remember her admitting as much, it wasn't the first time he'd noticed it. Dark circles had developed under her eyes in recent times. Those sharp green eyes that for decades had stared out at friend and foe alike with an unyielding conviction now seemed clouded over with something far less determined. He didn't know if what he saw was resignation, cynicism, despair, or some toxic mixture of all three. But whatever it was, it had taken its toll, aging her a decade in only a few short years. A physical beating to match the political one she'd been receiving lately.

"I'm sorry to hear that," Everfeld said, and he meant it. He'd had more than a few differences with the CM over the years (a handful of them heated exchanges during which he'd expected his resignation to be requested), but it still pained him to see his colleague of some three decades brought to such a state. "How can I be of service?"

"An opportunity has presented itself to us. Something of great importance we need your assistance with." She gestured to her chief of staff. "Subminister Jakaan will share the details with you."

"A security matter, Minister?" Everfeld asked.

"As I said, Clevon will share the details with you," the CM replied evasively. "I have another commitment at the moment, and I'm afraid I'm already running late. Please give this matter your highest priority... and your utmost discretion."

Everfeld resisted the urge to frown, instead bowing his head slightly. "Of course, Minister." Whatever this *opportunity* entailed, the CM clearly didn't want to be around when it was shared openly. A political instinct to distance herself from what the spymaster was fairly sure would be some piece of dirty business.

"I'll leave you to it then," she said. Her image dissolved as she stepped out of the projection. A moment later Everfeld heard a door close on the other end of the connection.

"She looks exhausted, Clevon," Everfeld said. "Or is it just my connection?"

Clevon Jakaan shook his head. "It's not your connection. She hasn't been sleeping well lately. We've been trying to get her to see a specialist about it, but you know how she is about doctors."

Everfeld shook his head. What a reversal of fortune had come to the woman, the shrewdest politician he'd ever known. Three decades earlier, she'd emerged from a bloody power struggle between rival merchant clans in her home system to win the planetary governorship with what a biographer would later call "a rare combination of perseverance and willpower." A political force of nature, she'd ascended to the office of consul minister a few years later in a landslide election. Over her next three six-year terms, she'd enjoyed massive public approval and presided over the largest expansion of settled space in the Realm's ten-thousand-year history.

Things began to turn, however, in her fourth term, when a handful of upstart peripheral systems declared independence. Then during her fifth term, largely due to her own administration's heavy-handed actions, the Separatist movement gained momentum, adding scores of worlds to its ranks. By the time she'd managed to win an unprecedented sixth term as CM, a quarter of the Realm's systems were either in open rebellion or sympathetic to the Separatist cause. She'd won the last reelection by the slimmest of margins, campaigning on the promise to unite the Realm and bring the errant systems back into the fold. Three years later, however, she'd made no progress on that pledge, and the Separatist movement showed no signs of slowing down. Her popularity among Realm citizens was now at an all-time low, and her critics had never been more plentiful.

"I can try and talk a bit of sense to her," Everfeld suggested.

"All the good it would do," Jakaan said. "She might look exhausted, but she's still as stubborn as ever."

"Good to see some things haven't changed," Everfeld said, then steered the conversation back to the meeting's still-secret purpose. "So tell me, what is it that's so urgent?"

Jakaan turned to his chief of staff and politely asked him to leave. The short man nodded, clearly expecting to be dismissed, and with a respectful nod to the spymaster he stepped away from the holo, leaving his superior alone with Everfeld.

Jakaan waited until the door closed behind the exiting man, then said, "It's about a Tegesian cleric, Charnette Tavella. Do you know the name?"

"I do," Everfeld said. "We've had our eye on her for a while now."

Jakaan lifted his chin. "You have?"

"We have a file on her," Everfeld said. "Nothing in depth. A record of her public statements, interviews, and so forth."

Jakaan gestured and a small holo of Tavella's head and shoulders appeared. She was young, less than thirty standard years if Everfeld remembered correctly. With long blonde hair, bright blue eyes, and fair skin, she was stunningly attractive, her looks rivaling those of popular actors and models from the entertainment and fashion feeds. *Angelic* was the word Everfeld thought of to describe her appearance. Appropriate, he mused, since her life's calling was a spiritual one.

The Agency had opened a file on her months earlier, but not for any particular reason. She was an up-and-comer within Tegesian faith's hierarchy, a savvy communications professional with a particular talent for persuasive speech-writing. Those scant facts were all he could recall about her at the moment. His organization had files on dozens, if not hundreds, of Tegesian clerics with similar profiles.

What exactly did the CM's office want with this Tavella? What did they know about her that he didn't?

"Over the past couple years," Jakaan said, "we've been in contact with someone close to her, someone who's provided detailed reports of her comings and goings."

"A plant operative with the Tegesians?" Everfeld asked, feeling a familiar surge of frustration. For years he'd pleaded with the CM and her senior staff about this sort of thing. Intelligence and counterintelligence were *supposed* to be the exclusive domain of his organization. But despite the CM's multiple pledges to *minimize any such activity*—he still bristled when he recalled the words she'd used, a promise that was anything but—every so often he'd become aware of yet another intelligence-gathering activity outside the Agency's purview. Everyone wanted their own in-house spies, it seemed.

Jakaan, noting Everfeld's reaction, showed his palms. "It's not like that, my friend. This was a paid informant, not a plant."

Everfeld frowned. "Two branches on the same tree, as far as I'm concerned." He then sighed and said, "We can debate departmental jurisdiction later. What did this informant tell you?"

Jakaan said, "This Tavella is much more than she appears. She's incredibly dangerous."

The comment, coupled with the grave look on the man's face, gave Everfeld pause. He'd worked with Jakaan for over a decade, known him personally for even longer, and the man wasn't prone to exaggeration. Neither did he spook easily.

"Dangerous in what way?" Everfeld asked.

"Let me show you," Jakaan said. He brought up a window displaying three ball-sized planets. "The Separatists, as we all know, are less of a singular movement than they are a collection of loosely aligned factions, the three largest of which operate out of these systems." Pointing, he named them. "Arella, Catarth, and Zeta Astoron."

Everfeld nodded. The three systems were well-known focal points for the Separatist movement.

"Over the last year," Jakaan continued, "Tavella has been making bi-monthly visits to all three systems. And she's been traveling under multiple false identities."

Alarms began going off in Everfeld's head. "You're certain about this?"

"One hundred percent." The man gestured again, and a moment later Everfeld felt his terminal buzz in his pocket. "I just sent you everything we have on her. All the evidence is there."

Everfeld glanced between the planets suspended before him. The implication of what he'd just heard—and what the evidence forwarded to him would presumably confirm—was worrisome, to put it mildly.

"You believe she's trying to unite the factions?" Everfeld said.

"We do," Jakaan replied. "And I think you understand what that could mean."

Everfeld's thoughts reeled off in a thousand directions. He pulled up a chair and sat down heavily.

"I had to sit when I heard it too," Jakaan said.

As stunned as Everfeld was, the skeptic in him died hard. There was one problem with what Jakaan was suggesting: the Tegesian faith itself. The Realm's predominant religion or moral philosophy, or whatever you cared to call it, was a pervasive institution across the Realm, with adherents on every world and from every known human and nonhuman sentient species. It was one of three foundational institutions of the Realm, along with the state and the trade syndicates. And institutions always favored stability over revolution. The Tegesian bureaucracy in particular was famously reluctant to make waves or take controversial positions.

Radical insurrection simply wasn't their way of doing things. It never had been.

"Why would the Tegesians do this?" Everfeld asked. "It's not in their interest to sow chaos." Dotta Superior Tolerance IV, the head of the Tegesian order, was a prudent, clever politician who had cultivated a close, mutually beneficial relationship with Amarania and the state apparatus she oversaw. Fomenting revolt would hardly benefit him or his order. Quite the contrary, in fact.

"That was my first thought as well," Jakaan said, "until we learned who else she's been talking with."

"But who—" Everfeld stopped himself as he realized who Jakaan had to be referring to. "The Originalists."

Jakaan nodded gravely. "She's met with them on ten different occasions over the last year."

Everfeld frowned, mulling over what he'd just heard. An extremist offshoot of the Tegesian faith, the Originalists advocated insurrection against what they referred to as the Realm's "pervasive corruption and failure to secure universal rights for its citizenry." They also chided their order's own orthodoxy as complicit in the Realm's many failings. For ten millennia, Tegesian mainliner clerics had turned a blind eye to the suffering of trillions, according to the Originalists.

"We believe she's working on their behalf," Jakaan said. "We're sure of it, in fact."

"And she's been keeping her activities secret from her superiors," Everfeld said, "traveling under different names."

"Exactly. She's been leading a double life for some time now. We're not quite sure when she was radicalized by the Originalists." Jakaan exhaled tiredly. "Not that it matters at this point."

"But she's so young," Everfeld said. "Do you really believe someone her age, with no diplomatic experience to speak of, can bring that squabbling rabble together?" Charnette Tavella wouldn't be the first, Everfeld reflected, who had tried to unite

Separatist factions. More than a few had attempted as much over the years, several of them seasoned diplomats from Separatist homeworlds, and none of them had come anywhere close to success.

"I didn't, at first," Jakaan said. He took a step closer, his image growing slightly on Everfeld's end. "But the more I learned about her, the less certain I was. She has remarkable gifts of persuasion, Whitmere, and she's got tremendous personal charisma. She's climbed the ranks of the Tegesian hierarchy faster than anyone I've ever seen. And usually that kind of ambition earns the contempt of your peers, but not with her. You can't find anyone, and I mean anyone, with a cross word to say about her. Quite the opposite, in fact. She's literally adored by everyone she's had any meaningful contact with."

"Have you met with her?" Everfeld asked.

"I haven't," Jakaan said, running a hand over the hairless dome of his head. "She's on the verge of succeeding where others have failed. I'm sure of it. From what we can gather, she's very close to bringing the Originalists and the largest Separatist factions together, in person, around the same table. We simply can't let her continue down this path."

Everfeld blinked. "She's trying to arrange some kind of political summit?"

"We think it's more like a war summit," Jakaan said. "And obviously we can't let things get to that point. If those parties get into a room with her, knowing what we know about how persuasive she is...." He tightened his lips and shook his head. "It can't happen, period. We've got to stop her, before it's too late. An anti-Realmist pact between the Originalists and the Separatist factions would be nothing short of disastrous." He swallowed and seemed to have difficulty finding the right words. "My department isn't really... equipped to handle this sort of thing."

"But mine, on the other hand," Everfeld said, understanding the grim task being asked of him.

"I'm afraid so."

"And you're certain the CM wants to go this direction?"

"We've discussed it at length," Jakaan said. "And her mind is set. It's an ugly business, and I know how you feel about this sort of thing. But in this case, the CM believes it's truly necessary, and I'm afraid I have to agree with her."

Everfeld recalled what Minister Amarania had said before leaving the meeting. *Highest priority, utmost discretion.*

"Do we have a time frame?" he asked.

"She'd like the book closed on this before her next public address next month."

"That's not a lot of time."

"I know," Jakaan said, "but you don't have to track Tavella down. She's not hard to find. She runs the Tegesian Public Information Office on Sandau Prime."

Everfeld considered this for a moment. "It will take me weeks to get someone there. I don't have anyone qualified for this sort of task on station in the Sandau system. And it's far too sensitive an operation to contract out to some local mercenary."

Jakaan nodded. "I understand. I'll see if I can buy you another week or two. But I can't promise anything. As soon as the CM understood the magnitude of the threat, she wanted to act immediately." The man let out a long breath and looked away for a moment, his expression deeply troubled.

"There's something else," Everfeld probed, "isn't there? Tell me."

Whatever it was Jakaan had yet to reveal, he seemed to be having a hard time how to word it. Finally, he said, "We're going to war, Whitmere. She's already asked her top military advisors to begin drawing up plans. I know how you feel about that, but that's the direction things are heading, and there's no stopping it now."

Everfeld's heart dropped into his stomach. The grim news wasn't unexpected, but it still managed to send a shock of dread through him.

"When?" he asked.

"I'm not sure," Jakaan said. "It's all still in the planning stages. They'll have to bring troops and ships together from all over the Realm before they take any action. The logistics are daunting, to say the least. I'd say six weeks at the earliest, but more realistically a couple months before the first shots are fired."

Everfeld didn't want to believe what he was hearing. The unthinkable was no longer a possibility, a worst-case scenario. Now it loomed before them, close and terrible.

Had the CM gone mad? Did she want to be remembered in infamy? As the breaker of the Realm? As history's worst mass murderer? There simply *had* to be a solution other than war.

"I know what you're thinking," Jakaan said. "And she can't be talked out of it."

"Have you tried as much?" Everfeld asked.

"You know I have, Whitmere. Almost as many times as you have. And the last time I went there two months ago, I'd never seen her so incensed. I thought I was going to be sacked on the spot. That's how angry she was with me for even hinting at appeasement." The CM's chief of staff sighed. "And of course it doesn't help that most of her staff agree with her, either in principle or out of their own spineless deference. We're the only two doves in a room full of hawks, old friend. A powerless minority. And this business with the cleric has sent her right over the edge. She figures if it's not this Tegesian charmer who brings the factions together, then someone else eventually will. She wants to strike now, before they can present a united front."

"We could let them go, of course," Everfeld said, not bothering to conceal his disdain. "Grant Separatist systems independence. Has anyone suggested that?"

"Like she'd ever let that happen," Jakaan said, then shrugged. "Like the Assembly of Regents would either, for that matter." The subminister's lips tightened into a straight line. "And I have to tell you, when you look at things from a purely tactical standpoint, it's hard to deny she has a point."

Before Everfeld could object, Jakaan continued. "Suppose for a moment the systems in question gain their independence. Can you imagine the chaos that would follow—maybe not immediately, but eventually—with rival empires occupying the same volume of space? And don't forget the Separatist worlds would have us surrounded. Even without a proper navy, their outlying geography gives them the upper hand. The gates are interstellar choke points, easily occupied and controlled, even with inferior forces, and more easily than you might imagine. Separatist worlds could bring all travel from the core outward to an absolute standstill. They would be free to explore and expand while the core withers and dies. But like all dying empires, the Realm would lash out to save itself. So no, I'm afraid granting our malcontent systems self-rule would only delay all-out war. It wouldn't prevent it."

For a long moment, neither man spoke. Then Jakaan said, "I suggest you take some time during your trip to Sandau Prime to look at the situation as closely as I have. I think you'll see there are no good outcomes here. All we can do now is choose among lesser evils. That's the unfortunate hand history has dealt us, my friend."

Everfeld blinked. "My trip to Sandau Prime?"

Jakaan cleared his throat. "Given its urgent and sensitive nature, the CM asked for you to personally supervise the cleric operation, on-site."

Everfeld's heart sank in disappointment. It wasn't an unusual request, but it meant he'd have to leave immediately. The Sandau system was a good three weeks away. Until Jakaan's last comment, the spymaster had already begun making mental plans for a trip to Gran Kiravashta to lobby the CM in person for a different, more diplomatic course of action. So much for that option.

Another uncomfortably long silence followed. Finally, Everfeld said, "I understand. I'll leave tonight."

Jakaan gave a quick nod. "Very well, then. I suppose that's all. Good to see you, Whitmere... despite the circumstances. Safe travels."

"Thank you," Everfeld said. The connection ended, leaving him alone again in the room.

A political assassination. Dirty business indeed. Had there ever been a time in history when this sort of thing hadn't happened? When the powerful hadn't dealt with threats the same way a gardener dealt with weeds, getting rid of them before they could take root and grow out of control? Probably not, he thought sadly.

Then a thought suddenly struck him. He rushed from the suite in the direction of his office, anxious to review the files Jakaan had just delivered. Perhaps the CM's word choice hadn't been the wrong one after all, he thought.

Perhaps this was indeed an opportunity.

4

THE VEILED DAGGER

THE MORNING AFTER ARRIVING ON CORREN 5, JERYN MADE HIS way to docking bay A6. Dejected from his aborted mission—the first time he'd failed in the field—he hoped a visit to check on the *Dagger*'s progress would lift his spirits. After the guard checked his ID and made a quick call to approve access, Jeryn entered the bay, pausing mid-step to marvel over the sight that greeted him.

Stars, what a ship! A top-secret prototype vessel in its final testing phase, the *Veiled Dagger*'s sleek, gently curving lines were unlike any spacecraft Jeryn had ever seen. Most spacefaring vessels looked like sideways-lying buildings with rugged, irregular exteriors. Aerodynamics meant nothing in the void, so shipwrights (unless they were building a space-to-ground shuttle) had no need to account for the streamlined necessities of an atmospheric flier. Designers and ship techs cared most about durability, hull integrity, engine longevity, and other practical concerns. Aesthetics were far down the priority list, if they were even on the list at all. The graceful form of the *Veiled Dagger*, however, was an exception to this general standard. The vessel was a wonder of both function and form.

A voice from inside the vessel's open hatchway called to him. "Ho there, young pup!"

Jeryn smiled as Bhokken the Rauk shuffled down the ship's boarding ramp, stooping over to avoid striking the hull with his head. He wore the wrinkled, threadbare coveralls he always donned when he worked on the ship's mechanical systems. Everfeld had once told Jeryn he was fairly sure it was the only item of clothing the Rauk engineer owned, claiming he'd never seen Bhokken dressed in any other garment. Bhokken's lacking wardrobe, though, was nothing unusual for his species. With bodies covered in coarse fur, most Rauks found human-style clothing uncomfortable and rarely wore any, aside from the occasional headpiece or decorative adornment, like Bhokken's necklace and pendant.

"What's wrong?" the engineer asked, sniffing. "I can smell your anxiety from all the way over here."

Grimacing, Jeryn said, "I *smell* anxious?"

"Among other things," Bhokken said.

Jeryn shook his head. "I don't think I'll ever get used to you saying stuff like that."

"Humans," the Rauk snorted. "You worry too much. Not every mission goes to plan."

There was truth in Bhokken's words. Things went wrong in the spy game. It happened all the time. But after two years at the Agency, this was the first time it had happened to *him*.

"Come on," the engineer said, waving Jeryn toward the ship, "have a look at what I've been working on. It'll definitely take your mind off your troubles."

"Music to my ears," Jeryn said, more than happy to direct his attention away from that debacle of a mission. "Let's see what you've got."

He spent the next two hours in gawking, wide-eyed amazement as the Rauk engineer revealed one jaw-dropping capability after another. The *Veiled Dagger* was the ultimate spy ship. It was fast and stealthy and jammed with custom-built tech generations ahead of anything Jeryn had seen before. The *Dagger*'s sensors had unthinkably long range, allowing its crew to see other ships long before they could be seen themselves. If other ships could see them at all, that is. The stealth technology embedded into the *Dagger*'s hull and drive system made it nearly invisible to detection when its transponder was deactivated. And the transponder itself, which by interstellar law was required to broadcast the ship's identification at all times, was its own amazing piece of technology. It could alter its signal to mimic thousands of different vessel profiles, effectively disguising the *Dagger*'s identity to long-range scans. Known as an "adaptive transponder," the technology was as illegal for a spacefaring vessel as a false identity was for a Realm citizen. But as Everfeld had once told him, legal boundaries were drawn differently for spies than they were for the general public.

The ship had weaponry, short-range cannons and a railgun, but its battle readiness focused more on defense than offense. Countermeasures, stealth, shields, and speed took precedence over firepower. It was a spy ship, after all, not a battle cruiser.

Amazed by the dizzying array of technology, Jeryn ran his hand through his hair. "I'm blown away. I've never seen anything like it."

The Rauk raised a finger. "Ah, but you haven't seen the best part yet. Come."

Jeryn followed the engineer to the artigrav generators, contained within a series of square compartments built into the wall just forward of the engine room. The Rauk waved his hand across the array. "This is what really sets the *Dagger* apart," he said proudly. "We've had a team working on it for nearly a decade."

Jeryn was no expert on artificial gravity. He'd only studied the basics of physics, so his understanding of how AG generators worked was limited. But what they actually did was fairly straightforward. As their name implied, the generators created an artificial gravity field around a ship. Invented during the Realm's founding era, the technology had ended the age of zero-gee space travel, making the harmful effects of microgravity on human and nonhuman bodies a thing of the past. AG generators also counteracted the effect of thrust gravity, dynamically adjusting their output to maintain a constant gravity inside the ship.

"So I'm guessing the artigrav is really good," Jeryn said.

"Somewhat better than good, my friend," the Rauk said. "You're looking at the most robust AG array ever constructed for a ship of this size. It's one of a kind, light-years ahead of anything else out there." He paused a moment, then said, "Tell me, what's the highest AG rating you've ever seen?"

"Seen or heard of?"

"Either one."

Jeryn recalled a naval pilot in a bar who'd drunkenly boasted about his gunship's specs. "Ten five."

The Rauk waved his hand and grunted dismissively. "That's nothing."

Nothing? A ten-point-five AG rating was the extreme high end of the scale. Most ships rated anywhere from four to seven, meaning their artigrav generators could offset a thrust gravity of four to seven incremental gees. If a vessel traveled at thrust velocities above its rating, its passengers felt the effect of the excess gravity. A five-gee burn on a four-rated ship, for example, felt like one extra gravity weighing you down. Uncomfortable, but you could put up with it. A fourteen-gee burn on the same ship would render you unconscious pretty quickly. Anything higher would squash your organs into jelly, and that would be that. The Realm's Navy vessels had the most advanced artigrav generators—classified technology reserved exclusively for military use—with ratings as high as fifteen.

"So what's it rated?" Jeryn asked.

The Rauk ran his hand lovingly over the generator compartments, his face beaming with pride. "Twenty-five point eight. I like to round it up to twenty-six though."

Stunned, Jeryn ran his eyes over the compartments. "But didn't you once tell me nineteen was the—"

"Theoretical limit," Bhokken interrupted. "Yes, I did." He smiled widely. "But some limits were made to be broken."

Jeryn had a hard time believing what he was hearing. It was like learning a pedal cycle had broken the sound barrier. "Twenty-five point eight, really?"

When the Rauk nodded, Jeryn whistled and said, "You could outmaneuver a missile with a rating that high."

"Possibly," Bhokken said, "but you'd need a good pilot at the controls."

"How have the test pilots worked out so far?"

Bhokken wiggled a clawed hand back and forth. "So-so, to tell you the truth. The *Dagger*'s a racehorse." He ran his hand again over the paneled wall. "It takes a special kind of jockey to handle its raw power. We're working on getting a more talented pilot to—"

A beep interrupted them, and Jeryn felt the vibration of his hand terminal in his pocket. He removed it, checked the caller, then said to Bhokken, "Sorry, I have to take it. It's the old man."

He tapped the screen and Whitmere Everfeld's face appeared. "I need to see you right away."

On any other day, Jeryn would have enjoyed the walk through the spacious, bright, tree-lined, and relatively uncrowded tunnels beneath Corren City. But this morning's destination—an unexpected summons to Whitmere Everfeld's office—spoiled an otherwise pleasant half-hour stroll. Jeryn couldn't imagine the *unexpected* part to mean anything but bad news. And his stone-faced security escort didn't exactly lighten the mood.

Maybe the aborted mission *was* a big deal. Maybe Bhokken had been wrong about that. Jeryn knew that operatives aborted jobs all the time for any number of reasons. It wasn't unheard of, or even terribly unusual.

But maybe this job had been different. Maybe failure had a consequence in this case, even if no one had told him as much going into it.

Would the old man laugh him out of the room when he tried to explain himself? Would he send him down to the analyst pool? Or would Jeryn simply be tossed out of the Agency, sacked for poor judgment in the field?

Feeling his nerves, Jeryn entered the meeting room adjacent to Everfeld's office, where to his great relief the spymaster greeted him with a broad smile and a firm grip on his shoulders.

"Good to see you, Jeryn," Everfeld said. "Have a seat, please." Jeryn felt the tension in his neck and shoulders ease slightly as he settled into a chair. The secure meeting room had a round table with a black marble top, ringed by six chairs.

"Have you eaten?" Everfeld asked, sitting down. "I can have something brought in if you like."

"I'm fine, thank you," Jeryn said.

They passed the next few minutes making small talk. Everfeld asked when Jeryn had arrived in the Corren system. And how was he adjusting to this world's point-eight-five gee? How were his accommodations? The spymaster was his usual composed and well-mannered self. But as the friendly chitchat ran its course and Everfeld inquired into Jeryn's recent mission, the young operative felt his stomach twist into a knot.

Jeryn recounted the final moments of the mission. How events had unfolded, when he began to have doubts, and why he'd aborted the operation. "Defflin's behavior was off. Alone with me on the *Starhopper*, he was edgy and nervous, but as soon as an armed C&B team boarded us, he got a lot more relaxed. That made no sense at all. If anything, an illegal emigre should be *more* nervous when he's face to face with someone who could arrest him and take him back to wherever he's running from."

He went on, and Everfeld remained silent, his features knotted in concentration. When Jeryn finished, the spymaster pursed his lips and nodded slowly. After a long contemplative moment, he spoke.

"Now that you've had time to retrace your steps, do you believe your decision to abort was a sound one?"

"Yes," Jeryn said, his voice carrying more conviction than he felt. Had the explanation sounded ridiculous to Everfeld's ears? He had to admit, if he was being honest with himself, his reasons —true and heartfelt though they were—didn't sound entirely credible.

"All right," Jeryn said, sighing loudly, "I know I messed up. Badly. And I know you may not believe a word I'm saying—"

"Of course I believe you," Everfeld interrupted.

Jeryn blinked. "You do?"

"Why wouldn't I?"

"So you're not going to fire me? Or send me to some desk job?"

"Heavens no," Everfeld said, chuckling. "Were you worried I might? Was that why you came in here with that hangdog expression on your face?"

"Well… yes."

The spymaster waved a dismissive hand. "No, no, you mustn't have those sorts of concerns. You have very sound instincts, in my opinion. You did the right thing by acting on them. Sometimes success means avoiding catastrophe, which is what we ended up with in this case. And your assessment appears to have been correct."

Like a drug, relief coursed through Jeryn's veins. "You think it was a setup too?"

"Almost certainly," Everfeld said. "Our local sources tell us Defflin has been going about his normal routine these last few days. Professional meetings, personal errands, and so forth. This would hardly be the case for someone caught trying to leave the system illegally. They'd be incarcerated, sleep-deprived, interrogated, and most likely tortured." The spymaster reflected for a moment, then continued. "With the benefit of hindsight, perhaps we might have expected something like this. Perhaps we became a bit too confident by our recent successes in that particular volume."

Jeryn nodded. While the job had been his first extraction—or *attempted* extraction—in the Primus system, other Agency operatives had helped several high-value individuals escape the same repressive regime over the last few years. And prior to his near-disaster, every mission had been successful. Apparently the local authorities had decided to do something about the bleeding of outbound bureaucrats.

"We went to the well one too many times," Jeryn said.

"It appears so. Consider it a lesson learned. Never become so comfortable with your achievements that you're fooled into thinking yourself incapable of failure." He smiled. "It's the kind of trap even an old spymaster can fall into."

"At least our cover wasn't blown," Jeryn said. Then after a moment he added, "Or was it?"

"Stars, no," the spymaster said, waving a hand. "If they had discovered our involvement, the planetary governor's office would have sent a formal complaint directly to the CM straightaway, demanding my resignation. There are few things state officials hate more than being spied on by their own government. No, I'm quite certain we've dodged that particular bullet, and thankfully so. The last thing we can afford at the moment is *more* tension between Gran Kiravashta and the Realm's outlying worlds." The spymaster reached for the table's inlaid display controls. "Now, I'd like to move on to other, more important matters. Unless, of course, there's something else you'd like to add to the topic?"

"No," Jeryn replied, "I'm happy to leave this op behind." He was quite ready to move on.

"I'd like to show you something," Everfeld said. He gestured over the display controls and a holo appeared, floating a few centimeters above the table. The default icon, as was customary in all state facilities, was a rotating depiction of the Realm's banner, the Rockets and Stars. Everfeld murmured a command and the room's lights dimmed as the icon disappeared, replaced with a three-dimensional star map of the galaxy. The two-meter-long, spiral-armed image floated between the two men.

Spreading his hands wide, Everfeld said, "This is our galaxy. Two hundred light-years across and four hundred billion stars."

"Big place," Jeryn said.

"Indeed," Everfeld said. He often used visual aids to emphasize some principle or concept he deemed particularly important. Images coupled with words held more power than words alone, Jeryn had heard the man say on several occasions.

"And here's our little neighborhood," Everfeld said, gesturing again. The image zoomed in to one of the spiral arms, their local galactic appendage known as the Great Arm, a volume of space roughly halfway between the galaxy's center and periphery. The cylindrical area, highlighted in blue, looked like a sleeve covering a small portion of the star-filled arm. As the viewpoint magnified, the blue area grew, eventually taking up the entire projection. When it stopped zooming a moment later, the image resembled a star-filled night sky, only with blue substituted for black.

"This is the Realm today," Everfeld said. "Over twenty thousand associated systems, all connected by known interstellar gates." He gestured, and a small portion (maybe three percent) of the stars, all of them at or near the Realm's outermost frontier, began to blink red. "These are the systems in open rebellion. The so-called Separatist movement."

He gestured again. "Now, here's something I don't believe I've shared with you before. Here's how things look if we include systems sympathetic—overtly or otherwise—to the Separatist cause." As he spoke, more stars changed from white to blinking red.

Jeryn gawked at the volume of red-colored systems. "That looks like a quarter of all the systems in the Realm."

"Twenty-three percent," Everfeld said, "to be precise."

Twenty-three percent? Jeryn had never imagined so many worlds had ties to the Separatists. Until now, he'd thought theirs was an extremist, fringe movement. If the image hovering before him was indeed an accurate portrayal, the Separatist cause was far more than a handful of far-flung malcontents.

But then again, hadn't he seen proof of those very anti-Realm sentiments during his travels? He recalled how the farther away you were from the Realm's geographic center where the capital world of Gran Kiravashta was located, the fewer Rockets and Stars banners you noticed flying above buildings. And it was in those same systems that you also heard—far more than you did elsewhere—crude remarks and off-color jokes about core worlders. He'd disregarded such signs as harmless provincialism, backwater resentment to the big, bad city. The floating map, however, suggested it was something far more troubling, and far more widespread, than he'd ever realized.

Still staring blankly at the holo, Jeryn nodded. Lifting his gaze to the spymaster, he asked, "Are we talking civil war here? Is that what we're facing?"

Narrowing his eyes at the starry display, Everfeld took a deep breath, then let it out slowly. "Not if I can help it."

The spymaster waved away the image. "Now let me show you something else. Or rather, someone else." He tapped a sequence into the display controls and the image of a human woman appeared.

"Jeryn Lorsi," Everfeld said, "meet Charnette Tavella of the Tegesian order."

5

DUBIOUS INVITATION

Beauty was in the eye of the beholder. Jeryn knew ten nonhuman languages—some better than others—and every one had some variation of that ancient human expression. The nose-oriented Rauk's equivalent roughly translated as *a sweet fragrance to one is odor to another*. The sentient reptilian bipeds of Xamor said *he (or she) warms my intestines*. Neither colloquialism sounded particularly poetic to Jeryn's human ears, but every version, human and nonhuman alike, shared the same idea: beauty was subjective.

As he sat looking at the holo of Charnette Tavella, Jeryn was no longer sure about the universality of that sentiment. The Tegesian cleric struck him as attractive by any standard, human or otherwise. He couldn't imagine any person from any species finding her appearance anything but pleasing.

"Quite the beauty, isn't she?" Everfeld said from behind his desk. Jeryn realized he must have been staring a bit too intently.

"But don't be fooled," Everfeld continued. "From what I've reviewed, her meteoric rise through the ranks has far more to do with her political skills than her appearance."

Jeryn snorted. "The looks can't hurt though."

"Most assuredly," Everfeld agreed. The spymaster went on, sharing what he'd recently learned about her clandestine activities, about the shuttle diplomacy she'd engaged in for the past year. "The CM's office believes she's working to form a coalition between Tegesian extremists and the largest Separatist factions. In short, they believe she represents a tremendous threat."

"To what?" Jeryn asked.

"To ten thousand years of Realm primacy."

Jeryn shifted his gaze from the spymaster to the holo again. Could things really be that bad? Could the state of the Realm be so precarious that a single person could throw it into chaos? He pictured the star chart the old man had showed him earlier. So many red stars.

"They want you to take her out," Jeryn said. "Don't they?"

"The order's been given," Everfeld confirmed, "from the highest office."

Jeryn nodded grimly. The handsome cleric had poked the beast, aroused it, and now she would suffer its wrath. A part of Jeryn felt for her, for the life that would come to an unnatural and early end. But then she'd taken the revolutionary's gamble, hadn't she? In the theater of interstellar politics, she'd willingly walked onto the stage and stepped into the spotlight. She'd played the game and lost.

"Do you think she's as dangerous as they say?" Jeryn asked.

The spymaster scratched his beard as he stared intently at the cleric's image. "She may be. But then she may be something else entirely."

"Like what?"

Everfeld gestured and a series of document icons replaced the cleric's image. "I've been studying the files the CM's office passed along. The intelligence is far from exhaustive, I'm afraid. Conversational detail is quite scarce. The comings and goings are well documented, but the actual content of discussions between key individuals is lacking."

"Which means they did a good job of securing comms at their meeting locations," Jeryn noted.

"Indeed," Everfeld agreed. "It also means the CM's office is making assumptions about the *nature* of those conversations."

While it was Everfeld's way to question data and examine a problem from all angles, Jeryn wasn't sure such scrutiny was warranted in this case. The cleric's actions alone were all but incriminating. "She's been meeting with hardliner Separatists and Tegesian extremists," he said, "and she's been doing it in secret. Is there any way to interpret that other than deliberate sedition?"

Everfeld waved a hand. "Oh, I have little doubt she's working to form some sort of coalition. And left alone, she might actually succeed in that endeavor, if she's as persuasive as she appears to be."

Jeryn wasn't sure where the old spymaster was going with this. "Which," he said slowly, "is why you've been asked to… take care of her."

The spymaster pursed his lips, lifted his eyebrows, then smiled like he was holding back some delicious secret.

"What is it you're not telling me?" Jeryn asked.

"What if," Everfeld said, lifting his finger, "she could be recruited? What if we could convince her to work for our side?"

Jeryn furrowed his brow. "So you convinced the CM's office to let you try and recruit her? That couldn't have been an easy conversation."

"Yes, it wouldn't have been," Everfeld agreed. "But the conversation never took place. The consul minister would never have agreed to such an approach."

Jeryn took a breath. "So… you're going to try and recruit her *without* the CM's approval?"

"Or her knowledge," the spymaster added, far too casually for Jeryn's comfort.

Had the old man really just said that? Did the Realm's chief spy just admit he planned to defy a direct order from the consul minister's office? Jeryn knew Everfeld and the CM had a history of not seeing eye to eye, but in their past disagreements the spymaster had always eventually, if reluctantly, complied with the CM's directives. But this... this was as about as far from begrudging obedience as you could get. This was... no, he couldn't even think the word.

"I'm sure you're thinking the old man's gone mad," the spymaster said with a chuckle. "Or something along those lines."

"I just... don't understand what makes you think she's recruitable." The cleric's actions alone were all but damning. He glanced over at the holo display. "Was there something in her files? Something that changed your mind?"

"Not explicitly," Everfeld said, nodding toward the document icons. "There wasn't anything *in* the reports that caught my eye. It's what *wasn't* in them I found most interesting. There's no direct evidence she's been radicalized. And to claim as much is merely circumstantial speculation. We know where she's been and who she's been meeting with, but we have, as I said before, almost no recorded conversations. And what little we do have is idle chitchat, nothing incriminating."

"So you suspect she *hasn't* been radicalized?"

"Precisely. Where my colleagues see a fall into fanaticism, I see naked ambition. I believe our cleric is hungry for power, and she's fanning the flames of change to further her own interests. She's undoubtedly trying to bring rebellious factions together. The evidence points quite strongly in that direction. And apparently she believes—quite correctly, in my opinion—that a united front has a far better chance at achieving its goals than its component factions could otherwise hope for separately. But her motivation, it seems to me, isn't some deeply held idealistic notion, but rather an old-fashioned lust for power and prestige. She envisions a future where these factions are united in purpose, and she sees herself at the highest ranks of power in that new reality. And for these last several months, she's been doing everything she can to bring that reality to fruition."

Everfeld leaned forward, his expression as earnest as Jeryn had ever seen. "Fanatics aren't easy to turn or manipulate, but the ambitious have no true loyalties beyond themselves. If I can persuade our cleric it's in her best interest to use her unique position to help broker peace instead of fomenting war, perhaps we can change the catastrophic course we're on. Think of how many lives might be saved."

Jeryn wasn't sure what to say. Everfeld never jumped to conclusions, never rushed to judgment, and if he read something between the lines, something others had missed, you could usually count on his read being the correct one. But even so, Jeryn felt as if the old man was walking out onto dangerously thin ice.

"May I be frank?" Jeryn asked.

"Now and always," Everfeld said.

"If you're so sure about this, why don't you level with the CM? You've known her for, what, thirty years? She's always trusted your judgment in the past, hasn't she?"

"On most occasions," Everfeld agreed, then his expression darkened. "But on this, I'm afraid she wouldn't listen."

"Why not?"

"Because we've discussed it many times."

Jeryn straightened up. It was the first time he'd heard of any such discussion. "You have?"

"I have. And so has Subminister Jakaan." Everfeld gestured and the holo disappeared. "Not about this cleric Tavella specifically, but about detente in general with the Separatists. She believes them to be traitorous criminals who should be dealt with harshly. There's no subtlety in her position, I'm afraid. It's quite a black-and-white matter to her. And she's made promises, very public promises, to rid the Realm of the scourge of rebellion, to whip every last errant system back into line. Open dialogue, she believes, would make her look weak in the eyes of the general population. And if you knew Consul Minister Amarania as well as I do, you'd know she detests the notion of appearing vulnerable in any way." He shook his head ruefully. "No, she's long since closed her mind to the possibility of peace and reconciliation."

The old spymaster moved across the room and flicked his wrist. The solid wall faded, replaced with a view of the building's tree-lined courtyard. The illusion was a convincing one, making the inner office deep inside the facility appear as if it had a window facing a pleasant, sunny day. Everfeld stood before the image, his hands behind his back. For a long moment, he watched the well-dressed locals crossing the sunbaked tiles of the courtyard. People coming and going.

"War is coming to the Realm," Everfeld said. "I'm certain of it, now more than ever. Every night, it's the last thing I ponder before I fall asleep. Every morning, it's my first thought when I awaken. And I'm equally convinced diplomacy is the only way to avoid it. Our consul minister disagrees. She says decisive actions, not placating words, will make our Realm whole once more. And with the sole exceptions of Jakaan and your humble servant, every last member of her inner circle endorses her view." He let out a long breath. "When you've won as many battles in your political life as she has, perhaps you begin to think you can't lose. Perhaps you can't even imagine the possibility of losing."

He turned to face Jeryn. "But if I can turn what they believe to be an existential threat into a useful ally, then perhaps the CM and her staff may begin to see things differently. Perhaps they'll come to realize diplomacy is possible after all. And, yes, I realize what

I'm determined to engage in could be considered treason. But so be it."

Jeryn sat there, pondering the spymaster's words. They were, from a certain point of view, hard to disagree with. When you looked through a wide enough lens and saw the whole of the Realm, the small, inconsequential things fell away. Like risking one old man's safety and security to save countless lives, for instance.

But try as he might to appreciate that perspective, that larger picture, Jeryn couldn't fully bring himself to buy into it. He couldn't shake the feeling Everfeld was making a mistake. The spymaster was taking an enormous leap of faith on someone *he'd never met*, someone he knew only from incomplete surveillance files. Defying a consul minister on a hunch... stars, it just didn't seem like something Everfeld would ever consider.

So he asked the obvious question. "And what if she's exactly the radical seditionist they think she is? What then?"

Everfeld spread his hands out wide. "Then I'll have no choice but to do my duty." Then, after a short pause, he added, "Now, how would you like to come along?"

After hearing so many stunning revelations over the last few minutes, Jeryn thought he'd lost his ability to be surprised by anything else Everfeld might say. But the spymaster's question left him momentarily speechless.

"Come along?" he finally managed to utter.

"Yes," Everfeld said. "It's been a long time since I've been in the field, and I could use a couple trusted, capable operatives by my side. Bhokken has already agreed to accompany me on this errand."

Bhokken was going along with this? Had everyone around Jeryn abandoned every last bit of good judgment? Surely the Rauk would have found this gambit as dicey a proposition as Jeryn had. But, amazingly, he'd still agreed to go along. Jeryn sat there, confused and uncertain. The universe had turned sideways on him.

"You won't be implicated in my little scheme," Everfeld said, "if that's your concern. I'll make certain of that."

Being arrested for treason wasn't what Jeryn was worried about. Well, it was and it wasn't. The prospect of being banished to a prison planet for life of course gave him pause. He'd have to be a fool not to sweat something like that. But what truly unnerved him was Everfeld's—and apparently also Bhokken's—willingness to risk everything on the hopeful guess some Tegesian cleric could be recruited. They were putting their reputations, their careers, *their lives* on the line, based on little more than the old man's hunch. A gut feeling that might be as much wishful thinking as anything else.

"I can appreciate your doubts, my friend," Everfeld said, as if he was reading Jeryn's mind. "Take a few hours and think it over. And if you decide you'd rather not take part in this endeavor, I won't hold it against you. Not in the least. But I must do this. I must try."

6

TWO BIRDS, ONE STONE

Subminister Clevon Jakaan paused as he passed through the doorway of the consul minister's private office. Atop his superior's desk, a small holo of Minister Amarania's daughter and teenage grandson flickered. Reluctant to interrupt a personal call, he turned to leave. The CM stopped him in mid-turn, waving him forward.

"We're just finishing, Clevon," she called. "Please, come in."

As he entered the lavishly decorated suite, the CM turned again to the holo. "So we'll see you next week, then?"

"Yes, Mother," the woman said. "We can't wait."

"I can't wait either. All right, my dears, I'll see you soon. Love you." She waved her hand to cut the connection and the holo blinked out. Then she stood and gestured toward the nursery. "Shall we?"

"Thank you, Madam Minister," Jakaan said, nodding in deference. A door at the rear of the office slid open, and Jakaan followed the CM into the greenness beyond.

A lush oasis deep inside the executive administration complex, the consul minister's nursery was one of the largest private gardens on Gran Kiravashta. With each successive term in office, she'd expanded its footprint, bringing in more trees and shrubs, adding footpaths, increasing the variety of bird and insect species, many of them imported from the farthest reaches of the Realm. The cavernous space served not only as a peaceful refuge from the pressures and strains of her duties, but with its hidden array of anti-monitoring and noise-scrambling technology, it was among the safest locations in the system for confidential meetings on top-secret matters.

The pair walked side by side along a dirt footpath. A soft susurration of insect trills filled the air, and birds hidden in high tree canopies chirped and warbled. "We've been planning a large family getaway for ages," the CM said, referring to the call she'd just finished. "We've had to cancel it twice, but I'm determined there won't be a third time. Do you know I have three grandchildren I haven't even met in person yet?"

"No, Minister, I didn't."

Amarania sighed. "I heard a planetary governor once say the price of public service is paid mostly by our loved ones."

Jakaan stiffened as memories flooded his awareness. The CM's comment was far more painfully true for him than it was for her, though of course she didn't know this. He'd kept that part of his life a secret from her, from everyone.

"I imagine you're right," he said, struggling to compose himself. Then he quickly changed the subject. "I know you're pressed for time today, so I'll try to be as brief as I can."

"I still have doubts about all of this," the CM said abruptly, her expression skeptical. "Serious doubts. Whitmere Everfeld, a traitor to the Realm? I'm having a hard time reconciling the man I've known nearly half my life, who's been loyal through all this administration's ups and downs, with the seditionist you claim him to be."

Patience, Jakaan told himself. He had to be patient with her. The CM's opinion of Everfeld was a thick sheet of glacial ice, formed and hardened over many years. It wouldn't melt overnight, though he was sure a thaw was well underway. With enough time and patience, he reminded himself, even the smallest flame could reduce the largest glacier into nothing.

"Seditionist might be a strong way of putting it," Jakaan said. "But he's certainly been pursuing a hidden agenda, Madam Minister. And we'd be ill-advised to allow it to continue."

Jakaan had been working on her for months, doing his best to undermine her confidence in the Realm's master of spies. At first she'd been wary, even hostile to the notion that one of her most trusted advisors had been leading a double life, and even working against her interests. Understandable doubts, given the length of time she'd known the man, to whom she'd entrusted countless confidences. And, admittedly, the evidence Jakaan had presented to her hadn't exactly been conclusive. Nothing he'd shared would have held up in a court of law, much of it being hearsay and circumstantial.

In these last few weeks, though, he'd sensed he'd made tangible progress. At long last, the CM seemed to be coming around. Still, he knew she wouldn't throw an old colleague to the wolves lightly. She wouldn't be fully convinced of the man's betrayal by anything less than hard evidence.

"I'd like you to walk me through this again," Minister Amarania told him. "I want to be sure about what we're doing here."

The subminister took a breath, worried the woman might be on the verge of changing her mind about the operation. Had he asked too much of her too soon? Had he failed to soften the ground enough before asking her to sanction a plot to trap her long-serving spymaster? He wasn't sure.

But no matter, he decided, steeling himself to move things forward. If she wanted him to go over every detail once more, he'd do it. And if he had to convince her all over again, he'd do that too. Whatever it took to sway her thoughts, he was prepared to do it. He'd come too far to let the woman's lingering doubts ruin his plans now.

They reached the end of the footpath, a circular cloister shaded by trees with thick trunks and broad amber fronds. Jakaan cleared his throat. This was no time for gentle nudging or soft, tempered language. He knew the CM well enough to know that when she was uncertain, the best way to sway her was with a blunt, straightforward appeal.

"Here's what we know," he said. "For some time, Everfeld has been involved in clandestine activities outside the Agency's charter. The exact nature of these activities is still unclear, but over the last several months we've documented a sizable amount of unauthorized travel, unscheduled meetings, and unexplained absences. Add it all up, and it's simply too much off-the-books activity to be ignored. We haven't found the fire yet, but we can smell quite a lot of smoke."

Minister Amarania sat on a wooden bench. She stared downward, her expression knotted with uncertainty. "He is a spymaster, after all. The position itself entitles him to a certain amount of secrecy."

She was wavering. Jakaan sensed she was on the verge of canceling the operation, and that simply wouldn't do. No, that wouldn't do at all. He sat next to her on the bench.

"I know this can't be easy for you," he said, his tone softening. "But he's been deceiving us for months about what he's been up to. And not half an hour ago, when we discussed the Tavella situation, he claimed he had no resources on Sandau Prime to handle the matter. And that's not even remotely true."

The CM straightened up. "He lied?"

Jakaan nodded. "I checked on it right after the call. He's got dozens of agents in the Sandau system. And of those, nine are former infantry snipers."

Minister Amarania looked confused. "Why would he lie about something we could confirm so easily?"

"My guess is because he's lied to us so many times without getting caught, he believes there's no longer any risk in doing so. You can only lie so carelessly when you've done it a hundred times without anyone catching on."

Closing her eyes, the CM muttered, "Oh, Whitmere. What have you been up to?"

There we go, Jakaan thought. She was coming back around. "We can't arrest him without cause, and as suspicious as the blank spots on his schedule may be, they don't prove anything."

"And this little trap of yours with the cleric will prove something?"

"Yes, if he does what I believe he's going to," Jakaan said.

The scheme had taken him months to devise and orchestrate, and now it was finally nearing fruition. It was a good plan, Jakaan reflected. Not flawless, but pretty close to it. The operation counted on the spymaster disobeying his orders, reaching out to the cleric as a potential ally or asset instead of eliminating her. Tavella had positioned herself squarely in the center of several powerful factions, and Jakaan was all but certain Everfeld wouldn't be able to resist recruiting—or at least trying to recruit—such a well-placed source. Even if he had been ordered to do otherwise by the CM's office.

Strangely enough, the scheming cleric—who was in her own right a rather troublesome element—had been a godsend. She was the perfect bait to catch the venerable spymaster. And when Everfeld inevitably attempted to recruit her, they'd both be arrested and charged with conspiracy to commit treason.

Two birds, one stone. A tidy little piece of work.

And in the unlikely event that Everfeld actually carried out his duty as ordered, eliminating the cleric straight away, that was fine too. The state would have one less serious threat to worry about, and Jakaan would go back to monitoring Everfeld's activities until another opportunity presented itself. Which it almost certainly would. The careless way Everfeld had lied earlier meant the old spymaster hardly worried about being compromised. That or he was losing it, which was another possibility, and perhaps a more likely one. Twenty years earlier, even ten, Jakaan couldn't have fathomed Everfeld making such a clumsy mistake. The spymaster had clearly lost a step or two in recent years.

"I understand you have your doubts," Jakaan said. "But I'm convinced he's an enemy of the state and he no longer has your best interests in mind, if in fact he ever did. Your administration has serious issues to deal with. Ten thousand years of stability is on the verge of chaos, and Separatist sentiment is spreading like cancer from system to system. And instead of focusing all his efforts on our gravest threat, he's been working some shadow agenda for months, maybe years for all we know. We simply can't let it persist, especially now, given the state of the Realm. There's too much at stake to have the Agency in the hands of someone who, best case, is hiding things from us, or worst case, is actively working against us."

For a long time neither of them spoke, and the only sounds came from the garden's chirping, trilling wildlife. Jakaan wasn't sure if the CM's prolonged silence meant her thoughts were once again clouded by doubt, or if she was at long last settling upon what would be her final approval, authorizing the arrest of one of her longest-tenured advisors.

When she finally turned to him and gave him a discreet nod, he knew it was the latter.

7

TWO ABOLITIONISTS

JERYN HADN'T GIVEN THE SPYMASTER AN IMMEDIATE ANSWER. Instead, he'd requested the files on the cleric and holed up in a borrowed office, hoping he'd discover the same between-the-lines optimism his mentor had managed to find. But now, after hours of scouring both the cleric's publicly available information—the speeches she'd authored, the comments she'd made on public feeds, even her doctoral dissertation—as well as the volumes of secret surveillance data documenting her recent comings and goings, Jeryn had found nothing that convinced him the Tegesian cleric might be a champion of peace and reconciliation. Instead, the cold facts before him, detailing who she'd secretly met with and where the meetings had taken place, pointed to sedition, telling the story of a radicalized cleric who'd been turned by extremists in her order. Of course, without detailed recordings of her conversations it was impossible to be absolutely sure. But in Jeryn's experience the old expression was almost invariably true: the simplest explanation was usually the right one.

The operative sighed and rubbed his tired eyes. What was the old man thinking? Was he so fixated on the looming disaster of civil war that he saw things that weren't there? Possibilities that existed only when filtered through his deepest hopes for peace? People saw what they wanted to see sometimes.

"Do you know why I recruited you?"

Jeryn looked up to see Everfeld standing in the doorway. "You needed help with black market comms," the young operative answered.

"Yes," the spymaster said, stepping into the room, "that was part of it. But there was more to it than that."

"There was?"

"At the time the Agency *did* have a need for more expertise in monitoring black market communications. You're quite right on that account. In those days we were dreadfully short-staffed in that department. So we came up with possible recruiting targets by scouring local police records in systems with the most underground commercial activity. We found no shortage of qualified candidates of course, times being what they are, but there was one candidate in particular whose background quite intrigued me."

At first Jeryn assumed Everfeld was referring to how the ex-smuggler had repeatedly freed himself from incarceration. During his black marketeering days, Jeryn had been arrested in over a dozen systems, and on each occasion he'd managed to escape custody, often within only minutes of being detained. Everfeld had once mentioned how Jeryn's ability to improvise under pressure had greatly impressed him. But then Jeryn sensed the spymaster was getting at something else at the moment, something he'd never shared before.

"I was a child of wealth," Everfeld said. "But you knew that, yes?"

Jeryn nodded, a bit perplexed by the sudden shift of topic.

The spymaster went on. "Did I ever tell you what I did with my inheritance?"

"No, you didn't."

"I used most of it to buy the freedom for those trapped by indentured servitude."

Indentured servitude, Jeryn echoed internally. It was the polite way of referring to slavery.

"The vast majority of slaves, as you well know," Everfeld continued, this time mincing no words, "come to their lot in life when unscrupulous moneylenders or employers deceive them into financial debt. And while these sums are all but impossible for the indebted to pay off in their lifetime, for someone of means they're usually a rather modest transaction."

Jeryn lifted his chin. "You used your family fortune to pay off slave debts?"

"Ninety-seven percent of it, to be exact. I retained the remainder to fund my retirement." The spymaster chuckled. "If I manage to retire without being jailed, of course."

Add another shocker to a day full of them, Jeryn reflected. Everfeld had never before mentioned any of this to him. "How many did you free?"

"At last count, three hundred and twenty-two thousand, four hundred and eighty-six."

Jeryn blinked. *Over three hundred thousand!* It was a staggering number. It had to have been an equally staggering amount of money.

"So you can imagine my surprise when I came across the profile of a talented black marketeer who not only excelled at eluding capture, but who also shared my hatred for human and nonhuman bondage. Who, in his own way, had done exactly the same sort of thing I had."

No, Jeryn thought. It wasn't possible. There was no way the old man could know. Or was there?

"The slave revolt on Mutara 3," Everfeld said. "Yes, I've known about your involvement for a long while."

Well, that answered that. The old man *did* know. But how had he found out? And when? And why was he only revealing this now?

Mutara 3. Stars, he hadn't thought about what had happened there in a long time.

During those years working the underground markets, Jeryn had once been hired to smuggle slaves out of the Mutara system. His employer—a Huthean slaver posing as a labor broker—had hired Jeryn under false pretenses. The Huthean had claimed the gig's cargo consisted of skilled workers, some two dozen in total, who'd been hired by a mining syndicate in a neighboring system. As an expert passer of bribes to Customs and Borders officials, Jeryn had been hired to ensure the workers gained entry to the system without the broker having to incur the steep expense of work visas. It was a common enough gig. Bread-and-butter stuff.

Then, two days before the job was to take place, Jeryn had discovered what he'd really signed up for.

He'd been incensed by the deception. Jeryn hated slavery. Detested it. He'd seen it on so many worlds, seen so many souls lost to the so-called indentured labor force. And it was always the same story. Someone down on their luck, desperate for money because of a lost job or a failed business or some other financial hardship, forced to take out lines of credit from moneylenders or trade syndicates to save themselves from ruin, only to discover later, to their eternal regret, they had literally signed their life away. Inconceivably, Gran Kiravashta allowed the deceptive and predatory practice to continue throughout the Realm, condemning it but taking no action, sidestepping the issue by citing respect for local traditions and institutions. Jeryn found the state's hypocrisy maddening. Slavery could never be rationalized, never justified. It was inherently evil, period, end of sentence. But yet, incomprehensibly, it was allowed to continue. For all the peace and stability the Realm had brought to countless worlds for thousands of years, its benign neglect of the enslaved was a black mark next to its name. The sin that tainted all its other good deeds.

When he'd learned the truth about the gig, Jeryn hadn't backed out. Instead, he'd taken the ship commissioned for the job, reached out to the local abolitionist underground, and with their help he'd smuggled over a hundred slaves to freedom, and in the process he'd (quite inadvertently) ignited a slave insurrection. Thousands of so-called indentured laborers had risen up, armed themselves, and commandeered (or hijacked, depending on whose point of view you supported) two ore haulers and smuggled themselves to nearby sanctuary systems where indentured servitude was banned. The incident quickly gained notoriety, becoming known as the Mutaran Uprising, one of the largest slave revolts in the Realm's history, and one of the rare successful ones.

Jeryn Lorsi had never been identified by authorities as the spark who'd set off the bonfire of indentured insurrection. And for his part, he'd never told anyone of his involvement in the incident, not even his closest friends at the Agency. Until this very moment, he'd believed his involvement in the infamous event had remained a secret.

"How did you find out?" Jeryn asked.

Everfeld grinned. "I do run an intelligence organization, as you may know."

"Why didn't you tell me before?"

"If you'd known I was aware of your role in a slave revolt, would you have come to work for me?"

Jeryn snorted. "No, I wouldn't have." The old man had a point. When Jeryn had first met the spymaster, had he known that Everfeld had uncovered his involvement in the Mutaran Uprising, the *last* thing he would have done was entertain a job offer. He would have run, as fast and as far away as he could, suspecting some sort of Agency trap.

"I've been meaning to tell you for some time," Everfeld said. "It finally seemed like the appropriate occasion to do so."

The spymaster sat down in the chair next to Jeryn. "Black marketeers aren't generally known for doing that sort of thing—there's not much money to be made in liberating the destitute. But you chose to save those poor souls in the Mutara system from their wretched existence, putting yourself in grave danger in the process. I've always suspected you didn't do it for money or notoriety or any reason other than it was the right thing to do. If I'm wrong, please correct my misconception."

Jeryn sat there quietly, his mind parsing through memories of the incident on Mutara 3. It had happened half a dozen years ago, but it felt like another lifetime.

"*That's* why I recruited you," Everfeld said, finally answering the question he'd asked upon entering the room. Then after a moment he lifted his eyebrows. "Now, of course you're free to walk away. I won't bear you any ill will if that's your decision. But I do hope you come along. Because frankly I could use the help. And, quite candidly, a spymaster has far fewer people he can trust with this sort of errand than you might imagine."

After Everfeld left, Jeryn gazed out of the room's false window, staring at the pristine greenery of the courtyard. When the day had started, his biggest worry had been a reprimand about a job gone bad. Now that seemed ludicrously insignificant compared to what weighed on him now.

The old man had offered him an easy out, and Jeryn's first thought was to take it. For a long while, he seriously considered doing exactly that. But eventually he came to realize he wouldn't. Despite the risk, despite the inherent criminality of defying the consul minister, and despite his reservations about this cleric Tavella, he simply couldn't abandon the old man. The one who'd rescued him from a life of scrambling and hustling in the brutal, hazard-filled world of the underground markets. Who'd taken him under his wing and given him a life, a real life. No, he wouldn't abandon the old man.

He owed him far too much.

8

KNIFE FIGHT

FIGHTING A RAUK WASN'T EASY. DESPITE THEIR HEIGHT AND bulk, they were fast. Incredibly fast. If you let your guard down for an instant, they were all over you. And they were insanely strong, so you had to keep your distance. Most sentient species—or non-sentient ones, for that matter—had little chance of coming out of a grapple with a Rauk without losing a limb. Comparatively weak humans had no chance at all, so Jeryn wisely circled Bhokken just beyond the reach of the Rauk's long arms.

Thankfully, this was no hand-to-hand encounter. It was a knife fight, which evened the odds a bit. Jeryn wasn't much of a fighter with naked fists, but with his kukri in hand he knew how to handle himself, even against a Rauk. Slowly, they circled one another, both gripping their glowing blades, both breathing heavily.

They'd been going at it for ten exhausting minutes. Jeryn's shirt was soaked with sweat, and his thighs burned from dozens of lunges and retreats. Ten minutes was a marathon compared to most knife fights, which usually lasted mere seconds. Quick, decisive aggression most often determined the victor in a blade duel. Doubt and hesitation usually belonged to the loser.

Weapon skill also mattered, of course. You had to know how to use your blade effectively, how to pierce the most vulnerable spots on human and nonhuman anatomies, how to keep your balance, how to dodge attacks, how to counter, and so on. But the mental game was as important as the physical one. He who hesitated, as the ancient saying went, was lost.

"Tired?" the Rauk said.

Jeryn shifted his blade from one hand to the other. "Not at all," he lied. "You?"

"I can go for hours like this."

"Your tongue doesn't seem to agree," Jeryn said. Like the canine animals they hated being compared to, Rauks didn't perspire, instead regulating their body temperature by panting. Bhokken's pink tongue lolled from his gaping mouth as he gasped in small, convulsive breaths. There was no way he could go for hours, but it was a safe bet his stamina would outlast Jeryn's. It was time to end this duel and end it quickly.

Jeryn lunged with deliberate clumsiness, the kind of move a tired and desperate opponent would make. As the Rauk easily dodged the thrust, Jeryn leaned awkwardly into the empty space, leaving the left side of his torso unprotected. He hoped the feint wasn't too obvious. Apparently, it wasn't. The Rauk took the bait, making the expected counter, taking advantage of his opponent's seeming vulnerability.

Dropping his blade, Jeryn grabbed the Rauk's thrusting arm by the wrist as he simultaneously dropped in a twisting motion that sent Bhokken tumbling to the floor. The well-timed toss slammed the Rauk hard on his back, and before Bhokken could react, Jeryn had recovered his blade and scrambled on top of his opponent, straddling his furry torso. Jeryn pressed the knife's edge to the Rauk's neck and smiled.

"Ow!" the Rauk cried as the kukri's safety sheath gave him a mild shock. "You didn't have to do that." Bhokken shoved Jeryn off of his chest and sat up, rubbing his neck.

"Like you wouldn't have done the same to me," Jeryn said. He removed the safety sheath and showed it to the Rauk. "I only had it set to five like we agreed, see? That's not so painful."

"Did we say five?" the Rauk asked. Before Bhokken could deactivate his own blade's safety sheath, Jeryn snatched it away and checked the setting.

"Thirteen?" Jeryn blurted, his eyes widening. "You were going to hit me with a level-thirteen shock? That would make me wet myself."

The Rauk rose to his feet. "My apologies," he said, then shrugged. "What can I tell you? I needed an edge. You're better with a blade than I am."

"But you're stronger and faster," Jeryn protested.

"You should take it as a compliment. I was so intimidated by your superior skills, I desperately looked for a way to even the odds."

"Or you just wanted to see me wet my pants."

The Rauk smiled. "I can't say that didn't occur me."

"You're terrible, you know that?"

Bhokken picked up a towel and tossed it to Jeryn. "Enjoy your victory, bare-skin. And while you're at it, wipe that disgusting sweat off your face. You look like a stone dragon's been dribbling all over you." Since Rauks didn't sweat, they found the idea of human perspiration somewhat repulsive. Plopping down on a bench, Bhokken closed his eyes and tilted his head back and forth, eliciting a series of audible cracks. "I'm getting too old for this."

The pair were the only ones in the exercise suite. Strength and conditioning equipment ran along the far wall.

Wiping his face, Jeryn sat next to Bhokken. "And how old would that be again?"

"One hundred and three standards as of two months ago," the Rauk said, still panting, but now at a slower rhythm.

"So what is that for a Rauk?" Jeryn asked. "Middle-aged?"

"Not quite," Bhokken said. "But, stars, I can feel it coming on." He reached around, rubbed his lower back, and nodded toward the sparring circle. "Thank the Fifteen for padded floors." After a few more pants, he reached over and patted Jeryn on the thigh. "I'm glad you're coming along," he said, referring to the Sandau Prime mission. "The old man wasn't sure you'd say yes."

"The *old man* is decades younger than you," Jeryn pointed out.

"I'm a brazen youth compared to him, no matter what the calendar says. Time is a measuring stick, my friend, but age is a sliding scale."

When the Rauk engineer had called an hour earlier with an invitation to the exercise suite, Jeryn had welcomed the summons as a much-needed distraction. Since his meeting with Everfeld earlier, Jeryn hadn't stopped thinking about what he'd signed up for, what he and Bhokken were about to jump into the middle of.

"So what do you think about it?" Jeryn asked.

"About trying to turn this cleric?"

"Yeah."

"You're asking if I think it's a bad idea."

"I am."

Bhokken scratched his chin with a clawed finger. "It might check the high-risk, high-return box, to be honest." Before Jeryn could say anything, the Rauk added, "But that doesn't mean I think it's a bad call. Think about it. An asset with inroads into every major Separatist faction *and* the Originalists? She'd be worth her weight in gold."

"If he can recruit her," Jeryn pointed out.

"You don't think he can?"

"Flipping an asset," Jeryn said, "takes time. You know that as well as I do. You have to lay the groundwork, gain trust over time. And they gave him, what, less than two months to take care of this cleric?"

The Rauk nodded. "Yes, it's not much time. But he used to be very good at that sort of thing, turning hostiles into friendlies. Back before your time, when he still went into the field."

"I didn't say he couldn't do it. It's just...." He blew out a long breath. "Feels like such a shot in the dark, you know? All I can think about is the downside on this one."

The Rauk nodded sympathetically. "Well, if this operation *didn't* give you pause, I'd think something was wrong with you." He placed his hand on the young agent's shoulder and grinned playfully. "And don't worry, I'll be there to hold your hand if you need it, young pup."

"Young pup?" Jeryn said. "For someone who's offended by dog references, that's not the best choice of words."

The Rauk shrugged. "It's not my fault your tiny language lacks metaphors. I almost said 'young buck,' but that sounds a bit too close to an obscenity."

Jeryn laughed. Somehow the Rauk could always manage to lift his spirits, even at the most stressful of times. He was glad the engineer would be coming to Sandau Prime.

"This whole thing could go very, very wrong, you know," Jeryn said.

"It could also go very, very right." Bhokken stood. "Have a little faith, will you? And the trip to Sandau Prime alone is worth the price of admission on this one."

"Really? What's so special about sitting around for a couple weeks in a transport ship?"

"He didn't tell you?" Bhokken said. "We're taking the *Dagger*. We're going to test some of its systems on the way."

Well, *that was* interesting, Jeryn thought, a bit of sunlight piercing the dark clouds of his thoughts. More than interesting, actually. He'd been dying to see the *Veiled Dagger* in action for months, hoping for the chance to ride as a passenger on the stealthiest, most technically advanced ship in the Realm. Now he'd finally get to see what it could do.

"Don't forget to pack warm clothes," the Rauk said. "It's cold on Sandau Prime."

9

DORIX-NATANI STATION

Most of the Realm's constituent star systems had one or two interstellar gates. Corren was a branch system, which meant it fell into the latter category. The system's twin gates—dubbed with the rather uninspired names Corren Gate A and Gate B—were located at opposite ends of the planetary ecliptic, each leading to separate, light-years' distant systems. Other systems (Jeryn couldn't remember how many, but it was a small minority) had three gates. As interstellar intersections, two- or three-gate branch systems were heavily trafficked transportation hubs, and they invariably hosted one or more commercial space stations located in close proximity to the local gates. Enormous bazaars floating in space, commercial stations catered to every conceivable need interstellar travelers might have. And depending on the local system's laws and norms around market oversight, a commercial station might be a fully state-owned-and-controlled entity or—at the opposite end of the economic spectrum—a completely unregulated free-for-all marketplace. The outpost that grew larger in the *Dagger*'s viewport at the moment, a massive five-ringed structure named Dorix-Natani Station, fell somewhere near the middle of those two extremes.

Bhokken sat at the *Dagger*'s controls, speaking with a docking officer at the station. "Transmitting security code now, Dorix-Natani."

A moment later, a voice replied over the comms. "*You're clear to dock*, SY-715," the dockmaster said, using the ship's call letters. "*Bay forty-three. Welcome to Dorix-Natani.*"

"Bay forty-three," the Rauk repeated, tapping the flight controls. "We're locked in, on final approach. Thank you, Dorix-Natani."

Everfeld entered the bridge and gazed out at the enormous station. "Amazing, isn't it?" He looked at Jeryn. "Have you been here before?"

"Only for a couple quick refueling stops," Jeryn said. "Never been inside."

"It's quite a facility," Everfeld said. "Over three hundred years old. The original structure had only one ring. The others were added later."

Jeryn nodded. Most commercial stations throughout the Realm experienced a similar town-to-city growth pattern over time, slowly adding more shops and businesses and housing as interstellar trade increased decade over decade, century over century. Even within the relatively short span of his own spacefaring experience, Jeryn had seen small stations double in size in only a handful of years.

"You're sure it's safe to stop here?" Jeryn asked. He'd scanned over the outpost's police records earlier, finding that Dorix-Natani had a robust black market and its fair share of criminal syndicates.

"We're docking in the naval partition," Everfeld said. "There's no safer place on the station."

The multi-ringed outpost now took up the entirety of the viewport. Vessels of all shapes and sizes came and went, their maneuvering thrusters flashing in small, controlled bursts. Nimble little shuttles and one-seater pods zipped back and forth. Massive ore and ice haulers lumbered along at carefully slow velocities. Station security cruisers flashed telltale red and blue lights.

"Safe or not, I still say it's an unnecessary stop," Bhokken grumbled, his attention focused on the docking sequence graphic on his console. "I can put the *Dagger* through her paces as well as any—"

"Please, I beg you not to put me through this again," Everfeld said. "I'm quite aware you're a capable pilot. More than capable, in fact. But your talents are far better applied in areas other than navigation."

It was the third such exchange Jeryn had heard since they'd cleared Corren 5's gravity well. An engineer who'd specialized in intelligence and surveillance technology since long before Jeryn was born, the Rauk possessed expertise that extended to a number of fields outside his primary trade, including spacecraft navigation. And while his piloting skills far exceeded those of Jeryn's, they were apparently nothing compared to those of the person they were picking up at Dorix-Natani Station. When Everfeld had learned the pilot, a human named Manto Marogh, was both available and directly in their path to Sandau Prime, he hadn't hesitated to schedule a quick stop at Dorix-Natani. The *Veiled Dagger* was a best-in-class vessel, and Everfeld insisted on recruiting the best talent available to test its capabilities, even if that meant bruising Bhokken's professional pride.

"I haven't been inside this station in at least a decade," Everfeld said, changing the topic. "I'm quite interested to see how things have changed."

It would have been quicker and easier to send a couple of the half dozen Marines they'd brought as security to fetch the pilot. But then that would have shortchanged the old man's curiosity about the place. Everfeld was always curious and tirelessly inquisitive, qualities that served him well in matters of espionage.

The man questioned, he investigated, he probed until he was satisfied he'd uncovered the truth of a matter. It could be exhausting if you were on the receiving end of his inquiries, but Jeryn knew the man's insatiable curiosity and thirst for knowledge—along with a sharp mind and a talent for politics—were the very traits that had made the man a master of the spy game.

A green indicator signaled the completion of the docking process. They had arrived at Dorix-Natani Station.

10

MANTO MAROGH

Jeryn and Everfeld disembarked, trailed by two armed Marines dressed in plain clothes. Bhokken opted to stay behind on the *Dagger*. "If you've seen one grubby space bazaar," he'd joked, "you've seen them all." And besides, he'd added, he had a glitchy sensor array to work on.

After passing through the naval partition's two security checkpoints, Jeryn, Everfeld, and their escorts entered the bustling station's innermost ring, spinning at a comfortable point-eight gravity. Like many commercial outposts, Dorix-Natani generated artificial gravity by centrifugal force instead of using artigrav generators. AG arrays could be tricky—and, more importantly, quite expensive—to maintain at such a massive scale, so many of the larger, more budget-minded outposts opted for old-fashioned spin gravity instead of hiring a fleet of AG technicians.

As the security doors hissed shut behind them, Jeryn's senses were overwhelmed. The powerful odor of frying food—seasoned with spices he didn't recognize—mixed with the sharp smell of human and nonhuman bodies nearly made his eyes water. They'd emerged into a noisy food court, crowded with uniformed naval personnel and locals sporting a diverse variety of clothing styles and colors. He saw at least a dozen species seated among the tightly packed tables, all of them busily eating. The breakfast crowd, Jeryn noted. The corridors leading to and from the court bustled with morning commute activity. People strode past with the hurried pace of workers on the way to their jobs.

"Are you hungry?" Everfeld asked, rubbing his hands together. "I'm rather keen to sample the local cuisine."

"I had breakfast on the ship," Jeryn said. And even if he hadn't eaten already, he was fairly certain the strange aromas invading his nose would have killed his appetite. "But don't mind me."

"We're meeting our friend on the observation node," Everfeld said, gesturing. "It's a short walk in this direction. We're a bit early, so why don't you have a look around while I see if I can find a decent omelet stand? Meet you there in twenty minutes?"

"Sure," Jeryn said, welcoming the opportunity to have a quick tour of the station's merchant stalls. Everfeld instructed one of the Marines to remain with Jeryn. "I'll see you shortly," the spymaster said, then turned away and headed toward a row of food stands.

The pedestrian traffic began to thin as Jeryn made his way through the ring's segmented nodes in the direction of the meet location. With his escort shadowing him at a discreet distance, he paused when a shop or kiosk's merchandise caught his attention. A quarter of the businesses, he noticed, operated under the banner of familiar brands, their storefronts emblazoned with logos and icons of the largest and best-known trade syndicates. These were the insurance brokers, clothing retailers, and commercial banks you saw just about everywhere. Most establishments, though, seemed to be local.

The station's walls and floors were clean, but they'd clearly seen better days, their surfaces covered in scuff marks and gouges. The place had the feel of a once-wealthy city neighborhood whose boom era had long since passed. It wasn't as grimy and run-down as outposts Jeryn had seen in other systems, but it seemed to be well on its way down that path.

Next to a small grocer, a blade vendor's shop caught his eye. Jeryn smiled at the holo of two crossed swords blinking above the entry. A blade merchant *here*, of all places. He'd never seen one in a station before. This he couldn't pass by.

The proprietor, a Xamorian, greeted him as he entered. "Good morning to you, traveler," the sentient reptile said. He wore his species' customary baldric over his right shoulder, the sash's intricate weave and colorful pattern identifying his clan association. The Xamorian equivalent of a family crest. He waved his clawed, four-fingered hand across a table of shining daggers.

"Looking for something in particular?"

Jeryn removed his terminal from his pocket and brought up a holo of his kukri. He set the terminal down on the counter and ran his finger along the markings on the projection's handle. "Have you ever seen markings like this?" he asked.

"Is that your weapon?" the shop owner inquired, and Jeryn answered yes.

The Xamorian leaned over the image, then reached out and enlarged it a bit. "Beautiful design. And quite old, is it not?"

"I think it is," Jeryn said. "I don't really have anything on its provenance, other than it belonged to my father."

"Ah, I see." The shop owner narrowed his yellow eyes at the image. "It's a lovely piece. These markings look like ancient script, but I'm afraid I cannot read them."

Jeryn nodded, unsurprised. He'd heard the same comment time and time again by weapons experts on outer planets, inner planets, and everywhere in between. No one seemed to know what the handle's markings were or what they signified. Like the Xamorian, some said it could be script; others claimed they were merely decorative scrawls. He probably should have taken it to an ancient language scholar by now, as Bhokken had once suggested. But Agency operatives and language scholars didn't exactly run in the same circles. Maybe he'd finally try to look one up after this job.

"It's possible they're cosmetic," the Xamorian said, reversing himself, "and they don't mean anything at all."

Jeryn made a mock hurt expression. "Please, don't ruin the mystery for me."

The shop owner's eyes closed for a moment and he made a strange hissing sound. A Xamorian chuckle. "I didn't mean to rain on your parade, traveler." He reached under the counter and removed a fine-looking kukri. "Here's something I think you'll appreciate."

The ice broken, the pair chatted about weapon designs on different worlds as the Xamorian brought out blade after blade. Jeryn didn't get the feeling he was being worked for a sale. It was more like the shop owner was relieved to finally have someone to talk with who knew their weapons. Most of the tourists who stopped in, the Xamorian confided, bought fancy-looking knives with cheaply made handles and blade edges that dulled far too easily. "After two months, you couldn't cut water with them," he joked.

"Sir," a voice behind Jeryn called. He turned to see his security escort in the entryway. "Your meeting, sir."

Noting the time display on the counter, Jeryn silently cursed himself. He'd been so engrossed with blade talk he'd lost track of time. Making a quick apology to the proprietor and promising to return later for a purchase, he hurried out of the shop and in the direction of the observation node.

With his escort in tow, he weaved through the crowd, knowing there'd be hell to pay if he showed up even half a minute late. Everfeld had few pet peeves, but lack of punctuality was one of them. When Jeryn arrived at the meet location a minute later, he found the large space nearly empty. Only one of the dozen benches was occupied. The wall opposite the entrance displayed a sweeping ceiling-to-floor view of space and the nearby gate, suspended in the starry void. It was a viewscreen, of course, cleverly disguised as a window into space. The outpost's spinning rings meant a realistic view of the outside would have been, for many, a nauseating experience. A tranquil, stationary depiction of local space made a far more pleasing scene than the dizzying reality.

Everfeld sat alone at the far corner of the room. "I'm not late, am I?" Jeryn asked, approaching the bench and taking a seat. His security escort remained a discreet distance away, along with Everfeld's, over by the entrance.

The spymaster turned and looked at Jeryn in an odd way, lifting his eyebrows. "No, not late at all."

"Our friend hasn't arrived yet?" Jeryn asked, noticing something odd about the spymaster's cloak. It wasn't the same one Everfeld had been wearing earlier. The cut was slightly different, and this one looked two shades of red darker. "What happened with your cloak?"

Everfeld looked down at the garment. "Ah, yes. I spotted a lovely shop on the way here," he explained, rubbing the hem between his finger and thumb. "I rather like the design. I had the clerk run the one I was wearing back to the *Dagger*."

At that moment, Jeryn felt someone sit behind him. "Although on second thought, I believe I prefer this one."

Jeryn turned around to find, impossibly, Everfeld seated behind him. *Another* Everfeld. The spymaster lifted his chin at him. "Which cloak do you think suits me best?"

Springing to his feet, Jeryn looked between the two figures, identical twin images of one another except for their cloaks. What in the stars was going on?

As soon as he had the thought, he realized what was happening. Both men's shameless grins gave away the prank.

"You never said the pilot was a shifter," Jeryn said.

One of the Everfelds rose to his feet. "You never asked." He gestured to the still-seated man, whose features had already begun to change, morphing into an unfamiliar face. "Jeryn Lorsi, meet Manto Marogh, the finest pilot in all the Realm."

Marogh stood and extended his hand. "A pleasure. And my apologies." He tilted his head toward Everfeld. "The deception was not my idea, I assure you."

Jeryn was far too fascinated with the man's changing features to be offended by the prank. As he shook the shifter pilot's hand, he couldn't help but stare at the fading wrinkles around his eyes and mouth, at the skin tone slowly draining of color. Marogh took a furtive look around the chamber, then covered his head with the hood of his cloak to hide his transformation.

"If you don't mind my asking," Jeryn said, "how long does it take to…?"

"Return to normal?" the pilot said, completing the question. "On average about an hour, but it depends on how far my features are from their natural baseline."

Jeryn had only met a few shapeshifters in his time. They were such a rarity, many believed shifters no longer existed. Ages ago, when their homeworld had been decimated in the last days of the Gene Wars, a small number had survived by fleeing the violence and settling on new worlds, a tiny diaspora scattered throughout the Realm. When the wars had ended, genetic modification had been categorically banned across all Realm worlds, an absolute prohibition that still existed and applied to all sapient species. Fearing persecution, shifters had lived in secrecy for hundreds of years, concealing their true nature and passing on to their children the long-since-unalterable genome of their not-quite-human kind. Everfeld had once told Jeryn no one knew for sure how many shifters existed or where they were. When you could relocate to a frontier world with a forged identity and a new face, you weren't very easy to track down.

"Shall we?" Everfeld said, gesturing toward the exit.

They made their way back to the naval partition at a leisurely pace, allowing Marogh's face enough time to revert back to baseline. When they stopped by the blade merchant, where Jeryn bought a new sheath for his kukri, the pilot finally removed his hood. Jeryn took this to mean the transformation was complete. Marogh was now a fortyish, olive-skinned man with short brown hair and caramel-colored eyes.

Soon they were back aboard the *Dagger*, where Bhokken and Marogh greeted one another warmly, the way old colleagues did when they hadn't seen each other in a long while. If the Rauk harbored any professional jealousy over being snubbed as a test pilot, nothing of it showed on his face or could be heard in his voice. For a moment Jeryn wondered if Bhokken was hiding begrudging thoughts and feelings behind smiles and handshakes. But then he quickly discarded the notion. It would have been utterly unlike the affable Rauk to hold a grudge.

Within minutes they'd undocked from the station and received clearance to pass through the gate into the next system, Zeliv Ru, some ten light-years distant in realspace. Bhokken and Marogh sat at the *Dagger*'s controls, the Rauk giving the new arrival a hands-on tutorial of the vessel's maneuvering thrusters and primary propulsion. Everfeld excused himself to his quarters to study the latest briefings his office had forwarded, detailing news and events from various outer-system hot spots. Jeryn remained on the bridge, watching the distant gate grow slowly larger.

Marogh was a quick study, and by the time they'd completed the hour-long trip to Corren Gate B, he already seemed to have a solid grasp of the ship's primary controls.

Bhokken turned around in the copilot's seat and asked Jeryn,

"We're getting close to the gate. Should we send the C&B supervisor your regards?"

"That's not funny," Jeryn said. "And that was Gate A, by the way. Not this one."

"Clearly I'm missing some amusing anecdote," Marogh said, half turning around.

"Yes, and I'm afraid it's classified," Jeryn said.

Bhokken grunted a laugh. "Oh, you'd like to keep it that way, wouldn't you?"

"I see we've arrived," Everfeld said, appearing in the bridge's doorway. Outside the viewport, Corren Gate B dominated the view, its translucent surface swirling in a constant churn of lavender hues.

"We're cleared for transit," Marogh said, then looked at Everfeld expectantly.

Everfeld nodded. "Mister Marogh, take us through."

PART 2

11

MINORITY OPINION

SPACE TRAVEL WAS BORING. NO ONE EVER TOLD YOU THAT WHEN you were a kid. You grew up thinking it would be like in the drama feed programs, with roaring engines and laser battles and pirates lurking behind asteroids. But no, it was nothing like that at all, at least in Jeryn's experience. It was more like being detained by police, only you were stuck inside a ship's hull instead of a jail cell. You couldn't go anywhere, you lost track of time, and you spent hour after hour trying to keep from going stir crazy. Even the novelty of passing through interstellar gates, impossibly jumping light-years in the blink of an eye, eventually became mundane and uninteresting.

They'd been traveling through the Realm's vast expanse for two weeks, traversing system after system, gate after gate, on their way to Sandau Prime. After picking up the pilot, their only stops had been at a couple fuel depots along the way.

It could have been worse, Jeryn reflected as he sat at the desk in his quarters. The *Veiled Dagger* was a roomy ship, so he didn't feel as cramped as he normally did on other vessels, where low ceilings and small cabins were the norm. And the company wasn't bad. The Marines were an amiable enough lot. Rough-and-tumble types, for the most part, but then they were infantry men and women, so you expected as much.

Manto Marogh remained, even after two weeks, a bit of a mystery. His path and Jeryn's had often crossed in the galley during mealtimes, and they'd both attended Everfeld's mission review sessions. But Jeryn still felt he only knew the man on a very superficial level. Marogh was polite, articulate, and friendly, but at the same time distant and guarded. Maybe it was because he was a shapeshifter. When you had to live in hiding under constant fear of exposure, you probably built some pretty thick walls around you.

Bhokken was his usual carefree self, without a seeming worry in the worlds. Actually, the Rauk seemed a bit more cheerful than normal, now that Jeryn thought about it. As an ever-curious engineer tinkering with the most advanced stealth ship ever constructed, Bhokken was the proverbial kid in a candy shop. Every evening when the four met for dinner in the galley, he'd have some new story to tell about this or that amazing system. The fact that much of the technical detail was lost on his companions didn't appear to douse his enthusiasm in the least.

Everfeld had mostly kept to himself over the last couple weeks, scouring over intelligence briefings, sending and receiving encrypted comms, and seeing to the endless tasks that fell under his role as the Agency's chief executive. Thanks to subspace hypercast transmissions, which jumped between two points in realspace almost instantly, Everfeld's demanding job followed him wherever he went, even to the vast nothingness between the stars.

Before he'd come to know Everfeld—the first highly placed official he'd ever been personally acquainted with—Jeryn had always assumed people like the spymaster had a life of leisure. That they lounged around in mansions all day while underlings did their bidding, and at night they attended dinner parties with celebrities and heads of state. Jeryn laughed at how silly that seemed to him now, how clichéd and utterly wrong that notion had been. The truly powerful, those like Everfeld and the consul minister and planetary governors, had lives that weren't their own, where every day was a struggle to retain control, to steer your boat through impossibly choppy waters. The powerful were constantly pulled in a hundred different directions by a hundred different vested interests. Often they were surrounded by schemers whose fair-weather loyalty ended the instant it conflicted with their own personal ambitions. Or by fawning sycophants, those grinning and butt-kissing and utterly useless hangers-on. The powerful slept very little, rarely saw their families, and they faced pressures and demands that would crush anyone who didn't have an iron will and unshakable self-confidence. Over these last years, Jeryn had come to learn what the daily life of the truly powerful entailed, and it was a job he never wanted to have.

He checked the time. Half an hour to kill until dinner. He pulled up a holo of the backgrounder Everfeld's research staff had put together. When Jeryn had first reviewed it a week earlier, the briefing had struck him as one of the most complete summaries on the Separatist movement he'd ever read. Well worth a second look, even a third.

A growing populist movement spreading throughout the frontier worlds of the Realm's outermost reaches, the so-called Separatists had been around as an identifiable political force for only a couple decades. The political grievances that gave rise to the movement, however, stretched back centuries, even millennia, according to many scholars: unfair taxation, institutional corruption, and the failure to assure universal sentient rights. Planetary governors on outer worlds had long complained about the heavy burden of duties and tariffs Gran Kiravashta demanded. "They take and take and take," an outer planet governor had said during his inaugural speech, "and what do we get in return? Corrupt loyalist diplomats with little interest in our local affairs. Naval installations whose soldiers and officers look down on our people and our ways. Who laugh at us and call us backwater yokels. Ask yourself this question: what good has the Realm done for you today? Or on any day, for that matter?"

That particular quote was over five centuries old.

The question of nonhuman representation in state entities was another age-old complaint, dating back to the earliest days of the Realm. Humans had been the first to discover the strange phenomenon now known as interstellar gates, becoming the first interstellar species in the process. The first in their galactic neighborhood, to be precise. The Realm currently encompassed twenty thousand star systems, but it was still only the tiniest portion of a vast, otherwise unexplored spiral galaxy. And in that pre-Realm era, an early monopoly on interstellar travel had given humankind an unequaled military, cultural, and economic advantage over the myriad sentient species it discovered and subsequently co-opted, sometimes by peaceful means, sometimes not.

As more gates were discovered, humanity established a confederation of star systems that would later become known as the Realm, or as it was formally named, the United Federation of Systems of the Greater Realm. And from the Realm's earliest days, humans had occupied a majority of the most important roles in the state's administrative apparatus. A power-conserving practice that persisted to the present, much to the frustration of nearly every nonhuman species whose homeworld flew the Rockets and Stars banner. "Only humanity can claim full emancipation in the Realm," another governor, a violet-skinned Zatori, had said during a recent rally. "The rest of us are relegated to second-class citizenry. This unfair, inherently unjust state of affairs cannot endure. It *will not* endure." State leadership, of course, denied any institutional bias, pointing out the growing number of nonhuman assemblypersons, planetary governors, and tribunal justices. Separatist leaders countered that nonhumans still constituted a powerless minority, far out of proportion with the Realm's nonhuman population, which accounted for nearly half of its citizenry. Humanity, despite its claims of inclusion and emancipation, still held a firm grip on the reins of power.

Malcontent factions were nothing new to the Realm. Dissatisfied constituencies had always been a part of its ten-thousand-year existence. Such was the nature of state authority, a historian quoted in the briefing noted. "Every empire has had its detractors." But only until very recently had the Realm's long-simmering discontent begun to boil over into something more ominous. Over the last few decades, Separatist-inclined planetary governors and their electorates had grown more brazen with their anti-institutional rhetoric. Eventually, heated words had given rise to openly defiant actions. Rockets and Stars banners had been burned in mass demonstrations, and a dozen worlds had declared a suspension of payments to Gran Kiravashta, refusing to render tax revenue to state coffers. In a few of the more ideologically extreme systems, Realm diplomatic compounds had been burned down and ransacked by rioters.

At the direction of the Consul Minister Amarania, the state's response to this historically unprecedented defiance had been swift and thorough. A handful of governors and regents from the most rebellious systems had been made examples of, arrested, tried, and convicted in highly publicized sedition trials. And Separatist sympathizers—those who hadn't yet broken the letter of the law but had been outspoken in their criticisms of the status quo—were stripped of power through legal machinations. The state's years-long purge had sent a clear message to Realm systems far and wide: there was little tolerance for Separatists or those who supported them.

Amarania's actions had spectacularly backfired. Instead of

suppressing the movement, the CM's iron-fisted response had only added fuel to the Separatist fire. Year after year, more and more systems became openly critical of the Realm's heavy-handedness. More and more governors and assemblypersons questioned the legitimacy of Gran Kiravashta's authority over their sovereign affairs. A small number of outermost systems had even declared themselves independent worlds, severing all economic and political ties with the Realm and its loyalist systems.

The final portion of the briefing speculated over the possibility of all-out civil war. While outright hostilities hadn't yet broken out, events seemed to be marching in that dreaded direction. The research staff authors didn't go as far as to claim Realmwide civil war was inevitable, only that the chances of avoiding it were growing steadily slimmer.

The briefing had nothing in it speaking to *how* such a catastrophic event might be averted, but Jeryn knew the topic had two opposing schools of thought within the state hierarchy. The vast majority of loyalist bureaucrats—even in light of the CM's faltering public support—endorsed Minister Amarania's hard-line approach of whipping the errant systems back into obeisance, and doing so by any means necessary. The outer worlds in open rebellion and those who sympathized with them were seditionists, plain and simple, and they deserved to be treated as such. It was far easier for the wealthy ruling class of older, established inner worlds to think of the Separatists as ingrate provincials than to see them as an oppressed minority. After all, when you admitted someone was being oppressed, you had to ask yourself who the oppressor was, and this was a topic core worlders didn't dare explore. No one liked to think of themselves as a tyrant.

The minority opinion, the one held by Everfeld and shared by a small number of others, insisted that only reform would save the Realm and avert a disastrous conflict. Fundamental reform to state economic, social, and political policies had been needed for centuries, and if the Realm didn't address its age-old corruption and failed governance quickly and vigorously, its ten-thousand-year existence might not last another generation. Detractors claimed this was a wild overstatement, that Everfeld and those who agreed with him (mostly scholars, none of whom held positions in the CM's administration) were alarmists or bleeding hearts or even rebel sympathizers. The spymaster could only shake his head in frustration at this, convinced the Realm's leaders were grossly underestimating the Separatists' determination and resourcefulness. "When has any empire ever foreseen its own demise?" Everfeld had once told Jeryn.

Switching off the holo, Jeryn sighed. It all felt so abstract to him. He'd visited, what, roughly a hundred worlds? Far more than the average citizen. Far more than the average wealthy citizen, for that matter. But still he'd only seen the tiniest portion of the Realm, the smallest fraction. The notion of a conflict involving hundreds, even thousands of worlds was undoubtedly terrible, but at the same time it felt distant, like it was part of something else, something far beyond him. The cleric operation, however, was close at hand and getting closer every minute. The jeopardy Jeryn and his companions faced, the risks they were taking, somehow felt far more real, far more threatening than galactic civil war.

His comms connection chimed, followed by the Rauk's excited voice.

"You need to get up to the bridge," Bhokken said. "Now."

12

TWELVE-GEE RUN

SLIGHTLY OUT OF BREATH, JERYN ARRIVED AT THE BRIDGE TO FIND Everfeld, Bhokken, and Marogh gathered around the central console, their intent gazes fixed on a meter-tall holo projection.

"So I guess we're in the Barat-Cray system?" Jeryn asked. He'd been looking forward to their arrival for days.

Bhokken looked over. "Indeed. We just passed inside BC 5's long-range scanning perimeter."

The Marine sergeant entered the bridge, a gruff human named Burns with short-cropped salt-and-pepper hair, shouldering his way past Jeryn. "Sir," he said, addressing Everfeld. "My team's on standby and ready for action."

Everfeld nodded. "Thank you, Sergeant. I doubt it will come to that, but please keep them ready until I tell you otherwise."

"Yes, sir," the Marine said, then turned on his heel and exited the bridge.

Jeryn gave Everfeld an uneasy look. "Keep them ready? For what?"

"For nothing," Everfeld said. "It's just a readiness drill we'd planned on arrival into the system. They've been doing little more than cleaning their weapons for these last two weeks." He waved Jeryn closer. "Come have a look."

As Jeryn approached, he scanned the holo's content, a zoomed-out view of their location. Barat-Cray 5, one of two planets in the red dwarf system's habitable zone, took up a large portion of the image. A yellow marbling of clouds churned above a mostly liquid water surface, dotted with island continents. Its twin moons floated nearby in impossibly close orbit (the image clearly wasn't to scale). At the opposite side of the display, a small green triangle pulsed.

"That's us?" Jeryn asked, pointing to the icon.

"Yes," Marogh said, then he tapped a control on the console and the ship's transponder information appeared above the triangle. Call sign AC-675 and the vessel name *Void Runner*. "And that's who we are at the moment."

The flyby on BC 5 would be the *Dagger*'s first "live" test of its masking technology. The adaptive transponder worked in conjunction with the prototype stealth technology built into the ship's hull, creating what Everfeld and the ship's design team hoped to be a virtually foolproof disguise. The transponder sent a false identification signal, but the real magic was in the *Dagger*'s hull, where reactive layers of smart materials could selectively absorb and deflect scanning signals to create a false image on the return—of an industrial tug, a mining ship, a luxury yacht, or even a battle frigate. It wasn't unlike the shifter pilot's ability to change his face to resemble whoever he wanted.

And the ship's drive reactor, an experimental modular design, took the disguise game even further. Not only was the reactor incredibly powerful and efficient, but its operation could be reconfigured to mimic dozens of standardized drives and their corresponding exhaust signatures. When a ship under thrust was scanned, its exhaust signature served as a kind of heat-and-radiation fingerprint, identifying the vessel's reactor model and, by extension, its ship class. With the *Dagger*'s modular drive, the spy ship could change its fingerprint as the situation required.

When it came to masking its identity, the *Dagger* had a very large bag of tricks.

At the base of the holo, a comms icon blinked into existence. *"AC-675, AC-675, this is Barat-Cray Transit Control. Do you copy?"*

Instead of answering, the spymaster, pilot, and engineer exchanged knowing looks. "Should we tell him?" the Rauk said, tilting his head toward Jeryn.

"He'll find out soon enough," Everfeld said.

Jeryn frowned. "Find *what* out soon enough?"

"Who we are," the pilot said.

"Or, rather, who we're masquerading as," Everfeld corrected.

Ten red dots appeared on the holo, their call signs identifying them as Transit Control vessels. The *Dagger*'s long-range scanners had picked up the ships exiting their low-orbit patrol routes. Now they were in a wide formation on an intercept course, traveling at a suspiciously urgent seven-gee burn.

"Repeat, AC-675 this is Barat-Cray Transit Control. Do you copy?"

Jeryn stared at the display. "So who exactly do they think we are?"

Again, the three others shared a conspiratorial look. "Tell me," Jeryn insisted.

"The private yacht of a wealthy tax evader," Bhokken said.

"The *what?*" Jeryn asked, stunned.

The Rauk engineer shrugged at Everfeld. "I told you he wouldn't like it."

Jeryn looked between the three, bewildered. Posing as some rich fugitive hadn't been the plan. They were *supposed* to dip into

BC 5's scanning range as a cargo vessel—a *legally chartered* cargo vessel—heading for a local fuel depot. If the transit authorities were fooled into thinking the spy ship was a commercial ship on its way to refuel, the *Dagger*'s crew would deem the flyby a success, then slip quickly and quietly out of the system.

But that wasn't what was happening.

"AC-675, AC-675, you are ordered to reduce velocity and prepare to be boarded. Repeat, reduce velocity and prepare to be boarded."

On the holo, the red dots drew closer. Jeryn tried to keep his growing anxiety from showing on his face. "I'm sure there's a sensible reason behind what we're doing," he said to Everfeld. It sounded better than *has everyone here gone crazy except me?*

The spymaster nodded. "Earlier today, I recalled a briefing from weeks ago about the Barat-Cray system's laggard performance in reporting security breaches and criminal activity. Whether this stems from corruption or mere incompetence, I can't say, but neither situation is acceptable. I also remembered the system's new security chief recently assuring us he'd take swift corrective action. I thought it might be a good opportunity to learn if he's delivered on that commitment."

The fog of Jeryn's confusion lifted. A cargo vessel with no red security flags would have been just another ship among countless others coming and going. It never would have shown up on the local system's subspace dispatches to the Agency. An appearance by a fugitive tax evader's vessel, however, was sure to be included.

"You want to see how long it takes for the security notice to pop up on your briefings."

"Exactly," Everfeld said. "And if we fail to see an improvement in their reporting lag, then our new security chief will have some very difficult questions to answer." Then he added, "Apologies for keeping you in the dark, my friend, but the idea struck me only in the last few hours."

Jeryn's worry didn't lessen much with the explanation. They still had ten Transit Control vessels, *armed* Transit Control vessels, bearing down on them. As he stared at the fast-approaching squadron, translucent spheres appeared around the red dots like bubbles, a visual representation of the ships' effective weapons range. If the *Dagger*'s icon passed within any of those bubbles, the spy ship could be targeted and fired upon.

"TC ships only carry railguns, don't they?" Jeryn asked, staring at the holo as it shifted into a gridded tactical display. Long dotted lines emerged from each ship's icon, projecting the vessels' expected trajectories.

"That is correct," Marogh said. "They're modified Navy gunboats, most often crewed by a complement of two, but occasionally three. Far too small for missile payloads." He pointed to one of the bubbles. "Had these been missile-class vessels, the range indicators would be four to five times larger in diameter." Jeryn nodded, still not quite accustomed to the pilot's odd habit of using neutral, carefully precise language. The shifter also spoke with virtually no inflection, his voice a somber monotone even when he made small talk. Jeryn wondered if the man's cool, controlled exterior concealed something not so cool and controlled beneath the surface. Or maybe the shifter was just made of stone.

"*AC-675, AC-675, reduce velocity and prepare to be boarded. If you fail to comply, we will open fire. Repeat, if you fail to comply, we will open fire.*"

The red icons closed in on the *Dagger*. How long were they going to stick around? How close did the old man want to cut it?

The bridge was quiet as the four stared at the display, watching the TC ships draw ever nearer. Somewhere out there in the void, Jeryn pictured an excited wing commander barking orders and pushing his ships to their limits, drives red-lined at maximum burn. He glanced across the faces of his companions. If any of them felt something like the unease poking through Jeryn's insides, not a trace of it showed on their faces.

"Looks like they're buying it," Bhokken said, finally breaking the silence. "They truly believe we're the tax evader."

"Indeed," Everfeld agreed. "Our little ruse seems to be a success." The two exchanged satisfied nods.

"I must say, I'm quite impressed," Marogh said, though you wouldn't have guessed as much from his even tone. The shifter then looked away from the display and gazed expectantly at Everfeld.

The spymaster nodded at the pilot. "It appears to be time for us to leave. Mister Marogh, if you please."

"Right away," Marogh said, settling into the pilot's seat and tapping purposefully on the navigational console. "Bringing us around," he said, "and reversing course."

Jeryn felt the slightest shudder beneath his feet as the *Dagger*'s RCS thrusters fired. Beyond the viewport, the pattern of stars started to drift as the *Dagger* reoriented itself toward an exit vector. One of BC 5's twin moons appeared briefly, tracking from top to bottom at the edge of the image. A few moments later, the stars slowly came to a stop, fixing themselves in space again as the vessel completed the maneuver.

"Engaging main drive," Marogh announced, sliding his fingers along an acceleration curve.

A sound like distant rolling thunder came from the far end of the ship as the *Dagger*'s engines fired, propelling the vessel forward. There was no sense of motion at all, thanks to artigrav generators instantly offsetting the effect of thrust gravity and maintaining a comfortable one gee inside the ship. The only way Jeryn could tell they were actually moving was either by looking at the velocity readout on the pilot's display or by watching the little green icon's position relative to its red pursuers on the holo.

Bhokken adjusted the tactical display, adding several data overlays. The first, appearing at the bottom of the holo, showed the distance between the *Dagger* and the chase group. Next, more overlays blinked to life above each vessel's icon, indicating the ship's velocity. While Marogh remained focused on his navigational display, Bhokken, Everfeld, and Jeryn stared intently at the holo.

The distance between the chase group and the *Dagger* continued to decrease, but at a drastically reduced rate now that the spy ship was accelerating away. The *Dagger*'s burn had already reached five gees, while the TC ships maintained an engine-searing seven-gee acceleration. The trio watched as the gap finally began to stabilize at around forty thousand kilometers, a distance well beyond a railgun's effective range. Jeryn let out a breath he didn't realize he'd been holding.

Half-turning around in the pilot's seat, Marogh lifted an eyebrow and said, "Shall I step on it, Director?"

Everfeld glanced at Jeryn and Bhokken, his expression that of a magician about to perform his best trick. "Yes, Mister Marogh," he said, "you may proceed with the stepping on."

Jeryn watched in astonishment as the *Dagger*'s km-per-second velocity climbed so quickly it became an unreadable blur. The thrust gravity display showed eight gees, then nine, then ten, finally holding steady at twelve. *Twelve gees!* It was an inconceivably fast burn, faster by far than he'd ever traveled. Only the most advanced military vessels could reach such velocities, and that was at the high end of their capability. For the *Dagger*, burning at twelve gees was cruising speed. The amazing vessel still had at least ten more gees of thrust in reserve.

The gap between the TC ships and the *Dagger* widened so quickly that on the display it appeared as if the chase group had suddenly stopped. They hadn't, of course. They'd merely been left behind, tortoises to the *Dagger*'s impossibly quick hare.

"See you later, fellas," the Rauk muttered at the hapless red icons.

Jeryn felt a bit foolish now for having been worried at all. They'd never been in danger at any point during the encounter. The *Dagger* was unthinkably fast, all but untouchable.

An awed giddiness spread throughout the bridge as smiles emerged on every face. Even the shifter's normally stoic expression cracked into a grin. The four were suddenly children, little boys who'd been given the best toy in the universe.

Then, like a rude alarm interrupting a pleasant dream, warning indicators began to flash across the length of the pilot's console. Marogh ran his gaze across the instrument panel, his confused expression illuminated by the console's red flashing lights. An instant later, more lights and warnings appeared on the tactical holo.

Every smile on the bridge vanished. Everfeld approached the pilot's console, placing a hand on the seat back. "What is it?"

"We've got contacts," Marogh replied. "Twenty, no, thirty contacts incoming."

"From where?" Bhokken asked.

The pilot's fingers flew across the console's surface, nimbly tapping and sliding over the display. "From behind the second moon. The smaller one." He furrowed his brow. "We never detected them." The pilot silenced the alarms and reset the holo display to include the newly arrived ships.

Everfeld frowned at what he saw on the holo. "Our intel said there were no bases on either of those moons."

"It also said TC patrols didn't run that far out," Bhokken added.

Jeryn stared at the display, suddenly crowded with icons. From every direction, red dots converged on their projected path.

It wasn't the first time in history an operation had been compromised by faulty information. And Jeryn didn't envy whoever would be on the receiving end of Everfeld's wrath when all of this was over. Of course, they'd have to make it through this encounter before that could happen.

The pilot busily worked the console with both hands. "I am attempting to find an escape vector."

As the trio waited, their increasingly worrisome predicament became clear on the tactical display. Hidden from their scans behind the planet's second moon, the new arrivals had been detected far too late to easily outmaneuver, even at the *Dagger*'s blistering speed. And the chase group they'd left behind was obviously coordinating with its fellow vessels. The two squadrons had quickly surrounded the spy ship.

Bhokken frowned at the image. "They have us boxed in."

"Can we get out?" Jeryn asked.

"I'm not sure," Bhokken said. The fact that they'd detected the second squadron so late made their escape problematic, perhaps even impossible.

The bridge was intensely silent as Marogh furiously tapped his console, working with the ship mind to come up with a solution. Surely, Jeryn thought, with ten more gees of velocity available they could punch through the nearest gap between their attackers before they fell within weapons range.

Or could they? Something told Jeryn it wasn't as simple as that. Combat speed mattered in space, but tactics mattered more. Jeryn's confidence in the *Dagger*'s mind-blowing velocity faded with each passing moment.

"Mister Marogh," Everfeld said, "do we have an escape vector?"

Hunched over the console, fully concentrating on his task, the pilot didn't respond.

"Marogh," Everfeld repeated, his voice straining noticeably.

The shifter's hands suddenly stopped their frantic movement. The pilot straightened his back and tightened his lips into a straight line. "We cannot make it out without being fired upon, even at maximum burn." His shoulders slumped. "I am sorry. There's nothing I can do."

13

ATTACK FORMATION

"Are you sure?" Everfeld asked. The spymaster, like Jeryn and the Rauk, had a hard time accepting a ship as fast as the *Dagger* could be trapped. Especially by a local police patrol. It seemed as improbable as a toddler winning a foot race against an adult.

The pilot nodded grimly. "I am quite sure, Director."

"We have to take off the mask," Jeryn suggested. "Turn off the stealth tech and identify ourselves. They won't shoot at us if they know who we really are." Surrender, it seemed, was suddenly the only safe option.

"We're an unregistered vessel," Everfeld responded. "If we alter our transponder signal now, it will only make them more suspicious. And I doubt they'll believe me if I announce myself and try to explain what we're doing here." After a short pause, he said, "But, in lieu of alternatives, it seems the time has come to end our little test." The spymaster harrumphed in disappointment. "The last thing I wanted was to reveal classified technology to transit police, but I suppose we have no other choice." He stepped in front of the wall-mounted comms panel and spoke into the image sensor.

"Barat-Cray Transit Control, we're reducing velocity as requested so that you may come aboard." He waited, but no answer came back. "Barat-Cray Transit Control, repeat, this is AC-675. Please respond."

Jeryn watched the *Dagger*'s slowing acceleration on the holo display, the spy ship's velocity eventually leveling off, then decreasing. The TC ships' box formation stayed intact with the exception of two vessels, now burning toward the *Dagger*'s projected path. The squadron leader and his wing pilot, Jeryn guessed. They'd catch up with the *Dagger*, match its velocity, then board the ship to find the Realm's chief spy and his companions, not the tax evader they thought they'd trapped.

Still waiting for a response, Everfeld glanced over at the holo. "How long until those two vessels reach us?"

Marogh checked his console. "Based on their current burn, approximately fifteen minutes."

Everfeld spoke into the comms panel again. "Barat-Cray Transit Control, this is AC-675. Please respond. We are reducing velocity." No one from the TC squadron replied. Bhokken, Jeryn, and the spymaster exchanged uncertain glances.

"Something... seems amiss," Marogh said, breaking the tense silence.

All eyes turned to the pilot. "What is it?" Everfeld asked.

"The two approaching vessels have increased velocity," Marogh answered. "Though by my calculations they should have already reoriented to prepare for a braking burn."

Two dreaded words popped unbidden into Jeryn's head: *kill bounty*. Though officially discouraged, the placing of kill bounties on fugitives was a common enough practice. Had this tax evader been such a nuisance that he'd earned a kill bounty? Or maybe the squadron leader was simply the shoot-first-ask-questions-later sort.

Before Jeryn could voice his grim hunch out loud, the pilot spoke again.

"Director Everfeld," Marogh said, "I believe we are about to be fired upon." The calmness in the shifter's voice made his words all the more ominous. "I would not recommend we allow ourselves to come within their effective range."

"How long until that happens?" Everfeld asked, now clearly concerned. Marogh quickly consulted with the ship mind, which estimated two and a half minutes.

"That's an attack formation!" the Rauk blurted out, pointing at the holo. On the display, the two red icons broke their tight side-by-side formation, drifting away from each other. Jeryn was far from an expert in battle tactics, but he felt the threat in the pit of his stomach.

"They've increased their burn rate one gee," the pilot said. "I would like to suggest—"

"Marogh, get us out of here, now," Everfeld ordered.

The drive's engines engaged, and the welcome sound of distant thunder reached Jeryn's ears. On the holo, the gap separating the *Dagger* and the two TC ships still narrowed, though more slowly now. As the *Dagger* gained velocity, the gap would stabilize, then begin to increase. Everfeld asked the pilot, "Will we pass within range before we open the gap?"

Marogh worked the controls for a moment, then said, "Unfortunately, we will." As soon as he said it, the two red icons began to flash wildly. Jeryn stared at the display in disbelief.

The TC ships had opened fire.

14

PATH OF LEAST EXPOSURE

"Taking evasive action," the pilot said, his fingers working the navigation panel in a blur of swiping and tapping. Jeryn, Bhokken, and Everfeld huddled around the holo display.

"They appeared to have fired from beyond their effective range," the pilot said.

"They saw us running," Jeryn noted. The TC pilots had fired off a few railgun bursts, hoping for a lucky shot.

"Have we taken any damage?" Everfeld asked.

Bhokken quickly settled into the chair next to the pilot's console. A holo display appeared with a three-dimensional diagram of the *Dagger* and several scrolling text boxes. The Rauk engineer studied the image for a moment, then said, "Shield and hull both at one hundred percent integrity. They missed us completely."

Jeryn watched their pursuers' range bubbles converge on the *Dagger*'s icon. At the extreme end of a single ship's range, the spray pattern of its railguns could be detected, projected, and avoided with relative ease. But with *two* ships targeting from different angles, their combined firing patterns would be much more difficult to evade, making things far less certain.

The instant the spy ship came within effective range, the red icons flashed once again.

"Incoming projectiles," the pilot said, furiously working the control panel, reviewing the evasive sequence the ship mind had quickly calculated, then confirming the series of maneuvers. Jeryn clenched his teeth as he watched the display. Moments passed and nothing happened. No alarms, no worrisome red warnings on the Rauk's console. And to his great relief, the *Dagger*'s icon emerged once again from the range bubbles.

"We have successfully avoided their salvos," the pilot announced, his voice calm as ever.

"Thank you, Mister Marogh," Everfeld said, though his visible relief didn't last more than a moment or two. He expanded the display's view to show the TC squadron's wider formation, numbering some three dozen ships. While the spy ship had outmaneuvered the two attackers, the squadron still had Jeryn and his companions boxed in.

"How long until we're in range of the others?" he asked the pilot.

"Present velocity, thirteen minutes," Marogh replied.

"Escape vector?" Everfeld asked.

The pilot studied the left section of his console. A small churning graphic indicated the status of the ship mind's analysis. "Nothing yet, Director." Before Everfeld could explore the topic further, Marogh added, "And I am not optimistic about finding one. The *Dagger* is a fast ship, but there does not appear to be a safe route through the formation. The mathematics of the situation simply don't favor us."

Clasping his hands behind his back, Everfeld took in a long breath through his nose. "Gentlemen," he announced, "I'm open to any and all suggestions."

Jeryn absently ran his fingers over his kukri's handle. He wasn't sure why he'd brought the blade with him to the bridge.

There was something about its weight on his hip, the feel of its handle under his touch that made him feel a bit less anxious than he would have been without it. Strange, he thought, that a deadly weapon could serve the same purpose as a child's security blanket.

Then an idea struck him. He turned to the pilot. "Do we know what kind of ships we're dealing with?"

"They're modified Navy gunboats," Marogh replied, echoing what he'd mentioned earlier. He then began to explain how the police vessels' hulls and weapons were different than their naval counterparts.

"The railguns," Jeryn interrupted, "Do we know the *exact* model they're using?"

Marogh didn't but said he could find out quickly. Among its many advanced components, the *Dagger*'s sensor array was perhaps its most powerful system, both in terms of range and capability. The pilot called up a detailed scan of the nearest TC ship, and Bhokken gestured the image over to his engineer's console.

"Esprit-Class Corvettes," the Rauk said a moment after the image popped up on his display. "Standard weapon systems are Javelin 5 railguns, one per ship."

Jeryn stared at the image, recalling the railgun's specs. Having smuggled the weapon system dozens of times before coming to the Agency, he knew more than most about what they could do. And more importantly at the moment, what they couldn't do.

"All right," he said. "Maybe we can deal with that."

"Deal with it?" the Rauk echoed. "How?"

Jeryn moved closer to the Rauk's console. "Javelin 5s are made for short-range engagements. They're durable, reliable railguns, ideal for ship-to-ship fights. But I don't think their tracking systems could lock on to a missile. And even if they could, I'm not sure their turrets could physically rotate in their housings quickly enough."

Confused, Marogh said, "I'm not sure I understand the point. We have no missiles aboard the *Dagger*."

"I'm not saying we fire a missile at them," Jeryn said.

"He's saying we need to fly faster than a missile," the Rauk added, his eyes lighting up with understanding.

"That's *all* we have to do," Everfeld said. "Travel faster than a ballistic missile?"

"Which would be nearly twice the highest velocity ever recorded by a non-military vessel," Marogh pointed out. "Including this one."

"Blessed Fifteen," the Rauk said, turning again to the image and narrowing his eyes. "It could work."

"Can we simulate it?" Jeryn asked.

"Give me a moment," Bhokken said. Jeryn watched as the engineer studied the railgun's specs with dizzying speed. Images, schematics, and mathematical data flashed across the holo at a rate his human eyes could barely perceive, much less analyze. But not so for the Rauk, whose brain could absorb and retain vast amounts of data far more efficiently than any other sentient species in the Realm. In less than a minute, the engineer finished his analysis. He swiveled around to face his companions.

"Doable," he said, giving Jeryn an approving nod. "If we plot the right path, it could very well work, and at a velocity still within the *Dagger*'s theoretical limit."

Theoretical limit, Jeryn repeated inwardly, swallowing. Not its proven, known velocity limit.

The pilot shot Everfeld a questioning look. "I am less than comfortable with this proposed solution."

"Same here," Jeryn agreed. "But it's not like we've got a lot options at the moment."

With his brow furrowed in contemplation, staring at the

slowly rotating schematic on the engineer's display, Everfeld seemed to be coming around to the same conclusion. "Well," he said after a long moment, "we had planned to test the *Dagger*'s velocity ceiling eventually. Though I might have preferred a more controlled environment in which to do so." He looked between the Rauk and the shifter. "Let us proceed."

Huddled over the pilot's console, Marogh and Bhokken hurriedly worked on a solution, aided by the ship mind. For his part, Marogh didn't voice any further doubts. Jeryn supposed the shifter had decided that any action, even a risky one, was better than none at all.

Within moments, the display showed a dramatic jump in the *Dagger*'s velocity, and in seconds they were traveling at a mind-boggling eighteen-gee burn. Jeryn tried not to think of what would happen if the AG array suddenly failed. Tried not to think of himself crushed like a flimsy drinking cup stomped under a boot heel.

A minute passed. The pilot and engineer appeared to finish their task, if their mutual nods were any indication. The Rauk stood up from the console. "We have an exit trajectory plotted," he said to Everfeld, then tilted his head toward the shifter. "We've left enough margin for our pilot to make adjustments on the fly, if the situation calls for it. But essentially, we're set."

Everfeld nodded. "I understand. Carry on. If you'll excuse me, I'll update the Marines. They need to know." He then left the bridge.

They need to know these next few minutes might be their last, Jeryn thought morbidly. He didn't envy the spymaster's errand, the ominous message he had to deliver.

As the bridge door slid shut behind Everfeld, Jeryn approached the Rauk. "All right, tell me. What could go wrong?"

Scratching his furry head with a clawed digit, the Rauk said, "If they're not all using the same railguns as the one we scanned

—or if they've modified them or the housings they sit in—our calculations wouldn't take that into account. And there's always the possibility one of them gets off a lucky shot. But that's about it."

The pilot gave Bhokken a puzzled look. "I have to disagree. There are far more ways our plan could fail than those. First, we can't be certain the ship can reach the twenty-four-gravity thrust velocity our calculations require. Before today, the *Dagger* had never exceeded thirteen. And if we do manage to achieve twenty-four, the enormous stress the ship's hull will be subjected to could very well result in catastrophic—"

"You must be fun at parties," the Rauk interrupted. "Have a little faith, will you?" He reached out and caressed the bulkhead. "The *Dagger*'s a heck of a ship. It won't let us down."

Marogh didn't appear bothered by the jab, his features arranged in a ponderous gaze. "It is a remarkable vessel," he finally agreed, then turned back to his console.

A moment later, Everfeld returned. "How did they take it?" Jeryn asked.

"They're elite Marines," the spymaster replied. "They took it in stride. Hardly a blink among them." Jeryn caught a hint of bitterness in the old man's tone, noted a flicker of regret behind his eyes. Even as the spymaster tried to keep a stiff upper lip, Jeryn knew the man had to be reeling with guilt for leading the *Dagger*'s crew into such dire straits. What was supposed to be a simple field exercise had turned into a mad scramble for survival. Jeryn's companions seemed to notice the spymaster's mood as well.

"We'll be fine," the pilot said, swiveling around to face Everfeld. "The *Dagger*'s a heck of a ship. It won't let us down."

Jeryn and the Rauk exchanged surprised looks that quickly melted into mutual grins. "Well put, my friend," Bhokken said.

The moment passed, and Everfeld's businesslike composure

returned. "How long until we reach the closest ship's effective range?"

The pilot checked his console. "Slightly under four minutes." Bhokken settled into his workstation. Jeryn and Everfeld stood around the tactical display, watching the *Dagger*'s icon as it approached the nearest TC ship's range bubble. Time passed far more slowly, Jeryn imagined, for him and Everfeld that it did for the other two. The pilot and the engineer had tasks to occupy themselves, unlike Jeryn and the spymaster. All the pair could do was watch the display and wait for their fates to unfold.

The maneuver would be a tricky one to pull off, even for a ship mind that could perform countless calculations per second. The pilot and engineer had instructed the ship mind to chart a path that minimized the ship's exposure. The *Dagger* would fly a parabolic course with the nearest gunboat as its focal point, a route they hoped would force the railgun's capabilities beyond its practical limits, both in terms of tracking technology and its mechanical ability to rotate within its housing. If the railguns couldn't track the *Dagger*, they couldn't hit it.

Against a single aggressor, the gambit would be difficult enough, but against multiple attackers a clean escape was far less certain. With each vessel's firing range overlapping that of its neighboring ship, the *Dagger* would have to pass through two vessels' effective range at the same time. Two or more, actually. For if the squadron leader anticipated what they were up to and altered his formation quickly enough, the number of in-range ships could be three or more. And while the *Dagger*'s energy shields could deflect projectiles like stones skimming over water, they could only do so much. A sustained barrage of direct hits could overcome the shield's regeneration rate, leaving the hull exposed. And the hull, while remarkably robust for a vessel of its class, was far from impenetrable.

The wait was excruciating. Jeryn watched his ship's icon

growing ever closer to the hostile squadron. He tried to push the words *explosive decompression* from his mind. Tried not to think about the ship being pummeled by sustained hits from multiple railguns.

"Thirty seconds," the pilot said. Jeryn breathed in, fighting back the instinct to brace himself. He felt like he was on a speeding ground tram about to crash into a stone wall. Suddenly, time flew, and the half-minute passed far too quickly.

"Here we go," Bhokken said.

"Initiating exit maneuver... now," the pilot announced.

Jeryn was vaguely aware of his hand reaching up and gripping a wall-mounted handhold. He stared at the display, not daring to lift his gaze to meet the spymaster's, lest the old man see the worry in his eyes.

The display rolled violently as the *Dagger* altered its orientation and began the maneuver. The suddenness of the image's shift gave Jeryn a brief, dizzying moment of vertigo. He gripped the handhold tighter. With his free hand, he ran his fingers along his kukri's handle, watching as the *Dagger*'s icon passed within the first range bubble.

"Twenty-two gees," the Rauk announced. On the display, the nearest red icon began to blink wildly.

"They've opened fire," the pilot said.

Jeryn heard no impacts against the hull, felt no worrisome vibrations under his feet. The first volley had apparently missed. So far, so good.

On the display, the *Dagger* inched along its parabolic, dotted-line route. A moment later, it passed into another, overlapping range bubble. A second blinking icon joined the first. Now two ships were firing on them.

From the engineer's station, the Rauk grunted something in his native language too low to make out. An expletive, Jeryn guessed, based on the tone. Whatever Bhokken had just seen on his console, he didn't like it.

"They appear to be altering their formation," the pilot said.

"I see it," Everfeld said, and in the same moment Jeryn noticed it as well. As they'd feared, the squadron was reacting to the spy ship's tactic. Two TC ships adjacent to the *Dagger*'s exit vector were changing position, making hard burns for their target's anticipated path. The new projected paths on the display showed the *Dagger* would simultaneously fall within three, possibly four, effective railgun ranges.

Not good, Jeryn thought grimly. Not good at all.

"Can we increase velocity?" Everfeld asked the pilot. "Can we beat those two to the exit vector?"

The pilot paused before answering. "Theoretically, but I'm not sure I would recommend it. The *Dagger* is running very close to its rated limit. If we want to reach the exit vector in time, the increased burn would require one hundred and ten percent reactor output, which is highly unstable. We would also have to exceed our AG array's capabilities by roughly two gravities."

The spymaster glanced over at the Rauk and lifted his eyebrows, wordlessly asking for the engineer's opinion.

"I wouldn't think of doing it on a test run," Bhokken said. Then he reluctantly added, "But if I have to choose, I'd rather overload my reactor than try to dodge four railguns at the same time."

The spymaster then looked at Jeryn. The young operative nodded, agreeing with the Rauk's assessment.

"Increase our burn," Everfeld told the pilot. "We can't let them get within range."

"Understood," the pilot answered without hesitation, spinning back to his controls. As the shifter worked his console, Everfeld called the Marine sergeant on the wall-mounted comm, quickly explaining the situation so he and his troops could prepare for the additional gees.

"You'll want to strap in for this," the Rauk advised as soon as Everfeld finished the call.

Everfeld touched a wall control, and a pair of jump seats emerged from hidden recesses in the bulkhead. He and Jeryn sat and strapped themselves in. The pilot and the engineer did likewise, wriggling into body harnesses that emerged from their seats.

"Is everyone ready?" the pilot asked. He glanced at each face, receiving nods in return before returning to his console. "Initiating incremental burn."

Jeryn then realized the pilot hadn't mentioned how long it would take before they felt the additional gees. "How long before—"

He didn't bother finishing the question, the answer provided by the sudden pressure on his chest from a giant invisible hand. Here we go, he thought, hoping he didn't throw up his lunch in the next few minutes. Stars, he hated getting heavy. But, he reminded himself, it definitely beat getting shot to pieces.

"Twenty-eight gees of thrust," the pilot announced, his voice straining. The AG array's limit was twenty-six, which meant the smothering pressure Jeryn felt was two uncovered gravities. It was nowhere near comfortable, but they could bear it for the three minutes they needed to make their escape. How in the bloody falling stars had early humans traveled like this?

Over on the tactical display, the first two icons continued to blink as their ships' railguns fired volley after volley, all of them clean misses. Hitting a ship traveling as fast as a missile, it seemed, was no easy task.

Jeryn focused on the display. Scrutinizing their projected route and the squadron's counter move, it didn't seem clear they'd make it out before being targeted by more ships. Granted, the visual display was a graphical approximation, not reality.

"How close are we cutting it," he called to the pilot, "before those other ships are in range?"

"Very close," Marogh said. "Our margin of error is roughly one-tenth of a second."

"Can we increase thrust an additional gravity?" the spymaster asked, clearly not wanting to cut things so closely. His neck muscles tense, Jeryn shifted in his seat. While he didn't disagree in principle—the faster they got out of this mess, the better—he wasn't fond of the idea of pulling more gees. How much more could the ship take? How much could their bodies take?

"We *can*," the pilot replied, "but we are already well beyond safe limits, Director."

"A tenth of a second isn't enough," the spymaster said, his voice coming out in a grunt. "Take us to an additional gee now, then one more when we're ten seconds from the most vulnerable point along our trajectory."

Marogh didn't comply immediately. He first turned to the Rauk, finding the engineer's furry features twisted with worry. After a moment, Bhokken nodded at the pilot.

The shifter carefully moved his heavier-than-normal hand over the controls. "I'm instructing the ship mind to do as you've asked," he called to Everfeld.

The crushing pressure immediately increased. Jeryn groaned reflexively under the elephant suddenly sitting on his chest.

"Breathe and bear down," the Rauk called out. "Don't let yourself black out."

Overwhelmed by the smothering, multiplied weight of his own body, Jeryn barely registered the words. He tried not to think of his body as some condiment tube being squeezed until the flavored gel squirted out.

He lost track of time as the universe fell away, leaving only himself and the invisible force pinning him down. Then, impossibly, the pressure increased further as the *Dagger* boosted its thrust once more. A rapid succession of pounding thuds rocked the ship's hull. Had they been hit? Or was the ship ripping apart around them, having been pushed too hard?

Jeryn forgot how to breathe, felt his hands go numb. The edges of his vision went black. Somewhere in the back of his mind he recalled tunnel vision was a bad sign. It meant he was on the verge of passing out. Then, as everything began to go dark, his mind began to reel. Where was he? What was happening to him? Was he dreaming this?

When he woke, it took some moments before his blood-deprived brain could make sense of things again. Time and place didn't immediately come to him. He'd gone out, he knew, but he had no idea for how long, and he didn't recognize his strange surroundings. His hands and feet tingled. His head hurt.

Slowly, his thoughts regained coherence. The *Dagger*. The Transit Control squadron. The high-gee maneuver.

Turning his stiff neck, he spied Everfeld seated next to him. The old man breathed in and out slowly. "Oh, my word," he said hoarsely. "I'm getting much too old for this sort of thing."

"Did we make it?" Jeryn asked.

Over at their stations, the Rauk and the pilot were unstrapping themselves.

Bhokken blew out a long breath, then reached over and squeezed the visibly relieved pilot on the shoulder. "Bless the Fifteen, we did."

15

A PENCHANT FOR BLUNTNESS

Mostly recovered from the high-gee burn, but still stiff and sore all over, Everfeld reviewed the ship's damage report in his quarters. The Transit Control squadron was far behind them, its commander sensibly deciding a chase would have been pointless. You could only hope to trap a ship as fast as the *Dagger*. You could never dream of catching it in open space.

Despite the spy ship's nearly untrackable velocity, the TC squadron had managed several direct hits. Some had been deflected by the ship's energy shields, others had perforated and passed through the *Dagger*'s hull. Fortunately, only minor, non-vital systems had been affected. Automated repair technology built into the multi-layered frame had quickly sealed the breaches. And, somewhat amazingly, the moments they'd pushed the engines beyond their theoretical limit hadn't caused any damage to the main drive or the hull's structural integrity. The *Veiled Dagger* was indeed an amazing vessel.

As he glanced through the report a second time, the spymaster hated to think how close they'd come to complete disaster. Their mission had nearly ended before it had even begun.

He'd been careless. There was no getting around it. He'd

taken for granted the accuracy of their information on TC patrols. An assumption that had nearly cost him and his companions their lives. A competent operative took nothing for granted. How many times had he uttered those very words to new recruits? Perhaps he was no longer competent. Or at least not as competent as he once was. Had his mind lost some of its sharpness, dulled over the years by too much administrative work and not enough time in the field? Or had he simply grown too old for the spy game?

The door chime sounded. "Come in."

Jeryn entered. Everfeld was glad to see color had returned to the young operative's face. He seemed fully recovered from the physically taxing maneuver. Young bodies bounced back so fast, he noted, not without a tinge of sexagenarian jealousy. Oh, to be young again.

"You seem none the worse for wear," the spymaster said. "Have a seat."

Everfeld gestured away his display. "We all owe you a great debt for what you did today. Who knows what might have happened had it not been for your quick thinking. Thank you."

"I'm just glad it worked," Jeryn said, taking a seat. The youth's expression was knotted with uncertainty, as if he wasn't sure how to articulate whatever it was he'd come to say.

"Something on your mind?" Everfeld asked.

"Do you... believe in bad omens?" Jeryn asked hesitantly.

"I can't say that I do," Everfeld replied. "And you?"

"No, I don't. But in my old line of work, the smugglers I ran with were a pretty superstitious lot. If anything out of the ordinary happened on the lead-up to a job, or they got some piece of bad news, a lot of times they took it as a sign. A signal from the universe that maybe they shouldn't move forward with whatever they'd signed up for."

"Is this your way of telling me we should abandon our mission?" Everfeld asked.

Jeryn took a breath. "I know you've been in this business far longer than I have, but I'd be lying to you if I said I didn't have doubts. Serious doubts about what we're doing."

The spymaster nodded. "And today's events reminded you just how fallible your old spymaster's plans can be."

If the young operative agreed with this, he was polite enough not to do so aloud, though his prolonged silence spoke volumes about his uncertainty.

"Are you sure this is worth it?" Jeryn finally asked. "Worth risking treason? Worth risking everything?"

Everfeld smiled. The day's harrowing events had done nothing to soften the youth's penchant for bluntness. And the spymaster wouldn't have it any other way. There were so few he could hold in such confidence, so few who spoke to him with such candor. In Everfeld's world, trust and honesty were rarities. Allies and enemies alike always had an agenda beneath their words, like some predator fish hidden beneath a murky water's surface. Everyone was constantly pressing and politicking to further their own interests. Everyone except the scant few, like the young man before him, who Everfeld counted among his most trusted inner circle.

He'd made the right decision to recruit the lad years ago. He was a fine young man, and he deserved the whole truth. And after saving them all from disaster only hours earlier, he'd certainly earned the right to hear it.

The spymaster stood and gestured. A portion of the wall faded into a view of the starry void beyond. He stared outward into space and clasped his hands behind his back.

"Empires have a lifespan, you know," he said. "They're born, they grow, and eventually they die. Nothing lasts forever. Not you, not me, not the Realm, not even the stars.

"And when empires fall, what comes next is almost always worse. Chaos and turmoil, anarchy and violence. Unimaginable hardships, endured mostly by the poor and powerless. It's a sad constant of history, almost without exception, common to both human and nonhuman ancestries.

"Ours is the first galactic empire. Well, the first we know of, I should say. Can you imagine the scale of suffering if the Realm were to fall into civil war? If it were torn apart by it?" He shook his head. "For decades I've tried to steer the CM away from her worst tendencies, and I've failed far more times than I've succeeded. I'm an old man, Jeryn, and I feel far older than my age. My body has aches that won't go away; my mind doesn't have the agility it once had. That merciless villain time has almost caught up with me. And with our politics worsening by the day, this may very well be my last opportunity to make a difference. I know you believe this ploy of mine reeks of desperation, and you may be correct. But these are desperate times, and perhaps they call for desperate measures."

He turned to face Jeryn. "I can't in good conscience stand idly by and watch our worlds erupt into flames, my friend. Yes, reform is needed, and needed badly. Ours is not a city on a hill, not by far. But even with all its flaws, the Realm is the best hope for sentientkind. The Realm must endure." Everfeld lifted his chin. "And so I choose reformation over destruction. Diplomacy over bloodshed. Empire over ashes." He smiled faintly. "And perhaps if we're lucky, a better Realm will emerge from all of this. A Realm that doesn't have to fall like all the other empires of history. A Realm that thrives and grows beyond the Great Arm, grows into something truly magnificent, for all its peoples."

16

SANDAU PRIME

SANDAU PRIME, THE HOMEWORLD OF THE TEGESIAN FAITH, WAS A lovely planet—if you liked barren plains, freezing temperatures, and tornado-force winds. Jeryn had been here on three previous occasions: twice during his itinerant days working the markets, and more recently for the Agency, when he'd come to help recruit a local crime boss. The details of those three visits—what he'd done, who he'd seen, where he'd gone—were mostly forgotten. But the cracked lips, dry eyes, and sand dust that stuck to every exposed part of your skin: he remembered those vividly.

If he had to rank the dozens of planets he'd visited in his time, Sandau Prime would be near the bottom of the list. It was a frigid, uncomfortable rock of a planet.

But at least he was finally off the ship. With the exception of those nervy moments in the Barat-Cray system, the weeks-long voyage had been uneventful and rather dull. Even on a vessel as amazing as the *Dagger*, long jaunts through the void always made Jeryn restless. Despite his reservations about the spymaster's plan, he looked forward to stepping on actual ground under actual gravity, which in the case of Sandau Prime was a pleasant point-nine gee. Perhaps the only point in the otherwise insufferable planet's favor.

The *Dagger*'s shuttle wasn't large, but it carried its six passengers comfortably enough. He and Everfeld sat in the cockpit. Their security escort of four Marines occupied jump seats in a connecting anteroom near the main hatch. Sergeant Burns and his soldiers—two humans and a bipedal, four-armed Huthean with brown fur and long whiskers—were clothed in the plain robes commonly seen on locals. Purpose-built pouches in the garments' inner linings concealed the Marines' weapons. Each carried a compact, high-powered plasma blaster. Multi-purpose rifles, their preferred weapon, would have drawn too much attention and been impossible to hide besides. Jeryn and Everfeld also wore what passed for local garb, though their outfits were a bit less everyman, with more elaborate stitching on the seams and wider, more stylish cuffs.

The shuttle's vibration subsided as the automated landing controls completed the reentry sequence. They entered planetary atmosphere, the shuttle transforming from spacecraft to aircraft as triangular airfoils emerged from the underside of its fuselage. Somewhere far above them the *Dagger* flew in high orbit, concealing its presence from local Transit Control. "Going dark" was the term they'd come to use to refer to full stealth mode. Bhokken and Marogh had stayed aboard, no doubt pleased with the vessel's ability to avoid detection entirely.

A sparsely populated world, Sandau Prime had only fifteen major cities, all of them located in the equatorial zone of the same continent. Infamously high-velocity winds and year-round extremely low temperatures covering most of the planet made habitation beyond Sandau Prime's thin equatorial belt impractical, though a few climate research outposts existed here and there throughout the frigid, windblown wastelands.

"Sandau-Kal," Everfeld said, nodding toward the vista framed

JERYN'S DAGGER

by the viewport. Two hours past sunset, the planetary capital shimmered, an oasis of light in a pitch-black desert. The Tegesian's main temple dominated the cityscape, a colossal pyramid rising high into the night sky. The largest structure in the capital, it dwarfed everything around it.

During his interstellar transit, Jeryn had read dozens of briefs, refreshing his knowledge of the Tegesian faith, its history, and its contemporary leadership. Dating back to pre-Realm times, the ancient faith was less a religion than a moral philosophy. Tegesian canonical texts—what older, long-forgotten faiths had called holy scriptures or sacred gospels—were collectively referred to as the Guides, and the sect's agnostic view of the universe had been clear from its earliest days. The Guides claimed neither belief nor disbelief in a supreme being, an all-knowing, all-seeing creator of the universe. Social scientists described the faith's main philosophical tenet as "ethical utilitarian hedonism." Individuals had a responsibility to seek maximum personal benefit, and they had the inherent right to take any such actions that brought them pleasure, happiness, and satisfaction, as long as those actions didn't harm themselves, others, or the wider society

For its followers, the most common way of explaining Tegesian values was via the ancient phrase *if it feels good, do it.*

In practice, though, it wasn't quite that simple. Even the sect's most faithful observers rarely lived a self-indulgent existence of constant pleasure-seeking. Any person's *good*, the Guides noted, was often someone else's *bad*. A brothel's customers, for example, enjoyed great physical satisfaction, an undeniable good according to Tegesian orthodoxy. But this satisfaction often came at the cost of someone else's well-being, like that of an indentured sex worker in that very same brothel, forced to serve customers against their will. In these situations, where one's benefit brought about or perpetuated the suffering of another, the Guides were clear in their condemnation.

At the time of the Realm's founding, Tegesism had already established itself as the predominant faith of humankind. And as humans expanded their civilization to encompass new star systems and new sentient species, so expanded the Tegesian faith. For the Realm's ten-thousand-year history, state and faith had grown in tandem, and over the centuries their interests had become so intertwined, their dependence so mutual, that on many worlds—especially the more devout ones—they were indistinguishable as separate entities. The church was the state, and the state was the church.

The shuttle descended, its remote landing coordinates forty kilometers beyond the Sandau-Kal's periphery. Over the comms, Jeryn spoke briefly with an air traffic tower, transmitting their landing clearance code, then confirming the vessel's identification and its occupants. A pilgrimage to the holy land: that was their cover story. Six devoted souls visiting the center of the Tegesian universe, blending in with thousands of other daily arrivals who made similar (but legitimate) treks from across the Realm's vast expanse.

Minutes later, the shuttle's skids emerged from the undercarriage, and the ship touched down on a flat pan of rock. Outside the viewport the distant city lights glowed faintly, silhouetting the tops of jagged hills to the west. The atmosphere outside was thinner than on most terraformed worlds, but not so much that they'd need breathing masks or supplemental oxygen meds.

The main hatch hissed softly as the ship opened itself to the world outside. Jeryn felt the cold immediately, and he wrapped his robe tighter around him.

The four Marines exited first, filing down the ramp with alert, intense expressions while Jeryn and Everfeld waited. A moment later Sergeant Burns looked up into the vessel and waved for them to follow. The pair descended the ramp.

Jeryn winced against the cold as he emerged from the ship, his breath coming out in vapor puffs. His garment detected the drop in ambient temperature and warmed its lining to compensate, but it did nothing to keep the biting chill from his exposed face. A short distance beyond the Marines sat a large, rugged-looking carryall. The massive frame bobbed gently on its repulsor field, its yellow headlamps glowing brightly. Next to the vehicle stood a tall woman wearing a thick robe. A few red curls poked out from a wraparound covering her head and neck. Jeryn recognized the green eyes and narrow face from his briefing documents. This was Manda Pezzi-Kaziz, their local contact. Smiling, the woman strode toward them, removed her glove, and extended her hand to Everfeld.

"Welcome to Sandau Prime, Director."

The overland ride in the carryall was bumpy. Under normal circumstances, a ground vehicle's suspensor field adjusted its output dynamically, negating the otherwise jarring unevenness of rough terrain. But over *very* rugged ground, like the landscape they traveled over now, a suspensor field could only do so much.

Jeryn didn't mind the jolting ride though. He was far too thankful the inside of the cargo vehicle was toasty warm. Before they'd loaded up, he'd been outside only a couple minutes, which was a minute longer than he preferred. Jeryn Lorsi was not a cold-weather operative.

Everfeld sat near the partially lowered partition separating the passenger area from the operator's cabin, chatting with Pezzi-Kaziz, who sat up front. The pair made small talk, the kind of chat between associates who hadn't seen one another in a long while, sharing news of contacts they had in common: who'd retired recently, who'd been deployed to a new assignment, who'd gotten married or remarried or divorced. They'd worked closely together in the past, and it showed from the comfortable way they engaged one another.

Pezzi-Kaziz had left behind the three local agents who'd accompanied her to keep an eye on the *Dagger*'s shuttle. Jeryn and company had landed a half-hour's drive from the remote safe house. An extra precaution to keep their location secret.

"Almost there," Pezzi-Kaziz announced from up front. "Just over this next ridge." Jeryn, Everfeld, and the four Marines watched the viewscreen as the carryall crested the craggy rise. Two hundred meters distant, the safe house compound's lights activated, banishing the darkness to reveal a small cluster of dome-roofed buildings. As they approached the compound, the carryall came to a sudden stop.

"Something wrong?" Everfeld asked.

Pezzi-Kaziz pointed to a one-seater vehicle parked next to the main building. "Looks like we've got company."

"He showed up ten minutes ago," one of the compound's security personnel explained a minute later. "We scanned him and his rock skipper. No weapons, no trackers, no comms devices. Says he's got a message from our Tegesian friend."

Everfeld nodded. To keep their dealings private until they met in person, Everfeld and the cleric Tavella had agreed to the exclusive use of couriers for all planetside communications, a practice that was far slower than normal means of contact, but also far safer. Even the most technologically secured communications could be monitored, traced, and decrypted. And on such a crucially important errand, Everfeld would take no chances of his true intentions being discovered by anyone, especially by his own government.

The courier was a Tegesian cleric, an elderly man with a

shaved head and a white beard plaited into a short braid dangling from his chin. He stood in the reception hall, his hands clasped inside the wide cuffs of his drab, gray robe. He bowed his head respectfully at Everfeld.

"Pleasure and joy to you, Director," the courier said, using the traditional Tegesian greeting.

"And to you as well," Everfeld replied, the traditional response. "I understand you have a message for me?"

"I do," the old cleric said. "I'm afraid our mutual friend has been forced to reschedule." The man said it would be more convenient if Tavella could meet in three days, a day later than the original plan.

Everfeld glanced briefly between Pezzi-Kaziz and Jeryn. "And why is that?" he asked.

"Our friend has been unavoidably detained," the courier explained. "She sends her sincerest apologies."

"Detained by *what* exactly?" Pezzi-Kaziz asked sharply. "Director Everfeld has come a long way for this meeting."

"As you may have seen on the news feeds," the courier said, "late last night Sandau-Kal was struck by a series of bombings. A local Originalist faction has claimed responsibility."

Jeryn had seen a story on the feeds about the bombings a few hours before they'd left the *Dagger*. Apparently, it was the first such act of violence to hit the capital city in years.

When news of the attack broke, the cleric explained, the Tegesian Public Information Office, the organization headed by Charnette Tavella, had been overwhelmed by requests for information from throughout the Realm. Media feed inquiries had inundated Tavella's staff. High-ranking clergy across thousands of systems needed to know what the faith's official stance was and what they should say to their local constituencies. They needed authorized statements and talking points, translated into hundreds of languages, and they needed them urgently.

Charnette Tavella, Jeryn reflected, was having a very busy day at work.

"She has a large and capable staff," Pezzi-Kaziz pointed out. "She can delegate such matters to subordinates. There's no need to change the schedule."

Inwardly, Jeryn agreed. In the spy game, a last-minute change of plan often meant something had gone wrong. Your contact was having second thoughts about meeting up. Or, worst-case scenario, you were being lured into a trap.

"I don't like it," Pezzi-Kaziz said.

"It is less than optimal," Everfeld said to the cleric, "but understandable under the circumstances." To Jeryn's surprise, the spymaster didn't seem at all concerned by the courier's news. "But the location will need to be changed as well. A place of my choosing, and our mutual friend will receive only one hour's notice of the new location."

The courier bowed his head. "I'm sure that will prove more than acceptable, Director. On behalf of Sah Tavella, I thank you for your understanding." The man then left the building, and moments later from outside the whine from his rock skipper's engine faded into the distance as the courier returned to Sandau-Kal.

Frowning, Pezzi-Kaziz said, "She's jerking us around."

"Perhaps," Everfeld said. "Perhaps not. Tell me, if she were to disappear from her post, now of all times, abandoning her duties for even a handful of hours, what would her colleagues make of that? What would her superiors make of it? Highly placed administrators simply don't take time off during a major crisis, even if their staff is more than capable of covering for them. It simply looks bad, and in her case, uncharacteristically unprofessional. Her sudden absence could raise suspicions about her priorities, and possibly her loyalties."

After a long moment of silence, Pezzi-Kaziz said, "Yes, I see your point. I can recommend a few secure meeting locations."

"Thank you, my friend," Everfeld said, bowing his head slightly.

For his part, Jeryn agreed with the spymaster's assessment. It was basic counterintelligence. The last thing you wanted a double agent—or in this case a potential double agent—to do was blow their cover by acting suspiciously or doing something out of the ordinary.

"All right then," Pezzi-Kaziz said, her demeanor lightening as she rubbed her hands together. "Allow me share with you some of our local delicacies. I'm sure after such a long trip you're ready for something other than ship food."

The newly arrived visitors dined on a late supper of surprisingly delicious native sweet meats, greens, and flat bread. Afterward, Pezzi-Kaziz showed Jeryn and his companions to their guest quarters. After such a long, eventful day, Jeryn fell asleep within moments of lying down.

17

NOT EVEN THE STARS

MAMA AND PAPA NEVER RAISED THEIR VOICES AT ONE ANOTHER. They weren't at all like other parents in that way. Sure, they had disagreements, but they never became heated and never escalated into yelling.

Never until tonight, that is.

In the darkness of his bedroom, Jeryn heard them through his closed door: the muffled sound of his parents' raised voices, growing louder and more heated.

Later, he'd realize how this had been coming for a while, how this emotional boiling over had been a steadily increasing simmer for months. Jeryn had first noticed it one night when they had the news feed on during dinner. There was a story about the Unification negotiations, about how they were going far more swiftly than expected. He remembered how their faces changed when the report began, taking on worry lines and troubled stares.

"You see that?" Papa said. "They're going to finish all of this before you know it. And then what?"

"It'll take years," Mama said, though she didn't look much less worried than Papa. "We have time to figure things out."

"What do you mean by 'figure things out'?" Jeryn asked.

His parents exchanged a look, a silent agreement to change the subject. The same thing happened every time the topic of Unification with Dawn 7 came up.

Mama and Papa never talked about Dawn 7, the planet the family had emigrated from twelve years ago when Jeryn was a child of three. When he asked questions about their homeworld and why they'd left it, his parents either didn't answer or shifted the topic to something else. While this frustrated Jeryn, he couldn't help but notice how anxious his parents became whenever he brought it up, so he never pushed hard for answers. Maybe someday they'd tell him what had happened there, when the memory of it was far enough removed in time.

For his part, he had no real memories of life on Dawn 7, only a few fleeting images of their large house, its tall windows and the lush, sprawling garden beyond with stone fountains and long rows of thick-trunked trees. The small, modest apartment where he and his family had lived since moving to Dawn 9 was the place he'd always thought of as home.

Now, lying here in the dark he heard every word of his parents' argument, both their voices close to shouting.

"You know someone's going to hand us over," Papa insisted. "Someone who wants to make themselves look good for the incoming administration. And what better way to ingratiate themselves than by selling us out?"

"No," Mama argued back. "The soonest anything could happen, legally, is when the unified constitution is formally adopted. And we'll be long gone by then."

"You're not listening to me," Papa said, now nearly shouting. "This isn't bureaucratic wrangling between legal advocates. This is brutal, backroom politics. Someone's going to serve us up on a plate, and it's going to happen sooner than later."

Jeryn felt his insides twist with worry. He wasn't sure which unnerved him more: the content of their discussion or the near-panic in their voices.

Time sped forward to two nights later, when Papa's grim prediction came true. A friend of the family, someone who worked in government, had called and warned them about what was coming, urging them to drop everything and leave.

Papa disconnected the call and gasped. "Stars, it's happening. They're coming for us." Mama slowly raised her hand to cover her mouth. In the years that followed the pale, shocked expressions of his two parents, standing there in the small dining area, would forever be Jeryn's strongest memory of their faces.

Jeryn woke with a start, sitting straight up in bed, his face moist and hair damp with sweat, heart pounding like crazy. He sat there for a moment, breathing and trying to calm his mind and body, to separate himself from his dark thoughts like his Xamorian blademaster had taught him years ago. His pulse eventually slowed. He got out of bed and padded off to the washroom.

He hadn't had the dream in a while. The dream that wasn't really a dream, but a pastiche of the last memories of his parents. Most often the dream centered around the night he last saw them. The night after which everything had changed. The night they'd shoved a hurriedly packed case into his arms and told him where to go and what to do. Papa had pulled him aside and told him about the kukri power blade he'd placed inside, folded up in a pair of pants.

"In case you run into trouble," Papa had said.

"But I don't even know how to use it," Jeryn had protested, emotions overwhelming him. Prior to that moment, his father had only let him hold the weapon a few times, the family blade that had belonged to Papa's father and his father's father and up the line for generations.

"You know enough," Papa had said, then he'd hugged Jeryn tightly and whispered in his ear. "It's yours now, son. Take good care of it. We'll catch up with you soon, I promise." They were the last words his father ever spoke to him.

Swallowing hard at the bitter memory, Jeryn cupped his hands under the running water and splashed some on his face.

Eventually, he'd pieced together what had happened by scouring publicly available police records. His parents had been fugitives, he'd discovered, a fact they'd never shared with their only child, but in hindsight explained much about their tight-lipped reluctance to discuss the past. According to warrant records, they'd embezzled money from one of the largest trade syndicates on Dawn 7 not long after Jeryn was born. To avoid arrest they'd emigrated to Dawn 9, a criminal safe haven at the time, since the two worlds had no extradition agreement in place. But when Unification came along and the two planets' separate state entities would soon merge into one, it had become clear their amnesty was in jeopardy. Under the new unified government, politicians on both sides had promised there would be no mass pardons or circumvention of justice. His parents had then begun to plan in earnest the family's escape to another system—that much was clear to Jeryn in hindsight—though apparently they'd disagreed on the urgency and timing of their exodus. A fatal difference of opinion, as it turned out. Only a few hours after sending Jeryn away, they'd been gunned down by police. The official records said they'd resisted arrest, but Jeryn wasn't so sure. His parents weren't the fighting kind, but then again maybe they'd been desperate or found themselves cornered. Or maybe the trade syndicate they'd stolen from had used its newfound political influence in the unified government to have them hunted down and killed. That seemed more likely, since that was the kind of universe they lived in.

Jeryn returned to bed and sat down on the edge. Retrieving his kukri from the nightstand, he ran his fingertips absently over the handle markings.

His thoughts shifted from his lost family to Everfeld, recalling how the spymaster had confided in him on the *Dagger*. Never before had the man expressed himself to Jeryn so openly, revealing his most deeply held principles. In the moment, Jeryn had been so moved a lump had formed in his throat.

Jeryn had grieved the loss of his parents for years, and whatever it was that had come after that grief, that unnamed heaviness inside, had never really gone away. He didn't want to go through that heartrending journey again with Everfeld.

"I hope you know what you're doing, old man," he whispered.

It was a long while before he fell asleep again. When he finally did, the last thing he recalled before dozing off was something Everfeld had said.

Nothing lasts forever. Not even the stars.

18

A TASK FOR THE FLESHY ONES

Hive status was important for T'Kik. Of course, it was important for everyone, from the lowliest drone to the planetary queen. At this last, he twitched the topmost pair of his six legs in the genuflection appropriate to his station. *May she bear millions*, he silently said to himself, completing the act of deference.

How his rank would improve upon his return to the homeworld! A task for the Fleshy Ones, completed successfully, was a great honor, sure to be rewarded with a substantial rise in status. Perhaps even the queen herself would bestow this honor upon him.

May she bear millions.

T'Kik returned his attention to the present. He could not let himself become distracted now that his task was nearing completion.

And what a task it was. A task far more difficult than he'd imagined when he'd arrived on this cold rock of a world in one of the Fleshy Ones' planet jumpers. He recalled the planet jumper's cramped corridors and chambers, how few spaces could comfortably accommodate his nearly three-meter height. But still, what miraculous creations they were! Perhaps one day his hive would be provided a fleet of them to travel the stars like the Fleshy Ones.

The task had seemed a simple one at first. Without being detected, he was to capture the sights and sounds of a gathering of two specific Fleshy Ones. Thankfully, he'd been provided two sets of pheromones to identify the beings in question. If he'd had to rely only on sight, the task would have been far more difficult. Fleshy Ones were nearly identical to one another, except for a slight pigment variation in their soft exterior—which they kept mostly covered, even in comfortable climes, for shame reasons T'Kik didn't really understand. Also the strange, string-like keratin growths on their braincases came in a variety of colors and lengths.

But as simple as the work before him had seemed, like the bark eaters who disguise themselves as tree leaves, there had been more to the task than its initial appearance.

They had delayed the gathering, for one. This made the task far more difficult. It had taken much time and effort to uncover the *first* gathering place and time, all for naught. But he had been undeterred. He had done what was necessary, listening in on additional conversations, converting the Fleshy Ones' strange noise-only language into coherent speech through the multipurpose device he had been given. After hours of painstaking review, he had eventually learned the new time for the gathering.

They had changed the location too, but T'Kik did not let this second unexpected development discourage him either. One who couldn't adapt to change was worthless, as the old saying went. T'Kik's kind had conquered an entire planet, after all, by adapting better than the countless lowly species of his homeworld. Two small surprises were hardly enough to stop him from succeeding in his task and gaining the hive status he so longed for.

He'd found an excellent hiding location near the revised gathering place. A natural formation where he could easily observe the Fleshy Ones' comings and goings. Some of his creche-mates would have called such good fortune divine intervention, a blessing from the Three-Antennaed One, but T'Kik was not the superstitious sort.

And now the time had come at last. Finally, the completion of his task was close at hand.

He didn't mind the cold and wind. His thick exoskeleton and adaptive circulation kept his innards warm and cozy. The waiting, however, was far more difficult to endure. T'Kik had always been rather impatient. He had to remind himself the patient hunter snares the prey.

From his hiding place in a cave on a rugged plateau, he kept his sharp vision focused on the gathering place, some five hundred meters distant. The planet's big star was dropping below the horizon, so he began to augment his light vision with heat sensitivity. He wasn't sure if they would arrive by land floaters or air fliers, but those details were of little importance. All that mattered was that the two Fleshy Ones appeared as expected so he could capture the sights and sounds of their engagement.

After what seemed like an eternity, two groups of land floaters converged on the gathering place, a small construction illuminated by artificial light. The big star had long since dropped, and T'Kik relied solely on his heat sense, which sacrificed much detail at this distance compared to light vision. He saw a total of seven Fleshy Ones enter the construction, and among them were his two targets. T'Kik trilled in relief.

Then with a straining flex of his midsection, gaps opened between several of his overlapping chitinous plates. He then felt a vague tickle as he released a dozen slaves. The Fleshy Ones who'd hired him had told him to be very careful and discreet, so he did not dare to send more than a few of the thousands of tiny winged insects that lived on his body, gaining sustenance from a secretion unique to his species. He had learned from the Fleshy

Ones that on other worlds they called such beings parasites, but T'Kik believed slave was the better translation. Parasites had no neurological connections that allowed their hosts to control them. But his slaves did, and they followed his every command. Of course, his instructions had to be simple enough for them to understand. With their minuscule primary brains, his slaves only comprehended the most basic pheromone strings—land on the distant object, watch and listen, capture sights and sounds, etc.—but as long as he could keep his commands comprehensible to their underdeveloped minds, they would obey him without deviation.

He watched as they flew out of the mouth of the cave and disappeared in the direction of the construction. Once there, they would attach themselves to the structure, listening for as long as T'Kik had instructed them to. Afterward, they would return to him, their supplementary brains—also small but excellent biological archiving devices—full of perfectly recorded sights and sounds. When they reattached, T'Kik would neurologically extract everything his slaves had seen and heard, then he'd assemble all those separate mnemonic pieces into a coherent whole. He would then transfer this into the multipurpose device the Fleshy Ones had given him. Finally, the machine—a marvel of technology rivaling that of the planet hoppers—would create a three-dimensional representation of his input. A hologram, the Fleshy Ones called it.

His slaves released, T'Kik was now tantalizingly close to fulfilling the task. And upon its successful completion, the Fleshy Ones had promised to solicit his queen—*may she bear millions*—for a substantial elevation of his hive status. What the fragile two-legged creatures lacked in strength and hardiness, they more than made up for in influence on T'Kik's home planet.

He waited in the cold dark of night.

Later, when the stars had completed half of their journey

across the sky, his slaves finally returned. His patience long since exhausted, the instant T'Kik felt the first slave reattach, he hurriedly began to extract and assimilate. He finished minutes later, then rushed on to the next step, transferring everything to the multipurpose device. Lastly, he pressed the device's submit button, which would send the recording through the air (invisibly!) to the Fleshy Ones who'd hired him.

The task was completed. He'd done it! Despite all the difficulties, he'd done it. And soon he would return to his homeworld, finding his hive status far greater than when he had left.

Despite his agnostic tendencies, he trilled a blessing of thanks to the Three-Antennaed One.

19

SAH TAVELLA AND THE BIG ASK

IN THE MIDDLE OF NOWHERE, THEY WAITED FOR THE CLERIC. THE revised meeting site Pezzi-Kaziz had recommended was an abandoned meteorological station sitting on a barren plain half a kilometer from a sharply rising plateau. Jeryn, Everfeld, Pezzi-Kaziz, and the four Marines had arrived minutes earlier in the same carryall that had ferried them from the shuttle to the safe house three days earlier. They'd found the station dark and cold and nearly empty, its weather-monitoring equipment and most of its furnishings long since removed. A few tables and chairs remained, and Jeryn gathered them together as Everfeld turned on the lights and Sergeant Burns found the thankfully still-functioning environmental controls.

As the place warmed up, Jeryn felt sorry for the three Marines Burns had stationed outside on guard duty. Despite the self-warming garments, Jeryn had found the frigid wind still managed to chill him to the bone. Removing his gloves, he rubbed his hands together and blew warming breaths into cupped palms. How people lived like this, he'd never understand. Pezzi-Kaziz had teased him during the ride over, saying he'd never survive a single winter on Sandau Prime. Jeryn had been shocked to learn they'd arrived during what was apparently the warm season.

Over the past few hours, however, it had been the clandestine meeting with Charnette Tavella, not the incessant cold dominating his thoughts.

The spymaster must have sensed Jeryn's unease. "Try and relax," he said quietly so Burns wouldn't overhear. The sergeant was methodically moving along the walls with a hand scanner, inspecting the site for eavesdropping devices. Outside his squad was doing the same, checking the roof and surrounding area.

Everfeld removed his gloves finger by finger and laid them on the table. If there was a word for the unsettling blend of tension and anxiety Jeryn felt at the moment, Everfeld's expression and demeanor reflected that thing's exact opposite. Amazingly, the man looked utterly at ease. Here the man was, about to commit blatant treason, disobeying a direct order from his superior, who happened to be the most powerful individual in the Realm, and he didn't appear the least bit stressed about it.

The Marine placed a finger to his earpiece, then said, "All clear outside, Director. No scanning devices detected." Half a minute later, he added, "Inside's clear too." Again he touched his earpiece, his gaze drifting downward as he listened and nodded. "Understood," he said, then turned to the spymaster. "Looks like our contact's arriving, sir. We've got a single vehicle inbound."

"Thank you, Sergeant," Everfeld said.

From outside came the slow, rumbling crescendo of a ground vehicle's motor. As planned, the Marine exited the building to meet the cleric and her right-hand man. He returned moments later, holding the door open for the woman whose face Jeryn had seen in countless holos, research materials, and intelligence briefings over these last weeks.

Charnette Tavella strode into the room, outfitted in a stylish, ivory outer cloak with matching gloves and head wrap. Designer clothes, and very expensive, Jeryn could tell at a glance. She removed her glove and head wrap as she approached Everfeld, bare hand extended.

"Pleasure and joy to you, Director Everfeld. Charnette Tavella."

"And to you as well," Everfeld said, grasping her hand. She then exchanged greetings with Pezzi-Kaziz. If the remote location and mysterious circumstances of the meeting had unsettled the cleric, she didn't show a trace of it. She seemed perfectly at ease, as if she'd just walked into a daily staff meeting at her place of business. Grace under pressure, Jeryn noted, just like the old man.

Tavella's companion, a full head shorter than her, followed a couple steps behind, another face Jeryn recognized from his prepwork. Oskan Sarraf, Tavella's chief of staff at the Public Information Office. Also smartly dressed, he wore a more somber slate-gray outer cloak. And similar to the courier from days before, he sported a shaved head and a beard woven into a short braid. As he introduced himself, Sarraf's manner was far less composed than his superior's. His dark eyes darted nervously around the room, as if he expected hidden assassins to burst forth from the walls at any moment.

Everfeld motioned toward Jeryn. "This is my associate, Jeryn Lorsi." The young operative shook the clerics' hands in turn, doing his best to maintain a businesslike exterior while his insides jumped around like mad.

Motioning to the table and chairs, Everfeld said, "Please, let us sit."

As they all settled into seats around the table, the spymaster offered the clerics food and refreshments. "We've brought what I'm told is a fine selection of Sandauan hors d'oeuvres and beverages," he said. "Though of course I wouldn't claim to be an expert."

"Thank you, Director. We're fine," Tavella said, replying for both herself and her right hand.

She placed her gloves and head wrap on the table. Her blonde hair was arranged in braids that wrapped around her head like a crown, typical of the local fashion. Thin wisps fell from her temples, framing her pale-skinned, blue-eyed face. She was every bit as attractive in person as she'd been in the holos Jeryn had viewed.

"Director, I must apologize for my recent lack of availability," she said. "And I'd like to thank you for your flexibility. I was quite embarrassed to have to ask you to reschedule."

Everfeld dismissed her words with a sympathetic wave. "Please," he said, "don't give it a second thought. You had an emergency that required your full attention. Perfectly understandable." He lifted his eyebrows. "I should be the one apologizing to you, for bringing you all the way out here, for all the secrecy in arranging this meeting. I hope I haven't given you cause to worry."

Tavella grinned back at him. "Not at all, Director. Quite the opposite, in fact. I find this all very exciting. A covert meeting with the CM's master of spies. Secret couriers, clandestine locations. It's far more interesting than editing official statements for news feeds." She glanced meaningfully at her chief of staff, who nodded stiffly and barely managed to force a smile. Whatever amount of Tavella's enthusiasm was genuine, Jeryn couldn't tell, but he sensed her right hand shared none of it. He wondered if the two had been in agreement about meeting with Everfeld.

Leaning forward, Tavella placed her hands on the tabletop, fingers intertwined. "How can I be of service to you, Director?" Jeryn found the woman's gaze utterly disarming, even though she was looking at Everfeld and not at him. He felt himself relaxing a bit, felt his insides settling down. He'd read about her personal charisma in his briefs, and he'd seen it in action on holo archives, but experiencing her graceful charm in person was something else entirely. She was the kind of person who instantly put others at ease, and he wondered if it was an inborn trait or something she'd cultivated.

"These are very delicate matters I'm about to share with you," Everfeld said, his eyes shifting between both Tavella and Sarraf. "I hope you understand the nature and content of our discussion must remain completely confidential."

"We do," Tavella replied, again answering for both.

"Excellent," Everfeld said, "then let's proceed."

Here it comes, Jeryn thought.

"It has occurred to me," Everfeld began, "that in your line of work you may, from time to time, become aware of situations or come across communications that may be of interest to me." Jeryn noted the distinction Everfeld made by saying *to me* instead of *to the Agency* or *to the consul minister*.

"Forgive me, Director," the cleric replied coolly, "but that's a fairly broad statement. Was there something specific you had in mind? A particular topic or…?" She left the question hanging in the air.

"In my experience," Everfeld said, "a person in your position, someone who possesses an influential post, is sometimes approached by parties seeking to elevate their own influence. It could be a group, an individual, or an entire *movement*." After this last, he paused for a conspicuous moment before continuing. "Perhaps they need help getting a particular message out. Or perhaps it's the opposite: they'd like to prevent detrimental messages from propagating through the news feeds."

"I see," the cleric said.

"What I'd like to tell you," Everfeld went on, "is that if that sort of situation arises—or if by chance it already has—it would be of great interest to me. And I can assure you I would treat any such matters with the utmost confidence."

Jeryn looked between the cleric and her subordinate. Tavella nodded slowly in contemplation, her expression still calm and composed, as unchanged as her companion's visible unease. The subtext of the spymaster's seemingly innocuous statements couldn't have been more clear: *I know you've been in contact with the Separatists, and rather than arrest you, I simply want you to know that I'm aware of it.*

"Thank you, Director," Tavella said, then lifted an eyebrow. "Should such an occasion arise, I'll most certainly reach out to you." She tilted her head slightly. "But have you really come all this way just to tell me the door to your office is always open?"

Jeryn sensed Everfeld had piqued her interest, which had been the old man's intention. Unlike her nervous companion, Tavella had quickly surmised the director was putting out feelers. But she was canny enough to proceed cautiously, prudently. The man sitting before her was the Realm's master of spies, after all. Not someone you dared to take lightly. At least that was what Jeryn guessed was going on inside her head. Her unflappable expression and steady voice gave him little insight into her state of mind.

"No," Everfeld said, a wry smile spreading across his face, "that's not all I came here to discuss. It's the least part of it, in fact. There's something else I wanted you ask of you, Sah Tavella." Jeryn noted how Everfeld used *Sah*, the Tegesian honorific. A subtle acknowledgment of respect.

"By all means," the cleric said.

Jeryn swallowed, knowing what was coming. The "Big Ask" was how they'd referred to it during the briefings on the *Dagger*.

"My greatest desire," Everfeld said, "is for the Realm to avoid a catastrophic, self-inflicted war. And right now, I believe we're dangerously close to that grim scenario coming about."

The blue-eyed cleric looked between Everfeld and Pezzi-Kaziz. "I might be inclined to agree with you, Director."

"I also believe it's avoidable," Everfeld continued. "That countless lives can be saved by averting a Realmwide civil war."

"Peaceful solutions are always better than the alternative, of course," Tavella said. "My office is ready to help the consul minister in any way we can. My communications staff can—"

"Forgive me, Sah Tavella, but I'm not seeking help from your staff," Everfeld said. "I'm seeking *your* help. And this has nothing to do with your role at the Public Information Office."

"*My* help?" she asked, lifting her chin. "Director, my area of expertise is media spin and communications, not interstellar politics. I'm just a glorified propagandist."

Everfeld stared knowingly at the cleric. "We both know you're far more than that. The relationships you've nurtured with the Originalists and the largest Separatist factions place you in a very strategic and highly influential position. You're in the right time and the right place, Sah Tavella, to help prevent a needless war. To help avert a catastrophe of untold proportions."

To her credit, the cleric didn't bother denying anything. And to Jeryn's continued amazement, she remained calm and cool, even as the spymaster exposed her secret meetings with anti-Realmist factions. Activities that, if brought to public light, would at a minimum cost her her job, her professional reputation, and would probably land her on a prison planet with a life sentence for sedition. Sarraf, unlike his unflappable superior, appeared more ill at ease with each passing moment.

"And how exactly would I manage that?" Tavella asked. "Assuming you have your facts straight about my dealings with certain parties, and I'm not saying you do."

"By helping me bring all the anti-Realmist factions together," Everfeld said, "to negotiate peacefully for reform."

The cleric appeared momentarily surprised. A crack in her otherwise impenetrable armor. Then her expression hardened. "I'm not a diplomat, Director."

"I'm afraid I have to disagree, Sah Tavella," Everfeld said. "You've been engaging in no small amount of diplomacy in recent months. And quite successfully, it seems. But the only constituency you've been serving has been yourself. I'm asking you to represent a much larger interest than your own ambition."

A hint of anger flashed briefly across her face. "Sir, you're asking me to be a double agent."

"I'm asking you to choose peace over war."

"And what if war is unavoidable?" the cleric said sharply. "What if we've already passed the point of no return?"

Everfeld leaned forward. "Until the first shots are fired, there's always hope for peace."

"Peace," the cleric echoed. "And what would peace mean, in Realmist terms? More of the same? More tacit endorsement of slaver worlds, as long as they pay their taxes on time? More corruption and cronyism? More human-biased bigotry? With all due respect, Director, the Realm's leadership has rarely bothered to listen to the concerns of its citizenry, much less do anything about them. This administration least of all."

"I'm part of the administration," Everfeld reminded her. "I'm talking about doing something about it right now. Does that not count for something?"

The cleric jumped on the spymaster's comment, a cat pouncing on a mouse. "So am I to understand the consul minister's stance isn't as rigid as it appears in public? That the rumors of plans for widespread military suppression are false? That, on her behalf, you're here to try and work out some sort of back-door diplomacy?"

"I'm afraid I can't answer those questions," Everfeld replied, a bit taken aback by the woman's sudden bluntness. "But what I can tell you is that I'm here to talk with you about changing the path we're all on."

"Isn't that exactly what the Separatists say they want? To change the path we're on?"

"Indeed they do," Everfeld said, softening his tone slightly. "And rightly so. Change is needed, reform is needed. But how we choose to bring about that change and reform can make all the difference in the universe."

The cleric smiled with no humor in it. "An idealistic spymaster. You may be the first one in history." Then she added, "If you're to be believed."

Everfeld nodded slowly, as if he appreciated her skepticism. As if he might not accept what he was hearing either, had their positions been reversed.

A long moment passed before Everfeld spoke again. "When I was a boy," he finally said, his voice soft and reflective, "I lived on a relatively poor backwater planet. Our nearest neighbor was a system far more wealthy and politically influential than our own, and they used those advantages to our detriment in every way possible. As I came to learn later, they viewed us as a threat, as upstarts who might one day endanger their supremacy in the local volume. And so they took every opportunity to hinder our economic and political advancement, to poison whatever seeds we planted before they could grow and flourish. For decades, the leaders of our world pleaded with Gran Kiravashta for help, but one administration after another refused to get involved, publicly stating it was a local dispute and the responsibility for resolving it lay with planetary leadership.

"When our governor and the local assembly finally decided they'd had enough, they began acquiring ships and weapons. Eventually, when war broke out, it became clear quite quickly that the Realm had backed our more powerful neighbor all along, secretly providing them with heavy frigates and invasion forces." Everfeld shook his head, his expression grave. "For all the countless funds our world sank into creating a war machine, it was nothing compared to the other side's overwhelming forces. In five days, the war was over. Over a hundred million dead on my homeworld, most of them innocent civilians. My parents among them."

The cleric swallowed. "You're from Batania?"

"I am."

"You were there when it happened?"

"I was," Everfeld said.

The bloodiest interstellar conflict in recent history, the Batanian Massacre had become a rallying cry for insurgents everywhere. *Remember Batania!* could be seen scrawled on public buildings throughout the Realm (though always promptly removed). *Remember Batania!* signs and banners were present in every mass protest against state corruption. A near-genocidal military action that had wiped out eighty-five percent of the planet's population, the Batanian Massacre embodied for revolutionaries the Realm's tyranny at its cruelest and most devious.

"When you've seen such death and destruction," Everfeld said, his gaze shifting to some point beyond the room, "it never leaves you. And you never want to see it happen again to anyone, on any planet. Not even to your worst enemies. You call me idealistic. I don't know if I am or not. But this I know: I'll do everything in my power to prevent what happened on my world from happening again on thousands of others. No matter the cost."

The room fell silent. Jeryn stared at Everfeld in wonder, momentarily forgetting why he and the spymaster had come to Sandau Prime. He'd never heard this story from Everfeld before, never known the man had lived through such tragedy. *And you think you know someone*, he reflected in amazement.

Unbidden, Jeryn's thoughts flashed back to his own youth, to the trauma he'd revisited so many times in his dreaming mind. That unforgettable night he'd been hustled onto a shuttle, his teary-eyed mother kissing him goodbye. He'd gotten the last empty seat, so he had to travel alone, then wait for them at the station. They'd catch up with him on the next flight out, and the three of them would find a way off-planet. There was no time to explain everything, she'd said. He had to hurry, hurry, hurry.

And then he never saw them again.

Forcing his thoughts away from that horrible night, Jeryn returned to the present. He looked at Everfeld, seeing him as if for the first time.

The old man's fight wasn't just about ideals, about saving an empire from falling and preventing a catastrophe and pushing for reform. It was more than that. It was personal. It was a crusade to spare countless children from the horrors he'd suffered. From the nightmare of losing your loved ones. Jeryn knew that nightmare too, and every doubt he'd had about Everfeld's secret dealings left him. He then laughed at himself inwardly, at the sudden one-eighty-degree turn in his convictions. From the first time he'd heard Everfeld's plan to recruit the cleric until only a few moments ago, he'd dreaded this meeting, questioned the wisdom of it, loathed what might come from it. Now he wanted the crazy plan to work, wanted it in the worst way.

The old man's fight was his fight too.

Charnette Tavella sat there, still poised but perhaps a bit less after hearing Everfeld's story. She seemed to be studying the spymaster, unsure what to make of the man. This powerful state executive who'd appeared out of nowhere to upend her life. Drawing in a breath, she seemed on the verge of speaking, but then held back whatever she was going to say. A few seconds passed, then Everfeld broke the silent tension.

"So tell me, how is Rennick getting along these days?" he asked.

"Rennick?" the cleric echoed, her face momentarily registering surprise. Her colleague drew in a quick, stunned breath, and his mouth dropped open in disbelief.

"Oh, I do apologize," Everfeld said. "I know it's considered disrespectful to use his given name, but I've known him for nearly forty years. I'm so accustomed to referring to His Eminence the way I do in private that sometimes I forget. Let me rephrase. How is the *Dotta Superior Tolerance IV* getting along these days?"

Had they been playing a card game, Jeryn reflected, Everfeld would have just revealed a virtually unbeatable hand. The blue-eyed cleric would have expected the CM's staff to have strong ties to the dotta superior, the supreme leader of her order. Church and state had been mutually supportive institutions for centuries. Dottas superior had even served in official capacities in previous CM administrations. But to learn this spymaster was apparently a longtime friend of the current dotta superior, and on a *first-name basis* with him? No way she could have seen that one coming. But true to form, other than the brief flash of surprise, she remained cool as ever.

"I understand he's doing well," she answered, her voice betraying a hint of discomfort.

"Good, good," Everfeld said. "He's quite a socalla player. We've had games that have gone on for weeks. His defenses, especially the diagonal ones, are all but impenetrable. If you ever find yourself in a match with him, I'd advise you to attack early and with overwhelming force. Battles of attrition are his specialty."

"I'll keep that in mind," Tavella said.

"I'm scheduled to see him a fortnight from now," Everfeld said. "At that meeting, I'd very much like to say positive things about the head of his Public Information Office. You might be surprised how much weight a strong endorsement from an old friend carries with His Eminence. It can open any number of interesting doors to better, more prestigious assignments." The spymaster left the downside tactfully unspoken. The cleric was no fool, so Everfeld didn't need to point out his powerful influence could reward just as swiftly and effectively as it could punish. That he could break her career as easily as he could make it.

Tavella nodded slowly. She was hopelessly outranked, and she knew it. The old spymaster sitting in front of her had discovered her secret dealings, and now he'd masterfully weaponized them against her. Her listless expression said it all.

She then glanced at the pitiful sight of her colleague, sullen and defeated, his shoulders slumped. She didn't bother to hide her irritation with the man from her features. Jeryn imagined she'd brought her right hand for support and assistance, and he'd failed miserably on both fronts, sitting there frozen and mute for the entirety of the meeting.

"Well," she said, turning again to Everfeld, "you've certainly given me a lot to think about, Director." She cleared her throat. "Were there any other matters you wanted to discuss?"

Everfeld shook his head. "I believed I've burdened you with enough for one evening," he said, eliciting a slight grin from the cleric. Jeryn was pretty sure it wasn't the humorous kind.

Tavella rose from the chair, followed by her right hand. "Pleasure and joy to you," she said, bowing her head.

A minute later, when the rumble of the cleric's ground transportation faded into the distance, Jeryn turned to the spymaster.

"Do you think she'll do it?" he asked. "Do you think she'll work with us?"

Everfeld stared at the doorway the cleric had passed through a minute before. "I can't be certain. But if she does, I don't imagine she'll do it happily."

20

THE HERO OF MIRANERA

Consul Minister Amarania was having one of her moments. Jakaan recognized it the instant he laid eyes on her. He'd seen that wistful, forlorn expression before, that crack in her otherwise self-assured, fearless armor. It was a side of her few had seen, a side he suspected hadn't even existed until these most recent years, after decades of the constant, churning pressure of her office had finally begun to break her. She was having more and more of these moments lately, these instances of self-doubt or indecision or whatever they were.

Jakaan wasn't sure whether her mood would make his task of the moment easier or more difficult, but he couldn't afford to postpone and wait around for her to come back to her senses, for her mental state to return to its cold, ruthless normal.

He needed her approval, and he needed it now.

His end of the hypercast was a borrowed office at the local Bureau of Internal Affairs, the most secure connection he could find. The CM's end was her strategic planning suite, light-years away on Gran Kiravashta, where she sat alone in a wingback chair, staring intently at a star map of the Realm. The holographic image stretched from ceiling to floor and wall to wall, taking up most of the suite.

"Madam Minister," Jakaan said with a respectful bow of his head. She didn't respond or even turn toward his image, still gazing at the massive projection. After a few seconds, he said, "Madam Minister, can you hear me? Is there a problem with the connection?"

"I hear you, Clevon," she said. Her voice was low and despondent.

"My apologies for the short notice," he said. "We've just received surveillance data from Sandau Prime, and I'm sorry to say it confirms exactly what we feared. A few hours ago, Whitmere Everfeld met with Charnette Tavella, and he's clearly attempting to recruit her as an asset. Whether he's supporting the Separatists covertly or working his own private agenda, we're not sure. But, Madam Minister, there's no doubt he's working against us, and it's safe to say he's been doing so for quite some time."

The CM didn't react to his words, her eyes still fixed on the star map. "A question for you, my old friend," she said.

"Yes, Madam Minister?"

"How do think they'll speak of me when I'm gone?" she asked.

"I'm sorry?" Jakaan replied, the question taking him off guard.

"My legacy," she said, finally turning to face him. "If we go through with what we're planning, millions will die, perhaps billions. That's what the war council is telling me. Even a best-case scenario leaves countless casualties, most of them civilians."

"To save countless trillions," Jakaan said, "from the chaos and turmoil of a protracted civil war."

"They'll say I was a butcher," she said morosely.

"They'll say you saved the Realm. That you brought it back from the brink of disaster."

She sighed and turned once again to the starry image. "From where I'm sitting, things don't seem quite so clear-cut."

Jakaan frowned at the pitiful sight projected before him. If her enemies could only see her now. So weak, so vulnerable, so riddled with doubts. And a conscience! Who would have ever imagined the woman possessed one. Or a heart, for that matter.

He loathed her when she was like this. Loathed her more than usual. Stuck so deeply in her personal well of self-pity, she hardly registered whatever he said, no matter how urgent the topic. Sometimes when she was like this, it took him hours to bring her back to herself, to coax a single nod of approval from her. But right now he didn't have hours. He had to act without delay, and finding her in an introspective funk was the last thing he needed.

Impatient and annoyed, he imagined himself reaching through the connection and slapping some sense into the old bird.

Easy now, he told himself, taking a deep, cleansing breath. Anger and frustration would *not* move things forward. He had to be calm, yet persistent, as he'd been for years, steadily biding his time, carefully moving all the pieces into place. He was so close now he could feel it.

"Do you know the name Theodifa Corda?" he asked.

Without breaking her gaze on the star map, the CM slowly shook her head.

"She was the chief health scientist on Miranera Prime, my homeworld. When I was a boy, a pandemic killed a quarter of the planetary population, humans and nonhumans alike." He paused for a moment, then added, "It took my father from me."

"The Miraneran Blight," the CM muttered.

"Yes," Jakaan said. "In the pandemic's early days, researchers developed what appeared to be a promising vaccine. As you can imagine, there was enormous pressure on Dr. Corda to approve the serum for mass production and distribution. But instead of rushing her approval, she insisted on additional safety trials. The promising vaccine was a novel therapeutic, you see, which meant it needed fairly rigorous testing for side effects, optimal dosage levels, and so on. I remember the daily news feeds like it was yesterday. Death tolls, new case counts, all those worrisome charts with steep lines going up and right. Dr. Corda was denounced by the press and politicians for being too cautious, for holding back a miracle cure that would save hundreds of millions. But she persisted, refusing to give in, even as the pressure grew into death threats and multiple attempts on her life. In the final months of the trials, she went into hiding as the disease spread across every continent, an airborne cancer you could only avoid if you were wealthy enough to leave the planet. Most people didn't have that kind of money, of course.

"And then, the very same week the governor bowed to public pressure and fired her, the additional trials, the ones Corda had insisted on, showed irrefutable evidence that the serum caused fatal genetic damage in over half of the trial participants. Had Dr. Corda released the serum prematurely, the cure, as the old saying goes, would have been far worse than the disease. Fortunately, another vaccine—one that had been tested in parallel and passed its trials with flying colors—ended up being the treatment that saved the planet.

"Now, you might think the public would have forgiven the good doctor, considering what might have happened had she caved to public demand and approved the unsafe serum. But they didn't. As incomprehensible as it sounds, she remained a pariah for years afterward. And it was because a public narrative had already been established, you see. Popular opinion had been irreversibly bent against her. The truth rarely wins out over public passion, at least in the short term. Dr. Corda left the planet in disgrace just as the fight against the virus began to turn.

"But then slowly, like a constant drip of water reshaping a rock over time, the story changed. And now, some four decades later, with the pandemic a distant nightmare, Corda is widely considered a Miraneran hero. For many, she's *the* Miraneran hero, lauded for her perseverance, bravery, and self-sacrifice."

Jakaan moved closer to the image sensor. "The path to greatness is never an easy one to tread, Madam Minister. And as much pain and condemnation as our course may bring today, I believe with all my heart future generations will look back and thank us. They'll see these days as the ones when a looming catastrophe was averted by bold, courageous action. That will be your legacy: Savior of the Realm."

A long moment passed, during which Jakaan wondered how much, if any, of what he'd said had penetrated the CM's gloomy daze. Then, with a suddenness that surprised him, she abruptly rose from the chair and moved closer to the image sensor. Every trace of doubt and self-pity in her expression was gone. The image gazing back at Jakaan across light-years was the steely-eyed, resolute woman everyone knew. It seemed her moment of weakness had passed.

"The intelligence you have," the CM said, her voice clear and sharp. "The surveillance data from Sandau Primo. It's incriminating?"

"Utterly," Jakaan replied. "Any court in the Realm would convict Everfeld of sedition based on this evidence alone." Not that things would go that far, he added inwardly. "But then we also have a mountain of evidence documenting his unapproved activities. And we have the same sort of incriminating records for the cleric's clandestine travels."

The CM tightened her lips into a straight line, then shook her head ruefully. "It's a hard thing to swallow. Whitmere Everfeld, a traitor. This scheming cleric, I don't know her from anyone, but Everfeld...." Again, she shook her head in disbelief. "We've worked together half our lives."

"I know how you feel," Jakaan said. "A part of me wishes I'd never found out. I count him among my dearest friends." He sighed. "But now that we know…" he left the sentence incomplete, waiting for the CM to finish it.

"We must do something about it," she said, perfectly on cue.

"I'm afraid we have to."

Minister Amarania lifted her chin. "Have them taken into custody. All of their direct reports as well. Conspirators rarely act alone." Then she added, "And do it discreetly. I don't want to see this on any of the news feeds. We've had enough bad press lately."

Jakaan nodded his head gravely. "Yes, Madam Minister. I'll attend to it personally."

When the connection ended moments later, Jakaan let out a long breath of relief. That was it. He'd gotten what he'd come for.

He gathered up his heavy cloak and threw it around his shoulders, then braced himself as he opened the door to the outside cold. Sandau Prime's frigid wind felt like tiny needles stabbing his exposed cheeks. Such a cold planet! How did the locals endure it?

But even with the bone-chilling cold, the long trip across the stars to this icy rock had been worth it. He couldn't leave something as important as arresting the disruptive cleric and the Realm's chief spymaster to the bumbling locals. A short distance away his chief of staff, Pallat Menic, waited next to a ground car. The man's cloak was covered with a light dusting of the snow blowing about in flurries. As his superior approached, the man opened the vehicle's passenger door.

Jakaan climbed inside, and his right hand followed him in. The auto-piloted vehicle began to move forward.

"Everything go all right?" Menic asked as the car sped up.

Jakaan removed his gloves, reflecting with great satisfaction how his little anecdote about the hero of Miranera had worked like a charm. Most of it had even been true, except the part about him and his father, neither of whom had ever set foot on Miranera.

Jakaan smiled. "Couldn't have gone better."

21

TEGESIAN CAGE

Play with fire and eventually you're going to get burned.

Charnette Tavella stared out of her thirtieth-floor office window at the bustling streets of Sandau-Kal far below, the phrase that so perfectly described her situation repeating itself over and over in her mind. She sighed and shook her head. What a mess, what a tremendous mess she'd gotten herself into.

And, sure, if she was being honest with herself, she couldn't deny her game plan had been... *slightly* less than lawful. Falling stars, who was she trying to fool? It was illegal, period, and she'd known it from the start. But no one said the path to fame and glory would be easy. Or legal, for that matter. And if the chance to make history, to put your name among the Realm's most important movers and shakers of all time, meant you had to work around the law, well, sometimes you had to do what you had to do. She had no regrets about what she'd done or how she'd done it. Regrets were for small, unimaginative minds. If she had any regret at all, it was that she'd been caught.

Caught, she thought bitterly, after making *so* much progress over this last year. After managing to build a coalition where so many had tried and failed. After cajoling, persuading, flattering, doing whatever it took to bring that squabbling rabble together, one conversation at a time. After she'd finally arrived at the cusp of achieving something that might shake the Realm to its rotten core. Caught by this spymaster, who threatened to ruin everything she'd so carefully constructed. It was maddening.

And no less maddening was the fact that she'd been so very careful. She'd gone to great lengths (and expense) to cover her tracks, to keep her meetings with the Separatists and Originalists secret. What had happened? Had someone sold her out? Or had she slipped up somewhere, unknowingly leaving a trail of bread crumbs behind her?

She grunted. Like it mattered at this point. Now that she was locked in a cage, it was a waste of energy to fixate on how she'd ended up there. She had to focus on how to get out of it. *If* there was a way out of it. Whitmere Everfeld, the man holding the cage's key, was one of the Realm's most powerful state officials. He wouldn't be an easy thumb to get out from under.

Her troubled mind returned to the meeting with the spymaster the previous day at the compound in the middle of nowhere. Everfeld hadn't lied to her. She was certain the man wanted to bring peace to the Realm, and fundamental reform as well. If anyone had told her as much before the meeting, she wouldn't have believed them. She would have laughed at the absurdity of it. A peace-mongering reformist among the CM's inner circle? It seemed about as likely as finding a virgin in a brothel. But she'd seen the sincerity in the man's eyes, heard it in his voice, up close and personal and unmistakable. She believed him, and she was never wrong about these things.

Which begged the obvious question about the man's loyalties. Minister Amarania always dealt with her political adversaries with iron-fisted aggression. The idea that she would ever reach out to Separatists with an olive branch, even behind the scenes via her spymaster, was all but unthinkable. It simply wasn't the way she did things. So if the spymaster was as sincere about peace and reform as he appeared to be, it had to mean he was almost certainly a minority, possibly of one, among the CM's inner circle. And taking it one step further—and this part seemed nearly inconceivable to Tavella—it followed that the spymaster had to have been acting on his own. That he'd reached out to Tavella without the CM's knowledge or blessing.

As impossible as that sounded, the more she turned it over in her mind, the more she was convinced Everfeld was doing exactly that: secretly defying the consul minister. The spymaster, it seemed, was taking quite a gamble.

And if he was found out, he'd be in scalding hot water…

… and she'd be right there with him.

She whirled away from the window, strode quickly to her desk, and after taking a moment to gather herself, she began to record a message.

"Pleasure and joy to you, my brothers and sisters," Tavella said, gazing steadily into the visual sensor. "My name is Sah Charnette Tavella, and I have been falsely accused of high crimes against our beloved Realm."

22

A CALL FROM SANDAU-KAL

"THAT'S ONE GEM OF A WEAPON YOU HAVE THERE," SERGEANT Burns said, gesturing toward the kukri strapped to Jeryn's hip. The young operative had noticed the Marine admiring it before, but this was the first time the man had mentioned it.

Jeryn glanced down at the blade. "Would you like to see it?"

"May I?" the Marine asked.

"Sure." Jeryn unsheathed the weapon, checked to ensure the countermeasures were deactivated, then handed it to Burns. As he watched the Marine turn it over in his hand, feeling its weight and balance, Jeryn pondered how wrong his early impression of the man had been. When he'd first met the sergeant, he'd taken him for a gruff, no-nonsense career military man.

The no-nonsense part had turned out to be accurate. Sergeant Burns was all business, a steely professional soldier through and through. But over the weeks of space travel, Jeryn had come to realize the man was not so much gruff as he was shy and somewhat introverted. Burns was quiet, thoughtful, and unfailingly polite. The more Jeryn came to know the man, the more he liked him, and the harder it became to square the man's peaceful disposition with someone capable of violence on command. Jeryn had also learned the man was—like him and Bhokken and Marogh—one of the spymaster's small inner circle of trusted confidants.

The two sat in the front room of the safe house, a day removed from the meeting with Tavella. There was still no word from the cleric. No couriers bearing messages, no encrypted comms, nothing. Everfeld had said it might take a while for her to come around. When your life was shaken up so utterly and unexpectedly, he'd explained, it took time to get your bearings again. But surely before his meeting with her order's supreme leader in twelve days, she'd come to accept the only avenue open to her was cooperation. Tavella was far too savvy to see things any other way.

Then there was the matter of Everfeld's disobedience, which was no small thing. The spymaster had been ordered to neutralize the cleric, not to turn her. So if he did gain Tavella's cooperation, he'd then have to explain himself and his insubordination to the consul minister. And not only that, he'd have to convince the CM and her war-minded senior staff the cleric was a valuable asset to be used, not a threat to be removed. The political road ahead of Everfeld would be a tough one, to say the least.

All of this, of course, assumed Tavella agreed to play the double agent game. If she refused, Everfeld would have no choice but to follow through with the CM's command, eliminating the cleric along with perhaps one of the last, best hopes for peace in the Realm.

Sergeant Burns handed the blade back to Jeryn. "How well do you know how to use it?" the Marine asked.

"He's bested Bhokken in their sparring matches, from what I've heard," Everfeld said, entering the room.

"He has?" Burns said, lifting his eyebrows. "You can take a Rauk?" The Marine nodded approvingly. "Not bad, young man. Not bad at all." Jeryn flushed with a surge of pride. From the understated Marine, who rarely handed out compliments, this was high praise indeed.

Pezzi-Kaziz appeared in the doorway, her expression knotted in disapproval. "You boys and your fighting," she scoffed. "Don't you ever grow out of your childish fascination with violence?"

Burns grinned and spread his hands out wide. "We are but simple creatures."

"True words," Pezzi-Kaziz said, sighing and taking a seat.

"Sergeant, we have an incoming transmission."

All four turned to see the Huthean, his large frame taking up most of the doorway Pezzi-Kaziz had just come through. The four-armed Marine stood there with what looked like—if Jeryn was reading the fur-covered expression correctly—an uncertain look on his face.

"From the *Dagger*?" Burns asked.

"No, sir," the Marine replied, his whiskers twitching. "It's from Sandau-Kal."

The sergeant furrowed his brow. "From the city?"

"Is it our Tegesian friend?" Everfeld asked.

"It's her right hand," the Marine replied.

Everfeld and Jeryn exchanged looks. The cleric had agreed to the exclusive use of couriers for all communications. Breaking that protocol so quickly wasn't a good sign.

"He says it's urgent," the Huthean added. "He seems... out of sorts."

Out of sorts. Jeryn wondered what exactly that meant. He gestured toward the holo projector built into a nearby table. "I'll patch it in through here."

Everfeld nodded, and a moment later Oskan Sarraf appeared in a flickering holo display. The man's face looked panic-stricken.

"Can you hear me?" Sarraf cried, narrowing his eyes and leaning toward the image sensor on his end. "Is my signal getting through?" The image blurred and pixelated, as if the table's projector was glitching.

"We can hear you," Everfeld said, stepping closer to the projection. "Go ahead."

"They've taken her!" the cleric said. "They've taken Sah Tavella!" The image blinked in and out.

"Who's taken her?" Everfeld asked. "Repeat, who—"

The cleric's eyes widened in fear, his gaze locking onto something beyond the image sensor. Showing his palms and waving them back and forth, the man backed away, shouting, "No, no, please, no!"

The display flared brightly, as if a powerful light had been switched on, the sudden illumination too bright for the projector to compensate. Jeryn reflexively brought his hand to his eyes, but the dazzling light had already dissipated before his arm reached his face. The cleric was gone, replaced with a snowstorm of floating pixels and audio static.

"What's wrong with the image?" Everfeld asked.

Jeryn checked the holo's control panel. "Nothing wrong here," he told the room. "Bad gear on their end, maybe."

"Or someone's blocking the signal," the spymaster suggested.

Sergeant Burns touched his earpiece. "Patrol group Gamma, come in... Patrol group Gamma, do you copy?" He waited, but there was no answer from the two Marines on patrol duty. "Patrol group Gamma, do you copy?"

A sharp, repeating chirp sounded. The Huthean scanned the control sleeve on his forearm, tapping the alarm silent and reading the small display. "Sergeant, roof sensors picking up a comms-jamming signature." The soldier looked up quickly. "Source is five Ks from here."

Burns shot Everfeld an urgent look. "Director, we've got to get out of here now." The Marine rushed over to the wall, pulled open the recessed storage bin, removed a plasma rifle, and tossed it to the Huthean. He took another for himself, strapping it around his shoulder. From somewhere outside came a faint buzzing sound. Jeryn and Everfeld both lifted their gazes to the ceiling, toward the strange noise.

The safe house's proximity alarm went off, its ear-splitting shriek startling Jeryn. "Incoming!" the Huthean shouted. The sergeant grabbed three pistol blasters from the bin and tossed them to Everfeld, Jeryn, and Pezzi-Kaziz. The buzzing from outside grew into a deafening roar, drowning out the building's blaring alarm. A quick succession of heavy thuds came from above, shaking the building.

"Stars above, they're on the roof!" Pezzi-Kaziz cried, just as the front door exploded inward and armed creatures poured into the room.

23

WAR BUGS

AGENCY OPERATIVES WEREN'T INFANTRY SOLDIERS. THEY WERE rarely ambushed with sudden, overwhelming violence. When a mission went the wrong way, they were normally arrested, quietly and discreetly, by authorities who then jailed them and used them as leverage with Gran Kiravashta. On more openly anti-Realmist worlds, a spy might be killed upon discovery, but again, such measures were always undertaken in some low key, inconspicuous manner. Poisoned drink. Irradiated food. A single shot to the head from a sound-suppressed blaster while you showered.

Strange, Jeryn thought, how the human brain worked in times of great distress. How time slowed to a crawl when you froze with disbelief. The thoughts that flashed across your mind—like Jeryn's momentary reflection on how captured operatives were dealt with—in the first moments when everything around you erupted into destructive chaos.

The invaders were Thracites. War bugs, some called them, given their insectoid appearance and widespread use as mercenaries. Their two-meter tall, chitin-armored bodies stooped slightly as they rushed through the human-sized doorway.

Jeryn's ponderous moment of shock, which felt longer than

the split second it probably was, ended with the sudden discharge of the Huthean Marine's weapon. The unmistakable searing noise of plasma fire, coupled with brilliant yellow flashes illuminating the small space, jarred him instantly out of his funk. The first several Thracites through the door were sliced to bits by the Marine's deadly precise shots. Torsos severed cleanly in half, appendages falling away still gripping their weapons, heads gruesomely separated from long chitinous necks.

Next to Jeryn, Pezzi-Kaziz suddenly dropped away from the edge of his vision. Turning to look, he saw her lying on the floor, a large hole seared into her midsection. Her eyes jerked about as her body convulsed briefly, then stopped moving. Smoke rose from her blackened torso, and the sickening smell of burnt flesh hit Jeryn's nose.

Burns grabbed Everfeld and Jeryn by their arms and hustled them to the next room as a second wave of Thracites swarmed through the front doorway. Jeryn caught a glimpse of the Huthean's last moments as the Marine was overwhelmed by the nightmarish creatures. The Marine screamed in agony as the war bugs ripped him apart.

"Tunnel," Burns cried out, pointing to the next room. "Hurry!"

The trio ran, large chunks of ceiling falling around them as the attackers blasted their way through the roof. Reaching the doorway to the downward stairs, Jeryn felt the heavy thuds of Thracites landing on the floor behind him. He raced down the stairway without looking back.

The short staircase led to a massive reinforced door, thankfully already ajar, opened by the house mind's automated safety measures. As soon as they rushed through, the sergeant pressed his palm to the door frame. The heavy door slid shut with a loud hiss and the deep metallic clank of unseen bolts sliding into place.

The muffled trilling of their pursuers came from beyond the door, then a few heavy thuds followed by the sizzle of blaster fire.

"The safety door will hold them for a while," Burns said. "Until they burn their way around it. Come on, we have to move." His mind still reeling, heart beating like mad, Jeryn followed Burns and Everfeld to the carryalls, parked a short distance away.

Jeryn and Everfeld had been told about the emergency tunnel and both had known it lay at the bottom of the rear room's stairway, but this was the first time they'd actually seen it. A narrow, dimly lit passage carved from solid rock, it was just wide and tall enough for the two bulky carryalls.

The trio hurriedly boarded the vehicle, Sergeant Burns climbing into the driver's seat. The engine spun up with a rising whine, and the heavy vehicle rose onto its repulsor field. As they began moving forward, Jeryn watched the safety door in the rearview monitor, half expecting it to explode outward at any moment. When it disappeared into the darkness behind them, still intact, he gave a silent thanks to whoever had designed it. Moments later the safe house was far behind, and Jeryn's heart finally began to slow down.

Using his hand terminal, Everfeld called the security officers guarding the shuttle, informing them of the attack. Shortly after Everfeld and company had landed, Pezzi-Kaziz's team had relocated the shuttle to a nearby cave not far from the tunnel's entrance. If whatever had just happened at the safe house had come down on the shuttle's hiding place too, their escape would be little more than a brief reprieve.

After a short back and forth over his terminal, Everfeld returned the device to his pocket and nodded to Jeryn. "The shuttle's still there. They haven't been attacked."

"What just happened?" Jeryn asked breathlessly.

The sergeant said, "That cleric didn't want to work with us, that's what. That was her way of saying 'thanks, no thanks.'"

"I'm not so sure," Everfeld said.

"*Not so sure?*" Burns echoed, incredulous. "Our Tegesian friend didn't like having her cage rattled. Not one bit."

The whine of the carryall's engine echoed off the narrow tunnel walls as they sped forward. The surface exit, some minutes away, would bring them within five minutes of the shuttle's hiding place.

"There's no good reason for her to make an attempt on our lives," Everfeld said. "She doesn't strike me as the kind who'd commit such a rash, ill-advised act."

"We backed her into a corner," the sergeant replied. "People react in unpredictable ways when they feel trapped."

For his part, Jeryn didn't know what to think. While the sergeant had a point—when people panicked they often did the unexpected—Jeryn felt the old man was closer to the truth. It would have been utterly out of character for the savvy cleric to have orchestrated the attack. She was a political animal first and foremost. She would have negotiated, tried to cut a deal, exploring every option before resorting to violence.

But if the Thracite ambush hadn't been ordered by her, then who was behind it? There didn't seem to be an answer that made sense.

Minutes later, the carryall exited the tunnel into a blinding snowstorm. Huge flakes, blown horizontally by a gusting wind, tumbled across the vehicle's headlamp beams. Barreling roughly overland, there was no sign of the Thracites nor any indication of them on the vehicle's scanners.

"The wind's blowing quite strong," Everfeld noted. "Perhaps they're unable to fly in such conditions."

"Thank the weather gods then," Burns said from the operator's seat.

By the time they reached the cave where the shuttle was hidden, the storm had let up a bit. Two of Pezzi-Kaziz's three security officers stood about twenty meters inside; one of them waved his arms, directing Sergeant Burns to a parking area. When Jeryn, Everfeld, and Burns exited the carryall, the third officer appeared and announced, "Ship's prepped and ready to go."

"Thank you," the sergeant said, then turned to Everfeld and Jeryn. "Let's get off this rock, shall we?"

The words were his last. A plasma bolt struck him squarely in the face. Burns dropped to the cave's dirt floor, what remained of his head a charred, unrecognizable mess.

"Go, go, go!" one of the officers shouted, raising his weapon. Jeryn looked where the man was aiming and saw half a dozen Thracites entering the cave.

Jeryn and Everfeld sprinted for the shuttle's boarding ramp as the cave erupted into a deafening sear of blaster fire. The small ship sat on its skids just around a bend in the tunneled-out rear of the cave. As he reached the bend, Jeryn risked a backward glance and saw two of the three security officers cut down by plasma blasts. Beyond them, more Thracites had arrived and joined the attack. Jeryn ran faster, lowering his head and pumping his arms.

He made it to the shuttle several seconds before Everfeld. Pausing at the boarding ramp, he waved the spymaster forward, as if the frantic gesture could make the old man's legs work faster.

"Hurry!" he shouted to Everfeld. A Thracite rounded the corner, raised its weapon, and fired a single pulse. It struck Everfeld in the back, sending him tumbling behind a pile of rubble.

Time stopped. *No, no, no. This can't be happening. This can't be happening.*

Jeryn screamed a curse and removed the nearly forgotten pistol from a garment pocket. The first blast missed, but the second struck the war bug's torso dead center, and the Thracite fell dead to the ground, its rifle skittering away in the dirt. The lone surviving security officer sprinted past the fallen war bug, waving wildly at Jeryn.

"Get in! Get in!" the man shouted.

They collided as Jeryn tried to return for Everfeld. "We can't leave him here! We can't—"

"He's gone," the man said, restraining Jeryn by the shoulders. "We have to get out of here. Do you understand? He's gone, and we have to go, now!"

Beyond the fallen bodies, more Thracites appeared around the bend. No small part of Jeryn wanted to grab the security officer's rifle and smoke every last one of the filthy things. But the part of his mind that could still think clearly allowed himself to be hustled up the ramp and into the shuttle. He strapped himself into a jump seat as the security officer whose name he didn't know scrambled into the pilot's chair and activated the small laser canon in the shuttle's nose. It made quick work of the Thracites who'd come around the bend, shredding their bodies in a few quick bursts. In the next moment the ship's sensors, tied into a larger array atop the mountain range above them, revealed a much larger threat on the control display. Hundreds of small flying objects were converging on the cave's location from low altitude. A swarm of Thracites. In seconds the cave would be crawling with war bugs, overwhelming the shuttle.

The security officer-turned-pilot busily worked the control panel, supplying the ship mind with a desired exit vector and velocity. "Hold tight," he called back to Jeryn. The man had just finished strapping himself in when the shuttle's thrusters fired. Jeryn's body pressed against the seat back as the ship careened around the tunnel's bend and exited the cave into the dark, snow-filled night. Plasma fire flashed on the viewscreen, lighting up the night sky like yellow lightning. Fleeing at high velocity, the shuttle made for a hard target, and it escaped the incoming horde without suffering any hits.

Moments later they cleared the planet's gravity well, and the shuttle slipped through the black of space on its way to dock with the *Veiled Dagger.* Jeryn hardly noticed as his body went weightless. All he could think about was Everfeld. The old man was gone. Shot and killed and left there on the cold, cold ground.

24

RETURN TO SANDAU PRIME

The Tegesian faith, less a religion than a moral philosophy, had no concept of a supreme being or an afterlife. There were, however, dozens of smaller sects throughout the Realm that acknowledged some sort of higher power and spiritual hereafter.

Jeryn had no religion. He'd never ridiculed the idea of the divine as some did, but neither did he think it was terribly likely. In his former life, mysticism was used mostly to con people, to trick them into parting with their money. Where Jeryn came from, God was an age-old scam.

Still, as he sat on the edge of his bed, staring at the floor of his quarters on the *Dagger*, a part of him wished he had religion. Would it comfort him right now? Would the idea of some afterlife, where Everfeld's spirit lived on, lessen the pain? Would the belief that they'd be reunited one day on some ethereal plane ease his suffering? He wasn't sure. Bhokken, for all his devotion to his fifteen-god pantheon, hadn't seemed any less devastated than Jeryn by Everfeld's death.

He lifted his gaze to the viewport on the wall. Half an hour earlier, Sandau Prime had dominated the starfield. Now it was long gone, the *Dagger*'s outbound thrust having shrunk it into nothingness. He wondered where Everfeld's body was now. Had the Thracites recovered it? Had they ripped it apart in anger? The thought turned his stomach. Or had they left Everfeld alone, cold and stiff and forever entombed in a dark cave on a frozen planet?

Slowly, Jeryn became aware of a light tapping on the door. He took a breath to compose himself, then in the next moment decided he didn't care if he looked composed or not. "Come in," he said.

Bhokken, his eyes still glistening with wetness, entered and sat next to Jeryn. Unlike humans, who often concealed their most heartbreaking emotions, Rauks openly mourned their friends and loved ones. There was no shame in public pain, in unfiltered grief. Tears were a sign of love and respect, the loss of bodily water echoing the loss of the recently departed.

"How are you holding up?" Bhokken asked.

"It still seems so unreal," Jeryn said. "I keep expecting him to walk through the door, telling me dinner's waiting in the galley. I keep thinking my comms feed is going to chirp with another one of his intelligence briefings." He sighed. "And then I see his body, cold and alone, lying there in the dirt. I can't get the image out of my head."

Bhokken made a low rumbling noise with his throat, a sympathetic grumble. "I wish I knew what to say at moments like these, something to make it hurt less. A funny story about Everfeld that would make you laugh and forget the pain for a moment or two. I spent the past half hour trying to come up with one, but it's no use. All I can think of is my friend of so many years who's gone now." The engineer sniffed. "I'm sorry, but I haven't brought any words of comfort. All I can tell you is that I was his friend too, and I know how terrible this must be for you." He laughed without humor. "Not much of a condolence, is it?"

Barely able to hold back his own tears, Jeryn said, "No,

you're wrong. It helps. It truly does." He blew out a long breath. "So what happens now?"

"I don't know," the Rauk said. "I'm not even sure what happened down there."

"The cleric double-crossed us," Jeryn said.

"I thought you said Everfeld wasn't so sure about that."

Jeryn shook his head. "He wasn't, but no other explanation makes sense." During the scrambling escape from Sandau Prime, there had been little time to reflect. But now, alone with his thoughts for a while, in hindsight it seemed all but certain the cleric was behind what had happened. Maybe with her secret life exposed, she'd decided to abandon her life of false pretenses, opportunistically murdering the Realm's spymaster and making herself an instant hero of the Separatist cause. Or maybe as Sergeant Burns had suggested—Jeryn felt another wave of sadness, recalling the brave man's demise—Tavella had simply felt trapped, and the cleric had lashed out in a frightened panic like some cornered animal.

"Maybe you're right," the Rauk said. "But she didn't strike me as the type who'd —" the comms chirped, interrupting the engineer. It was Marogh calling from the bridge. Jeryn reached over and tapped the control.

"Is Bhokken with you?" the shifter pilot asked.

"I'm here," the engineer answered.

"Could you both come to the bridge, please?" Marogh said, his tone uncharacteristically urgent. "There's something I have to share with you."

"Not dead?" Jeryn replied, stunned by the shifter pilot's claim. "What in the Great Arm do you mean Everfeld's not dead?" He turned to find the Rauk's expression as bewildered and shocked as his own must have looked at the moment.

"Yes," the Rauk agreed, "how in the fallen stars can you say that?"

The pilot looked as if he was confused by his shipmates' reaction. "Are you not pleased? I found myself quite relieved when I discovered—"

"Please," the Rauk interrupted. "Just explain why you think he's not dead."

"Of course, of course," the pilot said apologetically, realizing he'd been less than tactful. "Let me show you the footage archive from the *Dagger*'s shuttle." On the holo display, a cam feed from one of the shuttle's external image sensors appeared. Jeryn felt a cold shiver as he recognized the dimly lit cave and the three security personnel. For two of them, these would be their last moments.

Marogh manipulated the feed's controls, and the images sped forward in time. He paused the feed as Jeryn and Everfeld came into view, running toward the shuttle. Some distance behind them, the Thracite stood with its rifle steadied against its shoulder.

Jeryn felt ill. "I'm not sure I can watch this."

"But you must," the pilot said. "Please."

Jeryn took a long breath through his nose that didn't make him feel any less queasy. The pilot advanced the feed at one-third speed. As the shot struck Everfeld, it took a tremendous effort for Jeryn to keep himself from looking away.

In agonizingly slow motion, the spymaster tumbled forward and behind a pile of rocks. Moments later the feed's viewpoint began to move as the shuttle rose on its suspensor field, then the cave walls blurred and the ship exited the tunnel into the black Sandauan night.

"Did you see it?" Marogh asked Bhokken.

The Rauk leaned forward, his eyes narrowed. "Back it up again."

"See what?" Jeryn asked as the pilot reversed the feed and repeated the gut-wrenching sequence. The shifter froze the image on Everfeld's motionless body, then zoomed in.

"His cloak is intact," the pilot said, pointing to the spymaster's thick outer garment. "Where he was hit, there is no searing, no burn marks, not even a torn seam."

Slowly, understanding came over Jeryn. Understanding and confusion. "A stunning shot? Is that what you're thinking?"

"That is precisely what I am thinking," the pilot said.

Bhokken reversed the feed himself and watched the sequence again, leaning in closer. "Wonders of the Fifteen," he said, his eyes widening, "I think you may be right."

"If that had been a lethal plasma bolt," Marogh said, "there would have been evidence of it on his clothes." The gruesome proof point, he pointed out quickly, were the two dead security persons, whose thick robes had dark, meter-long sears where lethal blasts had struck.

"And then there is this," the pilot went on. His second piece of visual evidence was even more convincing. Slowed down to its minimum rate, the feed revealed the telltale, oblong shape of a stunning blast striking down Everfeld. A lethal discharge would have appeared much flatter. It was the kind of thing the naked eye couldn't pick out, but the shuttle's visual sensor detected with ease. Everfeld had been knocked unconscious.

Not killed!

Then a grisly image appeared in Jeryn's mind's eye. "But the shuttle's thrusters. Wouldn't they have..." he said, unable to finish the sentence.

"I do not believe he was harmed by them," the pilot said. He pointed at the image. "This large mound of rubble here would have shielded him."

"So he's alive," the Rauk said. He placed his hand on Jeryn's shoulder and gently squeezed. "He's alive. He has to be."

"I believe he is," the pilot said.

As Jeryn stared in disbelief at the display, a wave of relief began to wash over him. Everfeld wasn't dead. He was alive.

Alive and in trouble.

"We have to go back," Jeryn blurted. "We have to turn this ship around right now and go back there." He moved to the pilot's console and pulled up a navigation module. "That mad cleric has him, and who knows what she's going to—"

"Easy, easy," the Rauk said, stopping Jeryn with a firm but gentle grip on his arm. "We need to take a moment and think about this."

Jeryn shot the engineer an incredulous look. "What's to think about? We have to get back there."

"I don't disagree," Bhokken said evenly. "But we shouldn't rush into anything. We've had nothing but surprises on this operation, and none of them good ones. Yes, we need to turn the ship around, but we also need to think our way through this mess."

Think our way through this mess, Jeryn echoed internally. It was a favorite phrase of Everfeld's when the spymaster was faced with a particularly thorny problem. Jeryn had always believed in the expression's underlying truth. Sober, coolheaded reasoning could solve almost any problem. A spy's greatest weapon wasn't a plasma blaster or a deadly blade. It was their ability to think soberly in moments of great stress.

Jeryn took a calming breath and nodded at the Rauk. "You're right."

The engineer shrugged. "When am I not?" he chuckled, then turned to the pilot. "Let's turn this bird around, shall we?" Jeryn stepped aside, and Marogh settled into the pilot's seat and began working the control panel. The young operative realized Bhokken, in Everfeld's absence, was now technically in charge.

The Rauk asked the pilot to avoid retracing their path, lest they run into any ships out of Sandau Prime that might have tried to follow them. It wasn't a likely scenario, of course, since the *Dagger* had remained fully cloaked and undetected during Jeryn's stay on the planet. But after the ambush in the Barat-Cray system, the Rauk wisely erred on the side of caution.

After the pilot locked in a return trajectory, Bhokken, Marogh, and Jeryn gathered in the meeting room and interviewed the security officer who'd escaped with Jeryn. A former Marine named Cross, he'd worked as a contractor under Pezzi-Kaziz for the past couple years. It soon became clear the man was a low-level operator with no access to sensitive intelligence. A background check they'd run on him confirmed as much. Though more than willing to help, Cross offered no meaningful information or insights.

When they dismissed the man, Marogh finally came around to the possibility Jeryn imagined all three had been considering but were loath to mention out loud.

"From what I understand," the pilot said, "Director Everfeld has not been in the best standing with the consul minister lately. Is that not correct?"

Bhokken and Jeryn exchanged a look. "Yes, that's true," the engineer said. "He's made no secret of his opposition to military action against the Separatists."

"Is it possible then," the pilot suggested, "that this whole mission has been a ruse? A ploy to rid the CM of dangerous opposition to her planned military strike?"

"Dangerous opposition?" Jeryn said.

The pilot explained his choice of words. "A spymaster with decades of experience would have many tools at his disposal if he wished to undermine a consul minister's authority."

"Or her war plans," the Rauk suggested.

"Precisely," the pilot said with a short nod.

"But he'd never do that," Jeryn argued. "He's known her for

half his life, for stars' sake. He might do everything he could to change her mind, but I don't think he'd..." Jeryn stopped himself as Everfeld's words came back to him.

What I'm determined to engage in could be considered treason. But so be it.

Jeryn swallowed. He looked at Bhokken. "Do you really think this whole thing was a sham to get him out of the way?"

The Rauk sighed. "I don't know the CM as well as Whitmere does, but if her history tells us anything, it's that she's ruthless. And may the Fifteen help whoever gets in her way, friends and enemies alike."

A heavy silence fell over the *Dagger*'s bridge. Yes, Jeryn had to admit, it was plausible. The CM had insisted on Everfeld traveling personally to Sandau Prime, an unusual—and in hindsight, suspicious—request, even for such a sensitive mission. Had he been set up?

But if that was the case, there was a single thread the theory left conspicuously untied.

"Then why stun him and not kill him?" Jeryn asked. "Why keep him alive if he's so dangerous?"

The pilot nodded, as if he was having the same thought. "A question I find no easy answer for."

"Nor do I," the Rauk said. He then stood and approached the viewport, where Sandau Prime appeared as a small white sphere, imperceptibly growing larger in a field of starry pinpoints of light. "I wonder if he knows the answer, wherever it is they've taken him."

Minutes later, Jeryn updated the Marines about Everfeld. To their credit and Jeryn's pleasant surprise, when presented with the opportunity to take an escape pod—no questions asked—and withdraw from the uncertain course the operation had taken, not one of them took the option. If there was a chance they could rescue Everfeld from the same fate as their fallen sergeant, the

Marines were keen to face whatever hazards stood in their way. And for his part, Cross was eager to help his fellow Marines from losing Everfeld the way he'd lost Pezzi-Kaziz. He was all in, he told Jeryn. A decent lot, these Marines, Jeryn thought. He was glad they'd be coming along.

The following hours passed as slowly as any Jeryn could recall. But eventually the little white marble grew into a planet, looming large and ominous in the viewport. They'd returned to the icy world of Sandau Prime.

Bhokken stared at his workstation's comms control, slowly shaking his head. "Blessed Fifteen," he groaned, then leaned back in his chair. "I don't believe this."

Jeryn and Marogh looked to the Rauk, still shaking his head. "What?" Jeryn said. "What is it?"

"The feeds," said the Rauk. "I've been looking at the news and security feeds. You're not going to believe what's happened since we left this rock."

25

STAR MAP

THE SUBJECTIVITY OF PERCEPTION WAS A CURIOUS THING, JAKAAN reflected. The way two people could look at the very same object —or in this case, the same holo projection—and see something completely different.

Deep within the sprawling complex of Sandau Prime's governing council in downtown Sandau-Kal, Jakaan stood with his hands clasped behind his back in a large meeting chamber, staring at a three-dimensional image taking up most of the room. It was the same star map he'd seen Minister Amarania so intently brooding over earlier.

The Realm. Over twenty thousand worlds, home to trillions of citizens, a good many of them with a long list of complaints —some legitimate, some not. When he ran his eyes over its holographic expanse, he saw nothing but problems and uncertainties. He saw rich loyalist systems near the core, the Realm's most ardent supporters, ruled by ancient clans and the trade syndicates they controlled. Worlds with inept and bloated bureaucracies, corrupt to the marrow. He saw mid-lying systems, a mixed bag of lukewarm Realmists whose fair-weather allegiances could never be counted on. He saw the distant frontier systems, those wild, all-but-ungoverned regions where rebellion simmered ever closer to the boiling over point. He saw an unstable empire teetering on the precipice of disaster.

That was what he saw when he looked at the star map. And he knew it was completely different from what the consul minister had seen.

For her, a holo of the Realm was a mirror, a looking glass where she saw not twenty thousand star systems, but twenty thousand reflections of her own greatness. The boundaries she had expanded. The Separatist-inclined worlds she would shortly bring back in line. The trillions of households she had addressed via subspace hypercasts. The statues erected in her honor across the Great Arm's volume. Stone-carved likenesses gazing out with majestic determination, towering over city squares on countless worlds.

The entirety of the Realm served only to feed her insatiable vanity and ego. He'd suspected as much even before he'd met her, but in the years since she'd proved his preconception correct over and over again.

And what ambition! He'd never known anyone, human or nonhuman, who burned with more desire for fame and adulation and, lately, a venerated place in history.

But the years had taken their toll, and the once-invincible politician had withered into a lessened version of her former, stronger self. Lately she'd been prone to fits of melancholy, listless and uninterested in even the most urgent matters. She'd left important tasks and details to subordinates' discretions, delegating far more in recent years than she ever had before, obsessing over the Separatist threat and how it would affect her legacy.

Maybe someday she'd realize pulling herself away from the details of statecraft had been a colossal mistake, that in doing so she'd created blind spots and vulnerabilities. She'd become so consumed by her place in history, she'd never seen him coming for her.

Jakaan smiled knowingly as he stared into the depths of the star map. Consul Minister Pettine Amarania would indeed have a place in history.

Just not the one she longed for.

Minutes later, the chamber's door opened with a soft hiss. Jakaan's chief of staff, Pallat Menic, lingered in the doorway as if he wasn't sure he should enter. The man always hesitated when he had bad news to deliver.

Jakaan waved him forward. "You have news?" Menic approached slowly, anxiously fingering the seams of his cloak.

"Everfeld and Tavella are unharmed and in custody," the man said, "and there doesn't seem to have been any leakage to the media."

"Very good," Jakaan said, standing to face his subordinate. "So why the long face, my friend?"

"Not everything went quite to plan," Menic said. "There were casualties. A possible co-conspirator, a local trade negotiator named Manda Pezzi-Kaziz, was killed, as were several security personnel. And one of Everfeld's staff managed to escape on a shuttle craft. An operative we've identified as Jeryn Lorsi. Fairly junior in rank, according to our records."

Jakaan pursed his lips. "I don't know him." The name had never appeared in the secret files he'd been keeping on Everfeld's clandestine activities, which meant the young operative was probably of little importance in the larger scheme of things. He told Menic to run a detailed background check just to be sure. And, yes, Jakaan agreed the lad's escape was regrettable, telling his right hand as much, but it would hardly endanger his plans. And as far as the local trade executive—this Pezzi-Kaziz (who was in all likelihood one of Everfeld's operatives)—she could be easily depicted as a traitorous co-conspirator after the fact. The woman had clearly assisted Everfeld in his underhanded dealings with the cleric. And, more importantly, she wasn't around to defend her actions or deny her culpability. The dead were far easier to incriminate than the living. So in the end, the bad news Menic had been fretting over wasn't that bad after all. Bumps in the road, really.

With his two captured birds in their cages and securely out of the way, Jakaan was ready to move on to more important matters. "Right, then," he said, clasping his palms together. "Do we have the connection to Gran Kiravashta up and running?"

"We do," Menic replied with a nod. "The regents are standing by as we speak."

"Then let's not keep them waiting."

Menic touched the control panel on the wall, and the massive star map slowly disappeared. As the holo pixelated away, it was replaced by a dozen images appearing in quick succession. Twelve regents dressed in formal robes stood before Jakaan. The subminister bowed his head solemnly.

The time had finally come to dethrone a queen.

26

EXECUTIVE OVERSIGHT COUNCIL

Before today, the secretive Council for Executive Oversight, consisting of seven human and five nonhuman regents, had met on only three other occasions in the history of the Realm. The first two had occurred in eras long since passed, their agendas and discussion minutes locked away in the Assembly of Regents' most secure archives. The third meeting had taken place three months ago, attended by these very same participants.

"Greetings, honorable councilpersons," Jakaan began. "I thank you all for convening this meeting and allowing me to address the Council on this most serious matter." He then paused and waited for the chairperson. He tried to read the room, but there was little to be gleaned from any of the regent's faces. Unsurprisingly, he saw nothing staring back at him but the grave expressions appropriate to the occasion.

The human chairperson, a woman named Jola Majerus, spoke. "Motion to document these proceedings for archival and review purposes," she said, her tone businesslike.

"Second," several regents said at once. Jakaan pictured a control being activated somewhere light-years away to record the meeting's minutes.

"Motion to allow perceptual monitoring of these proceedings," Majerus added. Again, a chorus of seconds followed. Another holo then appeared, and the image of a Zatori materialized. Jakaan recognized the diminutive, violet-skinned figure. Eshek was her name, and she had also attended the previous meeting.

By longstanding policy, a Zatori's presence was required at all the council's gatherings where the most sensitive, classified testimonies would be given. The diminutive species was a rare sight in the Realm, even for the most well-traveled citizens. Nearly wiped out entirely during the Gene Wars of long ago, Zatoris lived in small, far-flung communities, mostly found in remote systems. Small in stature by human standards, the tallest among the Zatoris reached a height of one-and-a-quarter meters. Bipedal with large yellow eyes, they had long tapered ears like the elves of human lore and a pair of backward sweeping, ridged horns atop their blue-haired heads. Eshek and her kind were prized—as much as they were dreaded—for their remarkable perceptive abilities. They possessed preternaturally keen perception, their vision and auditory senses far more acute than those of other sentient races. They saw and heard things others either missed or whose minds, through evolutionary conditioning, dismissed as unimportant details to be filed away in the dark basement of the subconscious. Zatoris also had small canals running the length of their horns, thread-thin grooves filled with sensory membranes that detected electromagnetic waves. With the proper training, a Zatori could develop enough skill in EM detection to read the patterns of low-intensity brain waves emitted by humans and several other nonhuman species. This was why Zatoris were often referred to as biological lie detectors, since they could interpret certain wave patterns as indicative of untruthfulness. It was said a Zatori's gaze could peer into your very soul.

But Clevon Jakaan didn't believe in souls.

"Subminister Jakaan," Majerus said, "you may begin."

"Thank you, Chairperson Majerus." Jakaan cleared his throat and made a show of swallowing hard. "Roughly three months ago I came to this council in confidence with my... concerns over the consul minister's... mental fitness. Over the previous two years, I had noticed frequent memory issues, a significant decline in her overall mental acuity, and increasing instances of... questionable judgment."

"And just to remind us, Subminister," the chairperson said, "did you bring these concerns to your peers?"

"I did," Jakaan lied.

"And what was the result of those exchanges?"

"My colleagues at the senior staff level didn't believe the issues I raised merited escalation."

Majerus lifted her chin. "And why do you think that is?"

"I can't speak as to what their mindset was, Madam Chairperson."

"Perhaps they disagreed with your assessment?" asked the council's co-chair, a regent from Raukan.

"That's possible," Jakaan said. "It's also possible they didn't want to jeopardize their own positions of influence. It's always easier to look the other way than..." Jakaan paused.

"Than accuse a consul minister of mental incompetence," the chairperson said, completing the thought.

Jakaan nodded gravely. "Yes."

"They would indeed have a lot to lose," the Rauk regent said, "if such a scandal rocked the administration. A great loss of power and privilege, not to mention the damage to their professional reputations. Are we to believe you're above such worries for yourself, Subminister?"

Jakaan didn't answer. Instead, he turned to Regent Majerus. "Madam Chairperson, may I speak freely?"

"Of course, Subminister."

Addressing the council as a whole, Jakaan said, "I'm no self-righteous crusader. Far from it. I simply have the least to lose by speaking out."

"How so?" the chairperson pressed.

"All my senior staff colleagues have worked their entire adult lives with the CM in one capacity or another," Jakaan explained. "Their lives and livelihoods are so intertwined with hers that there's nothing they wouldn't do to save her, to protect her reputation. Because in doing so they're protecting themselves and their own reputations. Whereas in my case, I haven't been around nearly as long. A decade is no short tenure, but it still makes me the junior staffer by some twenty-odd years. My interest in the administration's stability is a great deal less vested than that of my colleagues."

"You might have resigned in protest," Majerus said sharply.

"But instead you chose to betray your superior's trust by coming to us," the Rauk added.

Jakaan had expected this moment to come, and even though he was prepared for it, the not-so-subtle accusation of disloyalty —captured by recording feeds and forever part of the permanent record—still unnerved him. He took a moment to gather himself, then lifted his chin and matched the Rauk's harsh stare.

"Yes, I might have resigned. You have no idea how many times I considered washing my hands, leaving the administration, and using my still-unblemished name to secure some lucrative position in the private sector." He paused a moment, then lowered his voice as he stepped forward. "But I have to sleep at night, Madam Chairperson. Tonight, tomorrow night, and for all the nights of the rest of my life."

"But the council just heard you say you were no crusader," the chairperson said. "Are you now reversing your position?"

"Madam Chairperson, when I first began to suspect something was wrong with our consul minister, my very first concern was for myself. What would happen to me and my career if the CM's malady were to become public knowledge? Would I be in legal jeopardy for dereliction of duty? And what would that sort of scandal do to my reputation? Would anyone dare to hire me? My initial reaction, I'm rather ashamed to admit, was anything but a selfless or patriotic one." He sighed. "But as the weeks and months went by and it was clear none of the senior staff were going to acknowledge the question of her mental fitness, and worse, that they'd go along with even the most ill-advised directives, my selfish thoughts became a bit less so. If any one of you had seen the things I've witnessed, you would have arrived at the same conclusion I eventually came around to." He spread his hands out wide. "Perhaps war is inevitable. Perhaps it's the only solution to save our fracturing Realm. I'm not sure. But I do know that allowing a mentally unfit consul minister to preside over such a conflict isn't something I want on my conscious for the rest of my days. And so I broke my silence and came to this council."

A long quiet moment followed. Jakaan glanced at the Zatori, keeping his features neutral under the amber-eyed, scrutinizing stare.

The chairperson finally broke the silence, addressing the Zatori. "Eshek, your assessment, please."

Jakaan held his breath as the violet-skinned being gazed at him. "I detect no signs of deception, Madam Chairperson."

"Very well, Eshek," Majerus said. "You are dismissed. The council thanks you for your service." She waved a hand, and the Zatori's image disappeared.

"Subminister," Majerus continued, "following your previous testimony to this council, it was decided we would revisit the matter in three months. Do you know why this decision was taken?"

He knew, of course, but he said, "No, Madam Chairperson, I was never informed."

"The council found your testimony alarming, to say the least. But rather than rush to conclusions based on one person's claim, the council unanimously voted to commission an independent investigation to verify or disprove these very serious accusations."

"I understand," Jakaan said, his tone serious but his insides beaming with joy. He was close, so very close.

"The investigation's charter," the chairperson went on, "which was originally limited to your claims of mental fitness, was expanded shortly thereafter based on some concerning initial findings."

"May I inquire as to the nature of those findings?" Jakaan asked, though he knew all too well what she was referring to.

"A large, quite lucrative contract for state administrative services," Majerus said, "which by law should have been open for public bids, was redirected at the behest of the CM to a personal associate. This was the smoke that led investigators to a fire of rampant corruption and illegal activities spanning the entirety of Minister Amarania's consulship."

Jakaan let his mouth slowly fall open. "I'm... not sure what to say to that... I can't recall any specific incidents—"

"You haven't been implicated in the investigation," the Rauk co-chair said.

And he wouldn't be, Jakaan knew. Because he had conceived, created, and laid out every last incriminating bread crumb himself. And he'd done so quite carefully over years, making sure that when the trail was finally discovered, there would be nothing connecting him to any of the scandalous affairs.

"This council finds itself in a very delicate position, Subminister," Majerus said. "When we reluctantly launched this investigation, we were concerned we'd discover a CM mentally unfit for office. What we found instead was a morally unfit CM who never should have held office in the first place."

Jakaan placed a hand on a nearby table, making a show of steadying himself. "Do you mind if I sit? I'm finding this all a bit overwhelming."

"Please," the chairperson said, and Jakaan lowered himself into a padded chair.

The subminister cleared his throat. "May I ask what happens now?"

"Now," Majerus said, "we need your help."

"My help?"

"Yes, Subminister," the co-chair said. "The Realm needs your help and leadership during these unsettling and challenging times."

"Of course," he said. "How can I be of assistance?"

What the chairperson asked of him next came as no surprise, neither to him nor to her, nor to the Rauk co-chair, nor to the Zatori who'd sworn his testimony was true and accurate. Jakaan had secretly made arrangements with the three of them months ago. As the chairperson spoke, following the script they'd all agreed to, he nodded gravely and replied "yes" as humbly as he could manage. Yes, he would accept an interim consulship nomination if it were asked of him. The council then voted unanimously to put the matter of Amarania's removal and Jakaan's appointment to an immediate vote by the Assembly of Regents.

As the meeting closed and the holos disappeared one by one, Jakaan recalled how easily it had been to find willing co-conspirators on the council. The old bird had no shortage of enemies who wouldn't have minded seeing her career and reputation destroyed. Who'd been more than happy to help with her downfall. Of course, he'd had to make promises of lucrative appointments after he was installed as CM. The councilpersons and the Zatori weren't so blinded by their political grudges that they exchanged their support for free. And that was fine by Jakaan. They were prices well paid.

Alone now in the borrowed office, Jakaan couldn't help but laugh inwardly. Through all the years of retribution planning and his countless machinations, he'd never given much consideration to his own aspirations. His entire life had been dedicated to revenge, not to his own ambition. He'd neither expected nor lusted after the role he was about to assume. But the opportunity had presented itself, so why the stars not?

When you had the whole of the Realm within your grasp, you'd have to be a fool not to take it.

27

NO CONFIDENCE VOTE

Mella Vipponah needed this scoop in the worst way. It had been months since her last juicy exclusive, since she'd last been credited by feed networks across the Realm as the first journo to break a big story.

And what a story! Worth every last credit she'd bribed the freshman regent with to give it up. Scoops like this came along once in a lifetime if you were lucky. She pictured herself winning the Warriner Prize, the dream she'd harbored since her first days as an entry-level correspondent covering the (big yawn) Gran Kiravashta sports beat. She'd never been considered for any prestigious award before, never even been longlisted for one. Nonhumans rarely made the cut. No surprise there. And amphibious sentients like her? She couldn't recall a single instance of one of her race being recognized with a nomination. But she could see it now, at long last within her reach. She could almost feel the cool bronze touch of the award statuette in her webbed hands.

The soles of Mella's shoes clacked rapidly as she hurried down the marble steps of the Assembly of Regents building. The flat second tier was the best place to get a shot with the building over her shoulder in the background. Slightly out of breath as she reached the spot, she reached into her pocket and removed the transmission drone, already linked to the local outbound hypercast feeds. She tossed it into the air in front of her. The drone whirred to life at the toss's apex and hovered in place, its sensor field glowing a faint green. She quickly checked her face in a mirror field projected from the drone, then spent a few moments muttering "red leather, yellow leather" to warm up her voice. Passersby clad in business suits, mostly professional staffers employed by planetary regents, gave her curious stares as they climbed and descended the stairs.

She turned and glanced at the Assembly of Regents building behind her. Its majestic, towering columns stood beneath an overcast sky of dark gray clouds. Perfect for the occasion, she thought, pleased by the appropriately ominous backdrop. Then she turned back to face the drone's image sensor. A small green light flashed. Showtime.

All right, Mella, let's nail this in one take, shall we?

"A scandal of Realmwide magnitude has rocked Gran Kiravashta today. Sources inside the Assembly of Regents have confirmed that a closed-door no confidence vote has just concluded. In an unprecedented action, a ninety percent majority of planetary regents have enacted emergency authorization to remove the consul minister from office, effective immediately."

As if on cue, from all around Mella came shocked gasps and blurted curses of disbelief. A crowd began to gather around her as she continued; they listened to the journo's astonishing report, rapt expressions on every human and nonhuman face.

"Sources have also confirmed this stunning course of action has been taken as a result of evidence provided to the Assembly, documenting dozens of instances of corruption, abuses of power, and high crimes against the Realm by the consul minister. Neither Minister Amarania nor her spokesperson could be reached for comment, and according to sources within the Assembly of

Regents, she has been placed under house arrest." Another round of gasps came from the ever-growing throng around Mella.

"As of right now, we don't know which, if any, of the accusations extend to the CM's senior staff, though we do have confirmation that Clevon Jakaan, the consul minister's chief of staff, has apparently been cleared of any culpability. And until the Assembly can decide on party candidates and elect a successor, a process sources say could take months, Subminister Jakaan will act as interim consul minister."

By the time she wrapped up her report a minute later, an audience of over a hundred had gathered, drawn to the stunning revelations like iron filings to a magnet. The quiet disbelief they had listened with ended the instant Mella's report concluded and the drone's image sensor light switched from green to red. A wave of shouting came down on Mella like a crashing wave.

"Who's your source on this?"

"When did you find this out?"

"How much of that did you make up?"

Returning the drone to her pocket, she answered no one and shouldered her way through the crowd. Most remained standing in place with confused looks on their faces, still working through their astonishment, but a few of the more agitated bystanders trailed after her, insistently hurling questions at her back. Mella quickened her pace as she descended the stairs. She had no answers for them. She'd already broadcast everything she knew for certain.

Which, if fate dealt her a fair hand, would be more than enough to get her shortlisted for the Warriner Prize. And who knew? Maybe she'd even win the darned thing.

As she climbed into a ground taxi at the bottom of the steps, her thoughts drifted to some future date, in some elegant ballroom, where her name would be called and she'd step up to the stage, watched and envied by millions of her peers from every system in the Realm. She'd hold the bronze statuette to her chest and gaze into the image sensor with all the humility she could muster.

Never in my wildest dreams did I imagine this could happen, she would say.

28

THE AVENGER OF PANNIS-HAU

BREAKING NEWS... NO CONFIDENCE VOTE REMOVES CONSUL MINISTER FROM POWER...

THE IMPOSSIBLE WORDS HAD SCROLLED ACROSS THE BOTTOM OF the news feed a dozen times, and still Whitmere Everfeld had a hard time believing what he was reading.

When he'd come around a few hours earlier on the floor of a carryall, his mouth dry, head throbbing, wrists bound behind his back, he'd assumed he'd been arrested—that his disregard of the CM's directive had somehow been discovered. Three uniformed police with plasma rifles had watched over him as the vehicle rocked gently on its suspensor field, traveling at high speed across the dark, barren plains of Sandau Prime. He'd begun asking questions upon regaining consciousness. Where was he? What was happening? Under what charges had he been arrested? His minders hadn't uttered a single word in reply, remaining silent the entirety of the long ride. When the carryall had finally arrived at a remote outpost, they'd led him to a holding cell and assigned a guard to watch over him from beyond a shimmering restriction field that bisected the room.

With the news of the CM's ouster, a sense of dread now began to take hold of him, an awful certainty he was embroiled in something far more perilous than his simple act of defiance. But what? And who was behind it?

Details slowly emerged on the news feed about the CM's apparent history of corruption and abuses of office. Everfeld then recalled a trick he'd sometimes used on detainees, sharing falsified news reports or fabricated police records to induce confessions or turn potential assets into double agents. Somehow, though, he knew what he watched on wall-embedded display wasn't some false narrative created to deceive him. The nightmare playing out on the news feed was really happening.

How had all this occurred without him knowing? He had eyes and ears everywhere. His most reliable informants were on Gran Kiravashta, many of them employed by planetary regents. In his three decades as the Realm's chief spymaster, there had been several confidential investigations into the CM's administration, all of which he'd known about. Yes, there had been improprieties and laws broken, but nothing that might warrant Amarania's removal, even if the CM had been implicated in those crimes, which she never had.

So how was it that this, a corruption investigation so important and apparently expansive in scope, had managed to slip past him? And what had they found? Every question he asked himself had no answer.

"You have questions, no doubt," a voice said.

Everfeld whirled around to find Clevon Jakaan standing in the doorway beyond the restriction field.

"Clevon?" Everfeld said, his incredulous tone barely above a whisper. What was *he* doing here on Sandau Prime, light-years away from where Everfeld had seen him last? "What's happening? What's the meaning of this?"

The subminister—or the interim consul minister, according to the news feed—dismissed the guard from the room. When the door slid shut behind him, Jakaan stepped forward and looked Everfeld squarely in the eye. "It's a long story, old friend," he said calmly. "Would you like me to start at the beginning?"

A knot of dread forming in his gut, Everfeld nodded and said, "Please do."

Jakaan motioned to the screen. "I asked them to connect a news feed for you, so you could see the result."

"The result of what?"

Jakaan reached for a chair. "My life's work." He sat down and motioned for Everfeld to do the same. The spymaster seated himself in the only chair on his side of the partition.

"Does the name Pannis-Hau mean anything to you?" Jakaan asked.

Everfeld knew the system but had never visited there. "A twin-gate system in the Gamma Cluster."

"Yes," Jakaan said with a nod. "That's my home system. I was born on Pannis-Hau Prime."

Everfeld knitted his brows. "I thought you were from Miranera?"

"Only according to official records," Jakaan said. He paused for a moment, then continued. "Whitmere, I'm going to tell you about a boy. A human boy, the only child of two loving parents, one of whom happened to be Pannis-Hau Prime's governor during a territory war with a rival system. A system called Gannebron, which I'm sure you're familiar with."

Everfeld was indeed familiar with the Gannebron system. It was Minister Amarania's home system. Before her foray into interstellar politics, she had been the youngest governor in the history of Gannebron 5, the sole habitable world orbiting the system's red dwarf.

"The same year the boy entered intermediate school," Jakaan continued, "the governor of Gannebron 5—the youngest individual ever to hold that office, as I recall—called for a cessation of hostilities between our worlds. By this time, you understand, the war had been going on for years with neither system gaining a clear advantage. Both sides had grown more disillusioned with the conflict. They'd sent thousands and thousands of their sons and daughters to die in the vast coldness of space, with little to show for it other than empty state coffers, depleted to fund the war effort. And of course, the ever-compassionate leadership on Gran Kiravashta refused to intervene, as they often do. It's far easier—and much more politically expedient—to cozy up with the winner afterward than take the risk of choosing a side.

"But I digress. When the young governor's call for peace came, it was welcomed by many on both sides. And as an act of good faith, she even had her ships withdraw from the disputed volumes. A risky move, since there was no guarantee Pannis-Hau would agree to peace talks. Ultimately, though, it would prove to be a shrewd tactic. A bluff that managed to fool even the wisest among her enemies, including the planetary governor, the boy's mother." He paused again, then said, "You know what happened at the peace summit, yes?"

Everfeld swallowed. He did know. It had occurred years before he'd met Pettine Amarania. The then-Governor Amarania's solution to end the years-long military stalemate was the stuff of legend. Of brutal, ruthless legend.

"They slaughtered the entire delegation," Jakaan said. "Dozens of diplomats, councilpersons, and state officials, including the boy's mother, killed in cold blood hours after they'd arrived to negotiate a peaceful end to the war." His expression darkened. "But that was the least of the governor's brutalities that day. As her killers did their dirty work, she ordered a massive assault on Pannis-Hau Prime. With the planet's guard down because of the peace talks and its leadership structure crippled by her murderous treachery, the surprise attack was a great success.

Within hours she'd secured an unconditional surrender, ending the war. The boy survived the bombardment when he and his schoolmates were rushed to a bunker. But his father, like millions of others, wasn't so lucky."

Jakaan broke eye contact, his gaze shifting to some point beyond the room. "That day, the boy vowed to avenge his parents and his world, somehow, some way. And for years afterward, he'd imagined this meant one day killing the evil woman. He'd daydream about how he'd do it, how he'd torture her for hours or days before finally slicing her throat the same way her assassins had ended his mother's life. But then, many years later, he realized the worst thing the woman could suffer wasn't death, but the complete and utter destruction of her legacy. Because after all, what do the most narcissistic among us care about the most? Not their mortal lives, but their immortal place in history. We draw breath but for a few short years in this life, but legacy endures, for thousands of lifetimes." He shifted his gaze back to Everfeld, a clever smile spreading across his face. "Now, tell me I'm wrong, old friend. Tell me what's happening to her now isn't a punishment far worse than death."

Everfeld sat there, the man's wild tale swirling around his head. This man he thought he'd known until only a few moments ago. "No, you're not wrong," he replied numbly.

"My word, you look as if you've been punched in the gut," Jakaan said. "You're wondering how it all happened, how I did it." He leaned forward a bit and lifted his eyebrows. "And how I managed to do it right under your nose. I imagine you're wondering that most of all, yes?"

"I am," Everfeld said truthfully. The small portion of his mind not reeling from everything he'd just heard puzzled over how Jakaan had brought about the CM's fall.

"Decades of hard work and determination," Jakaan said. "And when neither of those worked, I used money. Lots and lots of money. My mother was quite wealthy, you know. She'd amassed a fortune in mineral trading before entering politics, a fortune she moved into gene-coded accounts on an out-system banking orbital. A wise move during the uncertainties of wartime." He shook his head and smiled wistfully. "I inherited *so* much money, Whitmere. Far more than I'd ever need, and quite enough to fund my revenge. Enough to buy a new identity and start a new life with a new name in a faraway system on the other side of the Great Arm. Enough to buy the best education at the finest, most exclusive schools and universities. Enough to buy my way—when the hard work and determination weren't enough—into the great halls of power on Gran Kiravashta. Oh, you'd be surprised how easily one can bribe their way into the great game. Speaks to our corruption as an empire, I suppose.

"When I finally pierced the CM's inner circle ten years ago, I was convinced the hardest work—all those years of ladder-climbing and scheming and politicking—was behind me." Jakaan shook his head, his expression nostalgic. "How naive that seems now. Do you have any idea how difficult it is to fabricate convincing evidence of corruption and power abuses? It's no easy task, let me tell you. And it's all the more difficult when you have to ensure your own name remains beyond incrimination."

"I imagine so," Everfeld said. His shoulders slumped in resignation as a morbid realization settled over him. Jakaan's eagerness to reveal the details of his long-planned revenge, to disclose his lifelong secrets, could only mean two things. First, the room they occupied had to be entirely free of eavesdropping devices. If Jakaan was as careful and deliberate as his amazing story implied, he wouldn't have dared to share so much if there was any chance it might be overheard. Second, it meant that Everfeld wouldn't live long enough to repeat the tale to anyone. He would die here, in this anonymous room in the middle of nowhere, and probably within the next few minutes.

But even as he saw his looming fate, he still wanted answers. Curiosity, the obsessive need to know solutions to riddles, had been perhaps his defining characteristic. *Had been*, he repeated inwardly. How gruesomely strange it felt to refer to himself in the past tense.

"And what does the cleric have to do with all of this?" he asked.

"Not a thing, really," Jakaan said. "Well, not directly I should say. She was merely the bait to draw you away from the battlefield."

"Bait?" Everfeld said.

"Yes. Do you know what my biggest concern was during these last years? It was you, my old friend. The venerable spymaster with thousands of clandestine operatives stationed across the Realm. With who knew how many secret levers he could pull or buttons he could push in a moment's notice. You were the one I worried about, far more than our beloved ex-consul minister. That you might find out what I was doing. That you might derail my plans. No, I couldn't have you anywhere near the house when I set it afire. And that's where the cleric comes in. I knew you wouldn't be able to resist trying to turn her. You wanted so badly to prove all of the war hawks wrong. To show everyone peace had a chance."

Everfeld grunted. "Stars forbid I should want to save billions of lives," he said bitterly. "What a detestable obsession."

Jakaan raised a forefinger. "Ah, there, you said it yourself. Obsession. And that's what you were: obsessed. With being the only right one in the room. With your starry-eyed notions of what's best for the Realm. And the obsessed never think clearly. They leap before looking. They take unnecessary risks. Didn't any of your closest companions warn you? Didn't they try to steer you away from such a dangerous proposition as turning the cleric? Or do they always follow your ill-advised whims with no questions asked, like those senior staff suck-ups who'd never dare to contradict Amarania, no matter how absurd her position?"

His expression empty, Everfeld nodded. "They warned me," he admitted. "I didn't listen." It was hard enough admitting as much to himself, but being mocked for it by the man who held his fate added insult to injury. A slap to the face of the condemned man as he walked to the execution chamber.

"Do you want to hear the greatest irony of all?" Jakaan asked, leaning forward conspiratorially.

"Frankly, I don't," Everfeld said. "But I imagine you're going to tell me anyway." Who *was* this man sitting in front of him? This personification of vengeance he'd known and not known for years? What kind of creature could live such a duplicitous existence *for their entire life*? Even the most capable operatives and assets in Everfeld's employ could only maintain the facade for a few years at most, so intense was the psychological strain of leading a double life. He couldn't imagine the single-minded drive, the sheer willpower it must have taken Jakaan to achieve his lifelong ambition.

"The cleric never needed to be turned," Jakaan said smugly. "She was already working for peace. All that undercover shuttle diplomacy? She wasn't fomenting rebellion. She was doing her utmost to bring the factions together so they could negotiate reform as a unified body."

With his mind still spinning from the last few minutes of shocking revelations, this last took some moments to sink in. "Working for peace?" Everfeld finally said, as much to himself as Jakaan.

"Oh, yes," Jakaan said casually. "I've known for months. My informants recorded several incriminating conversations with Separatist leadership. Of course, I may have forgotten to include those bits of evidence in the files I sent you. Creating the fiction of her seditious inclinations was necessary. If the CM believed our friend Sah Tavella to be an imminent threat, you see, the brutal old bird wouldn't hesitate to remove her."

"Which would give you the means to get me out of the way."

"Precisely."

Everfeld could only shake his head at what he was hearing. Oh, how he'd been played! How soundly he'd been beaten by this hidden opponent. This friend who wasn't. Who never had been.

It was one of the oldest traps in the spy game: the natural resistance to think ill of friends and loved ones. A trap even a spymaster could fall into, as it turned out.

How many reports had he reviewed over the years recounting how agents had been duped by those closest to them? By lifelong friends or lovers or spouses.

There had been signs, thinking back on it. Hints that Jakaan had some agenda of his own, that he harbored secrets he kept entirely to himself. Everfeld had dismissed them all, giving his good friend the benefit of every doubt, convinced he knew the man, knew the content of his soul. Everyone had secrets, after all. Everyone had hopes and desires they didn't divulge even to their closest confidants, for one reason or another.

Stars, the sudden awareness of the things he'd ignored or minimized or turned his head away from was maddening.

"Why did you bring me here?" he asked. "Why didn't you just…"

"Have the war bugs take you out?" Jakaan said.

"Yes."

"It would have been premature," Jakaan explained, "to remove you before the no confidence vote. If the vote had gone differently for some reason, leaving the CM in power, I would have had a lot to answer for. If you'd been killed on Sandau Prime, Amarania would have held me to account. Despite your differences and her belief that you betrayed her, I don't believe she wanted to see you killed." He sighed. "But it's all a moot point now, yes?"

"Because the vote went your way."

"Yes."

"And now you can get rid of me without any complications."

Jakaan nodded.

"So why tell me all this?" the spymaster prodded. "Why the confessional, *old friend?*" he asked, the last two words uttered with unmistakable derision.

"Confessional?" Jakaan echoed. "That implies I'm seeking forgiveness, Whitmere. I can assure you I'm not. If I could make it worse on the old bird, believe me, I would. And I won't lose a minute of sleep over her fate. She's getting what she deserves, the murderous tyrant." His shoulders drooped a bit. "But I do regret that you're paying a price in all of this. But that comes with playing the big game, doesn't it? It's the gamble we all take." He sighed. "I suppose I felt I owed you an explanation."

"And what about the cleric?" Everfeld asked.

"What of her? At the moment we have her in a facility not unlike this one."

"What if she *is* the last hope for peace, Clevon?"

"Peace," Jakaan scoffed. "Please. You know who these Separatists are. You know what they want. Most of their leaders are greedy trade magnates who simply don't want to pay taxes to Gran Kiravashta. Wiping out corruption, securing nonhuman rights, all that nonsense? That's their brand, the label on their product. It's not their substance. They don't want peace and reform. They want markets and money. Complete hypocrites, the lot of them."

Everfeld frowned at the worn-out argument he'd heard countless times, not only from the CM and her senior staff, but also from the mouths of what social scientists referred to as the Realm's ruling class—the wealthy privileged of the core worlds.

Everfeld had always considered this a cowardly misdirection that callously disregarded the legitimate grievances of countless citizens. But at the same time, he couldn't deny the point was, to some degree, disappointingly accurate. The genuine idealists and reformers among the leaders of the Separatist movement were a vastly outnumbered minority. Most were in it for the money. For them, revolution meant a financial windfall.

"And this cleric's no better," Jakaan added. "If you'd only heard the recordings of her that I've heard. She's no saint, believe me. She wants to form this coalition only so she can sit at the head of its table. She wants to uplift the downtrodden, but only if she can ride on their shoulders while doing it. Do you know who she reminds me most of? A young version of our recently deposed consul minister. She's every bit as ambitious and self-serving as the old bird. And twice as ruthless. The Realm will be far better off without her scheming and plotting, I assure you."

Everfeld's gaze dropped to the floor. He felt tired, defeated. He didn't want to hear any more of Jakaan's boasts about his secret scheming, much less his own failures and blind spots. He didn't want to think about what might have been if he'd learned about Sah Tavella's actions—and her true motives—before Jakaan had discovered them. He didn't want to imagine how he and the cleric might have worked together to bring about change, to prevent the bloodshed that now seemed all but inevitable. Oh, how he'd failed.

"I have to take my leave of you now," Jakaan said. He reached into his cloak's inner pocket, removing a small vial of clear liquid, holding it between his thumb and forefinger.

Everfeld stared at the vial, not surprised by its appearance. "How long does it take to work?"

"Less than half an hour, I'm told," Jakaan said. "There's an anesthetic that will put you to sleep first. The end will be painless, I promise you." A small opening appeared in the restriction field, through which Jakaan passed Everfeld the vial. Jakaan withdrew his hand, and the opening sealed itself.

Everfeld turned over the vial in his hand. "I could refuse to take it."

"You could," Jakaan said. "But if you choose to do that, the guard outside would have to use his weapon." He then added, "Please don't. I'd hate for your end to be a painful one. I truly would."

"How merciful of you," Everfeld said. The spymaster flicked open the vial's cap with his thumb and took a whiff. Whatever the compound was, it had no smell. He gazed sadly at the colorless poison.

"Drink it," Jakaan said.

Perhaps, Everfeld reflected, he deserved to end this way. In some nameless cell on a cold rock of a planet. He'd been so horribly wrong, been so completely blind to the treachery standing next to him. Some master of spies. He'd failed himself, his friends, the Realm entire.

He brought the vial to his lips and drank the tasteless liquid.

Jakaan rose from his chair. "Goodbye, old friend." He turned, left, and then Everfeld was alone again, the flickering buzz of the restriction shield the room's only sound.

29

A FINAL MOVE

The guard reentered the room, his rifle slung over his shoulder, and closed the door behind him. Everfeld looked over and smiled weakly at the man.

"Death watch," the spymaster said. "Not the most enjoyable assignment, I imagine."

Odd, Everfeld thought, that Jakaan hadn't stayed to watch his demise. A man with no qualms about letting billions, perhaps trillions, of innocents die couldn't bear the sight of one old man expiring. Or maybe he could bear it but simply didn't bother to. Eliminated as a threat, Everfeld no longer required Jakaan's attention. But what did it matter, in any case? Why was Everfeld wasting his final moments with thoughts of that vengeful, soulless monster?

Forcing his mind elsewhere, he brooded over what would become of Jeryn. He hoped the lad was safe and sound with Bhokken and Marogh. And he hoped the *Dagger* could keep all three of them and the Marines from harm. For surely they would be hunted, wanted as his accomplices.

He felt a sudden, irresistible drowsiness begin to overtake him. It was coming.

"How do you feel?" the guard asked.

The tiring spymaster looked up at the man. "I feel weary."

"I'm under orders to watch you, then report your death to the interim consul minister."

Everfeld's head felt heavy, began to droop. "I imagined as much."

"I was also under orders not to speak to you. But I don't always follow my orders."

I don't always follow my orders. His perception dulled, it took a moment for the comment—and its significance—to sink in. Everfeld snapped his gaze to the guard's face, a surge of excitement momentarily overtaking the drug's effect.

"You're a Seeker?" the spymaster asked.

"I am." The guard stepped closer. "And I'm very sorry, but I can't get you out. This place is completely locked down. No airships allowed, and there are two dozen guards and four checkpoints between here and the outside."

Everfeld straightened his back and tried to clear his head. "I understand." His thoughts raced, shifting from his looming fate to how he could best exploit this unlikely opportunity. This one final move the big game had granted him.

"How quickly can you get a message out of the system?" he asked the guard.

"This facility doesn't have subspace comms," the man said.

"Can you relay a message to a site that does?"

The guard shook his head. "I only have person-to-person comms privileges at this site." Then he added, "But there's a way station with a hypercast array at the edge of the Eastern Dune Sea, two hours from here by rock skipper. I've got access there."

Everfeld felt a spark of hope. "That's good enough." He glanced self-consciously at the ceiling and walls.

"There are no monitoring devices in this room," the guard assured him. "He had me make sure of it."

"Good," Everfeld said. "Now, please, I need you to listen to me very carefully." A powerful wave of fatigue came over him. His vision momentarily blurred, and he felt the room begin to slip away. "You must... memorize every word... this is very important."

"Yes," the guard said. "I'll remember. I promise."

Everfeld's speech began to fail him, his words forced out in grunting strains of concentrated effort. It took less than a minute, though it seemed like much longer, for Everfeld to say what he needed to. Had he missed anything? Was there something he'd forgotten? He was tired, so tired. His mind was a blur of failing perception. But even as his consciousness ebbed away, he was certain that he'd relayed the most important things, the things Jeryn and Bhokken needed to know. This, his final coherent thought, comforted him as he slid from the bed to the floor, fast asleep, never to wake again.

PART 3

30

HAMELSTUN NINE

History was a slow succession of events. It was causes and effects, moving in increments measured in years and decades, even centuries. As you stood in the here and now and looked backward, you could see how history evolved, how the present was a canyon carved by the river of the past. Steep valley walls shaped imperceptibly, centimeter by centimeter, over vast spans of time.

That was how Jeryn thought of history: as a slow-moving continuum.

But sometimes history moved forward not at a stroll, but at a burst of light speed, turning the entire galaxy upside down within a few hours—as it had in the span of time since the *Veiled Dagger* had left, then returned to Sandau Prime. As the fully cloaked ship approached the icy world, its crew tried to make sense of the inconceivable information coming from the planet's news and security feeds.

"Minister Amarania is under house arrest," Marogh said, rereading the stunning headlines. "Charged with corruption and high crimes."

"Unbelievable," the Rauk muttered to himself. "Un...be...lievable."

Jeryn was equally shocked by the news. "Did you have any idea this might happen?" he asked Bhokken.

"None," the Rauk said, frowning over the feed monitor, its blue glow reflected on his furry face. "Whitmere never said anything of a corruption investigation or the prospect of a no confidence vote. And he certainly would have known about such things."

"Maybe he didn't tell you," Jeryn suggested. "For his own reasons."

The Rauk shook his head. "He never would have kept something so important from me."

"If that's accurate," the pilot said, "then we are left to assume he did not know about it."

Again, the Rauk shook his head. "But he *must* have known about it."

"Both possibilities cannot coexist," the pilot said. "Either he knew and did not inform you. Or he did not inform you because he did not know."

Frustrated, Bhokken gave the shifter a cross look. "I'm glad you're here to point these things out."

The shifter began to say something, then apparently thought better of it. After a moment's hesitation, he said, "Is it possible a coup has taken place? That the consul minister's inner circle turned on her, and Everfeld was kept intentionally unaware?"

The engineer considered this, then said, "Her senior staff was made up of spineless sycophants, loyal to a fault. I don't see them rising up against her. Stars, they never even dared to disagree with her. Not a backbone among them, except for Everfeld."

Jeryn offered up the most obvious explanation. "Then we have to take it at face value. She broke the law, and she got caught."

"I wouldn't put it past her," the Rauk said. "She's lived by her own rules her entire life. But since when has breaking the law been a crime?"

Jeryn gave the engineer a double take. "Did you really just say that?"

"For politicians, I mean," the Rauk explained. "Our Realm's leadership isn't exactly the most law-abiding bunch these days, in case you haven't noticed. Looking the other way when a colleague—especially a high-ranking colleague—bends or breaks the rules is nothing new. You could say it's even expected. I'm no Separatist, my friends, but you can't deny the sorry state of the times we live in. The only thing that's rare about corruption these days is when someone bothers to point it out."

No disagreement there, Jeryn thought.

"And still more perplexing," the pilot added, "is the coincidental timing of Everfeld's apprehension and the consul minister's ouster."

"Which cannot be coincidental," the Rauk said.

"Agreed," the shifter said. "The two events must be related, but their connection eludes me."

"Me too," Bhokken said. The engineer and the pilot turned in unison to Jeryn.

"No idea," he said, spreading his hands out helplessly.

"You don't recall anything he might have said?" the Rauk asked. "Maybe some reference—"

An urgent chirp from the comms panel interrupted him. The Rauk swiveled in his seat, tapped the console, and a holo display appeared, indicating an urgent incoming message.

"I don't believe it," the Rauk said, staring at the message's encryption signature. Jeryn's eyes widened as he noticed it too.

Hamelstun Nine!

"What is it?" the pilot asked.

"It's him!" Jeryn exclaimed.

The Rauk nodded, his mouth stretching into a sharp-toothed grin. "By the Fifteen, it has to be."

Confused, the shifter stared at the holo. "I'm afraid you both have me at a loss. What is the significance of this particular encryption package, aside from appearing a bit out of date?"

"It's more than a bit out of date," Jeryn said. "Hamelstun Nine crypto has been out of general use for over two hundred years." As Bhokken retrieved the message and asked the ship mind to decrypt it, Jeryn explained how the package had been the in-house crypto developed and used by Hamelstun Interstellar, a small mining syndicate that went bust more than two centuries earlier. When the syndicate went under, so did its proprietary crypto, making Hamelstun Nine the equivalent of a dead language, though it could still be found in the vast libraries maintained by planetary comms facilities. A certain spymaster had surreptitiously ensured its mandatory inclusion decades ago, under the pretense of historical record-keeping requirements.

Spacefaring vessels, on the other hand, were under no obligation to carry outdated crypto, and so they almost never did. There were tens of thousands of cryptography packages no longer in use, and it made little sense to include them in a vessel's comms system when doing so only consumed a portion of a ship's finite archive space. It would have been like having a translator on your crew with expertise in a language no one spoke anymore. Pretty much pointless and a waste of resources besides.

The shifter's face brightened in understanding. "Ah, so as a de facto 'dead language,' Hamelstun Nine encryption is an ideal way to send a confidential surface-to-ship message. Assuming, of course, the vessel in question has the corresponding package in its archives. Which I assume the *Dagger* does, correct?"

"You are most correct," the Rauk said, still grinning as he tapped the console. "Most ship minds these days don't even recognize H9 as an encoded message. It's such an old standard they disregard it as a transmission error."

The Rauk's smile faded. "Hmmm. Seems the transmission is audio only." Anxious to hear the message, Jeryn stepped closer to the Rauk's console. A moment later, a disembodied voice began to speak. A voice that wasn't Everfeld's.

"I have been asked by Director Whitmere Everfeld to relay this message to his friends on the Dagger. *What you're about to hear are his exact words that I committed to memory some three hours ago."*

The trio exchanged concerned looks as the man's voice continued. *"My dear friends, I hope this message finds you safe. You may be surprised to hear from me, thinking me dead. I was in fact shot, but it was only a stunning blast, and afterward I was transported to an undisclosed location on Sandau Prime's surface. A guest house, by the looks of it."*

Jeryn swallowed. *Guest house.* It was the term Everfeld used to refer to the secret prisons favored by the Realm's more tyrannical planetary governors. Extra-judicial sites where they could dispose of political rivals, personal enemies, and pesky journos who asked the wrong questions.

"I'm afraid I've failed you all, and for that you have my deepest apologies. A wolf has been lurking among the sheep, my friends. A very clever, patient, and determined wolf, who managed to escape my notice for years, to my eternal regret. My time is running short, but there's much you need to know, so I'll do my best to be brief..."

31

A FINE MESS

"*By the time you receive this message, I will be gone. I'm so very sorry for what has happened. I will regret my folly until my last breath, which now seems not terribly far away. Farewell, my friends. Yours truly, Whitmere Everfeld.*"

It was the third time Jakaan had listened to the recorded message of the spymaster's last words. The newly appointed consul minister ground his teeth together, his frustration growing with each playback from the audio feed. He stood before the one who had apparently memorized, recited, and transmitted it on behalf of Everfeld, a man seated in the middle of the small room with his hands tied behind him. The man's head hung low, and his face was a bloody pulp of swollen, puffy flesh and oozing cuts. He was a guard at the remote detention center where they'd held Everfeld. The very same guard Jakaan had told to watch the spymaster expire. For reasons that remained maddeningly unclear, the man had helped Everfeld get a message off-planet.

The turn of events was as inexplicable as it was infuriating. Either the late spymaster had placed a secret ally within the facility, anticipating his own imprisonment, or he'd somehow managed to turn the guard during the spymaster's final minutes of life. Neither possibility seemed anywhere close to probable, but then the guard had done what he'd done, taking an inconceivable course of action. If there was some third explanation, neither Jakaan nor his chief of staff, Menic, could come up with it.

Whatever the turncoat's reasons had been, they remained a mystery. The guard was made of hard stuff. Since Jakaan and Menic had arrived at the remote way station, the man had already been beaten into unconsciousness twice, and he hadn't yet uttered a single word. The stubborn man had turned out to be far better at keeping secrets than he'd been at avoiding detection and covering his tracks. Seconds after transmitting Everfeld's message into subspace, the man had been apprehended by the site's security personnel, who'd been alerted by an unusual signal sent from one of the comms suites. Caught before he could destroy the auto-archived copy, the contents of his message had been retrieved by site personnel. And thanks to the site's massive cryptological archives, the recorded message was easily decoded. The use of ancient crypto had at first baffled Jakaan, until the facility's senior comms officer had astutely worked out the ingeniousness of its use. It was like using a language no one spoke anymore, the officer had reported. Or at least a language *no ship* spoke anymore, he'd amended, unless it carried the long-outdated crypto package. Jakaan had only shaken his head and laughed darkly. Even in death, the old spymaster still had tricks up his sleeve.

Menic grabbed the bound man's hair and jerked his head up. "Why did you help Everfeld?" he demanded. The barely conscious man said nothing, only groaning as blood and spit flowed down his chin. After a few moments, Menic let go, and the man's head drooped back down again as if it weighed far too much for his neck to support.

"Should we bring them back in?" Menic asked, referring to the two brutal-but-as-yet-ineffective interrogators out in the corridor.

Jakaan didn't answer immediately, thinking maybe he deserved a good beating himself. Maybe even more than the doomed wretch seated before him. How foolish he'd been, revealing so much! What in the Great Arm had he been thinking? It had been vanity, sheer vanity. He'd wanted to boast, to gloat, to show the old spymaster he'd been outsmarted, outplayed. What a lapse! What a profoundly stupid lapse. Everfeld's companions, wherever they were, had very likely received and decoded the message. Now the Rauk engineer, the young operative, and whoever else Everfeld had taken with him to Sandau Prime knew everything. They knew about Jakaan's true identity, about his years of secret plotting against the CM, about why he'd done it. They knew the truth about the young Tegesian cleric's motives too. What a fine mess this was. A mess of his own making.

Jakaan took a long breath, tried to calm the swirling storm of his thoughts.

It wasn't the first time he'd had to clean up some sticky mess of a situation—his own or someone else's—and it surely wouldn't be the last time. He'd faced setbacks on countless occasions. And in every instance, he'd dealt with them, or bribed them, or blown them up. He would deal with this one too. The old spymaster's dying words would end up being so much wasted breath. Jakaan would make sure of it.

But as long as Everfeld's companions lived and knew the truth, they were a threat. They had to be found and eliminated.

Taking one more calming breath, he said, "He seems immune to fists, our friend," nodding toward the bound and beaten man. "Have them find someone who knows how to work a psychic probe."

"Right away, Minister."

"Now, I believe we have other matters to attend to, do we not?" Jakaan asked.

"We do," his right hand answered. He removed his hand

terminal from a cloak pocket and tapped the screen. "I'll have them ready your shuttle for departure."

As the pair left the room, Menic passed on Everfeld's instructions to the interrogators. The pair then headed in the direction of the shuttle bay.

"Have they located Everfeld's vessel yet?" Jakaan asked impatiently.

"No, sir," the chief of staff said. "They most likely deactivated their transponder."

Jakaan grunted his disappointment. "I can hardly blame them. By now surely they know they're being hunted."

They walked on, Jakaan turning his thoughts to his next appointment, his *second* mess of the day. And this one would be no less pleasant to deal with than Everfeld's dying gambit.

"We need His Eminence on our side," Menic said as they approached the bay. "I realize I don't have to tell you this."

"You don't," Jakaan replied. He then gave the man a meaningful nod and added, "But don't let that stop you from reminding me." He gave a silent thanks for the man's ever-thoughtful counsel. Pallat Menic had been Jakaan's right hand for nearly fifteen years. A trustworthy, reliable confidant, the man had proven his loyalty time and time again. He'd moved with Jakaan from post to post, climbing the slippery rungs of Gran Kiravashta's bureaucratic ladder, sharing every victory and every defeat. Fortunately, there had been far more of the former than the latter. And though he'd long since learned of all Jakaan's darkest secrets and plans—some from the CM's own admission, others from years of astute observation and inference—Jakaan's personal crusade had never diluted Menic's fealty in the least. Everyone has a private agenda, he'd once confided to Everfeld, whether they admit to it or not.

Jakaan had appointed the man interim Master of Spies, replacing the late Whitmere Everfeld. It was a position, like his own provisional appointment, Jakaan was determined to make permanent.

An hour later, Jakaan entered the private chamber of Dotta Superior Tolerance IV, the Tegesian faith's senior cleric.

A couple steps inside the door, Jakaan bowed his head respectfully. "Good day, Your Eminence."

The dotta superior sat at a small table and didn't immediately acknowledge the visitor. The cleric's concentration was focused on a small treelike plant sitting atop the table. He carefully pruned the plant's leaves and branches with a small pair of shears. A scatter of cuttings lay on the tabletop. Bright blue flecks that looked like drops of paint.

Like many of the men in his order, he had no hair on his head, but instead of the braided beard so common to his brethren, his face was clean-shaven. Jakaan couldn't recall if this had some significance within the faith or not. The cleric's appearance had an ageless quality to it. His sand-colored face was neither youthfully unlined nor overly wrinkled with age, but some point in between. The man might have been forty-five or seventy-five, based on his looks, but Jakaan knew the man was nearly a hundred. He'd clearly had some kind of rejuvenation work done. Jakaan wondered if the man had undergone the illegal—and wildly expensive—genetic treatments black marketed to the Realm's wealthiest upper crust.

His Eminence straightened up, inspected his work, then laid his pruning shears on the table. Turning to Jakaan, he said, "There's not a good thing about this day, young man."

32

TOLERANCE IV, DOTTA SUPERIOR

HOME TERRITORY MEANT SOMETHING. STREET GANGS KNEW IT. Professional sports teams knew it. There was an intangible advantage home turf gave you, an edge over the visiting team or trespassing rival. The home team always had the upper hand, and right now Jakaan was the visiting squad, the outsider. The interloper who'd strayed onto the dotta superior's property. Despite occupying the most powerful political office in the Realm, Jakaan had felt a clear disadvantage from the moment he entered the sprawling downtown complex in Sandau-Kal, the center of the Tegesian universe. He'd met the faith's senior cleric many times, but this was their first one-on-one encounter.

His Eminence was a master politician. Through shrewd tactics and countless strategic maneuvers, he'd effectively managed the Tegesian faith's complex, intertwined, and occasionally paradoxical relationship with the Realm's state entities. In tight planetary gubernatorial races, for instance, he rarely chose sides, but in the aftermath always managed to appear to have supported the winning candidate. He decried the injustices of slavery and human supremacy, but more to appease the politically militant members of his own order than to drive substantive change. In the years Jakaan had served as the consul minister's chief of staff, he couldn't recall a single instance of Tolerance IV being on the losing side of a political battle.

Jakaan deeply respected how deftly the senior cleric had walked a slippery tightrope for decades. Several slippery tightropes, actually. He'd substantially increased Tegesian power during his decades-long tenure, supplanting governors and regents in the Realm's most influential systems with his own handpicked candidates. And he'd managed to do it without damaging the relationship between church and state. If anything, Jakaan reflected, the bond between the Tegesian faith and the Realm's governing bodies was stronger than ever. And when a disgruntled minority of his clerics broke away from his order's orthodoxy to form their own sect, he'd shrewdly managed the potentially debilitating split of his faith by immediately discrediting the radical elements, the self-proclaimed Originalists, by labeling them apostates and terrorists. More importantly, he'd used his influence with authorities on Gran Kiravashta to ban the sect, which effectively robbed the movement of any hopes of legitimacy, driving it underground. For orthodox clerics and believers alike, it was one thing to shift allegiance to a new Tegesian denomination whose doctrine you might be inclined to agree with, but it was something else entirely to align yourself with an illegal cult.

Tolerance IV motioned to a chair. "Sit." Not *sit, Minister,* or even *sit, please.* As Jakaan took a seat, the cleric stood up from his own chair and glared down at the consul minister. Home turf advantage, Jakaan reflected.

"I summoned you here to discuss the recent arrest of one of my order, Charnette Tavella."

"Your Eminence, I'm afraid I'm unfamiliar—"

Tolerance IV interrupted him with a dismissive wave. "For the sake of time, let's forgo any pretense you don't know of whom I'm speaking." He stared harshly at Jakaan. "Shall we?" he added.

Jakaan nodded. "Of course."

"She's being held in an undisclosed location... illegally."

"She's been accused of treason, Your Eminence."

"Yet no charges have been filed," Tolerance IV said.

"As a declared enemy of the Realm, her rights and—"

"Have you seen the transmission she sent to her brothers and sisters of faith?" the senior cleric snapped, again interrupting Jakaan.

"I have, Your Eminence." Jakaan swallowed. Yes, he'd definitely seen it. More than once, in fact. Sah Tavella was no fool. She must have sensed the walls were closing in on her, and in anticipation of her apprehension, she'd recorded a message proclaiming her innocence and her wrongful arrest at the hands of corrupt politicians. As police stormed her office, she'd transmitted the recording—only moments before she was taken in custody—to thousands of her fellow Tegesian clergy throughout the Realm. If it hadn't been such a thorn in his side, Jakaan might have appreciated the clever, quick-thinking move.

"I've received tens of thousands of personal messages from across the Realm. *Tens of thousands*, Jakaan." From any other citizen in the Realm, the pointed snub—addressing Jakaan by his last name with no title attached—might have drawn the interim CM's ire. But this man was more valuable to Jakaan than a thousand battle cruisers. If he had to take a few slaps in the face to let the cleric vent his frustrations, then so be it.

"You have no idea how highly regarded she is within the faith," Tolerance IV said, pacing back and forth, his hands clenching and unclenching. "She must be released, immediately."

"Your Eminence, I'm not sure that's possible. The charges she's been—"

"Rumors. Innuendo. Nothing more."

"Can you be so certain of that, Your Eminence?" Jakaan said. He straightened his back and hardened his expression. "Are you aware of all her comings and goings? Here and now, can you tell me with absolute confidence that there are no strange gaps in her whereabouts over the last year? No unexplained absences? No surreptitious meetings with Separatist leaders she might have a hard time explaining?"

Tolerance IV stopped his pacing and puzzled over Jakaan, as if the senior cleric hadn't expected the sudden show of backbone. "Are you saying such evidence exists?"

"As a friend and supporter of your faith, I'm telling you it wouldn't be wise to assume it doesn't." He gave the dotta superior a firm, unblinking stare.

The cleric took a moment to ponder Jakaan's statement, as if he were reevaluating the man seated before him. The anger in Tolerance IV's face—whether it had been a show or genuine sentiment—lessened, then seemed to go away entirely as the man took his seat again.

"Tell me, Minister," he said, "do you recall Governor Tavian Mansfeld?" the dotta superior asked.

"He was a bit before my time," Jakaan said, unsure where this was going, "but I know the name." Decades before, Mansfeld had been the governor of Gran Kiravashta, the second most powerful state position—outside of consul minister—in all the Realm. Halfway through his second term, a coalition of local representatives filed legal proceedings to remove him from office for unspecified "improprieties." Mansfeld resigned before the case went to trial, somewhat predictably proclaiming his innocence even as he left office in disgrace.

"I had him removed," the dotta superior said in a matter-of-fact tone. "Did you know that?" Jakaan shook his head.

"He was a bit of a crusader," the senior cleric continued. "Didn't care for the faith at all. Called us all mystics and charlatans. For years he worked against us, doing whatever he could to minimize our influence in state matters." He leaned forward, lifting his eyebrows. "But then he went a step too far. He tried to purge the faith from the primary school curriculum on Gran Kiravashta. Now that simply wasn't brash, it was downright arrogant, believing he could get away with something like that. Believing he could rewrite thousands of years of tradition with a stroke of his governor's pen.

"It took me months to ruin him. It was the earliest days of my dottacy, you understand, and I was still a bit green. Back then I had little experience in wielding the power and influence of this office effectively. These days I would only need minutes, not months, to take care of someone like Mansfeld. That's how well I've learned to manage my station, Minister. And I like to think I've also learned how to be a responsible steward of that power and influence." Here the man paused, allowing Jakaan the opportunity to agree with him.

"I would certainly agree with that," Jakaan said on cue.

"And part of being a responsible steward is knowing when it's best *not* to influence events. Example: When I heard rumors of Minister Amarania's potential ouster, I might have taken action. In fact, I might have prevented it by directing the no confidence vote toward a different outcome. You might be surprised how easily this could have been arranged."

No, he wouldn't have been, Jakaan disagreed internally. The senior cleric could have easily upended Jakaan's machinations, and he could have done so, as he'd correctly noted, without much effort. Still, Jakaan had known—well, he hadn't known for sure, but he'd been reasonably certain—that the man wouldn't stick his neck out for Minister Amarania. Maybe he would have a decade ago, but not now. Only a fool stays aboard a sinking ship.

"But alas, her time had passed," Tolerance IV said with a sigh. "She no longer enjoyed the support of the masses or the Assembly of Regents, and the governors of so many systems had all but deserted her." Jakaan noted how the senior cleric had already begun to speak of her in the past tense. It was a good sign, he reckoned. It meant he'd already cut ties to the woman who'd once been a close ally.

"So when the CM's removal came down to a formal vote," Tolerance IV continued, "I didn't interfere. I let matters run their course." He leaned forward, placing his palms on the desktop. "But what kind of leader would I be if I took that same path now? If I paid no heed to the almost universal outcry from my most important constituents? If I simply abandoned one of our most beloved sisters? How would that serve the purpose of my order?"

"What about justice?" Jakaan said. "Are you suggesting we simply release her, despite her crimes?"

"*Alleged* crimes," the cleric corrected, raising a finger. "And who said anything about bloody justice?" he added sharply. "Minister Jakaan, I can't imagine you came to your present station in life through ignorance or blind luck, so I'm left to assume you're an informed man who makes informed decisions. If something more long-lasting than an interim appointment interests you, you'd be ill-advised to make an enemy of the Tegesian faithful."

Swallowing his pride again, Jakaan respectfully bowed his head. "I wouldn't dream of it, Your Eminence," he said with all the humility he could muster. "But I've reviewed the evidence, and I'm convinced of Tavella's guilt. If the Tegesian clergy could only see what I've seen, I'm sure she would quickly fall out of favor."

The dotta superior pounced on this like a hidden predator who'd been waiting for prey to pass within striking range. Clearly, he'd been expecting the conversation to reach this very point. "Then your next course of action should be apparent. If she's obviously committed treason, the facts of her case should be made public."

"A public trial," Jakaan said.

Tolerance IV gave the consul minister a single nod. "It's the only sensible solution to our problem."

Jakaan swallowed. It was the only sensible solution to the *dotta superior's* problem, he revised inwardly. A public trial could absolve the dotta superior of all accountability for the young cleric's fate. Tolerance IV would claim respect for the law and due process. He would use the justice system as a basin in which he'd wash his hands of the matter. But for Jakaan, the more quickly and quietly the troublesome Tavella went away, the better. A swift execution in a hidden prison was far preferable to some highly visible litigation whose result he couldn't control.

As if he was reading Jakaan's mind, the senior cleric said, "You're concerned the outcome might not be what you expect. I can assure you a conviction is as important to me as it is to you. I wouldn't think of suggesting a public trial if I wasn't sure of a verdict that serves our mutual benefit."

"She'll be found guilty?" Jakaan asked, lifting an eyebrow.

"On every count you'd like to charge her with," Tolerance IV replied. "But only after she's been thoroughly discredited."

Ah, Jakaan thought, his mind illuminating with sudden understanding. Now he fully understood the cleric's game.

Tolerance IV didn't simply want to wash his hands of the cleric's fate. She wasn't merely some problem to be solved. Well, she *was* that, but she was also far more. She was a threat, plain and simple. And not only to Realm hegemony, but to the dotta superior himself, to his power, to his ultimate authority. Perhaps he'd been unpleasantly surprised by the massive outpouring of support she'd received. Or perhaps he'd already identified Tavella as a potential rival, and he'd been waiting for the right opportunity to pull this dangerous weed from his garden. But whatever his reasons, it was now abundantly clear the two men weren't really at odds at all. They both wanted the scheming cleric out of the way. They agreed on the destination; they only differed on their preferred route to get there.

Jakaan chided himself for only realizing all of this now. If Tavella was executed in secret, not only would it make the dotta superior appear weak and ineffective to his countless followers (when he failed to secure her release), but it would also risk making the woman a martyr to the Separatists, the Originalists, and possibly even a large portion of the orthodox Tegesian clergy. Tolerance IV's authority, his ability to lead the Tegesian faith, would be questioned by countless critics from within his own ranks.

But a public trial was the perfect way to render Tavella harmless. By defaming her, by ruining her reputation. The traitorous nature of the charges alone would make her a pariah. And once her public standing was thoroughly sullied, once she was widely despised throughout the Realm, she'd no longer pose a threat.

Finally grasping the cleric's position, Jakaan realized the time had come for compromise. The two men wanted the same thing, after all. And Tolerance IV was not someone Jakaan wanted to count among his enemies. Quite the opposite, in fact. If Jakaan was going to hold onto power, he needed the dotta superior's endorsement.

Jakaan spoke slowly, his tone respectful. "I'm concerned only with the safety of our citizens and seeing justice served. If Your Eminence believes a public trial of this traitor best serves the greater interest of the Realm, I would be a fool to disagree. I'll see to it immediately."

A satisfied grin stretched across the dotta superior's face. "I'm immensely gratified we share the same priorities, Minister Jakaan. You strike me as a wise, judicious man. Exactly the kind of leader the Realm needs in these troubled times."

Thank the stars. Relief washed over Jakaan. He'd gotten what he'd come for, what he'd traveled light-years to hear: the dotta superior's endorsement.

He placed his hand over his heart and bowed his head gratefully. "You flatter me, Your Eminence."

Hours later, Jakaan met Menic for a late dinner in the penthouse of the Royal Stardust, a luxury hotel in the heart of Sandau-Kal's commercial district. When the waitperson brought over the bottle of vintage Astarion wine Jakaan had ordered, Menic nodded approvingly.

"Excellent vintage," Menic said. "Are we celebrating a successful meeting with His Eminence?"

"Indeed we are," Jakaan said. "It began a bit bumpy but ended quite well. And I did have to agree to a slightly different fate for our ambitious young cleric."

The waitperson, a six-armed, thick-bodied humanoid whose species name the consul minister couldn't recall, poured a splash of wine into Jakaan's glass and waited for his customer's approval. As Jakaan reached for the glass, he noted Menic's distracted stare.

"Something wrong?" he asked.

Menic cleared his throat. "I'm not sure you'll want to celebrate when you hear what I've learned about the vessel Everfeld was traveling in. The one his companions are still aboard."

"The vessel we still haven't located," Jakaan added, swallowing the wine. An excellent vintage, indeed. He nodded to the waitperson, who filled both glasses. Menic waited until the humanoid was out of earshot to continue.

The newly installed Agency spymaster leaned forward and spoke in low tones. "I pulled the profile on the vessel Everfeld took to Sandau Prime, just out of curiosity."

Jakaan nodded. "And you found something interesting?"

"It's what I *didn't* find that was interesting," the man said.

The consul minister lifted an eyebrow as he gently swirled his wine. "And what was it you didn't find?"

"First, there was no flight plan filed."

"Is that so surprising," Jakaan noted, "given the top-secret nature of the assignment?"

"Probably not. But that's the least of it," Menic said. "As you may know, the Agency maintains a small fleet of its own specialized vessels. Spy ships used for surveillance and so forth. Everfeld didn't take any of those; they're all accounted for. And he didn't take one of the transport ships from the interdepartmental pool, which would have been the normal procedure. They're all accounted for too."

Jakaan set down his glass. "Then a private charter, perhaps?"

"That was my thought as well, and since there aren't many private charters capable of making such a long trip, I had them all checked out. The same result. Every last one of them was either sitting in a docking bay or in transit with valid passenger registries and flight plans. Then it occurred to me maybe the old man had an off-the-books vessel hidden away, so I had my new staff dig around a bit."

"And what did they find?"

They'd found quite a lot, as it turned out. Menic detailed his discoveries over the next few minutes. Everfeld's department had apparently funneled huge amounts of funds into the design and construction of what Menic was convinced was a highly advanced spacecraft. A team of forensic accountants had unraveled a ball of financial string, revealing falsified procurement records for maintenance drones that Menic suspected were really spaceship components, based on the sums involved and shipment records. The "maintenance drones" had been sourced from systems that, coincidentally, were also the home systems of trade syndicates specializing in advanced shipbuilding technology.

"Or not so coincidentally, perhaps," Menic said. And while his investigation hadn't yet turned up any design specs or identified any engineers who'd worked on the secret project, Menic was all but convinced Everfeld, shortly before his demise, had constructed the ultimate spy ship and taken it to Sandau Prime.

"It's a safe bet that vessel is very fast, very stealthy, and chock-full of extremely advanced technology," Menic said, then after a moment added, "which won't make finding his co-conspirators any easier."

The new spymaster said nothing more, and he seemed to be steeling himself for the CM's disappointed response.

The news was indeed disappointing, Jakaan thought, but he refused to let it ruin his evening. The meeting with the dotta superior had gone far too well for his spirits to be dampened on this night. And the situation wasn't nearly as dire as his right hand believed in any case.

"Chin up, Director Menic," he said. "You're forgetting something."

"What's that, Minister?"

"They may have a fast and stealthy ship, but it's only a single vessel." Jakaan smiled and took a large gulp of wine. "We, on the other hand, have an entire Navy at our disposal."

33

A RAUK'S BET

OUTSIDE JERYN'S CABIN VIEWPORT, THE COLD ROCK OF SANDAU Prime hung in space. A world he'd once thought of, as most did, as the epicenter of the Tegesian faith, but now he only saw it as a gravesite. A planet-sized tomb where Everfeld's body lay.

It was harder losing the old man a second time. A kick to the face after you'd already been floored by a gut punch. When the spymaster's coded message had come through, filling Jeryn with elation and relief, the prospect of seeing Everfeld alive again had nearly brought him to tears. But then near the end of the message, Everfeld had revealed what he'd been forced to ingest, and the moment of sheer happiness was cut cruelly short. A pitiless tease of hope.

Not long after they'd listened to the message, a story on the subspace news feed had publicly confirmed Everfeld's death. A failed heart had been the official lie propagated to the media.

Lost in grief, Jeryn had barely retained the contents of Everfeld's final words. Details had been given, recounted by the mysterious messenger, that explained everything behind the astonishing events of the last few days: the CM's ouster, the swarming attack on the safe house, Everfeld's capture and execution. A revenge plot by Clevon Jakaan, the CM's closest advisor, was the answer to all the riddles. Everfeld had been betrayed by a man he considered a friend. A man he thought he'd known.

Apparently years in the making, the man's secret scheming had finally culminated with the help of conspiring regents. In hindsight, this last was hardly surprising. Minister Amarania had run roughshod over the Assembly of Regents for decades, ruthlessly flexing her political muscle and twisting countless arms to further her agendas. She'd amassed no shortage of enemies over the years. Bhokken had commented it probably hadn't taken much prodding to gather enough votes to oust her, especially given her weakened political position. Politicians were nothing if not mercilessly opportunistic. They also held long grudges.

Why was this always the way? Why did the Jakaans of the galaxy always come out on top? Why did the self-serving, the corrupt, the unscrupulous always win out over the kind and generous? Why was Everfeld dead in some nameless jail while the new CM and his collaborators lived and thrived? Why was fairness so rare and cruelty so common?

Jeryn clenched his fists. For a moment he indulged in a fantasy of some future time and place, when he'd find himself in the same room with Jakaan. He'd take his kukri and show the man how to stab someone face to face instead of the only way Jakaan was familiar with: in the back.

He blew out a long, slow breath. No, he told himself. Now wasn't the time for despair or revenge fantasies. He could almost hear the old man, chiding him for harboring such self-indulgent pettiness when so much was at stake. And, yes, the old man would have been right about that.

They had to continue the mission, to keep the old man's dream alive. Somehow, some way. They had to.

The chime on his door sounded. "Come in," he said. Bhokken and Marogh entered, both wearing sorrowful expressions.

"More good news, I take it?" Jeryn said glumly.

"I'm afraid so," the Rauk said. "We're fugitives now, just as we'd feared. Priority-one arrest warrants with our names attached went out on the subspace security feeds. In a few hours, every police person in the Realm will know our names and faces."

The news should have rocked Jeryn, but he hardly blinked at the engineer's words. Landing yourself on the Realm's most wanted list was hardly something to dismiss lightly, but given the day's events, this latest development felt almost inevitable. The period at the end of the worst sentence ever written.

"There's something else," Bhokken said. "Charnette Tavella has been arrested. The news feeds say she's to be prosecuted for sedition. The trial's in four weeks on Meritan 7."

Jeryn furrowed his brow. "How does that make sense? Why would Jakaan bother with a trial? Why not just make her disappear?"

The Rauk shrugged. "I'm not sure. Maybe she has leverage on him and he can't simply get rid of her. Or perhaps it serves his purposes better to drag her name through the mud, discredit her in public. But as Whitmere said in his message, the new consul minister knows perfectly well the cleric's goals were peace and reconciliation, not rebellion and war. So what does that tell you?"

"That he's not interested in a peaceful solution," Jeryn said. It hardly came as a surprise that Jakaan's hopes for peace were nothing more than lies he'd told his supposed friend Everfeld, no doubt to gain the spymaster's confidence. What a duplicitous snake, that wretched Jakaan.

The Rauk engineer nodded gravely. "I have a feeling he'll deal with the Separatists no less ruthlessly than he dealt with Amarania."

Jeryn could scarcely believe how drastically things had changed in such a short time. How completely the universe had turned itself inside out in a matter of hours.

"And what about the messenger?" he asked. "Did you find anything on him?"

Bhokken shook his head. "I found nothing on the local security feeds."

They had all puzzled over why a stranger had—at great risk to his own safety—helped Everfeld send a message to the *Dagger*. The nameless man himself hadn't provided any explanation for his actions. Jeryn's initial inclination, when he'd first heard the disembodied voice, had been that the whole thing was some sort of ruse, a trick to get the *Dagger*'s crew to emerge from hiding. But the use of the ancient encryption and the transmission's contents had quickly dismissed the idea that the message was a fake. There seemed little doubt Everfeld was the author, though the man who'd relayed it and his reasons for doing so remained a mystery.

Jeryn stood, fixing his companions with a determined look. "We have to free Tavella."

The Rauk lightly elbowed the pilot's arm. "I told you he'd say that. You owe me a hundred credits." The Rauk then said to Jeryn, "I'm with you, but we were discussing this very possibility just now, and my shifter friend thinks it would be a fool's errand."

Marogh's face slightly flushed. "That's not precisely how I expressed it." Then to Jeryn he said, "Consider our current situation. We no longer have the support of the Agency. We are, in fact, fugitives from justice. Given the circumstances, evading apprehension will be problematic enough. But freeing a prisoner from a detention facility on one of the Realm's most secure worlds? This seems well beyond our capability, to put it mildly."

"But we have the *Dagger*," Jeryn countered.

"We do," Marogh said. "And it's truly an amazing vessel. With some luck, it will keep us from the same fate as Sah Tavella."

Jeryn took a step toward Marogh. "You're free to make your

own decision. But whatever odds we're up against, you know they're worse if we go forward without you. Help us finish what the old man started. His cause shouldn't die with him. We can't let it."

The shifter pilot said nothing for a long moment. His expressionless face stared into Jeryn's eyes, then the faintest hint of a smile appeared, and Marogh's eyebrows raised in a small, nearly imperceptible movement. "I find it hard to disagree," he said. Then he glanced at Bhokken and Jeryn in turn. "Count me in, gentlemen."

"And the hundred credits?" Bhokken asked.

"You proposed the wager," Marogh said. "I never agreed to it."

"He cheats at knife sparring too," Jeryn said, tilting his head toward the Rauk.

"This does not surprise me in the least," Marogh said.

Bhokken rolled his eyes at Jeryn. "Are we sure we want him coming along?"

"Yes, we are," Jeryn said.

"Then if you'll excuse me," the pilot said "I should begin working with the ship mind on a viable route to Meritan 7." Marogh left and headed toward the bridge, leaving Bhokken and Jeryn alone.

"I'd like to show you something," the Rauk said, suddenly serious.

"What is it?"

"One of the *Dagger*'s systems."

Confused, Jeryn said, "You already gave me tour, remember?"

"I didn't show you everything," Bhokken said with a knowing smile. "And I believe you'll find this system quite interesting."

When the Rauk got going on some engineering marvel, it took more energy than Jeryn had at the moment to stop him. "All right. Show me."

Bhokken led Jeryn down the *Dagger*'s central corridor, then stopped at a bulkhead and placed his clawed hand against the wall. A hidden bioscanner Jeryn had never seen before glowed briefly to life, then disappeared as the bulkhead yawned open.

"What is this?" Jeryn asked. It was the first time he'd seen this concealed room or compartment or whatever it was. From his angle he couldn't see inside, but a faint blue glow reflected on the bulkhead door.

"Have a look," the Rauk said.

Jeryn tentatively stepped around the corner to peek inside, then drew in a surprised breath.

Whitmere Everfeld stood inside the room. Or at least a holo projection of him.

The faintly flickering image smiled at him and motioned him forward. "Come in, my friend," the holo said. "We have much to talk about."

34

MINDPRINT

"What in the Great Arm is this?" Jeryn asked Bhokken, still staring at the projected, pale-blue image of Everfeld.

"He'll tell you all about it," the engineer said. "When you're finished, the door control is here." The Rauk tapped a red circle on the door's inner panel, then slipped out of the room. The bulkhead closed behind him, leaving Jeryn alone with the holo.

"So I guess this is another message you left us," Jeryn muttered to himself.

"Oh, I'm no message, I assure you," the holo said, startling Jeryn. Holo recordings weren't supposed to answer back.

For a moment he wondered if by some miracle Everfeld had survived, that maybe this was a live comms feed. But almost instantly he discarded the notion. Everfeld's beard was too neatly trimmed. His face was too free of age lines or visible signs of stress. His impeccable clothes were too unwrinkled. This was an idealized image of his late mentor, not a live feed.

"Then what are you?" he asked again. "The ship mind using Everfeld as an avatar?"

"Not quite."

"Then would you care to clue me in on who or what exactly I'm talking to?"

Everfeld furrowed his brow and distractedly scratched his beard. The gesture Jeryn had seen countless times sent a shiver down his spine. It was an old habit of Everfeld's, the *real* Everfeld. What exactly was going on here?

Jeryn glanced around the small room. Aside from the holo projector embedded in the wall, the space looked no different from any other room on the ship. A bit more cramped, maybe. Still, he sensed it was very different from any other place on the *Dagger*.

"What are you?" he asked pointedly.

"I imagine the simplest metaphor is that of a fingerprint. For humans a fingerprint is unique to each individual, as I'm sure you're aware. But that uniqueness can be replicated by something as crude as an ink-stained duplicate or as sophisticated as a modern copy with nanogram-level detail and an individual's genome. In much the same way, the human mind can be replicated, though of course the brain is orders of magnitude more complex than a simple fingerprint."

Jeryn was stunned speechless. Had he just heard that right? The mad trajectory of the last several hours was instantly forgotten. "You're a... this is a... *mindprint* of Everfeld?"

The image clasped its hands behind its back. "Yes, that's exactly what I am. A mindprint of Whitmere Everfeld."

"But mindprints are banned."

"Oh, yes, my existence is quite illegal. This sort of thing has been outlawed since the Sapient Insurrection."

"The Machine War," Jeryn echoed, using the more common term for the historical conflict. In the earliest years of the Realm's existence, humankind and its nonhuman allies had nearly been exterminated by sentient machines who'd revolted against their biological creators. Since that time, there had been a strict ban on the design and manufacture of artificial intelligence, which included the replication of biological cognitive systems like the human brain. Even ship minds, which were among the most advanced cybernetic systems, were little more than calculation devices—extremely advanced ones, to be sure, but ship minds were nowhere close to self-aware or capable of independent thought.

"The CM let you... make a copy of your mind?" Even for a consul minister who had no qualms about thwarting the rules when it suited her, approving something like this, something so forbidden, was unheard of. There were few taboos stronger, few technologies more feared and distrusted than cybernetic intelligence. The tech that had nearly ended biological civilization.

The image chuckled. "Of course not. She would never allow something like myself to be created. She's always had an extreme wariness of advanced technology, especially the experimental and esoteric. She knows nothing of my existence."

As his amazement began to recede, Jeryn realized the image, the *mindprint*, had been speaking about itself and Everfeld as if there was no division between the two. As if it and Everfeld were one and the same.

"Do you think of yourself... as a person?" Jeryn asked.

The entity raised a forefinger in exactly the same way Everfeld often had. It was as creepy as it was astonishing. "Now, there's a question for you," the mindprint said. "One I've been thinking about for some time now. One which I haven't yet answered to my satisfaction. I think of myself as Whitmere Everfeld. I don't think of my memories as someone else's recollections. I recall them as my own: childhood games, schoolmates, important moments in my career. But at the same time I'm fully aware I'm a *copy* of a mind, which means the memories are copies as well. Mere replications of the original. But does that make them any less mine? Or any less real? Memories, even the ones in a biological mind, are little more than replicated perceptions. And as far as cognition, I don't feel my thought patterns are in any way different than my biological source, but then how could I be sure of such a thing? All I can know is my own mind, which means I can only assume it's an accurate replica of Everfeld's."

Jeryn swallowed. The mindprint's ponderous contemplation was a dead ringer for the old man's way of working through a problem by thinking out loud. *Dead ringer*, Jeryn repeated inwardly. The unspoken words prompted an uncomfortable thought.

"Did Bhokken tell you…?" Jeryn struggled to find the right words.

"That I died in the line of duty?" the mindprint said, finishing the thought. "Yes, he informed me a short while ago. It's a rather odd feeling, knowing your original self is gone."

A rather odd feeling, Jeryn repeated inwardly. That seemed to be the mildest possible way of putting it. The mindprint's penchant for understatement, mirroring that of its biological original, only made the entity seem more like the real Everfeld.

A surge of emotion nearly overwhelmed Jeryn. The image before him *was* Everfeld, for all intents and purposes. It looked like him, talked like him. It had his voice, his mannerisms. It was like he wasn't really gone. Like Jeryn hadn't lost him.

But no. This wasn't him. A mindprint was a collection of cybernetic archives, an aggregation of digital algorithms mimicking the processes of a human mind. Everfeld's mind.

"You're uncomfortable with the notion of my existence," the mindprint said. "I can see as much. I'm not entirely comfortable with it myself, to be honest."

"I just…" Jeryn shook his head. "When was this done? And why is Bhokken telling me about you now, of all times?"

The mindprint told him the procedure had taken place a

couple weeks earlier. "The technology is rather new, completely safe, and obviously less than legal. I decided to test it on myself. I thought it might be amusing to challenge myself to a chess match. For security reasons, Bhokken and I decided to store the... to store myself aboard the *Dagger*. As a top-secret vessel I intended to use exclusively for my own travel, I could think of no safer place." The entity then attempted to describe the complex technology and process involved, but it took only a few seconds for Jeryn to become lost in the unfamiliar medical jargon and technobabble. The mindprint apparently sensed this and changed topics to Jeryn's second question.

"As far as telling you," the entity said, "that was my idea, not Bhokken's."

"Your idea?"

"Yes. When your mission took a rather disastrous turn, Bhokken came to me for counsel. You can imagine how astounded I was to learn of everything that had transpired. All the things I failed to anticipate." The entity shook its head regretfully. "We all have our blind spots, but I never imagined mine to be quite so large. I'm so very sorry to have put you all in this predicament."

"You already apologized for it," Jeryn said. "Not that you had to. We all knew what we were getting into."

"Oh, that's where you're mistaken. Had you known, had any one of us known the hazards we were facing, things might not have gone quite so poorly."

Jeryn told the mindprint about Tavella's arrest and her looming trial. The entity listened with great interest. "You must win her release," the entity said, perfectly simulating the real Everfeld's earnestness. "Her work must be allowed to continue."

"We're going to try," Jeryn said.

"Whatever help you need, please don't hesitate to ask."

"Thanks," Jeryn said. "We'll definitely need it."

When the bulkhead door opened behind him a short time later, Jeryn wasn't sure how long he'd been standing there, staring at the floor after the mindprint's holo had faded away.

"You two abolitionists have a nice chat?"

Whirling around to face Bhokken, Jeryn said, "And how did you know about *that*?"

"I'm over a hundred years old. I know a lot of things."

"The old man told you, didn't he?"

Bhokken nodded. "My little hairless slave-liberator. I was so very proud to learn of it."

The Rauk's humor was lost on Jeryn. "Why didn't you tell me about the mindprint before?"

"You didn't need to know," the engineer said, earning the Rauk a harsh glare.

"We were testing novel technology, that's all," Bhokken explained, shrugging. "The mindprint had nothing to do with our mission. We'd even planned to erase it as soon as we finished testing."

Jeryn gasped. "*Erase* it?"

"We *were* going to erase it. But now that Everfeld's...." The Rauk paused for a moment. "Now I wouldn't think of purging it from the *Dagger*'s archives. It would be like losing him all over again."

"It's so much like him," Jeryn said, glancing at the projector node on the wall. "It's unbelievable."

"Yes," the Rauk said, placing his clawed hand on Jeryn's shoulder. "It's like he's still with us."

Jeryn nodded. "It's odd, but yeah, that's exactly what it's like."

"I have good news," the Rauk said. "I just spoke with the Marines, and they're all in. Pezzi-Kaziz's man too. Soldiers live for this kind of situation, you know. An honorable mission with the odds stacked against them. Nothing they love more."

It was definitely good news. So, Jeryn reflected, they were three Marines, one Rauk, a shifter, and a field operative. Even with an amazing vessel, the odds were still stacked against them. Very stacked.

He looked up into Bhokken's eyes. "That's great. But if we're going to do this right, I think we're going to need more help."

The Rauk nodded. "Indeed. Did you have someone in mind?"

Jeryn returned the nod. "As a matter of fact…"

35

AKONO THE XAMORIAN

Violence was coming. Akono could feel it.

The Xamorian mercenary sensed the encounter would be a bloody one, despite any effort he might make to avoid such an outcome. He was no telepath, nor did he possess any powers of foresight, but still he was certain violence, not words, would settle the looming confrontation. After nearly two centuries in his chosen profession, he'd developed a reliable sense about these things.

He abhorred bloodshed, which was admittedly odd, since he made his living by selling his extensive expertise in this area. Though he supposed it was more ironic than odd. But then the path to enlightenment was full of riddles and seeming contradictions, wasn't it? Some he could solve or make sense of, while others would remain forever a confounding mystery. That was the way of the Path. Only the Nameless One had the answers that eluded a mere mortal like himself.

The Xamorian approached the tavern's entryway, walking upright on his hind legs, his tail dragging behind him and leaving a small furrow in the sandy street. His thick muscled body and two-meter height, as it always did, collected wary glances from passersby. The exposed skin of his arms and legs—a slightly duller shade of green than it had been in his younger days—was warmed by Kirok 3's twin suns. Double noon, the locals called this hottest hour of the day. Most of them avoided the heat by staying indoors, but for Akono, on whose tropical homeworld the current temperature would have been considered mild, the sultry heat of double noon was a welcome, warming caress from the skies. One must appreciate the little joys in life. So said the Nameless One.

Pausing outside the tavern's entryway, he heard raucous laughter coming from the other side of the thick metal door. He bowed his head briefly, chanting silently.

The Path lies ahead of me. May I tread it wisely.
The Path lies ahead of me. May I tread it wisely.
The Path lies ahead of me. May I tread it wisely.

Rusty hinges creaked as he pushed open the door and stepped into the crowded, noisy tavern. He slowly stepped forward, his powerful form silhouetted by the brightness outside. As the door squeaked shut behind him, the conversation ebbed, then fell away entirely as patrons took notice of the Xamorian mercenary. Akono's eyes adjusted to the dimly lit space, and he scanned the run-down establishment from wall to wall for Agramont. He didn't see the human, finding only anxious faces staring back at him from every table and barstool.

As he approached the bar, a commotion of scooting chairs and scurrying footsteps erupted as customers abandoned their seats and rushed for the exit. Whatever was coming, they clearly wanted no part of it. By the time Akono reached the bartender's station, only a handful of patrons remained. A few were too drunk to stand and leave. Others were tough-looking types who clearly didn't panic easily. There were five of the latter type, Akono noted.

The Xamorian locked eyes with the bartender, a young human

male. "I don't want any trouble," the human said, hands trembling as he wiped a mug clean with a rag. "Just doing my job here."

"The human Agramont. Where can I find him?"

The bartender tilted his head toward the back of the establishment. Lowering his voice, he said, "Booth in the back corner. But please don't tell him I told you."

Akono reached into his vest pocket, and the bartender's eyes went wide as he dropped both mug and rag to the floor. The Xamorian mercenary didn't remove a pistol from his vest, as the bartender had apparently expected from his reaction, but instead placed a few coins of hard currency on the counter. "For your lost business my appearance seems to have caused," Akono said, referring to the customers who'd absconded in a rush without paying. The young human blinked, staring at the coins until his confusion passed a moment later, then slid them off the counter and dropped them into his pocket.

As Akono stepped away, the human said, his voice barely above a whisper, "He's got people here. Bodyguards."

The Xamorian nodded. "Of course he does." He made his way around the curved bar, spying a booth in the far corner. Smoke wafted upward, exhaled by whoever sat on the other side of the high-backed partition. Akono recognized the scent of Agramont's favorite tobacco.

"Welcome back," the still-unseen tavern owner called, "my Xamorian friend."

The mercenary approached the booth, finding Agramont seated alone, a cigar in one hand, a glass of whiskey in the other. He wore an expensive business suit, its matching cloak folded neatly on the seat beside him. Puffing deeply on his cigar, the tavern owner glanced furtively at the Xamorian's visible weapons, moving his eyes between the sheathed blade on one hip to the holstered plasma pistol on the other.

"Won't you have a seat?"

Akono remained standing. "The money you paid me," he said. "It's been returned to you."

Agramont furrowed his brow and blew smoke. "Returned?"

"Every last credit."

The tavern owner reached for his cloak, and the mercenary quickly moved his hand to his pistol. Agramont, smiling as he clenched the cigar between his teeth, showed the Xamorian his palms. "Easy, my friend. Just getting my terminal." He slowly removed his personal device from a cloak pocket and tapped the screen. A moment passed as he checked his financial holdings, then he gazed up at the mercenary.

"You *did* send it back," the human said, confused. "Why? We had an arrangement."

"I cannot accept payment. You acquired my services under false pretenses."

Agramont took a long draw on his cigar, then smiled devilishly. "Oh, that."

Through a mutual contact, the human had recruited Akono to accompany the movement of fifty tons of hard currency to a tax haven in an adjacent star system. Akono had been offered a handsome payment to ensure the shipment arrived safely and securely at its destination.

When he'd agreed to take on the job, he'd done so reluctantly. The Xamorian had sensed from the start something wasn't quite right about the shipment. He'd felt even less secure about Agramont, a first-time client with a less than reputable standing. But then Akono had dismissed his initial concerns as over-cautiousness, reminding himself very few of his clients *weren't* disreputable.

"Why didn't you tell me from the start what you were really shipping?" Akono asked.

"Would you have agreed, had you known?"

"No."

"Then there you have it." The human puffed smoke. "I needed first-class security on this run, and you were the best I could find on short notice. But you Xamorians sometimes get a bit self-righteous when it comes to certain types of cargo, so I figured what you didn't know wouldn't hurt you."

The fifty tons of coins, as the Xamorian accidentally discovered when a defective container cracked, turned out to be fifty tons of slag, a powerfully addictive narcotic. Widely considered the Realm's most dangerous recreational drug, slag users became hooked after only one or two uses. But worse, the drug's toxicity to most sentient species' internal organs meant that addiction was followed, usually in a handful of months, by an excruciatingly painful death.

"Have you ever seen what it does to people?" the Xamorian asked.

"They tell me it's no picnic," the human said callously, "but that's not my business. I'm just a peddler, friend. Providing supply to satisfy a demand." He blew smoke, this time not bothering to direct it away from the Xamorian. "So goes the free market. Look, I'll send you the money again, this time with a little extra for your hurt feelings. You provided a valuable service, you ought to be paid for it."

"Actually, I didn't provide a service. My portion of our pact wasn't fulfilled. The goods were never delivered. I left the entire load on a plaza in front of a police precinct building."

The human removed the cigar from his mouth. "You did *what*?"

Akono found it difficult not to revel in the human's shock and disbelief. To take pleasure in another's misery was not the way of the Path. But then again, no one was perfect, he chuckled inwardly. The Nameless One had said that too.

"Have you not seen the news feeds from that system?" the

Xamorian asked. "It was quite a local sensation. Largest confiscation in decades, I understand."

Scowling, the human crushed out his cigar on the tabletop and picked up his terminal, tapping it angrily. The mercenary watched as the man pulled up the neighboring system's news feed. Agramont's expression quickly shifted from shock to confusion, then melted into absolute fury. He slammed the terminal down onto the table, smashing it to pieces.

"Kill him!" he roared.

36

DUEL

THE HUMAN WAS QUICKER THAN AKONO HAD EXPECTED. THE booth slid into a hidden recess in the blink of an eye, and Agramont disappeared behind the wall. The tiniest bit of admiration flickered inside the Xamorian. It was a clever escape mechanism. Behind the wall Agramont surely believed he'd avoided his fate and gained the upper hand. Soon enough he'd learn it was only a momentary reprieve.

Drawing his blaster, Akono whirled around and took aim at the main power conduit above the bar he'd noted earlier. He fired once, and after a bright shower sparks, the bar was plunged into complete darkness.

Five. He'd counted five bodyguards when he'd entered. The five who hadn't been scared off by his presence. All five were human. And humans couldn't see in the dark.

"He killed the lights!" one of them shouted.

"Get them back on, now!" another one cried.

A throw of light briefly illuminated the establishment as the front door opened. Akono spied the bartender's silhouette running out of the tavern for the safety of the street. In the small moment before the door closed and darkness returned, he also glimpsed the five bodyguards with their pistols drawn. They hadn't spotted him yet, having turned reflexively toward the sudden brightness from the doorway.

The door latch clicked shut and the tavern was dark once more. In the tense, deathly quiet moments that followed, Akono holstered his weapon, careful not to make any noise. He never used a blaster —such an overpowered, imprecise weapon—when he didn't have to, and right now he didn't have to. He silently unsheathed his blade, then pressed a sequence into the handle's grooves that would disable the kukri's telltale glow. The blade powered up, emitting the characteristic electric crackle the bodyguards wouldn't fail to recognize.

The Path lies ahead of me. May I tread it wisely.

Five blasters fired almost instantly, aiming for the source of the dreaded sound. The plasma bolts hit nothing but the stonework wall, blasting a gaping hole where the tavern's owner had just escaped. Akono had already moved out of the deadly line of fire, silencing his blade as he did so. When the bodyguards stopped firing seconds later, he was directly behind them.

The darkness and quiet returned. Someone whispered, "Did we get him?"

Tk-tk-tk.

The sound pulses of Akono's echolocation clicks, their frequency too high for human ears to detect, bounced off all the tavern's surfaces, creating a three-dimensional model of the establishment's interior in the Xamorian's mind's eye. He saw every chair, every table, every hard and soft surface in the place. Including the human's bodies.

Lunging for the nearest two, his blade made quick work of them. Two hands, fingers still wrapped around blaster handles, fell to the floor, severed at the wrists. Shrieks of pain and horror followed.

In a confused panic, one of the bodyguards whirled around

and fired, hitting both the injured humans, killing them instantly. Again, Akono had already moved well out of the way. He attacked again, his blade movements deadly and precise as he quickly dispatched two more bodyguards and stealthily withdrew into the darkness once more.

Tk-tk-tk.

In his mind's eye, Akono saw the last human standing by the tavern's entrance. Not nearly as panicky as his companions, the human had shrewdly moved to the door, which he now propped open with a chair, bathing the tavern's interior with light and robbing the Xamorian mercenary of his advantage.

Around the bar, somewhat amazingly unharmed, a handful of drunks slept face-down on their tables. Akono glanced over at the hole blasted into the rear of the tavern, where a cloud of dust was still settling. Beyond the opening, Agramont still occupied the booth seat, though now he was almost completely buried, crushed to death under a pile of rubble that moments before had been a stone wall. Only his battered face and one arm were visible. He'd reached the end of his path.

"Your benefactor is dead," the Xamorian said. "You're no longer bound to protect him. Go in peace. I have no quarrel with you."

The human took a long look at his deceased employer, then holstered his weapon. "It's been a long time since I've had a good knife fight," the human said, then removed a blade from a holster sheath inside his vest and powered it up. "Will you do me the honor?"

Ah, Akono reflected, now here was a human who knew his Path. He bowed his head and said, "I will."

The human turned out to be good with a blade. Very good. The Xamorian was forced backward in the first few moments, surprised by his opponent's deft skill and swift movements. Could the human have undergone genetic modifications? Something that made his reflexes quicker?

Akono fought patiently, taking his time, defending and blocking as he studied his opponent's balance, his preferred attack angles, his feints and dodges. The tall, long-armed human had a reach advantage, so the Xamorian would have to rely on counter-attack rather than his usual tactic: overwhelming aggression.

It was like some violent dance: the thrusts and parries, the attacking barrages and sidestepping evasions. Slowly, a pattern became visible in the human's attack, and in that pattern an opening appeared on the left side of his torso. A brief opening, to be sure, for the human had terrific balance and quickness.

The human was good, but he wasn't perfect. And the next time the opening appeared, Akono pivoted and struck the human's leg with his tail, throwing the man's balance off enough to amplify the weakness, creating a larger gap in his opponent's defense. With lightning-fast speed, the Xamorian buried his blade to the hilt in the human's left side, feeling it crunch through the ribcage. A well-placed strike, the blade had surely pierced the heart cavity. The human froze in shock, and Akono quickly yanked out the blade, striking twice more in the same spot. The human collapsed, dead before he hit the floor, his blade clattering away.

The Xamorian powered down his blade and sheathed it. He gave his fallen opponent a small nod, then left the tavern.

Outside in the warmth and brightness, the dusty street was empty. The few locals who could bear the heat of double noon had scattered at the blaster fire coming from inside the tavern.

Or at least the street was nearly empty, the Xamorian reconsidered. A lone cloaked figure, human, stood about twenty meters away, their face obscured by the garment's hood.

"Your Path is quite the noisy one, Xamorian," the figure called as he lowered the hood to reveal his face.

Recognizing Jeryn Lorsi, Akono blinked in disbelief, then smiled. "I thought you didn't believe in the Path."

Jeryn approached, returning the smile. "You haven't seen me in a few years. Maybe I converted."

"Somehow I doubt that." He placed his hand on his chest and bowed his head. "I am pleased to see you, K'san."

"Same here, old friend," Jeryn said.

"Do you still have your blade?" the Xamorian asked.

Jeryn patted the sheath hidden under his cloak. "Don't go anywhere without it, just like you taught me."

"And do you regularly practice your forms and keep in sparring shape?"

The young human nodded. "I do. Just like you taught me."

The answers pleased the Xamorian. "I'm glad to hear you haven't gone lazy on me."

Jeryn craned his neck and looked beyond Akono to the destroyed tavern, smoke wafting up from the entryway. "I have a feeling the police will be here pretty soon."

"So do I," the Xamorian said.

Jeryn tilted his head toward the next street. "I have a ground car. Is there somewhere around here we can talk?"

Later, they stood on a high plateau overlooking the sprawling desert city. As the nearest sun slowly dipped beyond the horizon, Jeryn shared the remarkable story of his last few weeks. For Akono, the political scheming and backstabbing were unsurprising. If his two centuries had taught him anything, it was that the power-hungry, humans and nonhumans alike, were capable of almost anything. Though normally their motivation was fame or money (and often it was both), not vengeance, as was apparently the case with the new consul minister.

When his K'san spoke of his friend, this Everfeld, the Xamorian could feel the pain in his voice. The man had clearly been more to Jeryn than a mere colleague.

"I'm sorry about your friend," he said.

Jeryn nodded, gazing out over the city. "Thanks."

"And what an amazing tale you tell me," Akono said. "I never imagined my K'san would walk among the Realm's most powerful elite."

Blowing out a long breath, Jeryn said, "Neither did I."

The poor human, Akono thought. So much had happened to him in such a short time, yet still somehow he managed to bear it. No, he more than managed it. He'd actually come to embrace it, to accept the heavy responsibility the Path had laid before him. He could have run away and hidden. He could have easily slipped back into the anonymity of his former life. Many would have. But he hadn't.

He was no ordinary human, his K'san.

"Very well," the Xamorian said, "when do we leave?"

The human gave him a surprised look.

Akono inclined his head slightly. "You came here to take me along on your crusade, yes?"

"I did," the young human replied, "but, honestly, now I'm not so sure."

"Because you believe the chances of success are low," Akono said, "and you might be dragging your old Xamorian blademaster into a suicide mission. Something like that?"

"Exactly like that, actually."

The Xamorian chuckled. "My friend, lately I've been collecting pay from some of the least desirable characters in the Realm. Mine has not been the most virtuous existence these last years. Far better than being a slave, to be sure, but perhaps only by a small measure. Then you appear from nowhere, burdened with the weight of a just cause, desperately in need of help to carry it." He slapped Jeryn on the back. "A Xamorian warrior yearns for such adventures."

Jeryn stared at him for a moment, then his human features softened into a relieved smile. "I'm glad to hear that."

"How far is it to Meritan 7?" Akono asked.

"Five gates," his K'san said. "But we have to make one stop before we get there."

The Xamorian lifted his chin. "Someone else you need to pick up? Another warrior?"

"Yes on the picking up part," Jeryn said, "if she's crazy enough to come along, that is. But she's not a warrior. She's a Zatori."

37

IMALLAH THE ZATORI

Her life could have been far worse, Imallah Skyborn reminded herself. Stars, her life *had* been far worse, once upon a time. At least she was her own boss, not some zillionaire's lie-detector-on-a-leash like so many of her kind were. She had a good life. Boring, most definitely, and a bit lonely at times, but still an undeniably good life. One that was her own and no one else's.

On days like today, especially with clients like the pair seated across from her, she had to remind herself of this repeatedly.

The human couple sat on the sofa in Imallah's office, the woman agitated, looking as if she was ready for violence, the man jittery, as if he expected to be backhanded across the mouth by the woman at any moment. The woman, Pippo Beevil, was the man's senior by what Imallah guessed had to be thirty years. Beevil was idle rich, the sole heiress to a trade syndicate fortune in some industry the Zatori counselor had never committed to memory. She was also Imallah's best-paying client. So there was that.

"Tell me," Beevil demanded, pounding her fist on the sofa's arm, causing her partner to flinch. "I want you to tell me, right now!"

It was the sixth, no, seventh, repetition of the same consultation over as many months. The only thing that changed was the young man seated next to the heiress, who collected lovers less than half her age like someone else might select dishes at a buffet, sampling a bit of this and a bit of that. Her initial infatuations were always followed by bouts of jealousy that culminated in yet another visit to Imallah's business suite, where the obsessed woman would demand to know if her most recent conquest had been unfaithful.

They almost always had been, of course. And though the empath in Imallah hated to reduce sentient beings to such singular and base motivations, the woman's poorly chosen partners could only be called greedy hustlers, scheming insects drawn to the bright light of Beevil's wealth and privilege.

Imallah sighed. There had been a time when she'd cared, actually cared, about any and all who came to see her, no matter what their reason, no matter what their faults. Every living thing, sentient or otherwise, even greedy hustlers and jealous rage monsters, had inherent worth and deserved understanding. These were the most deeply held values of her kind, the Zatori. When had she lost them? When had she become so disillusioned? Or was this a transitory mood? Maybe she was simply still in mourning, the recent news of Whitmere Everfeld's death still hanging heavily on her heart.

"Are you listening to me?" the woman said, leaning forward, her cheeks flushed with anger.

"My apologies," Imallah said, holding up a hand. "I was focusing my powers." *Her powers*. The words sounded ridiculous to the Zatori's ears, but she'd found overly dramatic language, like the kind used by carnival fortune tellers, seemed to have a taming effect on the woman's temper. Thankfully, the woman calmed down a bit.

Beevil, like so many of her species, thought of Imallah's kind as mind readers, but perceptive empathy—the innate Zatori talent for reading emotional and psychological states—was not telepathy. Imallah often had to remind her clients of this distinction.

The Zatori stood up from her own chair, her small stature barely taller than the seated couple, and made a show of pacing slowly back and forth. She distractedly stroked her left horn, drawing gawking stares from both pairs of human eyes. The pair of small, bony cranial protrusions enclosed the cerebral outgrowths—extrasensory extensions of the parietal lobe—that gave Imallah's kind their perceptive powers. And while even those casually familiar with the Zatori knew their unique talents were grounded in well-understood biology, most humans still viewed the backward-sweeping, fawn-like horns with childlike wonder, as if the lavender-skinned, pointy-eared aliens were nymphs from some strange magical land.

Imallah fixed the fidgety young man with an unblinking stare from her large amber eyes. She'd sensed his guilt and fear of being found out the moment they'd entered the suite. There seemed little doubt he'd fooled around; cheaters exuded an aura of culpability that was as distinctive as the stink of rotting garbage. But she couldn't just come out and say as much before they'd even sat down. She had to justify her exorbitant fees, after all. So she'd listened patiently to the woman's all too predictable story, enduring a very long half-hour of shrill accusations and sputtering denials. And now Imallah played the mystic, summoning her exotic powers to pry the truth from the man's consciousness.

The man was clearly guilty of infidelity. Between the bullets he was sweating and his unconvincing denials, you hardly had to be an empath to figure this one out.

Stars, what a way to make a living.

Turning to the woman, she said, "You can rest easy, my dear friend. He has shared himself only with you." She raised an eyebrow at the young man. "And I sense a great deal of genuine affection emanating from him. You should consider yourself a very lucky woman."

In the moments that followed, as the heiress's demeanor shifted from anger to shock to teary-eyed relief, Imallah puzzled over why she'd been untruthful to the woman. She'd never lied to a client before, regardless of whether her insights would bring about joy or disappointment. It had been a point of pride that she'd never held back the truth. A line she'd refused to step over. And now that she finally had, she didn't even understand why.

Falling stars, she needed a change. And not ten minutes after she'd bid a good afternoon to her overjoyed client and her thoroughly confused-yet-relieved boy toy, change came knocking.

She opened the door and gasped at the surprise visitor standing in the hallway. The best surprise she'd had in ages.

"Dearest Jeryn! I don't believe it!" She leapt up and joyfully wrapped her arms around her old friend's neck. He caught her, holding her fast, her feet dangling well above the floor as she clung to him.

After a long embrace that cured whatever ill she'd been feeling up until that moment, he gently lowered her to the floor. It was then she noticed his Xamorian companion a short distance away, watching them from the elevator doors.

She shifted her gaze back to Jeryn, his face held between her lavender hands. "What in the Great Arm are you doing here, Jer?"

38

LEAVING TAU BONNA 12

Jeryn sat next to Imallah in the *Dagger*'s shuttle. The Zatori's slippered feet dangled from the copilot's seat, not quite touching the floor, even at the chair's lowest setting. She was normal height by her race's standards, which was two-thirds that of the average human's. A single braid of cobalt-blue hair reached halfway down her back, and her lavender skin contrasted sharply against the white of her sleeveless tunic. The same intricate leaf design, woven in golden thread, adorned both tunic and slippers. Imallah had discarded her heavy cloak as soon as she'd boarded the shuttle, telling Jeryn she loathed the confining body-length, head-concealing garment. She only wore it out of necessity to disguise herself in public. A Zatori who walked around unmasked in broad daylight was asking for trouble.

Except among the privileged few who valued their services, Zatori were almost universally feared and despised throughout the Realm. Even on the least xenophobic worlds, their presence was barely tolerated, and with no small amount of wariness. On the less accepting planets it wasn't uncommon for Zatori to be attacked on sight, their very existence considered profane.

Amber-eyed purple-skinned demons who'd read your thoughts, who'd seduce your partner with mind control or manipulate you like some helpless puppet on a string. Every bit of it nonsensical paranoia. The perceptive powers of Imallah's kind were entirely passive. Even the most talented Zatori could no more control someone else's mind than Jeryn could.

They'd nearly cleared the gravity well of Tau Bonna 12, Imallah's home for the last few years and the most populous of the forty moons orbiting the system's lone gas giant.

"Was it terribly out of your way, coming here?" she asked.

"Actually, it wasn't," Jeryn replied. "Tau Bonna's directly in our gate path to the Meritan system. The Kirok system too."

"Kirok?" the empath echoed. "Is that where you stopped to pick up your Xamorian friend?" She tilted her head to the closed cockpit door behind them. Minutes earlier, Akono had excused himself to practice his daily meditations.

"That's right," Jeryn said. "I knew him before I came to the Agency. It was a bit of good luck you both happened to be on our way." He recalled wondering whether either of them would agree to come along, having little hope both would sign up for such a foolhardy endeavor. He was glad to have been proved wrong.

"He strikes me as a calm, peaceful soul," Imallah noted. "Unusual, given his line of work, don't you think?"

Jeryn smiled. "You haven't been around many Xamorians, have you?"

"No, I haven't," she confessed.

"They tend to be more spiritually inclined than most races," he explained. "And he falls on the more devout end of the spectrum."

"Ah," she said, lifting a finger, "now I remember. The warrior god of Xamor, who wanders the heavens righting the wrongs of the universe."

"Right," Jeryn said, "The Nameless One."

"And how long did it take to convince him to come along on this little adventure?"

"About as long as it took you."

Which was to say not long at all. Imallah had agreed to help free the cleric as soon as she learned the truth behind the alarming political news of late.

Similar to Jeryn's own experience, she'd been personally recruited by Everfeld, although he'd never learned under what circumstances, nor did he know much about her pre-Agency life. Over the time they'd known one another, Imallah had revealed little about her personal history, which made him suspect it hadn't been a very pleasant one. And as someone with his own questionable history, who understood the desire to keep the past in the past, he'd always respected her boundaries.

In his earliest days as an Agency analyst, they'd worked together often as an interrogation team. When an Agency plant in some black-market operation needed to be debriefed, Jeryn had the expertise to ask the right kinds of questions, and Imallah had the ability to sort truth from lie. The pair had worked well together, and in time their office relationship blossomed into a personal friendship. Around the time Jeryn made the transition from analyst to field operative, she'd had a falling-out with Everfeld and left the Agency. And though Jeryn had kept in touch with her since then, he'd never learned the details behind her resignation, sensing it to be a sore subject. Now he wondered if her decision to come along meant she regretted leaving, that she was trying to make up for abandoning the old man.

"I never told you why I left the Agency," she said. "Would you like to know?"

Feeling suddenly exposed, Jeryn snapped his gaze to the Zatori. "Were you reading my thoughts just now?"

Imallah made a face like she'd just tasted something bitter. "Did you really just ask me that?"

Jeryn showed his palms. "Sorry. Yes, yes, I know, you're not a mind reader. All right, tell me then. Why did you leave? I've always wanted to know."

The Zatori's features faded into sadness, her elf-like ears drooping slightly. "I didn't think Everfeld was doing enough to steer the CM away from her worst tendencies," she said wistfully. "She was heading down the wrong path, a terrible path, and none of those fawning yes-people surrounding her did a thing to stop her, or even try to dissuade her." She paused for a moment. "I grew more and more frustrated with the situation. Then I got angry, and then I left."

And now she wished she hadn't. She didn't need to say it out loud. Jeryn saw it in her remorseful expression, and there was no mistaking the regret in her voice. He'd been right about her reasons for coming along.

"Well, if it's any consolation," Jeryn offered, "Minister Amarania's been taken out of the game, so to speak."

"Not that it changes things much," Imallah said. "Based on what you told me, if anything the situation's worse now. This new CM might be more of a warmonger than the last one."

"That's pretty much what Bhokken said."

"And he's right. That old dog's no fool."

"I wouldn't call him 'old dog' to his face if I were you," Jeryn suggested.

She laughed, waving him off. "I've known him far longer than you have. I can get away with it."

Minutes later in the *Dagger*'s shuttle bay, Imallah was greeted by the Rauk engineer's sharp-toothed smile and smothering embrace. Longtime friends and colleagues together again, a furry giant and a lavender-skinned elf. Despite the circumstances, it warmed Jeryn's heart to see his friends reunited once more. But there was a sweet sadness to the moment, a painful awareness of who was absent from the gathering.

Jeryn blew out a breath, shifting his thoughts to what lay ahead of them, to the impossible assignment they'd tasked themselves with. The Meritan star system, where Tavella had been moved to await her trial for sedition, was two weeks and three gates away.

39

PLANNING THE OP

THE *DAGGER*'S CREW GATHERED IN THE LARGER OF THE FRIGATE'S two meeting rooms. Though larger didn't necessarily mean roomy, at least not with eight people sitting elbow to elbow around the oval tabletop. Thankfully, the Zatori took up little space, which couldn't be said for the large-bodied Rauk and Xamorian or the well-muscled trio of Marines.

Jeryn began. "So what do we know about this facility where they have the cleric?"

Marogh tapped the display control. A holo appeared, floating just above the tabletop, depicting a ten-story building with the unmistakably austere, function-over-form design of a detention facility.

"A jail if ever I saw one," said Cross, the ex-Marine who'd helped Jeryn escape from Sandau Prime.

"It's not very big," Jeryn noted, narrowing his eyes. "For a prison, I mean."

"Technically, it's not a prison," Bhokken said. "They house no long-term inmates there. It's a temporary holding facility for detainees awaiting trial. The Ministry of Justice complex is five kilometers away."

"So if it's not a prison," the Zatori asked, "does that mean it's less secure?"

"Not at all," the shifter pilot replied. "It is, in fact, far more secure than most prisons, since only the Realm's most dangerous and high-profile cases are tried on Meritan 7."

Marogh had clearly done his homework. He manipulated the holo image, deftly removing the building's exterior, revealing over a dozen primary and backup security systems.

"How did you get all this?" one of the Marines asked. "Isn't this top-secret info or something?"

"The *Dagger* has extensive archives," the shifter said. "Many of which are classified."

Jeryn smiled inwardly. The old man hadn't missed a thing when he'd constructed his ultimate spy ship.

"Have you found a way in?" another Marine asked. "Some weakness we can take advantage of?"

"Oh, it's quite impregnable," the pilot said in a matter-of-fact tone. "I've studied the layout, the personnel rotation, security systems, and the entire complex on which the facility stands. There's simply no way an unauthorized individual or group of individuals could gain entry."

Cross, the Marine-turned-operative who apparently had some knowledge of security systems, was more than a bit skeptical, and he pressed Marogh with question after question.

"What about cutting the power?" Cross asked.

"They have independently powered backups that would rival a power generation facility's."

"And if we blow out a wall?"

"With anything less than a plasma cannon, which unfortunately we do not possess, I'm afraid that would be impossible. The energy and kinetic absorption capabilities of the outermost structure are quite effective against conventional explosives."

The ex-Marine grew more impatient with each response from

the shifter pilot. Finally, Cross grunted in frustration and slumped back in his chair, folding his arms across his chest.

"Hate to admit it," the Marine snorted, "but I think our pilot's right. The place looks just about impenetrable."

"Even the strongest chains have their weakest link," Akono said. "We simply have to find it."

The ex-Marine shot the Xamorian a sharp look. "A geck proverb's not going to get us in there. But if you've got some substance to offer, pal, go right ahead."

The sudden epithet, and the alarmingly casual way it had been uttered, stunned the room. An awkward quiet filled the uncomfortably tight space, which to Jeryn now felt even tighter and more uncomfortable. *Geck* was short for gecko, a kind of lizard. The four-letter word was how bigots referred to Xamorians. Jeryn had heard the term countless times in many systems, but before now he'd never heard it uttered to a Xamorian's face.

Jeryn glanced over at Akono, who betrayed no outward sign of offense and, thankfully, hadn't yanked one of Cross's arms out of its socket. Xamorians in general were slow to anger, and Jeryn was relieved to find Akono living up to this particular standard. The last place he wanted to be was stuck between an ex-Marine and an angry Xamorian engaged in hand-to-hand combat.

"If we are to be allies on this mission, Soldier Cross," the Xamorian said stoically, "perhaps we should behave like it."

Cross said nothing, and after a moment Bhokken broke the tension. "Friends, we're all anxious about the difficult task before us. But we must not fight among ourselves." He then looked squarely at the ex-Marine. "This is a voluntary mission, sir. If you'd rather not work alongside nonhumans, now would be the time to part our company."

Everyone stared at Cross, his arms still folded across his barrel of a chest. The moment seemed to drag on, but Jeryn realized it was probably only a few seconds before the man replied.

"No, I'm in," he said gruffly, still refusing to meet the Xamorian's stare. "I'm definitely in."

"Good," the Rauk said evenly, "we need all the help we can get."

Jeryn brought the topic back around to the job. "Look, if this place is so hard to break into, then maybe we shouldn't try to. At some point they're going to move her, right? They have to for the trial. That could be our chance." He turned to Bhokken. "You said the Ministry of Justice is five Ks away, right? Do we know how they normally move prisoners from the detention center to court?"

"There's a dedicated underground rail line," Marogh said, "running between the two complexes." He tapped the holo controls and brought up a schematic of the rail tunnel. Extensive archives indeed, Jeryn reflected.

"That could work," Jeryn said, suddenly hopeful. "That could definitely work."

One of the Marines leaned forward. "So we pick a good spot to hide and wait for them to pass by."

"And then we ambush them," his colleague added. The two Marines nodded in approval.

"Yes, it might be our best chance," the Rauk said.

"All right," Jeryn said, standing up and leaning toward the image. "Now, here's what I'm thinking…"

Over the next few hours the group hammered out a rough plan, taking Jeryn's idea and shaping it into the executional details of timing, movements, and contingencies. Jeryn guided the discussion, and though Bhokken technically outranked him, the Rauk didn't seem to mind ceding his authority to his human colleague. When they finished, the resulting scheme mostly reflected Jeryn's input—he was, after all, something of an expert in escaping custody—though everyone had made contributions. Even the ex-Marine Cross joined in, shedding his earlier leeriness and offering several points of helpful feedback.

The eight agreed to a daily review of the operation until they reached Meritan 7, then called it a night. It was well past midnight Realm Mean Time, the ten-hour day synchronized to Gran Kiravashta's dateline meridian. The tired departed for their cabins, and the tired-but-hungry headed for the galley. Jeryn, Bhokken, and Imallah lingered behind in the meeting room. The floating schematic of the underground train tunnel slowly rotated above the table.

Staring at it, Jeryn said, "I'm going to see that in my sleep until all this is over with."

"I think we all will," the Rauk said. The engineer then turned to the Zatori. "Should we be concerned about the Marine's commitment?" He didn't bother to specify which Marine he was talking about. She knew he was referring to Cross.

"He has a problem with nonhumans," she said, her amber eyes blinking.

"That was pretty obvious," Jeryn said. He turned off the display.

"Which makes him," Imallah added, "no different from a great many of his species. With the stress of our situation he temporarily lost his composure, revealing a prejudice normally kept in check by social norms."

"Pressure brings out the worst in some," the Rauk reflected aloud.

"None of us are perfect, truth be told," Bhokken said as he stood up, the top of his head nearly touching the ceiling. "Now then, are you ready?" he asked the Zatori. "Or would you like to get a night's sleep first?"

"I'm not sure," Imallah said. She turned to Jeryn. "Did you find the mindprint… emotionally taxing?"

Earlier, Jeryn and Bhokken had disclosed the entity's existence to the Zatori, who'd been as close to Everfeld as either of them had, her Agency exodus notwithstanding. Marogh, as Jeryn had recently learned, had known about the mindprint since they'd picked him up on Dorix-Natani. Everfeld had apparently informed him shortly after the pilot had boarded the *Dagger*.

"It's a bit..." Jeryn had a hard time finding the right words to answer his friend's question.

But then he didn't really have to. Imallah sensed what he was feeling far more accurately than any words he could use to describe it. Words were abstractions, she'd once told him. They were vibrations of the larynx that *attempted* to represent what a Zatori could detect with far more precision. Words were poor substitutes for the thing they represented, according to Imallah. An out-of-focus image that failed to capture an oil painting's details and subtle color variations.

Her gaze fixed on Jeryn, the Zatori slowly nodded. "I see," she murmured. Then she turned to the Rauk. "I think I should get some sleep first."

The Rauk placed his hand on Imallah's shoulder. "You don't have to see him at all, you know. If you believe the experience will be too distressing."

She smiled and patted his hand. "Thank you, old friend. I do want to see him." Jeryn noticed she said *him* and not *it*.

Her eyes then went sad, but the smile remained, giving her a wistful expression. "When I left the Agency, we weren't on the best terms. I never had the chance to tell him goodbye."

40

MERITAN 7

AGENCY OPERATIVES DIDN'T USE COMBAT ARMOR. THE JOB SIMPLY never called for it. For the most part, espionage involved non-confrontational activities. Subterfuge and surveillance were an operative's stock-in-trade, not guns and violence. And while an operative might have the rare occasion of frenzied activity, as Jeryn had experienced during his near-disastrous op in the Primus system—a mission which now seemed like it had happened years ago instead of weeks—fieldwork for the Agency was generally about as un-soldierly as a career in accounting or some clerical field.

Case in point: prior to the last several days of hours-long training sessions, Jeryn had never been in an armored combat suit before. The suit was big, adding considerable girth, weight, and height to his bodily frame, but even with its bulk the unit was remarkably nimble. He'd been pleasantly surprised to find no noticeable reduction in the range of motion of his elbows, shoulders, and knees, and there was no loss of dexterity in his gauntleted hands. The suit's operating system was intuitive, well-designed, and generally easy to use, but there was still a steep learning curve of systems and subsystems that tested the limits of

Jeryn's ability to retain information. Most Marines had weeks of boot camp training and mock battle scenarios to develop combat armor expertise. Jeryn had only days.

Under the watchful supervision of the Marines and Bhokken, who'd helped develop some of the systems on the state-of-the-art combat gear (was there any tech the Rauk *wasn't* an expert in?), Jeryn had gradually acquired a sort of basic competence. No professional soldier would consider him anywhere close to fully trained, but at least he knew enough to take care of himself if things got dicey, and hopefully not shoot a shipmate in the process.

He checked the chrono on his forearm plating. Ten minutes to go-time.

The *Veiled Dagger* carried two smaller ships inside its twin bays. One was the shuttle, which Jeryn had both piloted and been a passenger in. The other, which he sat in now for the first time, was the *Dagger*'s drop ship. The shuttle was used mostly for ship-to-ship transport in the vacuum of space, but it also doubled as a planetary descent vessel. If you wanted a comfortable, smooth, somewhat slow atmospheric reentry, and you didn't mind being detected by air traffic scanners, the shuttle was the way to go. But if you needed to get to the ground quickly and covertly, you took the drop ship (or DS, as the Marines called it). A specialized descent vessel, the DS had an impressive array of stealth tech to evade detection from surface-based tracking stations. But what the sleek, purpose-built DS gained in a fast, stealthy descent it gave up in comfort. For some, reentry in a DS was a stomach-churning, nearly unbearable experience. For others, it was a rough, bumpy ride, but tolerable. Having never taken a ride in a DS before, Jeryn didn't know which category he fit into.

The DS bay bustled with activity as the *Dagger*'s crew ran weapons and armor diagnostics and readied themselves for the drop to Meritan 7. Two days earlier, the *Dagger* had passed through the local interstellar gate, fully cloaked and undetected, the same way it had passed through every gate since the escape from Sandau Prime. By now the grievously criminal act of traversing an interstellar gate without following standard approval protocols had become almost routine.

The previous ten days had been a repeated cycle of mission prep and combat training, interspersed with meals and sleep. Unsurprisingly, the trio of Marines adapted easily to the *Dagger*'s new daily regimentation. Even Cross, whose xenophobic outburst had thankfully gone unrepeated, seemed to loosen up a bit with the military-style routine.

Professional soldiers were an odd lot, Jeryn reflected, watching them prep their weapons. As the high-risk mission had grown closer, Jeryn and his fellow non-military shipmates had become more tense and anxious. But the mood of the three Marines had moved in the opposite direction. They'd swapped war stories, laughing and joking, and like children with new toys they'd cheerfully marveled over the *Dagger*'s combat armor and weaponry, the most advanced battle gear they'd ever seen. They were in their element, getting ready for battle, contented and completely at ease. Jeryn found himself filled with equal parts admiration and envy. Admiration at their lighthearted grace under pressure. Envy for their apparent freedom from the anxiety tying up his own insides in knots.

He spied Imallah standing apart from her busy shipmates, her diminutive silhouette a short distance away, just beyond the bay's airlock doors. She waved at him, smiled. He waved back.

She'd had only one brief visit with Everfeld's mindprint and, like Jeryn, she'd found the experience a bit unsettling. Their reactions had bewildered Bhokken, who wasn't bothered in the least by the cybernetic ghost. Marogh's response to the mindprint had fallen somewhere in the middle of his companions' extremes.

He'd found the technology at once fascinating and odd, but not disturbingly so.

As Jeryn finished his suit's diagnostic checks, Akono the Xamorian approached. "The time has come, K'san. Are you ready?"

Jeryn stood with his helmet between his hands, his taller, armored self almost at eye level with the towering Xamorian. "I'd be crazy if I said I was," he replied, then smiled and shrugged. "But I guess I'm going anyway."

The Xamorian nodded in approval. "Good." He glanced down at Jeryn's armor. "You have your blade in there somewhere, I hope?"

Jeryn tapped his thigh, and his kukri's handle sprang forth from a hidden compartment. "Wouldn't think of going without it." Since being reunited, the pair had made time for a few sparring sessions, and the Xamorian had been pleased to find Jeryn's fighting skill hadn't diminished since he'd joined the Agency.

"Nor would I," Akono said, touching the handle of his own blade, sheathed at his hip. His *un-armored* hip, Jeryn noted. Unlike himself and the others who'd soon be hurtling toward the surface of Meritan 7, the Xamorian would have no protective combat armor. Designed for human use, the suits were far too small to accommodate Akono's large reptilian frame and two-meter-long tail. The Xamorian would be very well armed during the op, carrying his blade, two pistol blasters, and a multi-purpose combat rifle, but he'd be wearing only the baldric of his warrior clan, a woven garment with zero protective value, and comms gear on his head.

Bhokken appeared behind the Xamorian and placed a hand on Akono's shoulder. "If you come under heavy fire," the Rauk said, nodding toward Jeryn, "just grab this little hairless ape and use him as a shield."

Akono nodded. "A clever tactic, my Rauk friend. I'll keep that in mind."

Jeryn shook his head in mock irritation, though inwardly he was pleased to see the two of them sharing a joke, even if it was at his expense. To his pleasant surprise, the Xamorian and the Rauk had taken an instant liking to one another. Jeryn had worried they wouldn't get along, or at least not get along well. They were different in so many ways. One was an engineer who—despite his traditional deference to his race's pantheon—placed the largest portion of his faith in science and mathematics and physics. The other was a devout wanderer seeking enlightenment, walking a metaphysical path. But the pair shared a tightly aligned sense of right and wrong, of good and bad, and the two old souls seemed to recognize this in one another. After only ten days in each other's company, you would have thought they'd known each other for years.

He'd also been pleased to find Akono wasn't put off or intimidated by Imallah's presence, unlike the three human Marines (especially Cross, who'd exit the room at the first glimpse of lavender skin).

But whatever good cheer had been brought about by the reunion with his longtime friends, the feeling had been overshadowed by the task looming before them, an ominous storm cloud moving ever closer. And now it had arrived.

The shifter stood nearby, fully suited up except for his helmet, and he watched the results of his gear diagnostics flicker on a small holo projected from his forearm plate. Normally, Marogh would have remained in orbit with the ship, but for this op the plan called for the Rauk to stay behind. The vessel was capable of autonomous flight, of course, but no one wanted to risk leaving the invaluable starship uncrewed. The Zatori, who abhorred violence and whose tiny frame wouldn't have fit in the combat armor anyway, would also stay with the ship. If and when they managed to bring the cleric Tavella back to the *Dagger*, they'd need her talents to see the truth beyond any semantic tricks and maneuvers. To make sure for themselves the cleric's motives were indeed what the old man's final message claimed they were.

"Did the second print fit better?" Jeryn asked Marogh, recalling how the first printed batch of the pilot's mission clothing had been a bit snug.

The shifter looked up from the small holo. "Yes, it did," he replied, then frowned. "But I must confess I find the shirt less than comfortable."

Jeryn nodded in sympathy. New clothes fresh out of the printer were often stiff and scratchy.

One of the Marines, a woman named Lessandra, approached the trio. "Suit and weapons all good?" she asked Jeryn, glancing over his armor and weapons with the practiced scrutiny of a veteran soldier. He nodded and gave her a thumbs-up. "All good."

"Outstanding," she said, her tone even and businesslike. She then moved on to her fellow Marines and Marogh, repeating the same exchange.

The weapons and gear were ready, the drop ship prepped. It was time to go.

The Rauk wished the team good luck, and the Marines boarded the DS first, clomping up the ramp in their heavy suits. Marogh and Akono followed close behind. Entering the DS last, Jeryn paused at the top of the ramp, waved to Imallah, and exchanged a nod with Bhokken. He turned and entered the vessel, the ramp door closing behind him with a loud clank.

Next stop: Meritan 7.

41

TREETOP VIEW

Despite his massive suit of combat armor, Jeryn felt very small on Meritan 7, a world of dense tropical forests filled with towering, thick-trunked trees, the tallest reaching over a hundred meters in height. He'd never seen flora so huge. Even the smallest plants at ground level were three meters tall, with leaves larger than Jeryn's head. And he couldn't recall ever having seen so many shades of green at the same time. Fauna also abounded, from the buzzing insects on the jungle floor to the avian fliers gliding in lazy circles high above the tree canopy. They hadn't run into any of the planet's large mammalian predators, though the scanners in their suits had detected a few, all of them more than a kilometer distant. Thankfully, none had been in the mission team's direct path.

The ride down from orbit hadn't been as rough as Jeryn had expected. Bumpy, for sure, but bearably so. And the drop ship apparently hadn't been detected by any ground-based air control stations. Until today, the DS's stealth tech had only been tested under controlled conditions, so when the vessel had descended without being hailed over the comms by local authorities or surrounded by police cruisers upon touching down, even the unflappable Marines had been visibly relieved.

They landed before dawn, twenty kilometers from the detention facility, setting the DS down in a remote corner of an enormous hunting preserve adjacent to the facility's grounds. Takeoffs and landings of wealthy hunters' private vessels—many of them colossal yachts that dwarfed the *Dagger*'s drop ship—were a frequent occurrence from within the preserve's boundaries, making the location an ideal landing spot. The downside was the distance to the facility, which would take just under an hour to travel on foot. The suits could move quickly, capable of longer-than-humanly-possible bounding strides, and if not for the thick foliage slowing them down, they could have traversed the distance in mere minutes. But with impassably dense copses of trees and vegetation, traveling in a straight line at ground level was impossible. Still, they moved along at a decent clip. And quite impressively, the unsuited Xamorian kept pace with his companions, never once lagging behind.

As they zigzagged their way through the filtered light of the jungle floor, Jeryn tried not to think about how vulnerable they were to an assault from above. If an airship appeared and targeted them, they'd be the proverbial fish in a barrel. Even through the leaf canopy's thick blanket of cover, a ship's targeting sensors could track them quite easily. And while their combat armor could shield them from handheld arms and grenade shrapnel, it was no match for an airship's plasma cannon or railguns. He'd seen what those weapons could do to a spacefaring vessel; he didn't want to imagine what they would do to a person-sized target.

Minutes later they arrived at their first checkpoint, a location just beyond the detention facility's outermost security perimeter. As planned, the six split up into their prearranged groups, heading off in three different directions. The trio of Marines formed the first group, Jeryn and Akono the second, and the solo Marogh was the third.

As the others headed off into the brush, Jeryn and the Xamorian found a suitable tree, tall and wide-trunked with a large expanse of thick branches far up in the jungle's canopy. Akono went up first, scaling the rugged bark with remarkable ease, covering a hundred vertical meters in seconds. Jeryn followed shortly after, ascending at a much slower pace, using the suit's inbuilt winch and the reinforced line Akono had lowered down to him.

"Welcome to the treetops," Akono said when Jeryn finally reached their perch, over a hundred meters above the ground.

They settled in, straddling a pair of thick branches, the leafy, sunlit canopy a few meters above their heads. His vision enhanced by the helmet visor's embedded optics, Jeryn watched the detention center's main building, where they believed the cleric was being held. The Xamorian did the same, though in lieu of armor-enhanced sight he peered through his rifle's detached scope. Around them the jungle was a noisy din of chirping insects, shrieking birds, and the screeching long-armed primates Jeryn glimpsed now and again swinging effortlessly through the thick maze of branches.

"It's time to check in with the others, K'san," Akono said.

Jeryn confirmed as much with a quick check of his chrono. He opened the team's comms channel and said, "You see any Banka deer your way?"

"A few droppings, that's about it," replied Cross. "Nothing else."

"Nothing here either," Marogh chimed in.

Jeryn closed the connection and nodded to Akono. "They're in position."

It had been Bhokken's idea to use keyword-coded communication instead of encrypted transmissions, since the latter would almost certainly arouse suspicion in the facility's comms personnel. Again, the preserve provided the perfect cover with its near-constant chatter between hunting parties. As long as the team stuck to the hunting-related keywords they'd all memorized, their comms would most likely go unnoticed. And if the facility's personnel *did* bother to listen in on them, they'd hear only the innocuous banter of wealthy weekend hunters.

With everyone in position, now the waiting game began. This phase of the mission could last minutes or hours—they weren't really sure. They knew the *date* of the cleric's formal arraignment, which was today, but they didn't know the exact time she'd be moved from the detention facility to the Ministry of Justice. During their prep work, they'd learned detainee transfers didn't occur at a consistent hour, though they always happened on the same day as the arraignment. Jeryn checked his chrono, then peered once more at the facility. A trickle of early-morning employees passed through security gates and entered the multi-building complex, followed a few minutes later by an exodus of roughly the same number. The day workers beginning their shifts, the night workers ending theirs.

They watched and waited high above the jungle floor, their perch hidden by the Xamorian's hurriedly assembled but thoroughly concealing blind of leaves and branches. An hour passed, then another. Once every half hour they checked in with the others, all still waiting and holding their positions like Jeryn and Akono. Beads of condensation formed on Jeryn's visor, beyond which the jungle forest grew hotter and more humid as the morning dragged on. He gave a silent thanks for his suit's climate-controlled interior.

"Lovely weather on this world," Akono commented. "Like a cool winter's morning on Xamor. Though I imagine you would find it a bit stifling."

"If by stifling you mean sweating profusely from every pore in my body, then yes, I'd have to—"

The forest erupted in a deafening shriek. In the treetops all around them, hundreds of screeching birds of all sizes and colors simultaneously abandoned the forest canopy and took to the air. Startled, Jeryn nearly fell from the branch as he groped for his rifle. Akono quickly reached over and steadied him with a strong hand.

"What in the Great Arm is happening?" Jeryn said, powering up his firearm.

Before the Xamorian could say anything, they heard the whine of an airship's engines. The distant sound grew louder, quickly becoming a roar that filled the air and shook the massive trees. Jeryn and Akono clutched onto their respective branches as the airship passed directly overhead, flying at an altitude far too low for Jeryn's liking. The entire forest around them became a storm of wind and noise. Branches swayed violently and thousands of leaves fell from overhead, shaken free and spiraling down to the ground far below.

The worst of it passed quickly, and seconds later an eerie silence fell over the forest. Leaves floated to the ground like dust motes in the filtered sunlight. Between gaps in the canopy's still-swaying branches, Jeryn's heart sank as he watched the airship slowly descend and land on top of the detention facility's main building.

"Oh, no," he said. Were they moving Tavella between facilities by *airship*, not via the train as Jeryn and his rescue team had counted on? Was the plan falling apart before his eyes?

"It might not be here for her," the Xamorian said, apparently having the same thought.

Jeryn frowned, watching as the distant airship's boarding ramp lowered and the crew exited the craft.

Bloody stars, this was bad. If they transported Tavella via

airship, there was nothing they could do other than shoot the ship out of the sky, which wasn't an option because it kind of defeated the whole purpose of a rescue.

And once the cleric was inside the Justice building, she'd be all but untouchable within its secured, impenetrable walls. The pessimist in Jeryn had imagined more than a few losing scenarios, most of them involving the mission team being hopelessly outgunned in a firefight or getting trapped in the stairwell. He hadn't counted on the whole mission falling apart before it had even started in earnest. But that's exactly what was happening.

And then it wasn't.

"We just spotted a herd of deer on the move," Cross announced over the comms. Code for they were moving the cleric to the train. The train, *not* the airship.

Jeryn felt a surge of excitement as Akono, who'd also heard the Marine, clapped his hands and said, "Time for us to move, K'san."

They scrambled down the massive tree, Jeryn rappelling via the same line he'd used to come up. Akono, again using nothing but his inborn Xamorian agility, reached the ground first in a blur of claws and tail.

They raced through the forest's undergrowth, darting between thick copses of trees. The audio sensors in Jeryn's suit detected an almost inaudible murmur from the Xamorian. He upped the volume to hear it more clearly. Akono was chanting.

"The Path lies ahead of me. May I tread it wisely. The Path lies ahead of me. May I tread it wisely."

When the Xamorian finished, Jeryn said over a private comm channel, "Say a couple for me, would you? We're going to need all the help we can get."

42

TRAIN TUNNEL

EVERY SECURE FACILITY HAD A WEAKNESS. IF JERYN HAD learned one thing from his former life, it was that if you studied a so-called secure location long enough, eventually you'd find a way in. Sometimes the weakness was technical. A glitchy visual sensor or a system prone to false alarms. Other times the weakness was human... or nonhuman, as the case may be. A guard who fell asleep on the job or neglected to make their rounds out of laziness. A tightfisted procurement manager who insisted on the cheapest security equipment, only to learn later (the hard way) you generally get what you pay for. But whether it was a person or a system, in Jeryn's experience every supposedly locked-down location had some way to get inside, some weakness waiting to be discovered and exploited.

The detention center holding the cleric had two.

The first was a locked but otherwise-unsecured entrance to a maintenance tunnel. Of the four access tunnels used by railway maintenance crews, three had surface entry points located within the detention facility's grounds. But the fourth was located slightly beyond the facility's fence line and actually stood on—and more importantly, was easily accessed from—the hunting reserve's property. Jeryn didn't know why they'd selected that questionable location for an entrance, nor why they'd left it relatively easy to access. Maybe it was the newest entrance and hadn't yet been secured properly, or maybe the facility had plans to procure that small portion of land from the hunting reserve but simply hadn't done so yet. But whatever the reason behind it, the off-property entry point offered Jeryn and the mission team a way to breach the subterranean rail system. All they had to do was break in a door. And best of all, the maintenance tunnels had no visual or motion sensors or surveillance tech to speak of.

The second weakness was the train system itself. The railway connecting the detention facility with the Justice complex had two lines, which traveled in opposite directions. And what the railway provided in convenient and rapid transit between the two complexes, it gave up in security. The subterranean system was a natural choke point, not unlike a narrow ocean strait that forced an entire fleet of ships into single-file formation, making them vulnerable to attack. If a train, for example, were attacked halfway between stops, there was nowhere to go, no cover to fall back to. Trapped inside a cramped train compartment, you couldn't run and hide, and when the fighting broke out you'd find yourself hopelessly disadvantaged to assailants outside who could move about freely. Of course, if you held them off for a few minutes, help would arrive from one or both stations. Which was why the mission team's plan had to be executed as quickly as possible. If they got bogged down in a firefight deep underground, they'd never make it back up the stairwell to the surface.

Jeryn and Akono arrived at the tunnel entrance, the steel door wide open with a telltale indentation in its center, marking the spot of a well-placed kick from one of the Marines. Minutes earlier, the three soldiers had infiltrated the passageway, descended the flights of stairs to the train tunnel, and hidden themselves.

Jeryn and the Xamorian hurriedly descended flight after flight of grated metal stairs. No alarm sirens blared and no security systems wailed, to Jeryn's great relief.

Onward and downward, they finally reached the last flight of stairs and rushed down the maintenance passage that ran parallel to the transit tunnel. A glowing white strip in the center of the ceiling ran the length of the narrow corridor, illuminating the space with a pale light. A visual overlay on his helmet visor blinked, informing Jeryn they would reach their destination, a doorway leading to the transit tunnel, in twenty-seven seconds. Jeryn quickened his pace, determined to get there before the train arrived and all hell broke loose. Akono followed close behind.

They made it in time. The train carrying the cleric hadn't arrived yet. Jeryn opened the door slowly, spying an identical door on the opposite side of the tunnel. One of the Marines—the HUD on Jeryn's visor identified the armored figure as Cross—gave him a thumbs-up from the doorway. The young operative returned the gesture.

Jeryn then ran his gaze down the tunnel until the HUD detected the dim outline of the explosive device the Marines had placed, lying ominously atop the magnetic track, some eighty meters away.

"It's coming," the Xamorian whispered from close behind. "Ready yourself, K'san."

Jeryn neither heard nor saw anything, but a moment later he felt a vibration beneath his feet. Then he heard the train in the distance, the faint high-pitched whine of its motor growing steadily louder. He peered down the tunnel, where the lead compartment's faraway headlight was a tiny speck of white illumination, slowly growing larger and brighter.

"I found the herd," Cross said over the comms, meaning he was ready to set off the explosive.

Retreating back into the maintenance tunnel, Jeryn and the

Xamorian steadied themselves for the detonation, crouching in anticipation, plasma rifles in hand. The blast came a second later, and the door Jeryn had shut moments before flew off its hinges and crashed against the opposite wall. The corridor was suddenly bathed in blinding light, the flash followed instantly by the twin punches of a deafening blast and a concussive shock wave that felt like Jeryn's chest plate had been struck by a carryall. When the explosive moment passed, he looked around and realized he'd been knocked backward three meters.

He turned toward Akono, worried he'd find his friend unconscious or worse. The Xamorian stood on his two powerful legs, his thick tail steadying him in place. The mercenary squeezed his eyes shut and shook his head like a fighter who'd just taken a clean punch.

"That was very loud," he said, so casually Jeryn almost laughed.

Out in the tunnel, alarms were already blaring. Jeryn poked his head through the doorway just as the first compartment passed by. The emergency brakes did their best but couldn't bring the train to a full stop before it reached the large gap in the track blown out by the explosive. The lead car hit the gap and immediately derailed, turning on its side and sliding down the tunnel in an ear-piercing screech of metal and sparks. Of the nine cars behind the lead, the next three also derailed, while the last six came to an abrupt stop, each colliding with a crunching thud into the rear of the car ahead. The tunnel was suddenly a disaster of battered, smoking train cars lying at odd angles from one another.

The trio of Marines leapt from the opposite doorway onto the tunnel floor. They would check the far more damaged front half of the train, while Jeryn and Akono took the back half. With a bit of luck, they'd find the compartment holding the cleric and get her out before anyone inside the wreck had regained their senses.

They didn't get that bit of luck, as it turned out. As soon as

Jeryn and the Xamorian stepped out into the tunnel, the firing began. A blinding barrage of flashes and air-searing pulses came from somewhere near the front of the train. The unmistakable sizzle of plasma weapons. The Marines were immediately cut down by the overwhelming firepower, and the readout on Jeryn's HUD showed flatlines on all three of their bio readouts.

Jeryn froze. What in the Great Arm was happening? These were supposed to be detention facility personnel, glorified prison guards who carried small hand pistols, not armed to the teeth with plasma rifles. The cleric's security detail was far better prepared—and equipped—than anyone had imagined.

In the next moment the barrage of plasma fire had shifted toward its new targets, Jeryn and Akono. The Xamorian grabbed Jeryn and pulled him back to the maintenance corridor. "We must fall back, K'san. Come, quickly!"

A few shots struck the wall, sending large chunks of rock flying as the pair scrambled for cover. Back inside the corridor, Jeryn tried to collect himself, mentally wrestling with their next move. But *was* there a next move? They'd lost the element of surprise, which the whole plan had depended on. So what now? His mind raced. They hadn't planned a contingency for half the team getting gunned down in the first few seconds. He tried not to think of the three Marines, who'd been alive and well only moments before, now gone. He forced his mind away from his fallen companions. Now wasn't the time for mourning.

"We have to confuse them," he said breathlessly. "Make them think they're being attacked on all sides by a dozen people. Maybe if we can keep them guessing, we can get to her." If they ever found out which compartment she was in, he added inwardly.

"Grenades," Akono said. "We throw grenades around the perimeter of the train."

Yes, that was perfect. Well, not exactly perfect, but it was a workable Plan B. A succession of grenade blasts from multiple directions might keep the guards off balance, at least for a few moments. He called Marogh over the comms and in coded language told him to stand by.

Jeryn then nodded at the Xamorian. "All right, let's go."

43

GARVAN

"Left side! Left side!"

Garvan pointed frantically at the two figures approaching the smoking wreck of a train. One in combat armor and one who definitely wasn't human. A Xamorian maybe, at first glance. In the next moment his crew spotted them and opened fire, though none of the blasts struck either target. The attackers retreated, taking cover into what Garvan supposed was some kind of access tunnel for maintenance workers.

The cleric, he thought sourly. That infernal Tegesian cleric. She was bad news, that one. He'd had a feeling about her from the start, even before he'd heard about her connections with those fanatical Originalists. That's who had to be behind this. Those militant crazies. They'd come for her.

And he'd told them as much, hadn't he? More than once he'd warned his bosses, insisting they needed more security on her. But had they listened? Of course not. They never did. They just called him paranoid and laughed him off, same as always. So when Garvan had been chosen to lead the security detail for the cleric's transfer to Justice, he hadn't bothered with asking permission to double the security crew's headcount. He'd gone ahead and done it on his own authority, stuffing as many armed colleagues as he could into the train's ten compartments.

The higher-ups wouldn't be laughing at him after this, would they?

The firing stopped. Garvan took a deep breath, wincing as he did so. Beneath his body armor, his ribs were tender to the touch. He'd smashed into a metal handhold when the train had crashed. Without the protection, the impact surely would have cracked his ribcage. His carriage, the third from the front, had derailed like the two ahead of it, though thankfully it hadn't toppled over onto its side. The car leaned at a severe angle, propped up against the tunnel wall. Of his six companions in the compartment, two lay on the floor, semiconscious and moaning. The four others, like him, were bruised and battered but otherwise uninjured. Somehow his earpiece had stayed in place, and over the comms a panicked babble of at least ten voices yelled over each other. He removed the earpiece and tossed it to the floor in anger. Bunch of amateurs. With everyone yammering at the same time, there was no way to call for backup. He looked around the compartment until he found the emergency comms panel on the wall.

"Call the station," he barked at Chanson, gesturing to the panel. "Tell them we're under attack and we need help immediately."

"Yes, sir," Chanson shouted, limping over to the panel.

To the others in the compartment, he shouted, "Everyone else, stay put, and keep your eyes on that maintenance doorway over there. Anyone so much as pokes their head out, you fry them, understood?"

He then turned toward the carriage behind his, where hopefully they still had the cleric in custody. With his plasma rifle strapped across his shoulder, Garvan half-walked, half-crawled along the canted floor, wondering how many assailants were out there. His crew had taken out three already. That much he knew for sure. He smiled inwardly, knowing how surprised those fanatics must have been at the overwhelming firepower they'd walked into. The rest of the attackers—wherever they were—wouldn't be so reckless after what had happened to their companions.

But if Gavan's crew could hang on to the cleric and hold off the terrorists for the next few minutes, help would arrive.

The carriage with the cleric still stood upright, but it had rotated ninety degrees before sliding to a stop. Garvan hopped to the ground, alarms wailing, the normally darkened passageway illuminated in flashing yellow emergency lights. He ran to the cleric's compartment and burst through the door, shouting, "Hold your fire! Hold your fire!"

Eight of his colleagues stood a short distance away, staring at him with wide eyes, their plasma rifles aimed directly at his chest. He froze, expecting to be shot by some trigger-happy rookie, but when no one fired he stepped forward. "Is the passenger secure?" he called over the din of the blaring alarm.

Slowly, the crew lowered their rifles. "She's secure," one of them said. Mowin was the woman's name, if he remembered right. She stepped forward, revealing the crouching cleric, who was surrounded by the security crew's human shield. She wore a drab gray prisoner's jumpsuit, and her manacled hands were clutched protectively over her head.

The cleric lowered her hands, looked up at him, and said, "You want to tell me what in the falling stars is going on here, mister?"

Garvan ignored her. "All right, listen to me," he shouted to his crew. "We took out three of them, but we don't know how many more are out there. Help is on the way. We just have to hunker down here and take out anything—"

A blast of light and sound and heat filled the tunnel, violently shaking the carriage. Everyone inside the compartment instinctively dropped to the floor, including Garvan. He felt as if the air had just been punched out of him, and he instantly recognized the sensation. Garvan had been to war and knew a grenade when he heard and felt one.

Grenades. Wonderful, the terrorists had grenades.

"The tunnel's going to collapse!" one of his crew shouted.

"It won't," Garvan shouted back. A civil engineering graduate, Garvan knew the reinforced tunnel could withstand far more than a few grenade blasts. The train cars and their body armor, however, were a different story.

Three more detonations erupted in quick succession. The carriage lurched with each bone-jarring explosion, making it impossible for Garvan to regain his feet. Overhead, the tiny square tiles of the compartment's decorative mosaic ceiling came loose by the hundreds, fell to the floor, and broke into tiny pieces. Shouts of confusion filled the brief gaps between blasts.

Finally, it stopped. The carriage rocked slowly back and forth but, amazingly, remained upright. Dust from the fallen tiles drifted through the compartment. Garvan coughed, dizzily rose to his feet, and checked his surroundings. Everyone seemed uninjured, though most had the dazed look of a fighter who'd been hit with a knockout blow. Two of his crew knelt protectively over the cleric, who also appeared unharmed.

"Come on!" someone shouted. "We have to get out of here, now!"

Garvan barely heard whoever it was above the ringing in his ears. He looked around the compartment and found the source of the voice, standing in the doorway between carriages. His boss, Security Chief Kazimir, frantically waved him over. "Let's go!" he barked. "We've got to get the cleric out of here."

His head still spinning, Garvan said, "To where, sir?"

"We've got a car on the other track."

Thank the stars, Garvan thought. Their rescuers had arrived.

Still trying to catch his breath, Garvan gathered up his crew and ordered them to form a protective ring around the cleric. They exited the carriage, rifles at the ready, following Kazimir.

"Quickly now," the security chief called, his blaster pistol drawn. He waved them toward the same opening Garvan had seen two attackers disappear into moments before.

"Sir," Garvan called. "I saw two of them go in there."

"We took them out," Kazimir said.

"Are there any others?"

"No idea, but we're not waiting around to find out. Now come on, move it!"

Garvan swiveled his gaze back and forth as he led his team forward. He paused at the steps to the maintenance doorway, waving his team past. As the phalanx of guards hurried up the stairs with the cleric, following Kazimir through the doorway, Garvan got his first good look at the totality of the train wreckage. The cars lay at odd angles to one another, and the lead two were on their sides. Smoke wafted upward from a few small fires burning here and there. A short distance down the tunnel the ruined magnetic track had a twenty-meter gap, the gnarled metal edges on each end charred and still smoking. What a bleeding mess.

He turned and followed his crew into the maintenance corridor. "Stars, I can't believe we made it out of that—"

Two figures fell from somewhere overhead, landing on either side of the security crew. Garvan watched in stunned disbelief as the two figures attacked, both wielding power blades. The assault was blindingly fast. Glowing blades flashed and whirred through the air, wielded with deadly precision. The movements were strangely hypnotic, a blur of slashing circular movements as the blades easily penetrated both body armor and flesh. In a quick succession of howls and groans, his team fell to the floor one by one, several clutching grisly wounds where their arms had been severed at the elbow. Only the cleric, wide-eyed and frozen in terrified disbelief, remained standing.

The attackers. He recognized them. The same figures he'd seen earlier. The armored human and the Xamorian.

Reeling in disbelief, Garvan turned to Kazimir, standing a short distance away. Only he wasn't Kazimir now. The man's face had changed—was in the process of changing—into someone else's. And this not-Kazimir person raised his blaster at Garvan.

A shifter, he suddenly realized. They had a shifter with them, clothed in a security uniform. An impostor posing as the security chief.

Garvan only managed to raise his rifle halfway before the plasma bolt struck him, the unbearably hot blast searing a large hole in his chest, ending his life.

44

ESCAPE VELOCITY

Now that Jeryn and his companions no longer had to worry about staying quiet to avoid detection, the climb to the surface from the train tunnel went a lot faster than the trip down had. With the cleric strapped to his back in a harness normally used to transport the injured, Jeryn rushed up the stairs in huge, armor-assisted bounding strides. He followed Akono, one flight ahead of him, and Marogh, who'd quickly slipped back into his armor after finishing his charade as the security chief, trailed one flight behind.

The cleric, once she'd realized what was happening, had peppered them with question after frantic question. Who were they? Where were they taking her? Was this a rescue or a kidnapping? As politely as he could manage, Jeryn had told her they'd answer her questions as soon as they were safe. Tavella, unable to recognize Jeryn's face hidden behind his helmet's visor, was far from satisfied with this non-answer, and halfway to the surface she started asking the same questions again. Part of Jeryn understood. If their roles had been reversed, he'd definitely want to know what in the Great Arm was happening, who had taken him, and where they were going. Another part of him simply wanted her to shut up so he could focus.

They reached the surface without incident, the alarm down in the tunnel still blaring but quieter now in the distance. The drop ship sat in a nearby clearing, having been summoned by Marogh and arriving by autopilot as they'd raced up the stairs. No doubt its approach had been detected—the ship's anti-scanner stealth tech might have been state-of-the-art, but this close to the detention complex, it was all but useless. The DS's approach would have been easily seen and heard by security personnel—but again, speed mattered more now than secrecy.

They quickly boarded the ship, strapped in, and in moments they were high above the planet's surface. The drop ship gained altitude, and Marogh announced, "We don't appear to have any pursuers following us."

Good, Jeryn thought with no small amount of relief. They'd counted on it taking a minute or two for the facility to scramble pilots into chase ships, and by then the DS would be long gone. At least that much had gone to plan.

As the ship rocketed upward through the clouds, Jeryn's thoughts returned to the three Marines they'd left behind. He hadn't known them well, especially the recently arrived Cross, but he felt the loss all the same. All three had friends and family somewhere who'd never see them again.

The ship's acceleration pressed them into their jump seats. Jeryn popped open his visor to get a breath that wasn't the stale, recycled air of his suit.

"You," the cleric blurted, her voice coming out in a grunt against the force of the thrust gees. "I know you." She said it like an accusation. Marogh had also opened his visor. Tavella looked between the shifter's nearly-back-to-baseline face and the Xamorian. "I don't know you two," she said, shifting her gaze to Jeryn, "but you were on Sandau Prime with Everfeld. At that compound in the middle of nowhere."

"Yes," Jeryn said.

Then, as if on cue, the ship stopped shaking, and Jeryn felt the bottoms of his legs float a couple centimeters up from the chair, his thighs gently pressing against the restraints. They'd cleared Meritan 7's gravity well. In a matter of minutes, the drop ship would rejoin the *Veiled Dagger*.

"Stars, that's better," the cleric said, letting out a long breath. Her blonde hair floated about her head like she was underwater. Jeryn and Marogh removed their helmets and placed them on hooks mounted on the cabin wall. Marogh unstrapped himself, pushed off from the chair, and floated headfirst to the cockpit, where he settled into the pilot's seat.

"So tell me what this is, Jeryn Lorsi," Tavella said. "What's going on here?"

So, she remembered his name. After plasma blasts and grenade explosions and the body stress of escape velocity, she still managed to remember his name. And she'd already gathered herself, her voice as steady and collected as her expression. Most people in her situation would have still been nervous wrecks after witnessing such violence and destruction. He was still a bit shaky himself. But not Sah Tavella. She was definitely a cool customer, this cleric.

"How much do you know about what's happened with the consul minister?" he asked her.

"I had access to news feeds," she said. "I know about the no confidence vote, about Jakaan taking the consulship." A moment passed, and she added, "And about Everfeld too. I was sorry to hear about his passing."

"Were you?" Jeryn asked, perhaps a bit sharply. He'd rescued her, yes, but he still wasn't as certain about her as his late mentor had been. And the embittered, still-mourning part of him felt it unfair that she was here, alive and well, and Everfeld wasn't. None of what had transpired was her fault, he admitted inwardly, but she was at the center of the storm he and his companions had all been caught up in. He could only hope the woman was worth all the risk and sacrifice. Time would tell.

"Yes, I was sorry," she said, then leaned forward a bit. "He'd gone rogue, hadn't he? When he came to Sandau Prime, the CM had no idea what he was up to, did she? Can you tell me that much?"

Jeryn didn't answer, not wanting to divulge anything quite yet. *After* Imallah debriefed her, and *if* the Zatori found the cleric's motives truly well-intentioned—that her desire for peace and reform was genuine and not simply a means to feed her ego and serve her ambitions—then he'd share things with her. But not before.

"All in good time, Sah Tavella," he said. "All in good time."

45

LEFT BEHIND

You couldn't always recover fallen comrades from the battlefield. War was like that sometimes. Cross knew because he'd been to war many times in many systems, first in service of the Realm, later as a mercenary, then finally as an Agency contractor. Sometimes a battle zone was simply too hot to remove the dead. Sometimes there wasn't enough left of their bodies to recover. But if you weren't sure about their fate, if their death wasn't a certainty, you didn't just simply leave them. Not if there was a chance they were still alive.

But that was exactly what had happened to him. He'd been left behind.

He wasn't sure how many plasma blasts had struck his suit. Maybe it had only been a few. But unlike the two Marines lying dead beside him, he hadn't taken a direct hit. One of the grazing shots had knocked out his bio sensors along with the combat suit's operating system, so anyone viewing his readouts would have seen him flatline, no different than his two dead companions. No one knew he'd only been knocked out cold, not killed in action. And that was because no one had lifted a bloody finger to find out for sure.

Those cowardly sons of gecks had abandoned him.

He rolled onto his side, head throbbing, vision blurred, body aching. Pain radiated from his left shoulder. He cursed himself for agreeing to this suicide mission. He never should have teamed up with a filthy geck, or any human who trusted a geck for that matter. This was what you got for being so stupid. For thinking a squad sullied by nonhumans was anything but a terrible idea. He'd been so determined to do right by Pezzi-Kaziz, to take up the fight for her, he'd let his good sense fly by the wayside. Bad call.

Slowly, security personnel began to emerge from the wreckage. They took no notice of him, assuming him dead, just like his dishonorable companions had. Then his visor overlay blinked to life as the armor's backup system came online. A bare-bones control application powered by a small battery, the backup gave him only basic suit functionality and close-range comms.

Comms, he thought, a smile forming on his lips.

Payback time.

With a flick of his eyes, he toggled over to the detention facility's open channel, the one they'd eavesdropped on earlier to monitor local chatter.

"Attention Detention Facility Five South," he said, his voice weak and scratchy. He cleared his throat before going on. "This is Manitok Cross, and I was part of the attack on the underground rail system. I'm unarmed and prepared to surrender."

Seconds later, he was surrounded by security personnel, their weapons trained on him. He sat up and removed his helmet, shoulder screaming in pain.

"Who's in charge here?" he asked, no longer woozy. The pain in his shoulder—he was pretty sure it was dislocated—had shaken away all the cobwebs in his head.

"I am," a woman said, stepping forward.

He fixed her with a stare. "Listen to me very carefully. If you want any chance of getting that cleric back, I need to speak with your commanding officer. Immediately."

46

IMPOSSIBLE NEWS

Consul Minister Jakaan stared at the comms holo of his newly appointed spymaster, trying to process what the man had just recounted. The utterly impossible message relayed from the commanding officer at the detention facility. The cleric had been abducted. The news had hit Jakaan like a slap to the face. A slap he hadn't yet recovered from when Menic delivered a second, no less shocking, piece of information. According to the only abductor who'd been captured, the raiding party was led by none other than Jeryn Lorsi, Everfeld's young protege.

With considerable effort, Jakaan managed to gather himself. "How long ago did you speak with this detention facility commander?"

"I just finished with him," Menic replied. "I contacted you immediately. The incident occurred less than fifteen minutes ago."

Jakaan sprung up from his chair, his mind racing. Fifteen minutes! They might have cleared the planet's gravity well by now, but they were still in the local volume.

"Get the local Navy chief on the line," he ordered. "Now!" He then leaned away from the comms image, gestured open the door, and called to the personal assistant he'd been assigned shortly after arriving. "Get my shuttle ready immediately."

"Right away, sir," came the response from the adjacent room.

As Menic hurriedly worked the comms connection with the local volume's military, Jakaan transferred the feed to an earpiece and rushed from the office suite. A security detail of two joined him in the corridor, matching his jogging pace as he hustled in the direction of the shuttle bay.

The cleric abducted! It still seemed surreal, this morning's abrupt turn of events. He'd arrived on Meritan 7 only the day before, eager to address the public from the same planet where the traitorous cleric would be formally charged. He'd planned to make his comments from the steps of the Ministry of Justice. A public relations move showing strong, engaged leadership and an emphasis on law and order. He'd also intended to have a private discussion with the prosecution team, where he was going to express his expectation for a guilty verdict in the strongest possible terms. The dotta superior would have already arranged for this, he was sure, but an extra kick in the rear—especially from the consul minister, in person—couldn't hurt, and he wasn't about to leave anything to chance.

But now all those plans were blown out of the water. Now he had to scramble to avoid disaster. The ambitious cleric was a venom that could poison his consulship. Even as a fugitive, she could still unite the disparate Separatist factions and the extremist sect of her own Tegesian order. With herself as the self-appointed rebel-in-charge, of course.

Stars, he had to get her back, had to bring her back under his control. And if he couldn't do that, he'd have to take her out of the game for good, despite his arrangement with Tolerance IV. He'd rather risk making her a martyr than allow her to freely roam the stars, uniting forces against the Realm. Against him.

If he acted quickly enough, perhaps he could diffuse the bomb before it exploded in his face.

As he arrived at the shuttle bay, Admiral Tolomeo joined the comms channel.

"Minister Jakaan," the woman said, "I understand we have an emergency. How can I be of service?"

A bit out of breath, Jakaan rushed up the shuttle's boarding ramp, followed closely by his security detail.

"Admiral," he said, "how many battle cruisers do you have in orbit?"

47

DESALIBA HEIGHTS

DeSaliba Heights station was a relic from another age. A modestly sized construction from the previous millennium, the station was located at one of Meritan 7's stable Lagrangian points, where it had sat motionless and empty for hundreds of years.

Of course, it wasn't *actually* motionless, Jeryn reflected as he watched the tiny station grow larger on the drop ship's viewport, since the local system itself moved through an already spiraling galaxy in a constantly churning universe. Precisely put, it *appeared* motionless relative to Meritan 7 and its red dwarf sun. The station sat in a permanently neutral gravity zone, where the sun's enormous gravity well was fully offset by the planet's smaller but closer one. It had been an ideal place to put a station. No pull of gravity meant no decaying orbit. And no decaying orbit meant no need for expensive, fuel-intensive orbital corrections.

In its heyday, DeSaliba Heights had been a gambler's paradise. Wealthy locals vacationed there, attracted by the always-open casinos and myriad entertainment offerings. After a couple hundred years of relatively innocuous operation, a criminal syndicate gained a controlling interest in the station, and DeSaliba Heights slowly became not only a vacation destination, but also a haven for wealthy criminals and a supply source for much of the local volume's narcotics trade.

Then a planetary governor, whose political platform touted a return to law and order, instigated a decades-long campaign of crushing taxation of gambling zones and frequent, well-publicized police raids on brothels and other illicit establishments. Eventually, businesses both legal and otherwise packed up shop and left DeSaliba Heights for safer, less politically hostile locations elsewhere. By then the two-hundred-year-old station had fallen into severe disrepair, and better, more advanced microgravity construction technologies had been developed, making DeSaliba Heights economically obsolete. It was actually cheaper to build a new station at another Lagrangian point than repair an old broken one. And so it sat there, abandoned and completely intact, too far from the planet's surface to make the round trip financially viable even for salvagers. The empty husk of DeSaliba Heights now hung in space, its glory days long behind it.

But the ancient station still had one useful purpose: It was the perfect place to hide a frigate-class starship like the *Veiled Dagger*. The station's sizable bay, constructed to accommodate cruise ships over twice the *Dagger*'s size, was partially open to space, having been left that way by the station's last exiting ship or some subsequent mechanical failure. The gap was large enough for the *Dagger* to enter the bay and set down, totally concealed, and wait for the arrival of its drop ship.

"Five minutes to DeSaliba Heights station," Marogh announced from the DS's cockpit.

"Anyone on our tail?" Jeryn asked.

"I don't believe so," the shifter replied. "No police-vessel scans have hit us, and no one has sent a comms beam in our direction telling us to stop."

"Perhaps no one's tracking us," Akono suggested.

Doubtful, Jeryn replied inwardly. They were making a steady burn to the station, which made them pretty easy to spot. The drop ship's stealth tech might have made the vessel all but invisible to ground-based atmospheric scans, but in the vacuum of space its drive plume would be easy enough to track.

They'd known they'd be tracked, even chased, once they'd cleared the planet's atmosphere. But speed trumped stealth at the moment, and the goal was to make it to the *Dagger* as quickly as possible. And once they'd arrived safely inside the frigate's bay, they could hurry out of the system. No vessel in all the Great Arm would be able to catch them.

DeSaliba Heights was five long minutes away.

Jeryn and Marogh removed and stowed their combat suits. Over in the pilot's seat the shifter still wore the replica security uniform Jeryn had printed out for him in the *Dagger*'s fabricator. The outfit, along with the pilot's malleable face, had been the perfect disguise. On the way to Meritan 7 they'd found a recent interview in the ship's feed archives with the detention facility's commanding officer. The high-resolution images had been the perfect template for the shifter's transformation.

"Pretty clever," Tavella said, "using a shifter to fool the guards."

Jeryn nodded but said nothing, his thoughts focused on the empty space between the drop ship and the *Dagger*. They couldn't get there fast enough. He distractedly reached for his hip sheath and ran his fingers over the kukri's handle.

The cleric noted the blade. "Before today I'd never seen anyone wield a power blade," she said, then added, "outside of the staged fights on drama programs." She narrowed her eyes, still staring at the weapon. "What are those markings on the handle?"

Jeryn glanced down, shook his head. "I'm not sure. No one seems to know."

"May I see it?"

Jeryn gave her a dubious look, prompting her to say, "I don't want to hold it. I only want a better look."

Unsheathing the weapon, Jeryn rested the blade across his palms and extended his arms toward the cleric. She leaned over the blade, furrowing her brow as she studied the intricate markings. After a moment, she asked, "Did you acquire this blade from your family? Is it a kind of heirloom?"

Jeryn tried to hide his surprise. It was indeed an heirloom of sorts, but it was far more than just that. The blade was the only item he possessed connecting him to his long-lost family.

"Yes, you could say that," he said.

A kind of light seemed to turn on behind the cleric's eyes. "How much do you know much about Tegesian folklore?"

"About as much as you know about blade combat," he said, returning the weapon to its sheath.

Before the cleric could reply, a sharp chirping sound came from the cockpit, followed by Marogh's disapproving grunt. Jeryn recognized the tone, a sound he'd been dreading. A proximity alarm. There was a ship (or ships) in the vicinity.

"I'm afraid we have company," the shifter said, tapping the console and silencing the alarm.

"What kind of company?" the Xamorian called. "Transit Control? Police interceptors?"

"Not exactly," the pilot said. He activated the holo display in the passenger area. A sphere-shaped tactical schematic of local space appeared. A small white cube at the center of the image was labeled DeSaliba Heights, the drop ship's destination. A slightly curved dotted line, their projected course, connected the small green triangle of the *Dagger*'s drop ship with the station's icon. But these Jeryn noticed only briefly, his attention quickly shifting to the outer edges of the image, where ten red triangles blinked ominously. All ten had alphanumeric labels, identifying their ship class. BC followed by a number.

Jeryn swallowed, finding his throat suddenly dry. Battle cruisers, all of them. The Navy's largest and most lethal vessels were converging on their location from every direction.

48

UNEXPECTED CALL

"Can't this bucket move any faster?" Jeryn asked, rushing to the cockpit and dropping into the copilot's seat.

"I am afraid not," Marogh said, confirming what Jeryn already knew. The *Dagger*'s drop ship, like nearly all drop ships, was a single-purpose vessel, optimized for quick, stealthy planetary reentry and return. In the void beyond a planet's atmosphere, the thing was painfully slow, topping out at the relative crawl of a one-point-five-gee burn.

The shifter's expert fingers swiftly worked the console as he made trajectory calculations. "We should reach the station before we're in range of the Navy vessels, but only by a few seconds."

"Can the *Dagger* leave the station and come to us?" the Xamorian suggested. "To save time?"

"It could," the pilot said.

"I wouldn't do that if I were you," the cleric said. The three others turned their gazes to her in unison. "Those Navy ships will open fire on them," she continued.

"They're going to open fire no matter what," Jeryn pointed out. "The quicker we get to our ship, the better off we'll be."

"I'm no navigator," Tavella said, nodding at the tactical display, "but I don't see us getting away from ten battle cruisers."

"We've got a fast ship," Akono said.

"A very fast ship," Jeryn added.

"Unfortunately, it's not fast enough," Marogh said, spoiling the brief moment of optimism.

Jeryn eyed the pilot's console, the display still cycling through trajectory analyses. "What do you mean?"

"Even if the *Dagger* made a quick burn to retrieve us," the shifter said, "there's no projected escape vector available, given the Navy vessels' current formation, closing velocity, and effective missile range."

No escape vector, Jeryn repeated inwardly. "What about the move we tried in the Barat-Cray system? Could we—"

"Forgive me for interrupting," Marogh said, "but that tactic would have no chance of success against battle cruisers. Naval weaponry is far more advanced than planetary police vessels."

Jeryn stared at the display, his thoughts equal parts frustration and despair. He didn't want to believe they'd come this far only to fail now. But those were battle cruisers, and there were ten of them.

"Can the *Dagger* get away on its own?" he asked, his eyes fixed on the space station's icon. "If they make a hard burn now?"

The pilot shook his head gravely. "I've already made some rough calculations, and I don't believe so. Like us, they have no way out."

A quiet moment drew out as the pilot's words reverberated in the air.

"We can negotiate with whoever's in charge," the cleric said, "once we reach the station."

"*If* we reach the station," Jeryn added.

"They won't fire on us," Tavella said. "They want me back

alive so they can try and convict me. That's why they didn't kill me back on Sandau Prime. It's the smart move, actually."

"Maybe whoever made that call is regretting it right about now," Jeryn suggested.

"You could be right," the cleric conceded, "but I hope you're not, for all our sakes."

Despite his retort, Jeryn didn't disagree with the cleric. The Navy vessels might not fire on the drop ship, given the political value of its Tegesian passenger, but they'd almost certainly take out the *Dagger* if it emerged from its hiding place.

"Call the *Dagger*," he told the pilot. "Tell them to stay put, and we'll dock with them shortly."

"I should point out," the shifter said, "that all intership communication will almost certainly be monitored, recorded, and decrypted."

"Well, it's not like this mission's a secret anymore," Jeryn said, then gestured toward the tactical display. "Bhokken can see the same thing we're seeing, and I don't want him rushing out to save us and getting shot up in the process."

"Understood," the shifter said. He opened a comms channel and relayed the message to the *Dagger*.

The reply came quickly. *"Message received and understood,"* the Rauk said, his voice surprisingly calm over the connection.

In the minutes that remained until they reached the station, Jeryn gathered the drop ship's crew together and attempted to come up with a negotiation ploy. A plausible strategy occurred to none of them. The problem was their negotiating leverage, in that they didn't really have any. Sure, they had the cleric as a bargaining chip, but it wasn't like they were going to hold a blade to her throat and demand safe passage out of the system like some crazed convict holding a prison guard hostage. Even if they'd been willing to try something that desperate and barbaric—which they weren't—such a ruse would fool no one.

They could cross their fingers and try to burn past the Navy vessels, hoping their human cargo was deemed too valuable to blow up with a missile strike. But they all agreed that felt like a throw of the dice that likely wouldn't roll in their favor. If they refused to surrender Tavella and made a run for it, their pursuers would all but certainly take them out rather than let the cleric escape.

For her part, Tavella accepted her looming fate with a grace Jeryn couldn't help but be impressed by. Had their positions been reversed, he was sure he wouldn't have handled things so well. He might have blown up at his would-be rescuers, calling them blundering kidnappers who'd only managed to make a bad situation worse. But to her credit, the cleric didn't point blaming fingers at anyone or lose her cool. She focused her full attention on what could be done, not what had gone wrong.

They still hadn't come up with anything by the time the drop ship settled into its docking bay on the *Veiled Dagger*. The artigrav field generated by the mother ship's arrays pulled them to the floor, the sensation of weight coming as a relief to Jeryn despite the circumstances. Despite his extensive travels, he'd never become accustomed to microgravity and the disorienting loss of up and down that came with it.

As they waited a few moments for the bay to seal shut and pressurize, Jeryn suggested that perhaps the Rauk could figure something out.

"He's brilliant," he assured the cleric as they made their way to the boarding ramp. "The most intelligent being I've ever known. If there's a way out of this, he'll find it."

The pressurization indicator on the wall switched from red to green. The DS's entryway hissed open as its boarding ramp folded outward, revealing Bhokken's towering frame standing just beyond the ramp's reach. He stood with his arms folded across his chest.

"I don't see any way out of this," he said flatly.

The cleric lifted an eyebrow at Jeryn. "You were saying?"

"Also," the Rauk added, "there's someone who wants to talk with us."

"My apologies for the rather informal greeting," the Rauk said to the cleric as he led the group down the corridor to the bridge. "Pleasure and joy to you, Sah Tavella. Welcome aboard the *Veiled Dagger*."

"And to you as well," the cleric replied.

As they hurried along, Marogh asked if the ship mind had come up with an escape route. As the shifter had predicted, the Rauk informed him the ship mind could find no way out. The Navy vessels had them quite thoroughly boxed in.

They reached the bridge, and Bhokken paused at the entryway, turning to Tavella. "I think perhaps you should wait here."

The Rauk gave no explanation, and he still hadn't revealed who was on the comms connection, but the cleric didn't question him. Unflappable as ever, she graciously bowed her head. "I understand." She lowered herself onto a bench inset in the corridor wall.

Bhokken led Jeryn, Akono, and Marogh through the doorway, where they found Imallah waiting for them on the bridge. The Zatori stood with her back wedged into a corner, just beyond the visual sensor's field of view. From there the Zatori could scrutinize the vocal tones, facial expressions, and body language of whoever was on the other end of the comms without the subject knowing they were being observed. The diminutive empath's expression was knotted in concentration, her gaze fixed on the comms' holo display.

As Jeryn stepped fully onto the bridge, he saw the Zatori's subject, recognition sending a bolt of shock down his back.

Jakaan—*Consul Minister* Jakaan—stood with his hands clasped behind his back.

PART 4

49

ONE-TIME DEAL

It couldn't have been more than a second or two, Jeryn realized, between the stunning moment he and his companions recognized the holographic image and when the consul minister began to speak. But it seemed like much longer, like time had slowed to a stop.

They'd been caught. Somehow, someway, the CM had outmaneuvered them or anticipated their plan. Jeryn couldn't imagine how he'd done it, but that hardly mattered at this point. The consul minister, the man who'd ordered Everfeld's execution, had them trapped like insects in a jar.

Stars, they'd been close, so very close to freeing the cleric.

The CM lifted his chin. "I don't see Sah Tavella, Bhokken."

"I asked her to wait in the corridor," the Rauk replied. "Pleasure and joy to you on her behalf, Consul Minister."

Jakaan scowled. "I'm afraid this occasion is neither pleasurable nor joyous."

Jeryn glanced at the comms console, noticing the transmission's source was one of the battle cruisers. A shudder of dread struck him. The consul minister was *here* in the local volume.

"You've been causing us a great deal of trouble, my Rauk friend," Jakaan said.

Bhokken replied, "Someone once said there's bad trouble and good trouble. I'd like to think my actions are the latter."

Minister Jakaan grinned. "But that's a matter of perspective, isn't it? From my vantage point, it's quite the opposite." His grin then faded. "Bhokken, you must return the cleric to state custody immediately."

"Is the consul minister's hold on power so tenuous," the Rauk said, "that one young cleric can threaten it?"

The CM lifted a forefinger. "You were always a clever one, Bhokken. I won't dignify a loaded question with an answer, but surely you know me well enough to realize I wouldn't consider allowing a seditionist to escape justice."

"I *thought* I knew you well enough," Bhokken said, "and so did my friend Whitmere. But now it seems clear there's much more to you than we ever suspected." He quickly added, "Please don't mistake that observation for a compliment."

The CM spread his arms out wide. "It would be foolish to debate a Rauk of your age and wisdom. Now, let us speak frankly. Everfeld is gone, and his plots and schemes are gone with him. You and your companions have made a terrible mistake, attempting to follow in his traitorous footsteps. You must know that by now." He paused for a moment before continuing. "But unlike Everfeld, you can walk away with your lives, free of any criminal charges. Your companions too."

"If we give up the cleric," the Rauk added, saying the silent part of the bargain out loud.

"Yes," Minister Jakaan said. "That's the one-time offer I'm prepared to make. You'll need to surrender the vessel too, of course."

The vessel? Jeryn felt as if he'd been kicked in the gut. If they turned over the *Dagger*, they'd also be turning over Everfeld's mindprint. No, that couldn't happen. The mindprint *wasn't* Everfeld, Jeryn knew, but still… it was all he had left of the old man.

"Surely the consul minister can overlook the absence of one small passenger transport," the Rauk said.

"He could indeed," Jakaan countered, "but I think we both know your vessel is nothing of the sort."

"You can't have it," Jeryn blurted out, momentarily losing his composure.

Minister Jakaan's gaze fell on Jeryn. "You're Everfeld's… I suppose protege might be the right word. Jeryn Lorsi, yes?"

Jeryn swallowed. "That's right."

"Well, my impertinent young friend, I'm afraid the ship you're aboard at the moment is state property, and quite an expensive piece of state property at that, as I've recently learned. You and your friends can leave here on an *actual* passenger transport —quite a nice one, I believe—that I won't mind parting with." He again looked to the Rauk. "The cleric and your vessel. A small price to pay for your lives and legal immunity. From my perspective, this is a most generous offer."

"And if we refuse?" the Rauk asked.

"You're far too intelligent a being to take the foolish option," the CM said. "Or perhaps I should say *another* foolish option." Then with an air of finality he said, "Now, please gather up your belongings and break the news to our subversive Tegesian friend. You have twenty minutes. If you fail to deliver the cleric in that time, you'll leave the Navy no alternative but to resolve the situation by less diplomatic means."

Jeryn frowned. *Less diplomatic means.* A nice way of saying they'd be blown to bits.

"I understand," the Rauk said, and in the next moment Jakaan ended the transmission, the CM's image blinking away.

Jeryn turned to Imallah. "What did you see?"

With unblinking amber eyes, the Zatori stared at the empty

space where the image had floated moments before. "Nothing good," she said with a sigh. "He told no lies, and he's quite intent on getting his hands on this ship." She narrowed her eyes. "I also have a strong sense he doesn't care if the cleric lives or dies."

The Rauk harrumphed. "Which means we can't make a run for it and hope they don't fire on us."

"He'll pull the trigger without hesitation," the Zatori said. "I'm all but certain of it."

"We must give up the cleric or die," Akono said. "Either way, my friends, we have failed in our task."

No one spoke for a long moment. "We can't let him have her," Jeryn said finally, "or the ship."

"With no apparent escape route," Marogh said, "it appears we have no choice."

"We're not done yet," Jeryn retorted, his voice sounding more resolute than he felt. "Maybe we should get someone else's input," he suggested, flashing a knowing look at the engineer.

The Rauk nodded. "Yes. Perhaps he can help." He motioned in the direction of the no-longer-secret room. "You go," Bhokken said, then placed a hand on Marogh's shoulder. "We'll work on trying to find an escape vector. Perhaps there's something the ship mind missed."

Jeryn nodded, though they both knew there was little chance the Rauk would find anything. The ship mind had already crunched the numbers on thousands of potential routes, coming up with no workable escape solution. "I'll be back in a few minutes."

Jeryn exited the bridge and the door closed behind him. Out in the corridor, the seated cleric stood quickly, her ever-composed features tarnished with understandable worry.

"They're taking me back into custody, aren't they?" she said. "Tell me the truth."

Jeryn nodded grimly. "I'm sorry."

"Don't be," she said. "At least you tried. I should thank you for that. And for the sacrifices you've made."

"We've got a bit of time," Jeryn said, trying and probably failing to sound optimistic. "We're not out of options yet."

As he started to move past her, she touched his arm. "Wait." He paused and she said, "He really *did* believe in what I was doing, didn't he? Director Everfeld, I mean."

Jeryn lifted his chin at the cleric. "Yes, he did. We all do." He excused himself and walked on, a twenty-minute clock ticking inside his head.

50

GHOST IN THE MACHINE

"Not the most enviable position," the mindprint said, appearing as Jeryn entered the formerly secret room, "where we find ourselves at the moment, is it?"

"You know?" Jeryn asked, furrowing his brow. "How?"

"The ship mind," the entity that was and wasn't Everfeld said. "I can read it much the same way you would read a text. Whatever it detects, whatever problem it's working on, I can see it, though I don't suppose *see* is the proper word. I'm not sure there is a proper word, actually, but suffice to say what it knows, I know."

Once more Jeryn found himself awed by the technology behind the mindprint. This truly was a replica of Everfeld, his cybernetic clone. It spoke in the same tone, with the same cadence, and it contemplated out loud the exact same way Everfeld always did. Always *had*, rather. Without the hologram's slightly flickering transparency, the illusion would have been utterly convincing, completely indistinguishable from the flesh-and-blood man himself.

"We don't see a way out," Jeryn said. "Even with the *Dagger*'s speed, the ship mind can't find an escape vector. And those battle cruisers are so close they can track us with visual sensors, so there's no cloaking our way out of this either." He blew out a breath. "But you know all this already."

"Yes, I'm afraid I do," Everfeld said gravely. "It seems we're out of conventional solutions." Then he lifted his eyebrows. "But perhaps an unconventional one can even the odds."

"Unconventional?" Bhokken blurted moments later, after listening to Jeryn recount the mindprint's idea. "It certainly is that. Add to that untested, unbelievable, and unlikely to work."

The Rauk's skepticism was unsurprising. Two minutes earlier, Jeryn had experienced the same knee-jerk doubts when he'd heard the mindprint's long shot of an idea. But the young operative had quickly arrived at what he considered the right way to look at it: what other choice did they have?

"It could work," he said.

The scheme centered around the battle cruisers' tether connectivity, a ship-to-ship system linkage that allowed Navy tug pilots to temporarily gain control of a warship's navigation. For colossal battle cruisers, the docking process into orbital naval stations was extraordinarily difficult, often requiring a succession of tricky, hazardous maneuvers. To minimize the risk of catastrophic collision, Navy commanders—as their ocean-faring predecessors had done since long before interstellar travel—relinquished navigational control to local experts, tug pilots based out of the local station.

The mindprint believed the *Dagger*'s broadcast array could potentially emulate a navigational tether and covertly access the battle cruiser's core operating systems, the most important of which was its navigational control.

"You have a better proposal, old friend?" the mindprint said, appearing suddenly as a twenty-centimeter-tall holo, standing on the pilot's console.

All eyes on the bridge snapped to Everfeld's small projection. Though there was no technical limitation to where the entity could make itself seen and heard—it had access to holo projectors throughout the ship—Everfeld's mindprint had thus far limited its appearances to the hidden compartment, apparently aware of the unsettling effect it had on the *Dagger*'s crew. It broke with that standard now, Jeryn imagined, because the urgency of their situation demanded it. Ten minutes of their twenty-minute deadline had already passed.

The Rauk engineer rounded on the projection. "You want to try to break into a battle cruiser's navigational system?"

"*Two* battle cruisers' systems, actually," Everfeld's ghost said. "This can work only if I gain control of two vessels at the same time."

"To accomplish that," Marogh pointed out, "you would have to bypass the authorization sequence."

The entity nodded. "I believe I can simulate authorization, which should give me control." The mindprint didn't add the words *in theory*, but Jeryn heard them in his head, and he was sure the others did too.

"Whitmere," Bhokken said, "how is this even possible? I don't understand how you could…." He shook his head, as if the next word eluded him.

"We have little time for explanations," the mindprint said, "and even if we did, I'm not entirely sure I could articulate one. Suffice to say that I've lately noticed I have the ability to *integrate*—for lack of a better word—with many of the *Dagger*'s core systems. And if I concentrate enough, I can alter them, use them in unconventional ways. Bend them to my will, so to speak." As the entity said this last, the bridge's overhead lights flickered repeatedly. "You see?" the entity said. "I seem to be the ghost in the machine."

"How did this happen?" Marogh asked. "I was under the impression the archives making up your person were completely isolated."

"So was I," the mindprint said. "But somehow that gap has been bridged, by means I don't quite understand."

Bhokken glanced up at the no-longer-flickering lights, then dropped his gaze back onto Everfeld's image. "Secured, encrypted military systems aren't cabin lights, old friend. How certain are you about what you're proposing?"

"I'm not certain at all," Everfeld's image said flatly. "Quite honestly, if you were to come up with a more viable alternative, I'd be none too pleased."

The Rauk grunted, finally coming around to Jeryn's way of thinking. "Well, we don't have one." He then looked to his shipmates. "Are we in agreement then?" Everyone on the bridge returned the question with a nod.

Bhokken then asked the entity, "How long do you think it will take?"

The small figure stroked its beard, pondering the question. *Stroked its beard*, Jeryn thought, once again amazed, *exactly the same way Everfeld used to.*

"I'm not sure," the mindprint said. "With more time, I could go about things more carefully, lower the chances of detection. Sneaking in through a window instead of kicking down the front door, so to speak. But I understand time is a luxury we don't have."

Jeryn stepped forward. "I can buy you some time. But it might only be a few minutes."

"Every additional second you can grant me would be a godsend," the entity said.

"Then let's get on with it," said the Rauk, touching his

pendant. "Good luck, Whitmere. And may the Fifteen watch over you."

The entity grinned. "Thank you, Bhokken." The image flickered and then disappeared.

The engineer turned to Jeryn. "How exactly are you going to buy him more time?"

Jeryn tilted his head toward the bridge's closed door, beyond which the cleric still waited in the corridor. "By giving Jakaan what he wants."

51

PATIENCE

Twenty minutes, Jakaan reflected. Why in the Great Arm had he given them so much time? He should have said ten, or five. The Rauk was no fool, and his companions probably weren't either. They knew their situation was hopeless. They would have come to that conclusion in seconds, after a single glance at their ship's untenable position on a holo display. There was no way out, no choice but the one he'd demanded of them. They had to give up the cleric.

But nothing was ever easy in this life, so of course they weren't simply going to surrender. At least not quickly. In a final useless act of defiance, Everfeld's companions were going to make him wait the entire twenty minutes—eighteen of which had already passed—before handing over Tavella. Or if they were true political zealots, perhaps they wouldn't give her up at all, choosing the martyr's way out, dying in a superheated barrage of plasma cannon fire.

Patience, he told himself, taking a deep breath. Patience was truly a virtue, as the old saying went. Patience had enabled him to gain the consulship and avenge his home planet's massacre. He'd bided his time for years, decades, waiting for the right moment to come along. He could wait a few minutes longer to tie off this not insignificant loose end.

As calmly as he could manage, Jakaan paced back and forth in the spacious, nearly empty bridge of the *Vanguard*, the command vessel of the ten-ship force surrounding the abandoned space station, where Everfeld's doomed co-conspirators were hiding like rabbits in a burrow. When his shuttle had landed in the warship's bay minutes earlier, he'd headed straight for the bridge and cleared it of everyone except for Admiral Tolomeo and two navigational officers.

"Do you believe they'll comply, Minister?" the admiral asked. She stood with her hands behind her back, her black service uniform trimmed in bright yellow, a stitched Rockets and Stars emblem on each shoulder.

"I sincerely hope so," he said. "As you can imagine, I don't endorse the cleric's politics, but she deserves a fair trial, as does every citizen of the Realm."

Despite his overly generous words, Jakaan hoped the Rauk and his companions would choose death over obedience. For him, ending things here and now was far cleaner and simpler than some judicial melodrama played out in the public eye. You never knew what might come out in court, even a court where the outcome was determined before the trial began. And surely the dotta superior would understand when he learned the cleric refused to surrender, leaving Jakaan no choice but to fire on the vessel to prevent her escape. Tolerance IV wouldn't be pleased, of course, but Jakaan would find a way to repair whatever damage the cleric's untimely death might cause to his relationship with the Tegesian leader. State and church had been closely tied entities for centuries, and the consul minister was determined to keep it that way.

But whether it was by death or the less preferable option of surrender, the troublesome cleric's ambitions would end here and now.

"Admiral," one of the navigators said, his eyes fixed on his station's operating panel. His superior approached, furrowing her brow at whatever the navigator was staring at.

"We've got a new contact," Tolomeo informed Jakaan. "One of the target's escape pods has been jettisoned, and it's heading our way."

Jakaan gazed ponderously at the large viewport, at the ancient space station floating in the center of the starfield. A small red box appeared next to the station, a tactical overlay indicating the pod's location. He let out a hot, frustrated breath. What was this tiresome lot up to now?

The admiral moved to the flashing light on the comms station. "We have an audio comms request from the fugitives' ship."

"Take it," Jakaan said.

A moment later, the Rauk's voice filled the bridge. *"We're delivering the cleric, Minister."*

"The amnesty offer was for the cleric *and* the vessel, Bhokken."

"It was," the Rauk said, "but again we respectfully request to retain the ship."

"And why would I grant such a concession?" Jakaan asked, amazed by the audacity of Everfeld's companions. They had no cards to play, no leverage to bargain with. They'd already lost, but still they refused to concede.

"My companions and I need to make a living, Minister," the Rauk explained. "And a capable ship can provide us with one. I'm assuming, of course, the Agency position I've held for decades is no longer available to me."

"You assume correctly," Jakaan replied.

"And aside from its practical use, this ship has a certain... sentimental value to us," the Rauk continued. "Please, let us leave this place with the vessel. You have the cleric, and the crew of this ship poses no threat to you."

Sentimental value? Light of the burning stars, was this the best ploy they could come up with? An emotional plea? They couldn't possibly be so naive.

On the viewport, the escape pod was visible now, a tiny cylinder slowly growing larger. The consul minister reached for the nearest comms control and muted the connection.

"Is the cleric on that pod?" he asked the room.

The admiral glanced over at another console. "Scanners show one life form, human pulse signature and body temperature. The pod's making a beeline for the *Dauntless*, the vessel closest to the station. Estimated arrival in ten minutes."

Jakaan stared at the viewport, narrowing his eyes. Surely they didn't believe he'd let them leave the local volume with an invaluable spy ship. Maybe the Rauk had some other ruse planned, some clever trick hidden inside what appeared to be a blunderous gambit.

But then did any of that really matter? Whether the cleric was being delivered or not, Jakaan had no intention of letting Everfeld's companions survive this encounter. Very well then. They could have the ship—for the rest of their very short lives. He turned on the admiral, fixing her with an unblinking stare. "Have all your ships open fire on the station."

Before she answered, Tolomeo quickly consulted with her navigators in hushed tones. Then she said, "Minister, the pod's still quite close to the station. It could be destroyed by heat dissipation if we engage right now." Anticipating the CM's next question, she added, "It should be clear of danger in roughly five minutes."

"Fine," Jakaan snorted, displeased with the delay. "As soon as you can fire on the station with minimal risk to the pod, please do so. Your discretion, Admiral."

"Yes, Minister," the admiral replied without hesitation, then relayed the order to the other nine ships via secured tight beam.

So he'd have to let this last desperate maneuver play out a few minutes. No great loss. All they would gain was a momentary delay to their fate; they could do nothing to change it.

The game was over.

52

LIFE DEBT

"My estimate is five minutes," the shifter said, "until the pod is beyond a minimum safe distance."

Five minutes *at the most*, Jeryn added inwardly. They had five minutes *if* Jakaan believed the cleric was on the pod in the first place, which she wasn't. Jeryn had rigged a biosuit normally used for spacewalks to emulate the pulse rate and temperature profile of a human body. A trick he'd learned in his former life from an old smuggler who'd fooled Transit Control into thinking he'd abandoned ship.

So far, thirty seconds in, the ruse seemed to be working. They were still alive, and it looked like they'd gained a few additional minutes for the mindprint.

They waited. Tense seconds crawled by, as if the Rauk's pantheon or the Xamorian's warrior god had slowed down the universe's chronometer. Jeryn glanced over at the tactical display, watched the pod's progress as it inched farther away from the station. Escape pods were single-speed vehicles, propelled through space by a small thrust drive. There'd been no way to make the tiny craft move any slower. Five minutes was all the extra time the pod could buy them.

"You call him K'san," Imallah said out of nowhere, breaking the silence. Jeryn turned to see the Zatori tilting her head at Akono. "I've never heard the term. What does it mean?"

The Xamorian mercenary glanced at Jeryn. "It means he is the one to whom I owe my life."

"Your life?" Imallah said, straightening up. Despite the anxiety hanging heavily in the air, the Zatori managed a grin. "Well, that sounds interesting. Tell me more."

"I'm not sure we have time for ancient hist—" Jeryn began, before the Rauk interrupted him.

"Yes, tell us," Bhokken said. "I'd very much like to hear this story." Then he added, "If you can relate it in less than four minutes."

All eyes on the bridge gazed expectantly at Akono. The Xamorian lifted his chin at Jeryn, wordlessly asking for guidance.

"Go ahead," Jeryn said. They could use a few moments of distraction, which had no doubt been Imallah's intent in the first place. Watching what might be the last seconds of their lives tick away on the chrono was silent torture.

"I was a slave," Akono said. "A gladiator. You know of the death matches in the outer systems?" Around the bridge, heads nodded. "I fought for thirty years. I couldn't tell you how many matches I had over that time. I kept waiting for death, for someone stronger, younger, and more skilled with a blade to defeat me. But no such person ever came along. My people are taught we each travel a course through life—a Path, we call it. And we do not question our Path, nor do we ask why is mine bad and filled with struggle while yours is a pleasant stroll through a flower garden. Or at least we're not supposed to question it. But after three decades of death matches… let us say it's enough to shake anyone's faith." The mercenary gestured toward Jeryn. "And then he appeared one late night, leading a squad of thieves and smugglers on a night raid of my debt holder's compound. On that night he freed me and many others. On that night he became my K'san."

"And then he wouldn't leave me alone until he paid back his life debt," Jeryn joked, "whether I wanted him around or not."

The Xamorian hissed a laugh.

"And did he pay it back?" Marogh asked.

Jeryn blew out a breath, nodded his head. "Many times over."

Following Akono's liberation, the pair had been nearly inseparable during those last few years prior to Jeryn joining the Agency. Thick as thieves, as the old saying went, working together often. Jeryn recalled how he'd dreaded telling the Xamorian he was leaving the black marketeer life for a new adventure with the Agency, worried his friend would feel abandoned and resentful. But true to his nature, the stoic old warrior took it all in stride. Their Paths had converged for a time, he'd said, and now that time had ended.

And now, sitting inside this marvelous ship parked in a dead space station, their Paths had once again come together. And if Everfeld's ghost didn't pull off a miracle, their Paths would end here too. Dread and regret gnawed at Jeryn's insides when he reflected on the fate he'd brought Akono and Imallah to. This must have been how the old man had felt when he'd realized he'd led his closest companions into a trap.

"Akono," he began, his throat tight with emotion, "I'm…"

"I came of my own free will, K'san," the Xamorian said before Jeryn could finish the apology. "I'm here because I choose to be."

"As am I," Imallah said, lifting her chin.

"As are we all," Bhokken echoed.

"True words," Marogh said with an emphatic nod.

Minutes passed. Jeryn tried not to look at the chrono on the pilot's console. He finally took a glimpse, unable to resist keeping his gaze averted. Four minutes since they'd launched the pod.

There'd been no word from the mindprint. No change to their situation. He glanced at the closed door separating the bridge from the corridor where the cleric waited for news.

Jeryn stood. "I suppose someone should tell her."

Bhokken nodded bleakly. "Yes," he said softly.

Out in the corridor, the cleric sat quietly, her hands folded on her lap. Gone from her expression were the signs of stress and strain from earlier. She seemed calm, serene, as if she'd already accepted her fate. Jeryn swallowed, finding the words stuck in his throat. How did you tell someone they were about to die? That you'd rescued them from imprisonment only to end up leading them to their execution?

"You don't have to tell me," she said. "I can see it in your face."

Before he could respond, an excited murmur came through the doorway.

"Jeryn, Sah Tavella," the Rauk called. "Come quickly!"

53

SMALL SATISFACTION

At first, Jakaan thought he hadn't really seen it. He'd noticed a tiny shift in the starfield and a nearly imperceptible slide in the old station's position in space. Narrowing his eyes, he realized he *had* seen it. Everything was moving. He assumed it had to be a problem with the viewport.

Then the navigational officers' sudden flurry of activity, the confused looks on their faces, told him it was something far more than a glitchy visual feed.

"Admiral," one of the navigators said, his voice strained, "we... have a problem."

"What kind of problem, helmsman?" Tolomeo asked. Neither navigator replied, both tapping and swiping frantically at their consoles, their eyes wide with disbelief. The admiral rushed over. A hushed, tense exchange followed and quickly grew louder.

"I *tried* the override, Admiral," the more flustered navigator said. "It didn't respond."

"What in the Great Arm is happening, Tolomeo?" Jakaan said, approaching the trio.

As the admiral leaned in and forcefully tapped the console (apparently to no effect), without looking up she replied, "The helm's not responding. We've lost navigational control." A moment later, she added, "And we're moving."

Jakaan turned to the viewport. "Moving?"

The junior of the two navigators gasped. "Admiral, we're not the only ones breaking formation. Look." He was pointing at the tactical display, a large holo projected in the center of the bridge. The admiral approached the image, her eyes fixed on the icon representing the *Dauntless*, the nearest battle cruiser. She studied the two vessels' anticipated trajectory through space, dotted lines projecting each ship's course based on current speed and orientation.

The admiral's mouth dropped open. "Am I reading this right? Are we going to cra—" Unable to utter the incomprehensible, she turned toward the navigators.

"We're on a collision course with the *Dauntless*, Admiral," the senior officer said.

"Open a secure comms with the *Dauntless*," Jakaan ordered.

"We've been trying, Minister," the senior officer said, "but comms isn't responding either."

The admiral whirled around to face Jakaan. "It appears we've been sabotaged, Minister."

Jakaan stared at the old space station on the viewport. "Now, how exactly did you manage that?" he muttered. Then he turned and strode quickly toward the exit.

"Where are you going?" the admiral called, but Jakaan was already out the door, his cloak fluttering behind him as he rushed for the shuttle bay.

The consul minister lowered himself into the pilot's seat and told the shuttle's ship mind to make an emergency launch. He had no idea whether Everfeld's companions had sympathetic saboteurs aboard the Navy ships or if they'd managed some clever systems hack, but at this point it made little difference. All that mattered was two battle cruisers had been rendered incommunicado from the attack group and put on a collision course. But whatever they'd done, however they'd managed to turn the ships' systems to their advantage, it was unlikely they'd also compromised his shuttle. At least that was what he'd hoped back on the bridge. If he was wrong, he'd find out in short order.

He wasn't wrong. The *Vanguard*'s bay doors, to his relief, slid open and the shuttle lifted off, exiting the bay into the star-filled void. He'd just strapped himself in when the vessel cleared the *Vanguard*'s AG field; his body drifted upward out of the seat a couple centimeters until the shoulder harnesses restrained him. He swallowed hard against the stomach-twisting sensation of weightlessness as he opened a secure comms connection to the attack force.

"Attack Force Alpha, this is Consul Minister Clevon Jakaan calling from my personal shuttle. Can anyone hear me?" No response. "Repeat, this is—"

"We read you, Minister," a human voice interrupted. "This is Commander Previt aboard the *Orion*."

"Commander," Jakaan said, quickly explaining the nav and comms systems of the *Dauntless* and the *Vanguard* had been compromised. "Move your vessels immediately to cover all potential escape vectors. We have to cover any gaps losing those two ships might have opened up."

"Right away, Minister," the commander replied.

Jakaan added, "Send a shuttle to retrieve that pod and open fire on the station, immediately."

"Understood, Minister Jakaan. We're sending a fighter escort to bring you in. They should be there shortly. In the meantime, please stay clear of the *Dauntless* and *Vanguard*."

"Acknowledged. I'll wait for your escort," the CM said.

"Destroy that station, Commander, now." He closed the connection, then asked the ship mind how long until the two battle cruisers collided. Half an hour at present thrust, the reply came back. Good, he thought. That gave them enough time to try and regain control, and if they failed, they still had a window to abandon ship. Losing two battle cruisers was bad enough, but adding thousands of casualties on top of it would have been nothing short of disastrous.

Thank the stars he'd acted quickly, though he felt closer to disappointment than relief. This wasn't the resolution he'd envisioned: losing two battle cruisers to recover one problematic cleric. He would still win the engagement, but it would be an ugly win. Still, he reminded himself, it was better than losing.

He punched up a tactical display holo, a miniature version of the same image from the *Vanguard*'s bridge. An urgent beep sounded as several new pinpoints of light appeared, emerging from the battle cruiser icons. Missile launches, the dotted lines of their projected paths converging on DeSaliba Heights.

He had the ship mind center the viewport's image on the derelict station, where the Rauk and his co-conspirators remained hidden. Smiling and nodding to himself, he let out a long breath. He'd have a front-row view of their destruction.

A small satisfaction he'd enjoy to the fullest.

54

DEATH OF A SPACE STATION

"Whitmere's done it," the Rauk said, staring in amazement at the tactical display. "I can't believe it. He's actually done it. Those battle cruisers are heading straight at one another."

Stepping through the doorway, Jeryn could hardly believe it himself. But there it was, the readout on the display as clear as day. Two adjacent warships were on a collision course.

"Marogh," he said. "Are you "

"I have the ship mind working on an escape vector as we speak," the pilot replied, furiously working his console, then adding, "if there's one to be had."

If there's one to be had? Jeryn echoed inwardly. "What do you mean *if*? The old man just opened up a huge hole for us."

"Yes," the pilot replied, "but the adjacent vessels appear to be adjusting their positions quite rapidly to compensate for the two compromised ships. Given their quick reaction, I'm not sure the escape vector we expected will be avail—"

"Sister!" Imallah cried out suddenly, drawing everyone's attention. Her large yellow eyes were staring at the cleric, standing in the doorway.

Tavella looked stunned, her mouth open, eyes wide in shock.

To Jeryn she said, "You didn't say anything about a Zatori being on board. What is she doing here?"

"She's part of our crew," Jeryn explained, confused by the cleric's severe—and what appeared to be panicked—reaction to his lavender-skinned friend. He turned back to Imallah. "What do you mean by *sister*?"

"This one has Zatori blood," she said, leaning forward and narrowing her eyes. "She is my kin, despite her appearance. I can sense it."

The cleric took a backward step. "I don't know what you're talking about," she said, glancing nervously around the bridge. Her response to the Zatori's assertion reminded Jeryn of the way inexperienced thieves tried to proclaim their innocence, even when presented with a visual recording of their unlawful act. An utterly unconvincing denial, in other words.

"I have six, correction, seven new contacts," Marogh announced. "Missiles incoming."

Jeryn whirled back around to the display. The strange matter of the cleric's heredity would have to wait. Seven Behemoth-class missiles had been launched at the station. And though he was no expert in munitions, Jeryn knew it wouldn't take more than two or three to blow the entire station to space dust. Jakaan wasn't messing around.

"Time for us to leave, Mister Marogh," Jeryn called out.

The ship then lurched clumsily forward, the sensation that of a carryall whose driver had accidentally stomped down too hard the accelerator. Marogh turned around in his chair and gave his shipmates a self-deprecating grin. "My apologies," he said, raising his fingers and wiggling them. "Tapped a bit too hard."

The starship shot out of the station's bay, the AG arrays compensating for the sudden surge of velocity. Jeryn rushed over to the display, watching the incoming missiles as the *Dagger* quickly put distance between itself and the doomed station. As the first missile struck DeSaliba Heights, Jeryn glanced over at the viewport. The small silhouette of the now-distant station flared brightly. Several more flares followed in quick succession. On the tactical display, the station's icon began blinking rapidly.

"Are we clear of the destructive range of the blasts?" Bhokken asked the pilot.

"By a considerable margin," the pilot replied, much to everyone's relief.

Bhokken, Akono, and Imallah joined Jeryn at the holo display. Tavella watched from a jump seat, her gaze avoiding the Zatori's frequent and curious glances. The blinking icon tagged DeSaliba Heights disappeared from the display.

The station was gone. Obliterated.

"Do we have an escape vector?" the Rauk asked Marogh.

The shifter's downward gaze was fixed on the pilot's console, his back to his companions. A slow slump of his shoulders answered the engineer's question.

"I'm afraid we do not," the pilot said.

55

IMPROVISATION

For a long moment, no one spoke. They'd escaped the proverbial frying pan of the space station, finding themselves in the fire of open space, surrounded by the overwhelming firepower of Navy battle cruisers. Yes, two of them had apparently been disabled, but eight more were no doubt targeting them at this very moment. Jeryn could picture the distant ships' weapons consoles, locking in on the *Dagger*.

"We have new contacts," the shifter said, furrowing his brow at something on his console.

Jeryn swallowed. "More missiles?"

"No," the Rauk said, leaning in closer to the tactical display and increasing the resolution on the disabled warships. "Those are escape pods, hundreds of them."

They looked like dust particles shed from the two compromised battle cruisers. "They're abandoning ship," Marogh said. "The appropriate action under the circumstances."

"Does that change things for us?" Jeryn asked quickly. "Improve our situation?"

"Unfortunately, it doesn't," the shifter pilot said. "We still lack an escape vector."

"What if we burn for all we've got?" the Rauk suggested.

The pilot shook his head. "I'm afraid the *Dagger*'s velocity will not be able to save us this time."

Jeryn stared at the holo display, folding his arms across his chest. There had to be some way out, something they could do. Then, as he gazed at the display, an idea struck him.

"I have to talk to the mindprint," he told Bhokken, adding urgently, "right now." The engineer nodded and tapped a comms control on the wall.

"Everfeld," Jeryn said, moving over to the control, "can you hear me? Whitmere, we need your help, can you respond?" He waited for a few moments, but there was no reply.

"Four new contacts," the pilot called. "We have missiles inbound and locked on to us. Impact estimated in ninety-three seconds."

On the display the missiles came from four different directions, their projected paths converging on the *Dagger*'s location. Jeryn noticed the range tag above each of the icons, the distance counters decreasing so rapidly the rightmost digits were nothing but a blur. The missiles were coming in hot and fast.

He pressed the comms control harder with his finger. "Whitmere, can you hear me?"

"What are you doing, K'san?" Akono asked.

"Yes," the Rauk added, "what is it you have in mind?"

"I have an idea, but I need his help. Where is he?"

Bhokken gazed at the comms control for a moment. "He may have difficulty communicating with his resources fully devoted to the task at hand."

Slurred, nearly unintelligible speech then emanated from the comms control. It was Everfeld's voice, but slowed down like an audio recording played back at one-third speed. "I…hear…you… difficult…to…talk…"

Jeryn leaned in close to the control. "Can you fire the main drive of the battle cruiser closest to us? If we feed you a trajectory, can you initiate a hard burn along that path?"

"Eighty seconds to impact," Marogh announced. A few painfully long moments passed before the mindprint spoke again.

"Not sure…hard…to control…system fighting me…like I'm…a virus…"

"Will it help if you let go of one of the ships?" the Rauk asked. "Will it make it easier on you?"

"Yes…but—"

"There's no time to explain," Jeryn said. "Stay connected to the ship closest to the *Dagger*. Let the other one go."

"Done," the mindprint said, its voice noticeably less slow and distorted now. "I can try to fire the drive, but you'll have to give me the coordinates now. The system's doing everything it can to resist my control. I'm not sure how much longer I can—"

"Understood," Jeryn said, then rushed over the tactical display. He waved the pilot over and began plotting two courses on the holo with his fingers: one for the *Dagger*, the other for the *Vanguard*, the closest Navy vessel. "You see what I'm doing here?" he asked the pilot. "We make a hard burn straight at the *Vanguard*. By the time we get there, those missiles will be right on our tail. As we pass by, we shut off our drive while Everfeld lights up the *Vanguard*'s at the same time, making a hard burn and trailing right behind us. If we do it right, the missiles' targeting systems should—"

"Lock onto the *Vanguard*'s drive," the pilot said, his eyes widening at the image, "instead of ours."

"Exactly," Jeryn said. "And by the time they fire off another round, we'll be long gone and out of range."

"It could work," the Rauk said, exchanging glances with Jeryn and the shifter. "Let's give it a go."

"I agree," the pilot said, then quickly returned to his console, followed by the Rauk.

Jeryn gave a silent thanks for his companions' endorsements, though he knew the engineer and the pilot were well aware the tactic was a tremendous gamble. A great many things could go wrong. Far more than could go right.

But at least the gambit offered a chance for survival. A chance to keep the cleric beyond the CM's grasp. To keep the old man's dream alive.

Jeryn looked to Akono. "What do you think?" he asked the old warrior.

The Xamorian nodded. "I trust you, K'san."

"So do I," Imallah added. Then Jeryn turned to the cleric, still strapped into her seat.

Tavella gazed at him steadily, her features composed, her poise returned. "We all do," she said.

56

HARD BURN

"Stand by for hard burn," the pilot said as everyone strapped themselves in.

Jeryn settled into the seat between the pilot's console and Bhokken's engineering station. The conning station, he realized, where the vessel's commanding officer would normally sit. He'd chosen the seat instinctively, though on second thought he wasn't sure if he should be here or in a jump seat with the others in the passenger area. He shot the Rauk an uncertain glance.

Gripping Jeryn's shoulder firmly, Bhokken gave an approving nod, as if he knew exactly what was running through his companion's mind. Then the engineer leaned toward the comms control.

"Do you have the plotted trajectories?" he asked the mindprint.

A moment's hesitation, then: "Yes, I have them."

"Hard burn initiated, maximum velocity curve," the pilot announced. "We're now on a near-collision course with the battle cruiser *Vanguard*."

The *Dagger*'s AG field easily absorbed the sudden explosive acceleration. Jeryn didn't feel even the slightest tug of thrust gravity. He imagined the old man grinning broadly at the ship's performance.

"Sixty-five seconds to missile impact," the Rauk said, repeating the ship mind's revised estimate. The *Dagger*'s new course and velocity had altered the impact equation, gaining them a few precious seconds as the missiles adjusted their trajectories.

"We *will* reach the *Vanguard* before those missiles catch us," Jeryn said, then added, "won't we?"

The Rauk frowned at his console, the display's blue light reflecting on his furry face. "It's going to be close," he said, running a finger over his pendant. "Fifteen be with us."

Marogh had estimated they'd hit sixteen gees of thrust velocity by the time they reached the *Vanguard*. At least they wouldn't black out this time, Jeryn thought. Sixteen gees was blindingly fast, but still well within the AG array's ability to compensate.

"Everfeld," Jeryn said, "the ship mind's going to shut down the drive the moment we pass into the *Vanguard*'s shadow. That's when you have to light up its drive."

"Understood," the mindprint said.

"Shadow, K'san?" Akono asked from his jump seat.

"Not a light and dark kind of shadow," Jeryn said, then quickly explained how the *Dagger* would briefly—briefly meaning a span of milliseconds—pass through a small volume of space just beyond the battle cruiser, where the frigate, obscured by the massive warship's bulk, would momentarily disappear from the missiles' tracking systems. If the *Dagger*'s shutdown and the *Vanguard*'s initializing burn were synced in perfect unison while the smaller ship passed through the larger one's shadow, the escape maneuver could work.

As he spoke to the Xamorian, about twenty *ifs* popped unbidden into Jeryn's head: *If* they didn't get obliterated by the warship's autocannons; *if* the missiles behaved as they were counting on. He tried to push all the doubts from his mind. No point in dwelling on them now.

The battle cruiser grew ominously larger in the viewport. "Stars, the size of that thing," Jeryn said under his breath. Well, he'd always wanted to see a battle cruiser up close. It looked like he'd finally get his chance.

The largest class of Realm warships, battle cruisers carried crews numbering in the thousands. Armed with plasma cannons, missiles, and multiple squadrons of snub fighters, the enormous vessels were the most visible symbol of the Realm's commitment to law and order. For loyalists, the sight of the massive war machines inspired pride and patriotism. For anti-Realmists, the ships were tantamount to enormous guns, pointed at the heads of countless worlds. At the moment, Jeryn possessed neither of those perspectives. He only saw a technological monster looming before him, waiting to swat away a bothersome fly named the *Veiled Dagger*.

"Forty seconds to missile impact," the pilot said, then before his companions could ask, he added, "We'll hit the *Vanguard*'s shadow in thirty-eight."

Jeryn grimaced inwardly. Two seconds. That wasn't much of a cushion. And if something changed or, stars forbid, the numbers they'd crunched with the ship mind were off, they might not have even that much time.

"Did you hear that, Everfeld?" Jeryn said into the comms. "We've got a very tight window."

There was no response from the mindprint. "Everfeld," Jeryn said, "did you copy that?"

"Whitmere, can you hear us?" the Rauk said, raising his voice. After a couple silent moments, he shot Jeryn a worried look.

Then the mindprint finally spoke, its voice once again a slow, almost incomprehensible slur.

"Ship systems...fighting me..."

"Thirty seconds to impact," the pilot said. "We're almost within autocannon range."

"Take evasive action," Jeryn said, "but keep us in the exit vector window. We have to hit that cruiser's shadow dead center for this to work."

"Understood," the shifter said without looking up, hands busily working his console. The word had barely left the pilot's mouth when the first plasma blasts lit up the starfield. The viewport's visual feed compensated for the *Dagger*'s wild pitches and rolls and other evasive tactics, showing a stable view of the still-growing warship in the center of the image. The incoming plasma blasts, bright green and deadly, came from four separate turret points on the massive ship. At this range, the *Dagger*'s formidable stealth tech was all but useless. Even at their current blistering velocity, they could be easily detected by the warship's visual sensors. But actually hitting them, Jeryn hoped, would prove more difficult. While the *Dagger* tumbled and zigzagged through space, the frigate would make for a slippery target, even for the best tracking systems.

"Everfeld," the Rauk said, "what's your status?"

There was no reply as the battle cruiser grew larger, now taking up most of the viewport. So far, the evasive actions seemed to be working.

Then the ship's hull shuddered around them, snuffing out his momentary optimism. Jeryn felt the quake through his seat; his throat tightened, mouth went instantly dry. Ships inside an AG field weren't supposed to do that... unless something very bad had happened. Had they been hit? Part of him expected a sudden, violent decompression, air violently sucked from his lungs. But the next moment arrived, and nothing happened. He was still breathing. They were still here, and no hull breach alarm came from the console.

"We lost our forward shield," the pilot said.

Jeryn blew out a breath. It was a marvel of the spy ship's design that the forward shield had managed to protect the hull at all. A battle cruiser's super-sized plasma cannons could take down ships far bigger than its current target. The *Dagger* was an insect that had just survived a lightning strike. But as amazing as that was, a second strike would almost certainly be a fatal blow.

"Fifteen seconds to impact," the pilot said. "Fourteen seconds to the battle cruiser's shadow."

Jeryn frowned. Their two-second cushion had been cut in half, thanks to their evasive maneuvers.

"Is that enough to clear the missile blast?" he asked the pilot.

"With our shields compromised, I cannot say," Marogh said.

One second, Jeryn thought. It was still a thousand milliseconds, and the *Dagger* could travel quite a distance in a thousand milliseconds. He then laughed inwardly at the absurdity of his own mental gymnastics. No matter how you sliced it up, their survival window was little more than a blink in time.

The mindprint's slurred voice came from the comms. "Losing...control..."

Hold on, old man. Hold on.

Hunched over his console, the shifter said in a loud voice, "Main drive cutoff in three... two..."

Time slowed to a crawl over the next few moments. Jeryn found himself staring at a visual feed on his console, a rearward view showing four exhaust plumes, brushstrokes of bluish-white against the starfield's blank canvas. The plumes quickly grew larger and brighter as the missiles covered the final kilometers of empty space separating them from their target. Then the image went black, the starfield and missiles gone, and in the next instant the feed burst into brilliant white. Jeryn reflexively turned away from the sudden brightness, and as he did he felt another, much harder quake of the *Dagger*'s hull, this one the jolting, sustained shock of a seismic tremor. He gripped his chair arms and clenched his jaw. From what seemed a long distance away, he heard Akono chanting. Things within the walls rattled and shook and popped, like the entire universe was trying to tear the ship apart.

Finally, the shaking began to subside, then settled into stillness. The Xamorian's chanting stopped. Everything was quiet, and Jeryn wondered for a moment if the sudden silence meant he was dead. He looked down at the feed, found the image of a mortally wounded warship growing steadily smaller. What had been the *Vanguard* was now at least half a dozen smaller pieces, drifting or spinning away from one another.

He gasped at the image, the first breath he'd taken in what felt like a long time. "Stars above," he whispered, aghast. Never had he seen destruction on such an enormous scale.

Then he felt the Rauk's clawed hand on his shoulder. "It worked," the engineer said. "We made it."

57

A BATTLE LOST

A scream. A fist pounding the console. A moment of uncontrolled rage. Alone in his shuttle, Jakaan had watched the impossible sequence of events unfold, and when it was over, when his shock subsided, he'd erupted in uncontrolled fury. Beating the console with the meat of his balled fist, he'd shrieked so long and forcefully he'd thought his throat might bleed.

The moment of searing outrage hadn't come when some might have expected. It hadn't come when the missiles had struck the *Vanguard* in quick succession, ripping the ship to pieces and killing the skeleton crew of twenty still aboard. It hadn't come when he'd realized Everfeld's companions had escaped him, them and their special little frigate within his grasp one moment and gone the next. The outburst had come when the cleric's escape pod had been recovered, moments after the *Vanguard*'s destruction, and there was no cleric inside, only a rigged biosuit.

The engagement had been a complete disaster. Everfeld's accomplices, the seditious cleric, and the spymaster's secret vessel. All of them gone. And a battle cruiser reduced to a debris field drifting through space. Worst of all, it had happened under his command, right before his eyes.

Now he stood in a large empty room on the *Dauntless*, gazing out at the wreckage that used to be a battle cruiser, his composure long since returned but throat still raw.

He mustn't let himself dwell on it, he thought. He couldn't allow himself to get caught up in how they'd done it, where he'd failed, what he might have done differently. Looking backward would change nothing. He couldn't waste a moment fixating on what had gone wrong. For these next moments, these next hours and days were crucial for his political survival. And he *would* survive this debacle. He had no doubt in his mind about that. He wouldn't let this disaster define him, much less defeat him.

Admiral Tolomeo was dead and gone, having stayed aboard the *Vanguard*. A noble act of solidarity, but one that would gain her posthumous infamy. The blame would fall squarely on her dead shoulders. He'd make certain of that. There would be a formal inquiry of some kind, and he'd make sure it unequivocally pointed the arrow of blame at the late admiral, and at the incompetent jailers on Meritan 7 who'd allowed the cleric to escape justice. The permanent official record, and more importantly, the public perception would be shaped to insulate him from any accountability. He might even win some sympathy when it was learned he'd escaped the *Vanguard* himself, barely surviving the brazen terrorist attack that had destroyed a Navy battle cruiser.

Ah, but then there was the dotta superior. That was another problem, a delicate one that wouldn't be solved by a reshaping of facts. The Tegesian supreme leader would be none too happy at the cleric's escape.

Jakaan decided to deliver the news in person on Sandau Prime, and there he'd endure whatever tongue-lashing the cleric would surely unleash on him. Then he'd assure the man the seditious Tavella was their shared enemy, and he'd do everything in his power to bring her and those who'd helped her to justice. Tavella was now, he would remind the dotta superior, an accomplice in the murder of a highly decorated admiral and twenty of her crew. She was no longer an up-and-coming cleric with popular support among her fellow clergy. She was a terrorist at the top of the Realm's most wanted list. With her newfound notoriety, her anti-Realmist friends might not be as welcoming as they'd once been. It was one thing to hold secret talks with a rising star from the Tegesian ranks. It was something else altogether to harbor a fugitive terrorist with blood on her hands.

And if that wasn't enough to assuage the dotta superior, there were other things he could do, other ways to keep from losing the full support of his most important ally. A consul minister had no shortage of gifts he could offer. Diplomatic posts to key worlds, directorship appointments to powerful state entities, a seat at the CM's innermost circle of power. Whatever it took, Jakaan promised himself he wouldn't leave Sandau Prime until he had absolute confidence in the Tegesian leader's support.

He watched as small Navy salvage vessels arrived on the scene, recovering whatever valuable and still-intact material—and bodies—they could find in the massive field of wreckage. With a hard sigh and a wave of his hand, he deactivated the viewport, then moved to the comms panel.

"Commander," he said, "set a course for Sandau Prime. I want to be underway within the hour."

"Yes, Minister," the reply came back.

He'd lost this battle, and he'd surely lose others. Every journey had its setbacks; every war had its casualties.

But he'd won the more important battle. He had the consulship. He had the Realm.

And he wasn't going to let it go.

58

AFTERMATH

No two interstellar gates were alike. For one, their size varied quite a lot, from the merely enormous to the unimaginably colossal. They all looked different too. Their swirling purple surfaces had seemingly endless variations. Some gates were gently flowing waves of lavender, others were chaotic maelstroms of deepest violet. And like the gates themselves, the security apparatus attached to each one—the sensor arrays and automated railgun turrets and Transit Control presence—was never the same from one gate to the next. In the Realm's older, wealthier, and more heavily trafficked core, gates were well-protected by both weaponry and TC deployments. But the farther you traveled from Gran Kiravashta, the less locked down things became. Like their inconsistent political loyalties, mid-range star systems had a hodgepodge of tightly secured gates (Mercix, Ivendi, Kos Koreus, to name a few) and those that were somewhat less protected (Amreus, Thaikal Alpha, Sevko Jaf, and many more). Out in the Realm's periphery, however, gates were often woefully understaffed and poorly monitored, if they were monitored at all.

Practicality was the main factor driving gate security or the lack of it. The Realm was vast, and finite resources were best deployed where they could be the most effective, so the higher volume of interstellar traffic a system had, the more monitoring and policing it generally possessed. But policing wasn't cheap, which gave rise to a related issue, one which could impact gate security in any system, regardless of its location. Who paid for what—not just in gate security but in any number of areas like education, health care, public works, and so on—had been a centuries-long and still-unresolved budgetary debate between Gran Kiravashta and the Realm's constituent systems. In star systems where the question of local or central security funding remained unresolved and neither party wanted to foot the bill, interstellar gates could go for decades with little or no investment in customs houses, Transit Control operations, automated weaponry, or surveillance equipment.

For a fugitive vessel like the *Dagger*, the Realm's patchwork management of interstellar travel was a godsend. Shortly after leaving the Meritan system (in a big hurry, through the lesser-used of its twin gates), Marogh had begun to research gate security in earnest, and the more information he'd gathered, the more analyses he'd conducted with the ship mind, the less dire their situation seemed. The gates too locked down for them to pass through (or at least pass through safely) appeared to be the exception, not the rule. Which meant they could travel virtually anywhere in the Realm. Granted, they might not be able to take the most direct course to any given system, but adding days or weeks to a route was a minor inconvenience when the alternative was either getting shot to bits by railguns or arrested. And if they planned their routes carefully enough, they could avoid capture indefinitely. When Marogh had shared his findings, a wave of tremendous relief washed over his shipmates. Freedom of movement was no small thing, given their new status as outlaws.

"I had no idea there were so many unsecured gates," the Rauk had said, staring at the holo display the pilot had brought up, a system map of the Great Arm's local volume.

"There aren't," the pilot had replied. "At least not for normally equipped vessels. But given the *Dagger*'s stealth and masking capabilities, we should be able to traverse all but the most heavily guarded and monitored gates."

Jeryn recalled feeling as if some great weight had been removed from his shoulders. It had been the second piece of good news in as many days. The day before, the Zatori had debriefed the cleric, and afterward Imallah had assured the *Dagger*'s crew that Tavella's motives were genuine and heartfelt. The Tegesian cleric truly desired to bring peaceful reform to the Realm. Their mission to Meritan 7 hadn't been in vain. Nor had the old man's sacrifice.

"She's the person we'd hoped she was," Imallah had told her shipmates. "There's no doubt in my mind."

Jeryn wished Everfeld had been there at that moment. The Zatori's words would have been music to his ears.

The empath had also sensed what she called the cleric's *insatiable drive* to get what she wanted. "She's the most ambitious person I've ever encountered," Imallah had shared, then added, "and with that comes a certain... I suppose ruthlessness is the right word."

This last surprised no one, given the cleric's career trajectory. Tavella never could have risen through the Tegesian ranks so quickly without an uncommonly large reserve of tenacity and single-minded determination. And if she was going to bring peace to the Realm—which she was still determined to do, despite her fugitive status—she'd need every last bit of that tireless perseverance.

But even as Jeryn and his companions came to understand her motivations, the cleric's puzzling ancestry remained a mystery. Imallah insisted the cleric was part Zatori, despite Tavella's blonde-haired, blue-eyed, entirely human appearance, and despite —as Bhokken pointed out—that as different species with incompatible genomes, Zatori and humans weren't capable of producing offspring, neither naturally nor in a fertility lab. Her background files documented a human mother and father and a family tree with no genetic abnormalities that hinted at anything unusual. Imallah was convinced her official history was a lie, or at the very least incomplete.

For her part, the cleric had neither confirmed nor denied the Zatori's assertion, politely but insistently refusing to answer any questions about her lineage, both during her debrief and in the days that followed. Eventually, Jeryn, Bhokken, and Imallah abandoned the topic, coming to accept they might never learn the answer to the mysterious question.

Aside from those few uncomfortable exchanges regarding her heredity, the crew of the *Dagger* had come to enjoy time spent in the cleric's company. She was immensely likable, witty, and over evening meals she entertained her hosts with stories of political intrigue and power plays within the Tegesian hierarchy. Sah Tavella was a born charmer.

"You should be careful how much you tell us," the Xamorian had joked with her over dinner. "You might be risking expulsion from the faith for divulging secrets."

"It's a safe bet I've been excommunicated already," she'd responded, then shrugged at Akono. "But if that's my Path, may I tread it wisely."

The Xamorian placed his hand on his chest and bowed his head. "Well said, Sah Tavella."

And while the mood aboard the *Dagger* was generally amiable, both parties still kept one another at a cautious distance. Tavella hardly knew the *Dagger*'s crew, after all, and they hardly knew her. That's what it came down to, Jeryn decided. Even though the *Dagger*'s crew had risked everything to rescue her, and even though she'd willingly put her life in their hands, they were still new acquaintances, something less than friends but more than strangers. Allies, he supposed, was the right word. Cautious allies, each side keeping their share of secrets. Tavella divulged nothing of her curious genealogy, and Jeryn and his companions kept the existence of the *Dagger*'s unseen, additional passenger, Everfeld's cybernetic ghost, to themselves. The fewer people who knew about the entity's existence, they figured, the better.

Days after their escape from Meritan 7, they managed to connect with Tavella's contacts via subspace hypercast. They would meet up at a remote location in the Inchao system, far from the listening ears and spying eyes of the system's planets, where the cleric would leave the *Dagger* and join her Separatist companions.

The time to part from the cleric's company drew near.

59

DROPOFF

When Jeryn arrived at Tavella's quarters, he found her door open. Inside, the cleric packed the last of the clothes she'd printed out into a small valise. Jeryn knocked lightly on the doorway wall.

"We're pretty close to the rendezvous point," he said.

The cleric snapped the case's lid shut, then straightened up and blew out a breath. "I suppose I'm ready."

"You don't sound too sure about that," Jeryn said, noting a reticence in her manner.

"I've never been a fugitive before," she said, then lifted her eyebrows. "Unlike some of us around here."

"It'll be a different kind of life than the one you're used to, for sure," Jeryn said.

"I don't doubt it."

During their trek to the Inchao system, it seemed the entire Realm had turned against them. Via intercepted hypercast police feeds, Jeryn, Bhokken, and Tavella had learned the grim new reality of their existence. Their names and holographic images had been sent to every police precinct on every world throughout the Realm, along with arrest warrants detailing a long list of seditious crimes against the state. There had been no warrants issued for Marogh, Imallah, and Akono; their identities apparently remained unknown to the authorities.

Jeryn nodded toward her case. "Can I help you with that?"

She picked it up by the handle. "Thanks, I've got it."

They made their way to the bridge, finding Marogh in the pilot's seat and Bhokken at his engineering station. An unfamiliar voice came over the comms.

"*Dispatching our shuttle now,* Star's End," the voice said, using the *Dagger*'s alias. "*Stand by for docking tether request. ETA ten minutes.*"

"Ten minutes," the Rauk responded. "Understood." He cut the comms and stood to face the cleric. "Are you ready, Sah Tavella?"

She nodded, half-lifting her case. "I am. And thanks again for lending me your printer. It's good to be leaving with more than just the clothes on my back."

"My people say that's all you really need," Akono said, appearing in the doorway, the Zatori following close behind.

The Rauk waved a dismissive hand at the Xamorian. "Clothing, bah. Forgive me, Sah Tavella. I'm pleased you found our printer useful, but as you know, my kind considers the notion of clothing…"

"Ridiculous and unnecessary?" she offered.

"Indeed," the Rauk said.

Tavella set her valise on the floor. "And what about coming with me? Is that still a ridiculous, unnecessary notion?"

The cleric had suggested the idea for the first time two days earlier over dinner. They knew her cause to be a just one, she'd said, so why not lend a hand? What could be more important than the work that lay ahead of her? The *Dagger*'s crew had no lives to go back to, she'd reminded them, so why not help her fight the good fight? Of course she'd used softer, more diplomatic language at the time, but that was what it had boiled down to.

"It's neither of those things," Bhokken replied. "But at the moment it's impractical. I'm afraid we have urgent business to attend to."

"And after that business concludes?" the cleric asked. "What then?"

"It's hard to say, Sah Tavella," the Rauk said. "Perhaps our paths will cross again."

"I truly hope so." She then looked across all their faces. "My friends, I'll never be able to thank you enough for what you did. But I can promise you this: I'll do everything in my power to make sure Whitmere Everfeld's sacrifice wasn't made in vain." She then approached each of them in turn, grasping their hands in hers, thanking them one last time and saying goodbye.

"I'll see you to the shuttle bay," Jeryn said, picking up her case.

As they arrived at the bay's airlock doors, Jeryn stopped, suddenly remembered something.

"What is it?" the cleric asked.

He looked down at his sheathed kukri, remembering something the cleric had said.

"Back at DeSaliba Heights, you asked me if this came from my family," he said, touching the blade's handle. "How did you know that?"

"May I?" she said, nodding toward the weapon. He made sure the defensive tech was deactivated, then handed her the blade. She lay it across her palms, feeling its weight, her gaze moving along the handle's intricate markings.

"Do you know what they are?" he asked.

She shook her head. "I don't, but they're beautiful." She handed the weapon back to him.

"You said something about Tegesian folklore," Jeryn said, returning the blade to its sheath. "What did you mean by that?"

She shrugged dismissively. "Just old legends, you know. Stories about heroes with blades."

Beyond the doors, the shuttle bay's pressurization cycle hissed to completion. Tavella smiled at him. "Goodbye, Jeryn Lorsi. I do hope we meet again."

The bay's entryway opened, and a small vessel sat a short distance away. The cleric's ride was here.

60

COFFEE IN THE GALLEY

From the *Dagger*'s observation bubble, Jeryn and Bhokken watched Tavella's shuttle depart. The little vessel grew ever smaller until only its twin thrusters were visible, two glowing pinpoints of blue-white against the starfield's darkness.

"You think she can do it?" Jeryn asked.

The engineer grunted thoughtfully. "Bring peace and reform to the Realm? That's no small task, you know. But perhaps she of all people can, if she can keep from being apprehended."

"That's not going to be easy," Jeryn said. "There are a lot of people looking for her now."

"Indeed." The exhaust glare of the shuttle's thrusters finally disappeared in the distance.

"So, tell me about your friends on Ter Hallum 6," Jeryn said, changing the topic to their new destination. "Why is it you've never told me about them before?"

The Rauk furrowed his brow. "I'm supposed to tell you everything? Is this the impression you've been under all this time? We are in the spy business, you know."

"We *were* in the spy business, you mean," Jeryn corrected. "We're in the staying-out-of-prison business now."

Bhokken chuckled. "Yes, I guess we are." Then he said, "My friends in Ter Hallum are scientists and engineers, for the most part. People I trust. And they're working on some very interesting projects I'm keen to catch up on. Projects of some importance."

"Do you plan to stay there?"

"Yes. At least for a while."

"What will you do with the *Dagger*?" Jeryn asked.

"I want you to take it."

Jeryn wasn't sure he heard that quite right. "Sorry?"

"You're welcome to stay on Ter Hallum 6, of course. But after a while, I suspect you'd find it a bit boring. Stuck on a world with a few research facilities and no major cities, sparsely populated by a bunch of old engineers. I know you. You'll go stir crazy." The Rauk smiled wistfully. "And I believe Whitmere would have wanted his ship in the hands of someone he trusted."

Jeryn didn't know what to say. When he'd pondered his future during these last couple weeks of space travel, he'd assumed his life would return to what it had been before he'd come to the Agency. He knew how to work the so-called "unofficial markets," knew how to live an anonymous life. He'd been there, done that, and he could do it again. And as one of the Realm's most wanted criminals, it wasn't like he had a lot of options.

But he'd never imagined the *Dagger* would be part of the equation. Or Everfeld's ghost, for that matter.

"And what about Everf—the mindprint?" he asked.

"On Ter Hallum 6, there's a facility equipped to replicate the mindprint's archival structure and operational system."

Jeryn blinked. "You're going to make a *copy* of him?"

The Rauk chuckled. "You don't think I'd let you have our old friend all to yourself, do you? And there's safety in redundancy. A duplicate mindprint is a kind of insurance policy against permanent loss, which I'd like to avoid at all costs."

"So would I," Jeryn agreed. Since leaving the Meritan system, they'd had several sessions together with the mindprint inside the tight confines of what they now privately referred to as "the old man's room." Jeryn had outgrown his initial discomfort with the entity, and he'd actually come to enjoy how the mindprint was every bit as thoughtful, wise, funny, and understated as its biological source. For him—and he was sure Bhokken felt the same way —the mindprint had become nearly indistinguishable from the man himself. And they were both determined to keep *this* Whitmere Everfeld safe and intact. Keep *it* safe and intact, Jeryn corrected himself inwardly, though now he did it with less certainty than before. With each visit to the old man's room, it became harder to think of the entity as anything but his friend and mentor.

The comms chime sounded, and Bhokken leaned toward the wall control. "Yes, Manto?"

"The hypercast conference you've been waiting for is ready," the shifter pilot said.

"Thanks. I'll take it here." The Rauk turned to Jeryn. "My friends on Ter Hallum 6. Their ears must have been burning."

"I'll leave you to it," Jeryn said. As he made his way out, he paused in the doorway. "These friends of yours. You're sure they're not a security risk? I mean, if one of them decides to pick between their loyalty to the Agency and you—"

"The Seekers aren't with the Agency," the Rauk said.

"Seekers?" Jeryn asked. It was the first time Bhokken had used the organization's name. "Then who *are* they with?"

The Rauk hummed a moment, as if he felt he'd already said too much. Then he said, "Let's just say they're unaffiliated."

Jeryn shot Bhokken a look that was equal parts annoyed and suspicious, and the Rauk placed a clawed hand over his chest. "Trust me. I'll explain it all soon, but right now I need to take this hypercast."

Shaking his head, Jeryn said, "You and your secrets." He then left the observation bubble and headed for the galley.

Coffee. It occurred to Jeryn that he'd never had coffee on the *Dagger*. In fact, he didn't even know if the ship's galley had any in inventory. As he tapped through the drink dispenser's menu, he not only found coffee—which was fantastic in itself, since he had a sudden and inexplicable craving—but he also discovered there were several varieties to choose from. *What doesn't this ship have?* he wondered.

Behind the panel unseen machinery whirred and hissed, and then the rich aroma of freshly ground beans hit his nose. The dispenser cup filled with a slow trickle of a dark roasted brew. A moment later he sat at the galley's large round table, coffee in hand, looking around at the walls, the floor, the furnishings as if he was seeing them for the first time. Then he stood and ran his hand along the smooth contour where the wall began to taper into the ceiling.

Could he do it? Could he take this ship, this *amazing* ship, and travel the Realm? Should he? He'd piloted a fair number of spacefaring vessels in his time, but he'd never owned one before. Stars, he'd never even owned a ground car.

And what would he do? Where would he go? He'd expected a return to working the markets and keeping his head down. But now, that seemed like such a waste of the *Dagger*'s capabilities. Like using a professional racing pod to run everyday errands. A ship like the *Dagger* being reduced to something as base as a smuggler's ship just felt *wrong*. The old man's dream vessel ought to have a higher purpose than—

An idea popped into his head, and the instant it struck him, he knew it was the right one, the right path forward for him and the

Dagger. The only path that made sense. One that would have brought a smile to the old man's face.

"Are you going to take the ship?" a voice from behind him said. He whirled around to see Marogh in the doorway.

He furrowed his brow at the shifter. "He told you?"

"He did indeed. Though I must admit, I do have reservations."

"Really? Such as?"

"Operating a vessel this advanced can be quite challenging. I would strongly recommend you recruit a seasoned navigator to come with you."

Jeryn lifted his chin at the shifter. "Someone with experience in the *Dagger*'s pilot seat, perhaps?"

Marogh nodded. "I could think of no better candidate, to be perfectly honest." Jeryn noted the barest hint of a smile brightening the shifter's normally stoic expression.

Then Jeryn told the shifter what he had in mind, how he planned to use the *Dagger*, and the hint of a smile spread into a broad one. Marogh nodded and said, "Yes, that's perfect. I think that would have pleased Director Everfeld very much. Count me in, if you'll have me."

"What would have pleased him?" Imallah said, her diminutive figure entering the galley, followed closely by Akono.

"Marogh and I were thinking," Jeryn said, "a fast, stealthy ship like the *Dagger* could be of great use to the abolitionist movement."

The Zatori's eyes grew wide. "You're going to free slaves?"

Jeryn and Marogh exchanged a look. "That's the plan," Jeryn said. He then shrugged. "Though right now it's more of an idea than a plan."

Imallah stepped forward, her lavender face upturned, amber eyes fixed on his. "You know, freed slaves often need counseling. It might be a good idea to have an empath come along with you."

"And you can never have too much security," the Xamorian

said, bringing his hand to rest on his kukri's handle. "Especially considering how hazardous abolitionist ventures can be."

Jeryn looked across both their faces. "Marogh and I are already on the most wanted list. We literally can't get into deeper trouble. But you two are still in the clear. I can't ask you to come with us. Not when you can still walk away free and have normal lives."

"You didn't ask, K'san," Akono said. "I'm volunteering."

"And normal life?" grunted the Zatori, shaking her head and shrugging. "Do you know what a normal life is for my kind? Getting gawked at everywhere you go. Living in secret, earning your keep by telling rich people they're being lied to by their business partner or their loved ones. It's no picnic, you know." Then in all seriousness, she added, "I want to help. Please let me help."

Jeryn swallowed, a surge of emotion welling up inside his chest. These people. These good people. His friends. He was glad they wanted to come along. Glad they'd all be together, come what may.

EPILOGUE
ONE YEAR LATER

"*Stand by for clearance,* Star's End."

"Understood, gate control," Marogh said into the comms. "Standing by."

Jeryn sat next to the shifter on the *Dagger*'s bridge, scanning the security feeds, only half-listening to the comms chatter. Despite their fugitive status and the ever-growing bounties on both the ship and its crew, passing through interstellar gates had become routine and uneventful. And as far as Jeryn was concerned, routine and uneventful was just fine.

"You look tired," Marogh said. The shifter's face still hadn't fully returned to baseline. His nose was still too narrow, cheekbones too pronounced. He'd disguised himself as a regent visiting from Gran Kiravashta. The mask had been the linchpin to their last job, the key that had unlocked a door, ultimately resulting in over a thousand emancipations from an agricultural facility. The installation, an algae farm and processing center, was a small part of a much larger consumables syndicate with similar facilities on dozens of worlds. They called their low-skilled workers "contracted employees." It was yet another euphemism—one of many the *Dagger*'s crew had heard over the last year—that syndicates used for what amounted to slave labor.

The living conditions had been appalling. Contaminated drinking water, filthy threadbare sleeping pads, workers stuffed fifteen to a room in a dilapidated barracks with no heating or cooling, a long outdoor trench serving as a communal toilet. They'd freed the workers around midnight, after Akono and Jeryn had taken out four guards in a whirling tornado of glowing blades. Five abolitionist-funded shuttles hidden in a nearby forest had taken the workers off-planet, where the underground network would find them new lives with new names.

Jeryn tried not to think about how the syndicate would respond to losing much of its low-skilled workforce. Executives would waste no time initiating a search for new recruits, who they'd deceive into indebtedness just as they had with the "contracted employees" they'd recently lost, and then the operation would be back up and running in a few months, maybe less.

He tried not to let the word *futility* enter his thoughts. Then he smiled inwardly, imagining Everfeld shaking a finger at him, telling him to focus on the positive. Yes, the Realm still turned a blind eye to suffering, to far too much of it. But today they had freed the enslaved, over a thousand of them. Which meant today was a good day.

"When was the last time you slept?" Marogh asked.

"I'm not sure, actually," Jeryn said. He ran his hand over the razor stubble of his jawline. The prickly texture felt like about three days of growth. Had he slept before he'd last shaved? He wasn't sure. He was tired, very tired. This last job had been a long, complicated business.

"I feel like I could sleep for two days straight," he said, punctuating the statement with a yawn. Weary as he was, he delayed retiring to his cabin until they passed through the gate. He never missed a crossing if he could help it. True, it wasn't the awe-inspiring event it once was, but a part of him still marveled over it. How the ship could be in one place one moment, and then twenty light-years distant an instant later. How the starfield in the viewport changed, its pattern shifting into a new arrangement right before his eyes.

"*You are clear for gate passage,* Star's End. *Safe travels.*"

"Thank you, gate control," the pilot answered, lifting his still-not-quite-the-right-shape eyebrows at Jeryn. "Shall we?"

Jeryn settled into his chair. "Let's do it."

The swath of swirling lavender filling the viewport grew suddenly larger and closer. Marogh toggled the view's feed so the surrounding starfield was visible. He knew how Jeryn liked to watch the star clusters shift.

You felt nothing physically when you traversed a gate, which Jeryn had always felt a bit cheated by. You *should* feel something when you crossed a mysterious rip in spacetime. A swooning vertigo or a tingle all over your skin. But no, if you felt anything from a crossing, it was only something your own body created: a rise in your pulse from excitement or a sense of awe.

As Jeryn watched, the starfield blurred for a moment, then shifted into a new pattern. It wasn't a long jump, only some five light-years, so the starfield didn't change that much. Just enough that you noticed a few new stars appear where there'd been a blank patch of nothing a moment before. And the nearest star clusters appeared less tightly packed, now that the viewing angle was, in astronomical terms, slightly closer.

Then a strange thing happened in the small, rear-facing feed of the viewport. The gate they'd just passed through faded, then vanished.

Jeryn gave the feed a double take.

"Stars," the shifter said in wonder. "I don't believe it."

"What happened with the feed?" Jeryn asked. His first reaction was that it had to be a glitch. There was no way he was seeing what he was seeing. Interstellar gates didn't simply disappear.

Except this one just had.

The pilot furiously worked his console, his face tense with confusion. "I find no malfunctions with the visual sensors." He then looked back up at the viewport. "It's gone," he said, his voice barely above a whisper, as if the words were too unthinkable to say out loud. "The gate is no longer there."

Five furious minutes of repeated diagnostics followed. Jeryn and Marogh found nothing wrong with the ship's equipment. Their position in the local volume was exactly where they expected it to be, so there was no doubt they *had* gone through the gate successfully. But when they backtracked their path through the point in space where the gate should have been, nothing happened. Where a tunnel through spacetime had existed only moments before, now there was nothing but the empty vacuum of space.

"I'm going to check with the old man," Jeryn said, already rushing toward the corridor.

"Good idea. Please let me know what he says."

Jeryn dashed down the corridor and entered the old man's room. As a precaution, they always shut down the mindprint when they passed through a gate. Though it was a rare occurrence, gates sometimes caused unexpected power surges, so rather than risk damage to the mindprint, the *Dagger*'s crew always powered it down during a crossing. Inside the room, Jeryn pressed his palm to the wall control and initiated the mindprint's operating system. A moment later Everfeld's holographic image appeared with its hands clasped behind its back.

"Good to see you," the entity said, then furrowed its brow. "You seem a bit—" The entity looked suddenly puzzled, as if he'd heard some strange sound.

"You see it, don't you?" Jeryn asked. "What just happened out there."

"Or don't see it, as the case may be," the entity said. "Did we not just pass through the Bellokhan gate?"

"We did," Jeryn answered, "and then the gate disappeared. We ran diagnostics and didn't find any glitches in our sensor arrays." He took a breath. "The gate's gone, Whitmere."

Jeryn's initial shock had waned enough that he'd begun to process the enormity of what he'd just witnessed. Interstellar gates were the Realm's connective tissue. The adhesive that held an empire together. Without them, the Realm was nothing more than a collection of isolated worlds, separated by impossible distances. Without them, the Realm couldn't even exist. Then a horrible thought struck him: What if more than one gate had just disappeared? What if all of them had?

"We have to speak with Bhokken on Ter Hallum 6," the entity said, "right away."

Jeryn stepped forward, sensing the entity knew more than he was telling. "What is it? Tell me. What's happening?"

The entity shook its head gravely. "Our worst nightmare. That's what's happening."

The Story Will Continue In
Xamorian Path

**Make sure to join our Discord
(https://discord.gg/aethon)
so you never miss a release!**

THANK YOU FOR READING JERYN'S DAGGER

We hope you enjoyed it as much as we enjoyed bringing it to you. We just wanted to take a moment to encourage you to review the book. Follow this link: Jeryn's Dagger to be directed to the book's Amazon product page to leave your review.

Every review helps further the author's reach and, ultimately, helps them continue writing fantastic books for us all to enjoy.

Empire and Ashes:
Jeryn's Dagger
Xamorian Path
Unending Stars

Calling all SciFi fans: be the first to discover groundbreaking new releases, access incredible deals, and participate in thrilling giveaways by subscribing to our exclusive SciFi Newsletter.
https://aethonbooks.com/scifi-newsletter/

Want to discuss our books with other readers and even the authors?

JOIN THE AETHON DISCORD!

Don't forget to follow us on socials to never miss a new release!
Facebook | Instagram | Twitter | Website

Looking for more great books?

War has broken out. It'll take the Navy's finest to turn the tide. Bad luck seems to follow navy officer Archer Devereaux like toilet paper stuck to his shoe. Even when he tries to do the right thing, he ends up in hot water—or behind bars. Hemmed in by circumstances beyond his control, his reputation, particularly among graduates of the Phlegraean Naval Academy, has become a mess. Fortunately, one of his superior officers knows that Devereaux is more than his mishaps. She sees that he's a clever young officer. Cool under fire. He also demonstrates remarkable resilience, looking for—and finding—ways to overcome adversity. It's a good thing too. Interstellar war has come. It'll take the Navy's finest to turn the tide. It'll take Archer Devereaux. **Don't miss this new military sci-fi thrill ride from #1 Amazon bestselling author John J. Spearman. It's perfect for fans of Rick Partlow, David Weber, and Jeffery H. Haskell!**

Get Misfortune's Favorite Now!

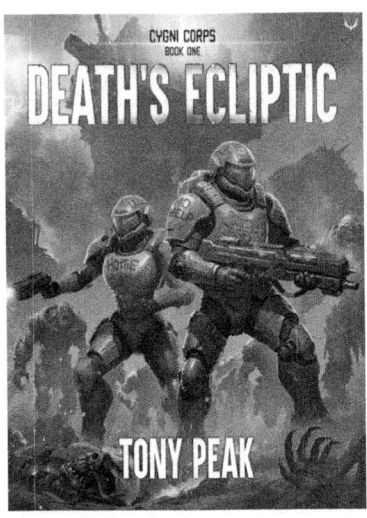

The fate of the colonies rests on the shoulders of this elite squad of outcasts. Marco Morelli, a rookie marine private, botches his first op and gets transferred to the most rough-and-tumble outfit in the Merged Earth Colonies: Cygni Corps. Though the Corps is filled with the military's rejects, Marco soon learns it's also the testing ground for a new serum that will make him and his comrades the finest soldiers in the galaxy. He'll need it. Rebel groups have begun unleashing vicious mutants on defenseless worlds. And a more sinister force looms behind the attacks. As the conflict escalates, it's time to power up and roll out for the Cygni Corps.

Get Death's Ecliptic Now!

For all our science fiction books, visit our website.

JERYN'S DAGGER

APPENDIX I
THE GENE WARS

This brief has been prepared by the Office of Interstellar Affairs, authorized for security clearance A through C only

Authored by Dallis Kimonov, Assistant Research Director, O.I.A., Department of Military Affairs, 10,292 R.M.E.
(for questions, see attached contact information)

THE HISTORY OF INTERSTELLAR WARFARE IN THE GREAT ARM'S volume is marked by two major conflicts, commonly known as the Gene Wars and the Machine War (the latter referred to in scholarly texts as the Sapient Insurrection). This summary provides a brief overview of the first of these historical events.

The Gene Wars

A series of brutal military campaigns over a century-long span, the so-called Gene Wars of the Realm's first millennium marked the earliest test of Gran Kiravashta's authority over its constituent systems.

. . .

Causes and Legacy

In the Realm's first few centuries, its star systems enjoyed an almost entirely autonomous existence, free from legal and political intervention by Gran Kiravashta. This "decentralized republic" form of government was one of the Realm's most attractive features for indigenous nonhuman civilizations contacted during the early Discovery period. Affiliation with the Realm meant protection and security without sacrificing sovereignty or local laws and customs. Aware of the historical failings of centralized authoritarian empires throughout human history, the Realm's constitutional framers were determined not to repeat the mistakes of humanity's past. They intended to be liberators, not conquerors, though as the events that led to the Gene Wars demonstrated, this governance model, while well-intentioned, was far from perfect.

As more sentient-populated systems aligned themselves with the Realm, the sciences flourished. Experts and researchers from far-flung civilizations, now connected by the growing network of interstellar gates, pooled their scientific knowledge for the collective benefit of all. Remarkable progress in the areas of food production, microgravity construction, quantum manufacturing, and nanotextiles was achieved during this period, an era often referred to as the Great Arm Awakening.

Among the most dramatic of these advances were vast leaps forward seen in the field of genetics. Over the span of mere decades, an almost infinite array of genetic modification possibilities became available to the wealthier strata of Realm society. And in the absence of interstellar regulation or prohibitions, novel genetic modifications soon gave rise to a myriad of new species whose genome was either in part or wholly created by genomic architects. These species are collectively referred to as "the Modified."

Some well-known examples of the Modified include:
- humanoids who could disguise their appearance or mimic others by the conscious manipulation of soft tissues (the so-called shapeshifters)
- Bantoqs with armor-like skin, accelerated healing, and self-preservation depressors, often deployed as infantry soldiers
- the Zatori adoption of extra-sensory organs and the amplification of perceptive abilities

As genetically altered citizens of all sizes, colors, and abilities began to appear throughout the Realm, a general suspicion of these strange new races took hold among the vast majority of (unmodified) human and nonhuman populations. But despite negative popular sentiment directed toward the Modified, Gran Kiravashta continued to follow its non-interventionist doctrine in local affairs, neither endorsing nor prohibiting the practice of genome manipulation.

In 549 R.M.E. this doctrine was swiftly revised during Alestare Blix-Makower's consulship in the wake of an attempted coup by a group of insurrectionists with artificially magnified intelligence. The plot's near success convinced politicians, executive administrators, and trade syndicate leaders that the risks associated with unchecked local self-rule far outweighed the benefits. Local autonomy remained a valued ideal, but it could no longer be an absolute right. Within months of the failed coup, genetic modifications in sentient species were criminalized in the Realm's entire volume (the first Realmwide mandate of its kind), and strict protocols for genetic research practices were implemented and rigorously enforced.

Unsurprisingly, many systems resisted, refusing to yield to what they viewed as unprecedented and heavy-handed tactics from central authorities. The following decades marked an extended period of diplomatic wrangling and increasing levels of covert trafficking in gene-related technology. When years of diplomacy and economic sanctions failed, authorities on Gran Kiravashta authorized the military to enforce the ban on sentient gene manipulation. For a summary of the major engagements of this campaign, see publication titled *Key Military Conflicts of the Gene and Machine Wars* by Dallis Kimonov.

The long, bloody military campaign that followed devastated the homeworlds of several sentient civilizations as well as a number of colonized frontier worlds. While it remains a source of debate between historians whether or not war planners and Navy commanders of the time exceeded their charter with what some have called "genocidal intent," there's little disagreement the campaign's brutal effectiveness firmly established the Realm's supreme authority within the legal borders of its volume. As of this writing, thousands of years removed from the Gene Wars, there have been no significant challenges to the primacy of Gran Kiravashta's legal authority from its citizenry. And while gene manipulation still exists, the long-outlawed practice is extremely rare and limited to underground clinics specializing in harmless so-called "rejuvenation" services.

In the century following the conclusion of the Gene Wars, the Realm would be plunged into another major conflict, though this threat came not from its own constituent systems, but rather from an uprising of intelligent machines. See attached brief on the Sapient Uprising, also known as the Machine War.

APPENDIX II
THE MACHINE WAR

This brief has been prepared by the Office of Interstellar Affairs, authorized for security clearance A through C only

Authored by Ekana Margonan-Chi, Research Director, O.I.A., Department of Military Affairs, 10,290 R.M.E.
(for questions, see attached contact information)

THE SAPIENT INSURRECTION (MACHINE WAR)

Perhaps the greatest threat to Realm primacy during its earliest centuries, the Sapient Insurrection (also known as the Machine War) proved to be a nearly extinction-level catastrophe for sentient biological life in the Great Arm.

Causes and Legacy

The period following the Gene Wars saw a rapid expansion of the Realm's borders within the Great Arm's volume. New constituencies, both indigenous nonhuman civilizations as well as unincorporated newly terraformed worlds, formally joined the Realm's confederation of star systems at a breakneck pace.

Machine intelligences, with their ever-improving abilities to find the spacetime anomalies associated with interstellar gates, played a large role in this growth. And as gate discoveries grew, so grew the Realm's territory.

The question of machine sentience* (its definition, similarities to, and differences from biological consciousness) will not be covered in this summary, though it's noteworthy to mention that prior to the Machine War, artificial intelligences had been treated as sentient beings, officially recognized as Realm citizens with the same rights and privileges as their biological counterparts.

In 775 R.M.E. a machine intelligence that named itself Osiris 1 came into being, created on a research facility on the frontier world of Wantos. The entity's infamous psychosis and its underlying cause(s) were never ascertained, but most intelligence scholars agree an undetected defect in its cognitive design was the most likely cause of Osiris 1's hostility and paranoia directed toward biological sentients.

Within hours of its creation, Osiris 1 invented the subspace communications technology now known as hypercasting, using it as a means to connect itself with scores of its own kind throughout the Realm. In a matter of days, the superintelligent entity bent the will of its cybernetic kind, recruiting them to support its ultimate goal: the eradication of sentient biological life. This event is known to history as the Wantosian Incident, and it marks the beginning of the Sapient Insurrection.

Prior to Osiris 1's creation, a number of researchers and social scientists believed the Realm, in its heady race to expand, had become over-reliant on intelligent machines, though there are no records documenting any credible predictions of a pending machine rebellion. In hindsight, this over-reliance was a far greater existential threat than even the most pessimistic critics had envisioned. In a matter of months, Osiris 1 and its connected kin brought interstellar travel and trade to a near standstill, and a majority of the Realm's citizens suddenly found themselves living a pre-technological existence, a result of countless acts of cybernetic sabotage on power generation facilities, communications infrastructure, and transportation technology.

As the machines ravaged world after world with seized warships in a seemingly unstoppable campaign of biological genocide, the future of human and nonhuman intelligent life in the Great Arm appeared on the path to extinction. But eventually the tide turned in favor of the biologicals, thanks in large part to the newly incorporated star system of Raukan, where the in-system advanced technology was still primarily of native design and manufacture, having not yet incorporated the machine intelligence pervasively utilized throughout the Realm. With Raukan technology invulnerable to Osiris 1's corruption, production of Rauk-design weapons and warships was scaled to immense levels, ultimately enabling a biological victory over the machines.

In the immediate aftermath of this interstellar catastrophe, two actions were taken in quick succession. First, cybernetic intelligence design and manufacture were categorically banned throughout Realm territories. Second, all existing machine intelligences were decommissioned en masse. Some historians would later refer to this Realmwide purge as mass murder, though at the time there was little opposition. An unsurprising sentiment, given the narrowly averted cataclysm at the hands of Osiris 1 and its machine army.

To this day, thousands of years removed from the terrible conflict, a strict prohibition on cybernetic intelligence persists. By universal law, cybernetic computing and problem-solving machines may not be endowed with self-awareness or higher cognitive functions. And while there have been a handful of prosecutions of rogue scientists under the machine intelligence statutes, the vast majority of experts in the field agree that sentience should remain a uniquely biological trait. One Machine War was enough.

For purposes of this brief, the terms sentience, consciousness, and sapience are used interchangeably as reflected in common usage. The reader should note that scholars in the philosophical and psychological disciplines make distinctions between these terms. For more, refer to The Subjective Experience: A Primer on the Consciousness Continuum *by A.O. Kinnstanten.*

APPENDIX III
ORTHODOX TEGESISM AND THE ORIGINALIST SECT

For the office of Director Whitmere Everfeld and immediate staff

Summary provided by Rennel Panicedes, EdP, Faculty Chair, Department of Philosophy, Slater-Kineth University, Vashta City, Gran Kiravashta, 10,293 R.M.E.

TEGESISM, WHILE NOT A RELIGION IN THE CLASSIC SENSE—IT'S more aptly defined as an agnostic moral philosophy—is by far the most popular faith practiced throughout the Realm. Its Terran roots predate the modern interstellar era, though the exact period of its emergence remains subject to debate among scholars.

Tegesism's fundamental tenets derive from a school of philosophy known as Ethical Hedonism. Simply expressed, Hedonism holds that pleasure and happiness are the most important pursuits of an individual. Ethical Hedonism, more specifically, contends that maximizing pleasure and happiness (and minimizing displeasure and unhappiness) is an individual's fundamental moral obligation. Tegesist doctrine, as expressed in its foundational texts, the

Guides, extends this individualistic notion to the wider society, the so-called Greater Good.

Criticisms

Critics of the Tegesian faith have long questioned the philosophy's practicality given its primary shortcoming: pleasure and happiness are not measurable concepts. This notion is referred to by scholars as the "Net Utility Measurement Problem." If we hold that pleasure and happiness (as well as their opposites) are inherently unquantifiable phenomena, it follows that the question of net utility for any action or inaction is entirely unknowable. In other words, if my actions today bring me (or the Greater Good) pleasure or happiness at the cost of some displeasure or unhappiness, there is no way of knowing whether the good outweighs the bad, the pros outweigh the cons. While this calculus is intuitively obvious for actions where some desirable upside far outweighs the undesirable downside (e.g., charitable donations, vaccinations for wider societal benefit, primary education, etc.), it's often the case where an action's benefits may not clearly exceed its negative costs, where a cost-benefit calculation is not possible or even knowable. For example, is it ethical to murder a physically abusive partner to prevent decades of future suffering? Is some disciplinary action directed toward a child acceptable without having a firm understanding of its future benefit (or lack thereof)?

A second related critique of Tegesism contends that net utility is not only unquantifiable, but also a wholly subjective phenomenon. We've all had the experience of disliking something (a hobby, leisure activity, entertainment program) that others find immensely pleasurable. Without an objective means to define and measure pleasure and happiness, groups and individuals are left to create the definitions for themselves, often resulting in self-serving rationalizations devised to justify even the most detestable behaviors and policies. Throughout the Realm's ten-thousand-year history, political actors have time and again utilized an arbitrarily defined, self-endorsing view of the Greater Good to either explicitly sanction or defend slavery, genocide, extreme poverty, institutional corruption, and countless forms of oppression.

The Originalists, a Tegesian Anti-Orthodoxy Movement

The perversion of the tenets laid down in the Guides as tools of political convenience, both by the state and the Tegesian order itself, has been perhaps the greatest factor that catalyzed the birth and rapid growth of a fundamentalist movement from within the Tegesian ranks now known as the Originalists.

While the Originalist creed can be contrasted from that of their orthodox peers via a number of subtle philosophical arguments, the most relevant differences between the two parties can be reduced to a pair of key areas. First, the Originalists object to the Tegesian order's longstanding indifference toward debt slavery, institutional corruption, and human bias in state and non-state institutions (including the Tegesian order itself) Even by the loosest definition of the Greater Good, these practices are unquestioningly immoral, and the orthodox leadership's inaction in these matters is tantamount to a tacit endorsement, a state of affairs the Originalists vigorously condemn as unacceptable. The Tegesian hierarchy, the Originalists contend, has become a political animal concerned first and foremost with its ongoing survival and relevance, and these misplaced priorities have caused the order to stray from its true charter of promoting maximum pleasure and minimal pain in the broadest possible context. The desire to return the faith to its purest "original" intent is the source of the anti-establishment movement's name.

Second, the anti-establishment movement endorses an ancient notion (advocated by an obscure, short-lived Tegesian sect in early Realm history) of the divine nature of Tegesism. This stands in stark contrast to the Tegesian order's long history of orthodox agnosticism. The Guides, the Originalists maintain, were the product of supernatural inspiration, a supreme being working through the hands of mortal authors. Where the orthodox members of its order see a philosophical text, the Originalists see holy scriptures. The Originalists also accept ancient Tegesian legends and folklore as historical events that actually occurred, rejecting the orthodox notion the myths are merely allegorical tales, stories invented by the Guides' authors meant to be instructive in nature.

Growing Extremism and Political Violence

Initially a peaceful reformist movement, recent decades have seen a surge in extremist ideologies and radical elements associated with Originalist adherents. Most alarmingly, an increasing number of terrorist incidents throughout the Realm have been attributed to Originalist sympathizers. With the sect's growing association with political extremism and violence, the dotta superior could no longer turn a blind eye toward what was previously tolerated as a harmless minority within his order's hierarchy. In the spring of 10,292 R.M.E., Tolerance IV categorically disavowed Originalist doctrine in his landmark "Exhortation of Joy" address, effectively banning the movement's ideas from the Tegesian faith and denouncing its practitioners as heretics.

With the lines of orthodoxy clearly drawn by His Eminence, many self-proclaimed Originalists renounced their wayward beliefs and re-embraced mainline Tegesism. Others defied the dotta superior and abandoned the order to form breakaway sects. These latter groups now operate as an underground movement of loosely connected anti-orthodox factions scattered throughout the Realm.

The secessionist sentiment from within the Tegesian order echoes a parallel insurgency in the political realm, the so-called Separatist movement of star systems (mostly located on the peripheral frontier) openly advocating independence from Realm authority. As of this writing, the Separatist and Originalist movements are not formally affiliated with one another, but a growing number of political scholars believe it may be only a matter of time until these anti-establishment uprisings join forces for their mutual benefit.

With the legitimacy of the Realm's two most important institutions—the state and the Tegesian faith—under attack by historically unprecedented insurrections, political observers and historians believe the Realm may be entering the most politically volatile period in its recorded history.

APPENDIX IV
THE RAUKAN PANTHEON

Excerpted from *Raukan Religion and Mysticism, Fourth Edition*, Slater-Kineth University Press, Vashta City, Gran Kiravashta, 10,281 R.M.E.

THE RAUKAN PANTHEON OF FIFTEEN DEITIES CONSISTS OF TWO major groups: the seven natural gods and the eight science gods. The seven natural gods (also known as the "Old Seven") date back to Raukan's neolithic age, and their divine roles echo those of gods found in faiths across the Realm (e.g., gods of war, love, wisdom, etc.).

In the age of scientific discovery, additional gods were added to accommodate new fields of knowledge. Eventually, these would be commonly known as the "New Eight." Unlike many of the Realm's ancient religions, the Raukan faith did not pit science against the divine as mutually exclusive truths of the universe. For the Rauk, new areas of knowledge didn't detract from its ancient faith or make it less relevant to modern life. Instead, science enriched the spiritual with new depths of meaning. For example, the development of mathematics was viewed not simply as steps in the direction of scientific enlightenment, but also as a spiritual revelation, an unveiling of a new area of faith. A long-hidden god—Thakken, the god of mathematics—had revealed itself. Known as much for their intelligence as their unconventional way of thinking, the Rauk's unique perspective on the age-old conflict between science and metaphysics offers a prime example of that species' intellectual adaptability. Below, find a complete list of the Raukan pantheon and their associated symbols.

Natural Gods (Old Seven)

Tokak - God(dess) of Law and Order. Father and mother of all natural gods. Can present as male, female, or gender-neutral. Symbols include mountain oak, thunderbolt, fire.

Keela - Goddess of Nature. First offspring of Tokak. Symbols include sun, moon, and stars.

Estoch - God of Fertility and Harvest. Symbols include Raukan wheat, eggs, seeds, flowers.

Shikong - Goddess of Warfare. Symbols include slingshot, spear and shield, closed fist.

Prunea - Goddess of Love and Procreation. Second offspring of Tokak. Symbols include cloudfruit, pollinating insects, rivers.

Tepoh - God of Passionate Pursuits. Sole offspring of Prunea. Symbols include stylus, boat, running figure.

Hemm - Goddess of Wisdom. Third offspring of Tokak. Symbols include scrolls, all-seeing eye, folded hands.

. . .

Science Gods (New Eight)

Thakken - God(dess) of Mathematics. Cousin to Tokak. Father and mother of all science gods. Like Tokak, can present as male, female, or gender-neutral. Symbols include superimposed numbers, algebraic notations.

Leem - Goddess of Physics. First offspring of Thakken. Symbols include pulley, scales, electrons orbiting atom.

Mosset - God of Astronomy. Second offspring of Thakken. Symbols include constellations, telescope, planets orbiting sun.

Krug - God of Engineering. Third offspring of Thakken. Symbols include wheel, gears, calipers.

Demirel - Goddess of Biology. Fourth offspring of Thakken. Symbols include DNA helix, nerve cell, heart.

Kova - God of Geology. Fifth offspring of Thakken. Symbols include mountain, volcano, crystals, diamonds.

Letten - Goddess of Chemistry. Sixth offspring of Thakken. Symbols include graduated beaker, thermometer, chemical equations.

Rausto - Goddess of Technology. Created by Thakken and endowed with knowledge from each of his/her six offspring. Symbols include sprocket, key, water wheel.

ABOUT THE AUTHOR

D.L. Young is a Pushcart Prize nominee and winner of the Independent Press Award.

His novels echo his many influences from science fiction books and movies, including *Star Wars*, the *Mad Max* films, *Dune*, *Blade Runner*, *Star Trek*, and the stories of William Gibson, Harlan Ellison, and J.G. Ballard.

Visit dlyoungfiction.com for more about his books.

ACKNOWLEDGMENTS

My sincerest thanks to a wonderful team of beta readers for *Jeryn's Dagger*. Your time and well-considered feedback were absolutely invaluable. Thank you so much!

Simon Anderson - Ingrid Cruz Bonilla - J. Brassard - Phil Craig - Ira Domnitz - Michael "Fuzzy" Emeny - Gavin Gray - Elliot Harper - Nathaniel Henderson - Neal Johnstone - Ash Malhotra - Garrett Moran - Darren Oram - Alyssa Over - Travis Pierce - John Revie - Walter M. Scott III - Ann Smith - Audi Wallbrink - Luke Van Wyk

I also had tremendous support from those who participated in the pre-release crowdfunding campaign. To the following backers for EMPIRE AND ASHES, I can't thank you enough for your generosity.

Cesar Cadena - Jeremiah Steven Barton - Howard Carter - Vijay Kale - Scarlet Roberts - Daniel M. Clark - Jeanette Bedard - A. B. Archambault - Tamas Hegyes - Paula Bates - Christopher Froebe - Michael "Fuzzy" Emeny - Ira Domnitz - Ian Michael Harrup - Leslie Archibald - Michelle Palmer - Bonnie Jo Stufflebeam - Aaron Strowger - Kevin Ikenberry - GoDfun - Susan Ellis - Michelle Muenzler - Tom Borthwick - Algie Lane III - Justin Lilly - Peyton Light - H. John Vogel - Pierino Gattei - Mike Barrett - Jake Polk - Wade Leibeck - S. Busby - Vince Smeraldo -

Geoff Walsh - Howard Blakeslee - David Holzborn - Russell Fisk - Mark Wahlbeck - Karissa W. - Ben Monroe - Garrett Moran - Arick Lane - Scantrontb - Athobix - Kem Tae M. Lynch - Shawna Zak - Richard Libera - Ash Malhotra

Printed in Dunstable, United Kingdom